THE REMEDY

ALSO BY SUZANNE YOUNG

The Program

The Treatment

The Recovery

Just Like Fate
with Cat Patrick

THE REMEDY

SUZANNE YOUNG

SIMON PULSE
New York London Toronto Sydney New Delhi

SIMON PULSE
An imprint of Simon & Schuster Children's Publishing Division
1230 Avenue of the Americas, New York, NY 10020
First Simon Pulse hardcover edition April 2015

Jacket designed by Russell Gordon
Interior designed by Michael Rosamilia
The text of this book was set in Adobe Garamond Pro.
Manufactured in the United States of America
2 4 6 8 10 9 7 5 3 1
Library of Congress Cataloging-in-Publication Data
Young, Suzanne.
The Remedy / Suzanne Young. — First Simon Pulse hardcover edition.
p. cm.
Companion book to: The Program and The Treatment.
Summary: Seventeen-year-old Quinn provides closure to grieving families
by taking on the short-term role of a deceased loved one, until huge secrets
come to the surface about Quinn's own past.
[1. Death—Fiction. 2. Grief—Fiction. 3. Identity—Fiction.
4. Memory—Fiction. 5. Science fiction.] I. Title.
PZ7.Y887Re 2015
[Fic]—dc23
2014039699
ISBN 978-1-4814-3765-3 (hc)
ISBN 978-1-4814-3767-7 (eBook)

For my mother, Connie

And in loving memory of my grandmother
Josephine Parzych

THE REMEDY

PART I
BEASTS OF BURDEN

CHAPTER ONE

IT'S TIME TO SAY GOOD-BYE. I SIT IN THE ARMCHAIR closest to the door and fold my hands politely in my lap. The room is too warm. Too quiet. My mother enters from the kitchen, her left eye swollen and bruised, small scratches carved into her cheeks. She limps to the plaid sofa, waving off help when I offer, and eases onto the patterned cushion next to my father. I shoot him an uncomfortable glance, but he doesn't lift his head; tears drip onto his gray slacks, and I turn away.

I begin to gnaw on the inside of my lower lip, waiting in silence as they consider their words. This intervention-style farewell is hardly the format I imagined, but the moment belongs to them, so I don't interfere. I cast a longing look to where my worn backpack waits near the door. Aaron had better not be late picking me up this time.

"Are you sure you can't stay another night?" my father asks, gripping his wife's hand hard enough to turn his knuckles white. They both stare at me pleadingly, but I don't give them false hope. I won't be that cruel.

"Sorry, but no," I say kindly. "This is where we say good-bye."

My mother pulls her hand from my father's, curling it into a fist at her mouth. She chokes back a sob, and I watch as the stitched wound on her cheek crinkles her skin.

I reach for my own tears, trying to appear sympathetic. *You'll never see your parents again,* I think. *Isn't that sad?* But all I can muster is a bit of blurry vision. It seems a little heartless, even to me, that I can't mourn their loss. But I've only known these people for two days. Besides, the clips on my hair extensions are driving my scalp mad. I reach a fingernail in between my red strands and scratch.

My mother takes a deep breath and then begins her rehearsed good-bye. "Emily," she says in a shaky voice. "When you died, my life ended too." A tear rolls slowly down her cheek, slipping into her dimple before falling away. "I couldn't see beyond my grief," she continues. "The counselors told me I had to, but I could only replay those last minutes in the car. This horrible loop of pain—" She chokes up, and my father reaches to rub her back soothingly. I don't interrupt. "And then you were gone," my mother whispers, looking at me. "I loved you more than anything, but you were torn away. I tried . . . I tried so hard, but I couldn't save you. I'm sorry, Emily."

I'm a barely passable version of Emily—different eyes,

smaller chin. But my mother is grieving, and through her tears I'm sure she thinks I look identical to her dead daughter. And maybe that resemblance pains her even more when we're this close.

"I love you too, Mom," I say automatically, and flick my gaze to my father. "And thank you, Dad, for all you've done for me. I was very happy. No matter what, I'll always be with you"—I put my hand on my chest—"in your hearts."

The words are dry in my mouth, but I stick to the script when I can't personalize my speech in some other way. Ultimately, this is what they wanted to hear—or rather, what they needed to hear to have closure. They wanted me to know I was loved.

My phone buzzes in my pocket, but I don't ruin the moment to check it. We're past deadline and it has grown dark outside, but I won't leave until I'm sure my parents will get through this. I wait a beat, and my mother sniffles and wipes her face with her palms.

"I miss you, Emily," she says, and her voice cracks over my name. "I miss you every day." The first tears prick my eyes, the honesty in her emotions penetrating the wall I've carefully built. I smile at her, hoping it lessens her ache.

"I know you loved me," I say, going off script. "But, Mom . . . this wasn't your fault. It was an accident—a terrible, tragic accident. Please don't blame yourself anymore. I forgive you."

My mother claps both hands over her mouth, relief hemorrhaging as her shoulders shake with her sobs. This is it—her closure. She needed relief from her guilt. My father climbs to his feet and motions toward the door. I stand to follow him, but pause and look back at my mother.

"I'm safe now," I continue. "Nothing can ever hurt me again. Not one thing." I turn to leave the room, my voice barely audible over her cries. "Good-bye, Mom."

My assignment is complete.

I follow my father to the front door, and when we reach the entryway, I rummage through the shredded middle pocket of my backpack and pull out a sweatshirt. I yank the Rolling Stones T-shirt off over my tank top and hand it to my dad . . . or, rather, Alan Pinnacle.

For the past two days, I've been wearing his daughter's favorite clothes, eating her favorite foods, sleeping in her bed. I'm the Goldilocks the bears took in to replace the one they lost, even if it was only to say good-bye.

Alan looks down at Emily's black shirt and pushes it in my direction. "Keep it," he says, staring at the fabric like it's precious. I widen my eyes and take a step back.

"But it's not mine," I say quietly. "It belonged to your daughter." Sometimes parents become confused, and part of my job is to keep them grounded in reality. Martha sits on the couch, staring toward the window with a calmed expression, but I worry that Alan is having an emotional breakdown.

"You're right," he says sadly. "But Emily isn't coming home." He holds up the shirt. "If this is still being worn, in a way, her spirit will be out there. She'll still be part of the world."

“I really shouldn’t,” I say, although if I’m honest, that T-shirt was my favorite part of this assignment. But we’re not supposed to keep artifacts of the dead. It opens up the possibility of lawsuits against the entire grief department, claims of unprofessionalism.

“Please,” he murmurs. “I think she would have really liked you.”

It’s just a shirt, I think. *No one’s ever been fired over a shirt.* I reluctantly take the fabric from his hand, and Alan’s face twists in a flash of pain. Impulsively, I lean in and kiss his cheek.

“Emily was a lucky girl,” I whisper close to his ear. And then, without waiting to see his expression, I turn and walk out of Emily Pinnacle’s house.

The night air is heavy with moisture as I step onto the wooden slats of the front porch; cool rainy wind blows against my face. The headlights of a car parked down the road flick on, and my muscles relax. I’m glad I won’t be hanging around for a ride; Aaron usually sucks at being on time. I reach into my hair and begin to remove the extensions, unclipping them and then shoving them into the bag on my shoulder, where I stuffed the Rolling Stones T-shirt.

The car pulls up, and I hold my backpack over my head to protect myself from the rain. I throw one more glance toward the house, glad neither parent is looking out the window. I hate to break the illusion for them; it’s like seeing a teacher at the grocery store or a theme-park character without its oversize head.

I open the car door and drop onto the passenger seat of a shiny black Cadillac. It reeks of leather and coconut air freshener. I turn sideways, lifting my eyebrows the minute I take in Aaron's appearance. I pretend to check my nonexistent watch. "And who are you supposed to be?" I ask.

Aaron smiles. "I'm me again," he says. "It was a long drive. I didn't have time to change clothes."

This was one of those rare moments where Aaron and I were on assignment at the same time—a mostly avoided conflict. It was probably a good thing that I was running late tonight. I scan my friend's outfit, holding back the laugh waiting in my gut. He's wearing a dark brown corduroy jacket with a striped button-down shirt underneath. Although Aaron's barely nineteen, he's dressed like an eighty-year-old professor. Sensing my impending reaction, he steps on the gas pedal and speeds us down the street.

"Twenty-three-year-old law student," he explains, turning up the volume on the stereo. "But his real love was math." He shoots me a pointed look as if it sums up his assignment completely. "The counselors are really pushing my age, right?" he asks. "Must be this sweet beard." He strokes his facial hair and I scrunch up my nose.

"Gross," I say. "You're lucky Oregon celebrates its facial hair; otherwise you'd be out of work." Aaron's smooth, dark skin disappears every No Shave November, but that ended five months ago. I'm partners with a Sasquatch. "When are you getting rid of that thing?" I ask.

"Um, never," he says, like it's the obvious answer. "I'm looking fine, girl."

I laugh and flip down the passenger-side mirror. The light clicks on, harsh on my heavy makeup. I comb my fingers through my still-red shoulder-length strands. Emily's hair was ridiculously long, so I had to wear itchy extensions.

"Too bad," Aaron says, motioning to my reflection. "I liked your hair long."

"And I like that special blazer. You sure you can't keep it?"

"Point made," he concedes. We're quiet for a moment until Aaron clears his throat. "So how was it?" he asks in a therapist's voice, even though he knows I hate talking about my assignments. "You were super vague on the phone," he adds. "I was getting worried."

"It was the same," I answer. "Just like always."

"Was it the mom?"

"Yeah," I tell him, and look out the passenger window. "Survivor's guilt. There was a car accident; the mother was driving. After arriving at the hospital, the mom ran from room to room, searching for her daughter. But she was DOA." I swallow hard, burying the emotions that threaten to shake my voice. "All the mother wanted was to apologize for losing control of the car," I continue. "Beg her daughter for forgiveness. Tell her how much she loved her. But she never got the chance. She didn't even get to say good-bye. Martha had a hard time accepting that."

"Martha?" Aaron repeats, and I feel him look at me. "You two on a first-name basis?"

"No," I say. "But I'm not calling her Mom anymore, and it seems cold to call her Mrs. Pinnacle." When I turn to Aaron, he looks doubtful. "What?" I ask. "The woman washed my underwear. It's not like we're strangers."

"See, that's the thing," he says, holding up his finger. "You *are* strangers. You were temporarily playing the role of her deceased daughter, but by no means are you friends. Don't blur the lines, Quinn."

"I know how to do my job," I answer dismissively. My heart beats faster.

Although all closers take on the personality of the dead person, I'm the only one who internalizes it, thinks like them. It makes me more authentic, and honestly, it's why I'm the best. "Don't be judgy," I tell Aaron. "You have your process; I have mine. I'm completely detached when it's over."

Aaron chuckles. "You're detached?" he asks. "Then why do you keep souvenirs?"

"I do not," I respond, heat crawling onto my cheeks.

"I bet you have more than hair extensions in that bag."

I look down to see the edge of the T-shirt peeking out. "Not fair," I say. "The dad gave that to me. It doesn't count."

"And the earrings from Susan Bell? The flashy yet clashy belt from Audrey Whatshername? Admit it. You're a life klepto. You keep pieces of them like some whacked-out serial killer."

I laugh. "It's nothing like that."

Aaron hums out his disagreement and takes a turn onto the freeway. It'll be at least forty-five minutes until we're back in Corvallis. I hate the away assignments, but our town is fairly small, and we don't have nearly as many deaths as Eugene or Portland. But being away can mess with your head. Nothing's familiar—not the places or the people. A person could forget who they really are in a situation like that. It's high risk, and the return is always more difficult after being cut off completely. But it's our job.

Aaron Rios and I are closers—a remedy for grief-stricken families. We help clients who are experiencing symptoms of complicated grief through an extreme method of role-playing therapy. When a family or person experiences loss—the kind of loss they just can't get over, the kind that eats away at their sanity—grief counselors make a recommendation. For an undisclosed sum of money, clients are given a closer to play the part of a dead person and provide them the much-needed closure they desire.

At this point I can become anyone so long as they're a white female between the ages of fifteen and twenty. I'm not an exact copy, of course, but I wear their clothes and change my hair and eye color. I study them through pictures and videos, and soon I can act like them, smell like them, *be them* for all intents and purposes. And when a family is hazy with grief, they tend to accept me readily.

I stay with them for a few days, but never more than a week. In that time, my loved ones get to say everything they needed to but never got the chance to, get to hear whatever they've told the counselors they needed to hear. I can be the perfect daughter. I can give them closure so they can heal.

I'm saving lives—even if sometimes it's hard to remember which one is mine.

"So what have I missed?" I ask Aaron. When he called me earlier to set up my extraction, he tried to talk, to reconnect me to the outside world. But I was with the family when my phone buzzed, so I fed Aaron some bullshit excuse to get off the line. Now I'm desperate for a reminder of my real life. I rest my temple on the headrest and watch him.

"Not much." He shrugs. "Deacon's been texting me nonstop. Says you're not answering your phone."

"Well, he's not supposed to contact me, is he?" I point out. Our guidelines state that we only consort with our partners or our advisors while on assignment—it keeps us from breaking character. But the fact is, I could have responded to Deacon's texts. I just didn't want to.

My eyes start to sting and I check around the front seat and find a bag of open trail mix stuffed into the cutout below the stereo; salty-looking peanuts have spilled into the cup holder. My father will kill Aaron for bringing those in here. And for dirtying up his Cadillac. We always use the same car for extractions. It serves as a reminder of our real life, something familiar to bring us home.

I hike my backpack onto my lap and start rummaging through until I find the case for my colored contacts. Although I'm not deathly allergic to nuts, they irritate my eyes and make my throat burn. Aaron's usually pretty good about not eating them around me. I guess he forgot this time—which is understandable. Assignments tend to leave us confused. At least for a while.

"I think Deacon's worried you'll run away without telling him," Aaron continues. "It makes him crazy."

"Deacon never worries about anything," I correct, resting my index finger on my pupil until I feel the contact cling to it. "And I don't know why he's asking you. If I planned to run away, you wouldn't know either." I remove the film and place it back inside the case before working on the other eye.

"Yeah, well, he worries about *you*," Aaron mutters, clicking the windshield wipers off now that the rain has eased up. "And whether you admit it or not," he adds, "you worry about his ass all the time too."

"We're friends," I remind him, reliving the conversation we've had a dozen times. "Just very good friends."

"Whatever, Quinn," he says. "You're hard-core and he's badass. I get it. You're both too tough for love."

"Shut up." I laugh. "You're just mad we get along better than you and your girlfriend."

"Damn right," Aaron says with a defiant smirk. "It ain't cool. You two—"

"Stooooop," I whine, cutting him off. "Change the subject. Deacon and I are broken up. End of story." I stuff my contacts case back into my bag and drop it down by my feet. The traffic has faded from the freeway, leaving the dark road empty around us.

"I'm not saying you should hate each other," Aaron continues. "But you shouldn't want to bone every time you see him either."

"You have serious problems, you know that, right?"

"Mm-hmm," he says, nodding dismissively. "Yeah, *I'm* the one with problems." He whistles out a low sound of sympathy, looking sideways at me. "You've both got it bad," he adds.

"No," I tell him. "We're both better off. Remind Deacon of that next time he's checking up on me." Aaron scoffs and swears he's staying out of it. He won't, of course. He thinks we're still pining for each other. And . . . he may not be entirely wrong. But Deacon and I have a very platonic understanding.

Deacon Hatcher is my ex-boyfriend turned best friend, but more important, he used to be a closer. He gets it. Gets me. Deacon was my partner before Aaron, almost three years side by side until he quit working for my dad eight months ago. He quit me the same day. The breakup may have wrecked me a little. Or a lot. Deacon and I had shared everything, had a policy of total honesty, which isn't exactly easy for people in our line of work.

I hadn't even known he'd ended his contract with the grief department when he told me we were over, said he'd moved on. I assumed he meant with another girl, so we didn't speak for over a month. I'd been blindsided, betrayed. Only thing left for me was closure, and I was damn good at it. I absorbed more of my assignments' lives, their families' love. I rebuilt my self-esteem with their help, their memories. Then my father assigned Aaron as my new partner.

The next day, Deacon showed up at my front door, saying how sorry he was. Saying how desperately he missed me. I believed him. I always believe him. But every time we get close—the very minute I fall for him again—Deacon cuts me off, backs away, and leaves me brokenhearted by the absence of his affection. Whether it's his training or his natural disposition, Deacon *is* charming. The kind of charming that makes you feel like you're the only person in the world who matters. Until you don't anymore.

I'm tired of the push and pull that continues to crack and heal over the same scar. I told Deacon that I was done letting myself be vulnerable to him, that he was ruining me. The thought seemed to devastate him. So Deacon and I agreed not to get back together, but acknowledged that we couldn't stay away from each other either. Best friends is the compromise. It lets us go to the very edge of our want without actually going over. And that works for us. We're totally screwed up that way.

From the center console Aaron's phone vibrates in the cup holder. He quickly grabs it before I do, and rests it against the wheel while he reads the text. After a moment he clicks off the screen and drops his phone back into the cup holder. "Myra says hello," he says, glancing over. "She's *super* excited for you to be back."

"I'm sure," I say, flashing him an amused smile. Aaron's girlfriend is barely five feet tall, with wide doelike eyes and a red-hot temper. She used to hate me—which, under normal circumstances, could be understandable. I spend *a lot* of time with her boyfriend. We're over it now, and the entire situation became a running joke between me and Aaron. And although Myra might still hate me a *little*, she's one of my closest friends. But everything will change soon. This is Aaron's last month as a closer—his contract ends in four weeks. After that, he and Myra are going to run off and live some deranged life in one of the Dakotas.

"Any chance I can talk you into dropping me off at home first?" I ask Aaron in a sickly sweet voice. "I've been dreaming about my bed for the entire weekend. Emily had a futon."

Aaron whistles in sympathy. "Sounds tough, Quinn. But I already called Marie to let her know we're on our way." He smiles. "And you know how much she loves late-night debriefings."

False. Marie absolutely hates when we come by after dark.

I exhale, dreading our next stop. I just want to go home, tell my dad good night, and then crash in my bed. Unfortunately, none of that can happen until we register our closure and confess our sins. Our advisor, Marie, has to interview us before we're allowed to return to our regular lives. There are procedures in place to make sure we don't take any grief home with us, take home the sadness. It's the old saying: misery loves company. Yeah, well, grief can be contagious.

CHAPTER TWO

THE DOOR TO THE FIFTH-STORY WALK-UP APARTment is always stuck, and Aaron has to ram his shoulder against it to get it open. He stumbles in, turning back to flash me a smile.

So strong, I mouth, making him laugh. I follow him inside, and then close and lock the door. I pause to look around. I haven't been to Marie's house in at least a month, but it's just as cramped as I remember. Exactly the same. Wall-to-wall antique furniture, ornate chairs and thin-legged tables. Layers of incense hang in the air; red tapestries are tacked over the window, casting the room in soft light from the lamps. The place is shabby chic—much like its tenant.

"You're late," a raspy voice calls from the kitchen. I catch sight of Marie's bare shoulder and thin long braids as she opens and closes kitchen cabinets in search of something.

"Quinlan was being nice again by giving them extra time," Aaron calls. He drops onto the worn velvet sofa and kicks off his shoes. I scowl at him for ratting me out so quickly, and remove my sneakers before Marie can yell at me for disrespecting her apartment. "She's too kindhearted," Aaron adds. "Tell Quinn she's too kindhearted." He rolls his head toward the kitchen, and Marie pokes out from behind the cabinet door.

"Stop being so nice," Marie scolds, and then goes back to what she was doing.

"See." Aaron holds up his finger to me in warning before working his arms out of the sleeves of his blazer. He carefully folds the fabric over the back of the couch.

I roll my eyes. "I was doing my job," I clarify, sitting on the painted chair near the door. "Check with the Pinnacles—I'm sure I'll get a glowing review."

"Don't worry," Marie says, coming out of the kitchen, carrying a tray. "We always check." She smiles at me and then sets the tray on the coffee table. There's a small teapot; the smell of mint wafts up from the cups. My stomach turns. That's not regular tea—not here. It's a medicinal cocktail that will compel me to tell the truth once I drink it. Luckily, I have nothing to hide.

Marie hands Aaron a cup. "Guess I'm first," he murmurs, and gulps his drink quickly. He sucks in a breath to cool down his mouth. "Nasty," he says with a shiver, and sets the cup on the table.

"I'll get the paperwork," Marie announces. She walks

toward the home office, her anklets jangling above her bare feet, her long braids clicking as they swish across her back. Marie Devoroux is in her late thirties with dark brown skin, piercing black eyes, and an effortless beauty that allows strangers to trust her. She's been my advisor since the beginning. I can still remember being a little girl on her lap, telling her about Barbara Richards—a nine-year-old who cracked her skull while riding her bike. I sipped peppermint tea and told Marie how sad it made me when Barbie's mother cried. I had a hard time adjusting to the grief in the beginning.

Marie's a bit less patient now, especially with me. She and my father have been at odds over a case neither will talk about. I'm not sure when it started, but it's clear Marie is on the verge of leaving the department altogether. I don't know what the counselors will do if she does.

Marie reemerges a moment later with folders and a voice recorder. She takes a spot next to Aaron on the couch, flipping her hair over her shoulder before she sorts through the file with DEXTER REED printed on the tab.

I pick up my warm teacup, swirling around the liquid. I'm not sure I could hate the taste of mint any more than I already do. Eleven years of drinking this stuff will do that to a person. I take a tentative sip and then gag. Marie gives me a dirty look like she's offended, and I hold up the tea in cheers before downing it, gagging again.

Aaron starts recounting his short time as the distinguished law student Dexter Reed. It took less than twenty-four hours to bring a person's entire life to a close. Which is good, I guess. Otherwise Aaron would have been late picking me up. Again. I don't listen to the story—although it's not a huge deal if I do. Hearing his experience won't make me sad, not like reenacting it can. That's why we're here with Marie. Closers aren't allowed to go home until we process the grief. We take that burden from the clients, help them heal. But we can become affected, taking it on as our own pain and suffering. Our extreme method of therapy isn't without its risks. The counselors don't want that to happen, so we talk to advisors. God, sometimes we talk so much I want to cut out my tongue.

I smile, leaning back in the chair. The tea must already be working. Even my thoughts are honest.

Aaron's voice drones on, and I contemplate the evening, the taste of peppermint thick in my mouth. Things could be worse, I guess. I could actually be Emily Pinnacle.

Only certain kinds of people can become closers. There are currently fifteen of us in Oregon. Different ages, races, and genders. Enough to cover the demographic more or less. We were all selected by the grief counselors because we have certain traits: adaptability, mimicking skills, and a healthy dose of detachment. We don't feel the same way other people do—almost like we're numb. Or at least most of us are. While the rest of the world is bent on sharing their feelings, we study them. We learn to copy behavior patterns, facial expressions. We learn how to become other people.

Over the last couple of years there's been a societal push to restructure our mental health institutions. As a result, people have become more cognizant of their emotions. Oregon was the first state to restructure. They placed counselors in every school, but many thought the districts still weren't doing enough to keep their children safe. There was kid-on-kid violence at an alarming rate and little that could be done to stop it. Some districts shut down for good in favor of homeschooling, with online therapists assigned to help students through hormones and homework. People have their counselors on speed dial. They talk about *everything*.

The latest news claims that society's leveling out now—finding a perfect balance with the development of better coping mechanisms. Although not a widespread practice yet, the grief department is slowly growing, the idea of closers becoming more and more appealing to those suffering from loss. I don't question the ethics of what we do because, ultimately, I'm helping parents come to terms with their new lives. And don't we all deserve the chance to move on?

"Quinlan," Marie calls, her chin lifted as she studies my expression. "Your turn." The room tips at a slow rock, and I'm not sure how much time has passed. I glance at Aaron just as he wipes his cheeks and sniffles hard.

"Be right back," Aaron says quietly, and leaves the room. He's going to lie down in the spare room until I'm done, let the tea wear off. Marie told us once that advisors didn't always use the tea—a cocktail of sodium amytal—because they trusted closers to tell the truth about their assignments. But through trial and error, counselors discovered they could make faster progress with reentry if we didn't lie all the time. They made a policy change, altering the entire system of advisement in order to prevent mistakes, like us bringing home the sadness we were meant to alleviate.

I hate that tea. I don't like being forced to do anything, even to tell the truth. But it's not like I have a choice. My contract isn't up for six more months.

"Sit," Marie says, pulling out the file with Emily Pinnacle's name on the tab. I move to the couch and face her. "How are you feeling?" Marie asks conversationally.

"Exhausted," I respond. I put my arm over the back of the sofa and get comfortable. There's no telling how long this will take. Marie opens the file and jots something down. She resets her recorder and places it on the table.

"Quinlan McKee," she announces for the recorder, and then smiles kindly at me. "Quinn," she says in her therapy voice. "Tell me about Emily Pinnacle."

I furrow my brow, contemplating. "She was quiet, polite. I read through her diary three times, flipped through photo albums, and studied her social media profiles. She didn't have a boyfriend, but she had an intense crush on Jared Bathman. She never told him," I say. "She should have, right?" I ask. Marie hums something noncommittal, and I continue. "She was worried he wouldn't like her back," I say. "But the day she died, he finally talked to her at the basketball game. She was so excited. On the way home she texted her friend and told her the entire conversation. But she never made it home." I look down into my lap, tears pricking my eyes. "It wasn't fair. It wasn't fair that Emily had to die at sixteen."

"You're right," Marie agrees. "It says here that her mother became very distraught after Emily's death. The father hired us because she had become unstable, erratic. The counselors were very concerned about her well-being. What did you observe?"

"Heartbreak," I murmur. "I saw a lot of heartbreak."

"And how did it feel?"

"It was a deep, dark hollow in my chest. It felt like hopelessness." I look up to meet Marie's eyes. "I started to think that I was never going to see my parents again—her parents," I correct. "I was scared. I didn't want to be alone. I didn't want to die." Tears roll down my cheeks as grief and loss submerge me. "Now I'll be alone forever." I tried to keep these feelings at bay when I was Emily, but now I can't lie. I can't hide from myself.

Marie reaches to take my hand, squeezing to reassure me. "*You* will see your father tonight, Quinn. You didn't die—Emily Pinnacle did."

"It could have been me," I say, shaking my head. "They all could be me."

"No," she says. "You're Quinlan McKee. You live at 2055 Seneca Place in Corvallis, Oregon. You're seventeen and you drive a beat-up old Honda that your father won't replace." She reaches and touches my cheek to draw me back into reality. "And you're alive, Quinn," she whispers. "You're here, and you're alive."

I let her words soak in, thinking about my crappy car—the

check-engine light that won't shut off. After a moment I'm rooted back in place. Back in my life. I clear the tears and grab a tissue to blow my nose. When I'm cleaned up, Marie resettles on the couch.

"Do you want to tell me about the T-shirt?" she asks.

My stomach drops and I shoot a betrayed look toward the back room. "Aaron told you?" I ask, angry that he's called me out twice since we've been here.

"He had to."

It's true. Even if my friend wanted to keep a secret, he couldn't here. "Why were you asking about me in the first place?" I demand. "I don't like being spied on, Marie."

"I thought we talked about this," she says, ignoring my comment. "Taking things—retaining possessions of the dead. It isn't healthy and it's against the rules."

"Emily's dad gave me the shirt. I didn't steal it." My emotions are starting to bubble up, but not the sadness I felt earlier. This is different—it's anger, defiance.

"I didn't say you did," Marie clarifies. "But why would you keep Emily's shirt? Does it hold an emotional attachment?"

My thoughts swirl as I fight the impending effect of the tea. Admitting an emotional attachment to the family could send me straight into therapy. *This* is why I hate talking about my feelings.

"I just really liked the shirt," I say, relieved at the words. Relieved . . . that I just told a small lie. I don't react, even though my heart races. It wasn't a huge lie—but it was evasive.

The truth is that everything I keep has significance, even if it's only slight. That T-shirt reminds me of my dad, Emily's dad, and how he bought it for me on my birthday two years ago because he loved the Rolling Stones. We have pictures of us smiling, arms over each other's shoulders. They may not be my memories, but I like them. And I want to keep them.

Marie studies me, and for a moment I think she can tell that I've skirted her question. I'm not sure how I could have, though. When she's not looking, I glance at the teapot, wondering if the dose was lighter. Or maybe just what was in my cup. Marie writes a note in my file and closes it.

"You're cleared to return home," she says, and gives me a closed-lip smile. "But don't keep anything else, Quinn. It might make the counselors think you're too emotional to handle the assignments."

"I'm a coldhearted bitch, Marie," I say. "Promise."

She chuckles, and pats my knee before standing. "Oh," she adds. "And don't be too hard on Aaron. He didn't want to tell me about the shirt. It's a new line of questioning your father added in. Aaron had to tell me the truth."

"Then why didn't you ask me about him?" I say, confused.

"Because the questions are only about you." Her expression is unreadable, unapproachable, and then Marie spins—her braids swinging—and walks back to her office.

Aaron and I are quiet as we get into the Cadillac and start toward my house, where Aaron's car is parked. Marie's words clog up my mind, and I wonder why my father would add in questions about me. Why he's checking up on me. I'm also concerned. Although I didn't lie, I wasn't completely honest. Did Marie . . . did she do something different this time? Am *I* different this time?

"I'm sorry," Aaron says in a quiet voice from the driver's seat. He doesn't look over, but he's raw—a little shell-shocked from his debriefing. "I didn't want to tell her."

"What did she ask?"

He swallows hard, tightening his grip on the steering wheel. "We went through the events like usual, but at the end she asked if I noticed anything odd when I picked you up. I didn't know what she meant at first, but she asked if I thought you were growing too attached to the clients. I . . . I told her about the shirt." He looks over, his dark eyes miserable. "I didn't mean to, Quinn."

"It's fine," I tell him, mostly to alleviate some of his stress. "She wasn't even mad."

Aaron's eyes narrow slightly before he turns back to the road. "That's good, I guess." He pauses. "Did she ask about me?"

"Nope," I say. His mouth flinches with a smile, but he quickly straightens it. Aaron doesn't want anything to mess up his contract. In just a few weeks he'll have his lump-sum payment, enough to start over somewhere else. He hasn't been a closer for nearly as long as I have, but then again, my father is the head of the department, so I've gotten double the pressure to continue. I'm jealous that Aaron will be gone soon, living his own life. Sometimes I wonder if I'll ever have that, or if my father will find a way to keep extending my contract.

The typical contract is for three years' time, although many closers sign on for a second term. Rarely beyond that, though. It's not recommended, because the stress puts a closer at risk for a whole host of problems—like losing oneself completely. I'm on my fourth contract. Even now, I couldn't say which of my favorite childhood memories actually happened to *me*. The lines blur. Occasionally, I look through old photo albums, but there are a few pictures that don't fit with my memories, and vice versa.

One of my most confusing memories is that of my mother—her shiny dark hair and wide smile, even as she lay in a hospital bed, obviously sick. I would crawl up the white sheets to be next to her, and she'd read me a story, tell me she loved me, and kiss my hair.

But *my* mother had blond hair and blue eyes. She was delicate and pretty, and then she was gone. She died in a car accident, and I never saw her in the hospital, never saw her after that day. I can find no pictures of the other woman from my memory, and when I ask my father, he insists I must be remembering an assignment, even though he can't pinpoint exactly which one.

That's part of my problem—the lives of my assignments blend together after a while, blend with mine. That uncertainty haunts me on occasion, especially when I'm deep in my role playing and longing for a connection. Then again, they all haunt me, all the girls I've portrayed, so I try not to dwell on the reality too much.

My most recent contract expired when I was fifteen, but somehow my father convinced them (and me) to sign another one. He's always logical, and it's hard to argue with him. It's even harder to disappoint him. In the end I'll get four times the money, plus a bonus. He says I'll be able to pay for college outright, be able to buy a house. He tells me I'll be set for life. Although those things sound nice to him, I think I'd rather go to prom or something frivolous like that.

Corvallis still has two open high schools, but I don't attend anymore. Closure kept me away too much. Online high school just doesn't have the same drama. The biggest scandal I've seen was when the servers crashed and the teachers had to reset our passwords. Deacon went to my old school until he dropped out. I never understood why he wanted to quit; I would kill to go back to regular high school.

Aaron takes the exit for my house, and I groan. I'm angry about my father checking on me, and I don't want to show up so pissed off. "Want to swing by Deacon's?" I ask. Aaron shakes his head.

"Myra's waiting up for me. I can drop you there, though."

"What about your car?" I ask.

"I'll park the Caddy and hop in my ride before your dad can even look out the window," he says. "Let him know the keys will be in the visor."

I agree, and settle back against the seat when Aaron passes

the turn for my house. My father is probably at the kitchen table with a cup of coffee so he won't sleep through my arrival home, but I don't mind making him wait a little longer. That's what he gets for spying on me. Now that the stress of going home passes, I realize how incredibly tired I am. How drained.

Like my soul is wearing thin.

CHAPTER THREE

DEACON OWNS A LITTLE CRAFTSMAN-STYLE HOUSE close to the college. He exited his contract eight months ago, but he still got paid for his first three years. He gets nothing for the extra year he put in because he broke the second contract. He ended up putting the money down on a home, which was way more responsible of him than any of us expected. He also dropped out of high school and got his GED instead. Deacon's parents died when he was a baby, and my father found him in foster care. An angry fourteen-year-old boy who he thought would make a perfect closer. Deacon was good, too—almost as good as me. His charisma draws people in, even if it's only a facade.

Aaron drops me off, still quieter than usual. I know he's feeling guilty about turning me in for the T-shirt, but I'm too tired to convince him I'm not mad about it. I get out, saying I'll call him tomorrow, and then watch as he drives away.

A headache has started, and I rub my eyes with the heels of my palms and then climb the front porch of Deacon's house. I knock, my backpack weighing me down. I slide it onto one shoulder. Although I've only been gone a weekend, I feel like I haven't seen Deacon in months.

It's a weird side effect of returning: It's like I'm an actor in my own life. Like I'm not the real one. It takes about twenty-four hours to become me again.

The door partly opens, and Deacon rests his hip on the frame and looks me up and down as if he has no idea who I am. He's wearing gray sweatpants with CORVALLIS UNION HIGH SCHOOL printed up the leg, his hair all askew. He's shirtless, whether for effect or for comfort I'm not sure.

"I wondered if you were coming by," he says finally, pushing open the door wider to invite me in. I touch his forearm in thanks as I pass and drop my backpack at the bottom of the staircase.

"I don't want to go home yet," I say, turning to him. "My father's being a dick."

"I'm so surprised," he responds easily.

For the first time since leaving Marie, I'm overwhelmed by a mixture of anger and sadness. The loneliness hits, the loss. I miss the way Mr. and Mrs. Pinnacle would dote on me and call me their little girl. I miss how badly they wanted to keep me. Or maybe I just miss being part of a regular family.

Despite everything Deacon and I have been through, we still have a total honesty policy, most of it unspoken. Without a word he holds open his arms, and I step in to him, rest my cheek on his chest. His fingers slide over my arm, stroking my skin and showing me affection to help ease my ache. After a long moment, the comfort sets, and I pull away.

"Thanks," I say, stepping back. Deacon shrugs like it's no big deal, and I brush my hair out of my face. "Mind if I crash for a bit?" I ask him.

He smiles wryly. "Bed or couch?"

I laugh, and in answer I walk into the living room and pull the blanket off the back of the couch to spread it over the cushions. Deacon comes in and drops into the chair next to me, watching as I lie down and get settled.

"Are you hungry?" he asks. "I can make you something."

"No," I say, tucking my hand under my cheek. This feeling of abandonment, I don't think it happens to other closers—it didn't happen to Deacon. But for me it's getting harder each time. That's why I sometimes come here before going home—even when I don't plan to. I'm afraid for my father to see me like this. I'm afraid of what he'll do if he does.

Deacon moves to sit on the floor next to the couch, and lays his head on the cushion next to mine. "You've still got red hair," he whispers. "I like it."

"I'm washing it out the minute I get home," I say, staring back into his warm brown eyes. He smiles.

"You're right. I hate it," he agrees. "You look better as a

blonde." I smile, curling up and moving closer. "Aaron texted me earlier," he says. "Told me you lifted a T-shirt from the family."

Damn it, Aaron. "It wasn't like that."

"Wouldn't care if it was," Deacon says. "I was just wondering about the T-shirt. Band?"

I laugh. "Yeah. Rolling Stones. One with the big tongue."

"Nice."

We're quiet for a little bit and my eyes start to get heavy, even though my mind won't stop racing. Deacon reaches over to slide a strand of hair behind my ear. "Although effective," he says quietly, "your method of closing isn't good for you, Quinn. You shouldn't take it all on like that."

"I know," I tell him. "But what can I say? Sometimes my heart still beats."

He smiles. "Then it's a good thing I ripped mine out. It was a pain in the ass. Much like you. Be right back." He stands and leaves the room. I hear him moving around in the kitchen, and then he returns with a glass of water. He holds out the drink and a tiny white pill that he says will help me sleep. I sit up and take both appreciatively.

"You should think about changing your methods," he continues when I lie back down. "If not for you, then maybe for my peace of mind." He covers me with the blanket and kisses my forehead. "Yell if you need me, okay? Unless you want me to stay."

"No, you get some sleep," I tell him. We pause for a long

moment as he decides whether or not I mean it. I smile softly. "You're a good friend," I murmur.

This makes him chuckle because it's our new go-to phrase whenever either of us has the inclination to discuss the possibility of hooking up. Keeps us grounded. "It's too bad, right?" he asks, straightening up. "Bet it's hell looking at this face all the time." He models his jawline, narrowing his eyes.

"I can barely restrain myself most days," I say. "But, luckily, you talk. And the spell is broken."

"Asshole," he says with a laugh. We say good night, and then Deacon goes upstairs. I listen to the creaking floorboards above me as he walks across his room, silence when he gets into bed.

Some days I really do wish it would have worked out with us—times like now, when I'm all alone. I could lie to myself—slip into his bed tonight and pretend we're different. But in the morning Deacon would be cold, act like it was a mistake. I'd rather not tear open that old wound. We're better off this way, just like I told Aaron.

I close my eyes, and in the quiet I think about my future: six more months of pretending before I can live my life full-time. But even then, I have to wonder if anyone will ever want me, love me—the real me. Or if they'll only ever want me as someone else.

"Quinlan," Deacon says from somewhere close by. "Quinn—your dad's here."

My eyes fly open, and it takes me a minute to recognize

my surroundings. The room is dim, but lights from a car in the driveway filter in from behind the blinds. I sit up and stretch. When I didn't come home, I'm sure my dad knew exactly where to find me. Deacon certainly wouldn't have told him. My dad kind of hates him, and the feeling is entirely mutual.

Okay, "hate" is too strong a word for their relationship. When Deacon was younger, my dad held him up as the example for all of us. But toward the end, Deacon became defiant, and ended up spending almost every return in therapy. My father thought he was becoming a liability, and then boom—Deacon had a meeting and was out of his contract early, a fact I didn't learn until after we broke up. My father asked me to stop hanging out with him, but neither Deacon nor I liked that idea.

"Did he come to the door?" I ask, standing and folding the blanket to lay it over the back of the sofa.

"No," Deacon responds. "But he called my phone a few times and then showed up. He beeped the horn, which I'm sure my neighbors loved."

"You were always his favorite."

Deacon snorts a laugh and then leaves to grab my backpack from the bottom of the stairs. I slip on my shoes, readying myself for an explanation. Although I've come to Deacon's upon return before, tonight was later than usual. It's probably two in the morning. There's a slight twinge of guilt as I think about my father worrying. I may be angry that he was checking up on me, but I didn't mean to hurt him. He's my dad. I love him despite his fatherly instincts.

I walk to the front, my head still foggy from the sleeping pill, and Deacon slides my backpack over my shoulders, hugging me once from behind. "Call me tomorrow," he says before opening the door. "Tell Dad I said hi."

"Night," I say, and thank him before walking out the door.

When I get on the front porch, I hold up my palm to deflect the light from the car. My dad switches to the orange glow of the parking lights and I start toward him. I can just make out his silhouette behind the wheel. I might be imagining it, but his posture looks pissed.

I have to remind myself that I'm the wronged party here—he was spying on me. But by the time I get to the car, my resolve has faded and I apologize the minute I climb into the passenger seat.

"I fell asleep," I tell him. "I didn't mean to stay this late."

"I don't think I want the details, Quinn," he says shortly, and flicks on his lights. "Not to mention your partner left a bunch of trail mix in my car."

I snort a laugh, but quickly cover my mouth when my father glares at me. He puts his arm around my headrest and turns to back us out of the driveway. He cuts the wheel hard before spinning around and jetting forward, squealing the tires of the car. Yeah, I'd say he's a little pissed. And it has nothing to do with Aaron's lack of consideration.

He doesn't speak again right away, but I watch him, waiting for the lecture. His powder-blue sweater is wrinkled like he pulled it on as an afterthought while storming out the door. I wonder if he's still wearing a pajama top underneath. His thinning hair is just the same, and his wire glasses catch the glow of the streetlights as we pass under them. His tight expression and forced silence give away his mood.

"I apologized," I say after another agonizing moment of quiet. "Is there something you'd like to say to me, Father?"

He glances over, looking annoyed that I'd even joke around. I lift my eyebrow, letting him know I'm being entirely serious—well, except for the *Father* bit.

"Yes," he says, turning away. "Stop hanging out with Deacon."

"No deal," I say, slapping my palm on the dashboard like I'm a game show contestant. He doesn't laugh, but the corner of his mouth does hitch up before he purposefully straightens it. I pause, the betrayal starting to thicken in my veins.

"You do owe me an apology," I say more quietly, and lean back in the seat, turning to look out the window. "For spying on me."

He doesn't deny it immediately, and an ache develops in my chest, spiraling down to open a hole in my gut. I clench my teeth and wait for an explanation.

"I'm protecting you," he admits. "You've stopped talking to me about the assignments; I needed another safeguard."

"You could ask," I say. "You could just ask, Dad."

He exhales, and looks over. "You're right. I'm sorry. I'll let Marie know she can stop the questions. I was just . . . worried."

"Well, I'm home now. So you can put your cape back in the drawer." He chuckles, and the mood in the car warms. "And you don't have to be so mean to Deacon," I tell him. "He's not a terrible influence. A bad one, sure. But not terrible."

He glances at the time lit up on the dash. "It's two forty-seven in the morning, Quinn. Please don't give me indigestion before bed."

"Gross." We both laugh, our fight ended. By the time we get home, after an obligatory ride through the drive-through, we're joking about Aaron's facial hair and how my father should send him an official letter to cease and desist its growth before the next assignment.

The front porch light is blazing, the sky above us a midnight blue because of the overcast sky. I have a moment of assimilation as I pause in my foyer—the entire layout perfectly planned for reentry into my life. There are pictures of me growing up, baby blond braids and a gap-toothed smile. My mother, who I can't remember, blows out birthday candles next to me. There's a coat hanging on the rack above the shoe bench. It's dark blue with flannel trim, hung there year-round even though I haven't worn it in years. It's always there to ground me. Mirrors on both sides of the room so I can check my reflection. I walk toward the kitchen through a tunnel of Quinlan McKees.

I kick off my shoes and then step over them, hearing my father tsk as he leans down to pick them up behind me. Now that I'm home, I can't wait to get back to our boring old routines—the kind that remind me that I'm real. Three nights in a row of delivery pizza. Bad made-for-TV movies together on a Saturday night. The discussions of where to go on the family vacation we never have time to take. Those are the things I miss when I'm gone—the mundane. The only time we both forget that I'm a closer. I toss my crumpled white takeout bag on the kitchen table and sit down, ravenously hungry. I'm only one bite into my burrito when I notice the cup of coffee, half drunk, across from me at my father's seat. The closed file with a pen next to it. My stomach sinks.

I spin around just as my father enters the room. His expression is solemn and he slips his hands into his pockets. I'm completely stunned. This is why he wanted me home so quickly.

"No," I say, disbelieving. "I can't go. It's too soon."

He nods in agreement, but there's no change in his resolve. "I'm sorry, but they need you," he responds. "You leave the day after tomorrow."

CHAPTER FOUR

ABOUT FIFTEEN YEARS AGO, RENOWNED PHYSICIAN Arthur Pritchard built on the idea of role playing in trauma counseling by embedding therapists in people's lives. He figured out that grief sometimes led to depression and thought that if he could eradicate one, he could lessen the other. Working under Dr. Pritchard, my father used the initial theories and expanded on the research. Closers were established and sold as a remedy for the brokenhearted, the cure for grief. Of course, grief isn't *curable*, but it can be treated. Controlled. Eventually, my father and Marie, who was his assistant, took over the grief department entirely, selling their services to those who could afford the peace of mind. My dad set up safeguards to protect the closers, to protect me. And one of the strictest rules of all is that closers never have back-to-back assignments.

When the department was first created, closers were paid per assignment rather than on contract. As a result, many took on multiple roles to make extra cash. But then Alexander Kell happened. He leaped off the fifth-floor roof of the hospital where his mother worked. He'd recently finished three long-term jobs back-to-back, and his advisor had stuck him in therapy indefinitely to control his erratic behavior. Just before he jumped, Alexander told his mother he'd rather be dead than start over again.

The next month, Felicia Ross disappeared from her dorm room while on assignment at college. She was playing the part of an incoming freshman—the parents wanting her to attend the first day of school since their real daughter never got the chance. Felicia had only been home from her last assignment for a week when my father offered her this one. She was gone four days later, and no one has heard from her since.

As more and more closers ran off, the effect was devastating to both my father and the others in the grief department. Contracts with strict guidelines were created to keep closers from overworking. Those rules were established for our well-being, and I can't imagine why my father would want to break them now.

I drop my burrito on its wrapper, my appetite thoroughly stomped out. He wouldn't ask this of me if it wasn't important, but I'm still jarred by the request. At the same time, the closer part of me is curious. I've been on too many assignments to count, but I've rarely been sent out in the same month, let alone the same week. Why now? Why her?

My father sits across from me at the table and slides the file in my direction. He takes a swig of his cold coffee without wincing. I drag the folder in front of me and scan the name on the tab.

CATALINA BARNES

I open the cover and flip the photo right side up to study my new assignment. I'm immediately struck by her eyes—a deep dark brown with false lashes and winged eyeliner. They sparkle, but they're also thoughtful and interesting. I'll have to wear colored contacts again to hide my blue eyes.

"She died a little over a week ago," my father says, reaching to take a page from the file and setting it in front of me. It's a death certificate. I scan it and find the immediate cause of death listed as "undetermined." I've never seen the death certificate before; they're not usually in the file. Already I can tell Catalina's different—there are more therapy notes from doctors who have studied her case. I glance up at my father, but he's searching through the file for another picture.

"These are Catalina's parents," he continues, tapping the photo of a typical suburban couple. "They're not coping well," my father says. "I've been treating them myself, but this is one of the toughest cases I've ever had. They've made themselves sick over it, and they need closure." He takes off his glasses to pinch his fingers across the bridge of his nose. He looks exhausted. I glance down at the picture.

The mom appears to be in her thirties, short hair and soft features. She seems sweet, like the kind of mother who packs lunch bags with notes that say I LOVE YOU. The father is big and stocky, a teddy-bear type with a bushy mustache and graying brown hair. They're both lovely, and I'm immediately sorry that they've lost their daughter. I'm sure they loved her a lot.

"How did she die?" I ask quietly, flipping back to the picture of Catalina. My father seems taken aback by the question. Although I usually know how the assignments died (car accident, for instance), it's morbid and disrespectful to ask for details. And it makes playing them that much more difficult. To be her, I have to imagine her alive. Alive and breathing with thoughts and desires and goals. Otherwise I'm just another counselor.

"We're still waiting for the autopsy results," my father says. He pulls out another picture, and I feel the weight of his stare. "This is about more than Catalina's family, though," he says, snapping the corner of a photo as he lays it in front of me. I immediately turn to him, confused and alarmed. "This is Catalina's boyfriend," he says. "He's part of the closure."

"What?" I ask, looking back at the picture. Closure is typically for family only. This guy . . . I study him, noticing the way he sits next to Catalina on a bench, how he stares at the side of her face, his expression a portrait of admiration. Catalina smiles for the camera, but her boyfriend seems utterly consumed by her. There's a small twinge of longing, and I push the photo aside and turn to my dad.

"I can't do that," I say. "Parents and siblings are hard enough. Hell, I don't even interact with their friends. And this guy loved her. Look how he's watching her," I tell him, pointing to the boyfriend's face. "What if he tries to kiss me or something? How am I supposed to handle that?"

"The same way you defuse any situation," my father says seriously. "You redirect, you reassert the relationship ending they require, and if that fails, you contact Marie for further intervention."

"A boyfriend," I repeat incredulously, glancing down at him. "What's his name?"

"Isaac Perez."

There are all sorts of competing emotions in my heart, the main one being fear. As a closer, I've occasionally had to deal with overattached parents. Okay, I've *often* had to deal with overattached parents. But this would be different. This is a peer, a boyfriend, a guy who's probably made out with Catalina a hundred times, shared secrets with her. Parents ultimately know the difference between me and their daughter, their flesh and blood. Add hormones to the mix, and I'm not entirely confident in the outcome of this closure.

"Dad, I don't think—"

"He's refusing therapy," my father says quietly. A quick chill shoots up my arms, hollows out my chest. As someone who hates talking, I can understand the aversion—but refusing therapy is insane.

"Refusing?" I ask, just to make sure I'm clear on the stakes. My father nods.

If Isaac refuses therapy but continues to decline, they will admit him to the psychiatric ward of the hospital. It's what they do for people at risk—people refusing help—based on the new codes established for mental health stability. This boy will be committed, and no one knows how long it will be before he's let out again. I think of his admiring expression and hate the idea of him being locked away.

"Isaac is only part of the assignment," my father says, folding his hands on the table in front of him. "The parents are our main concern for now. They have another child, but she's completed therapy and achieved success. She doesn't want to be a part of the healing process, so she's living with relatives during your stay."

"And how long will that be?" I ask. My last assignment was two days, and now that I'm home, I'm ready to get back to my real life. My father's quiet for a long moment, and I lift my eyes in his direction. "Dad? How long?"

"The assignment is for two weeks."

I gasp, free-fall into confusion and panic. "That's too long!" I say. "You can't . . . what? Dad, we're not allowed—"

"We're making an exception. Quinn, I can't tell you how important this assignment is. If there was anyone else . . ." He stops, pink rising on his cheeks. His response makes me pause. He doesn't think this is a good idea either.

"You know this is dangerous," I say. "Why is Catalina Barnes so important? She's not the first dead teenager in Oregon, Dad." *Ouch.* The words are insensitive, and I wince at my own callousness. Although I try not to get attached to my assignments, I know more than anybody the gravity of their situation. They're not coming back. Their lives are over, and it's a tragic thing.

My father's shoulders stiffen, and he pushes the papers back into the folder and closes the file. "You're right," he agrees. "But this request is coming from beyond the department, from my boss. If you don't think you can help the Barnes family, we'll contact the other advisors again. See if another closer can be brought in in time. But it's not likely. This one is flagged for immediate intervention."

The words echo through the room. It's rare that my father's boss asks a favor. Only Deacon has ever met Arthur Pritchard, and he quit soon after. "This is dangerous," I repeat quietly. "So why me?" I'm scared of losing myself, but I'm also scared of failing the family. Failing my father.

"You're the best."

"But I'm your daughter."

My father lowers his eyes, his expression tightening as he struggles with the same thought. When he looks at me again, all I can see is how much he cares about me. How I am his pride and joy—his greatest achievement. His belief in me never wavers.

For the last eleven years, I've completed every assignment he's given me without fault, except for the occasional taken item. I don't screw up. My father is truly devoted to his patients, devoted to their well-being—and he counts on me to help them. He's a good man, and I'm ashamed of my selfishness, guilty now that my father has made it clear what's at stake. I swallow hard, nodding that I understand.

"Why two weeks?" I ask. "Why so long?"

"It's all in the file." He taps the closed folder. "Quinn," he says, leaning into the table. "I know I sprung this on you, but I promise you're strong enough. I wouldn't have asked otherwise."

"Is this why Marie was asking Aaron about my state of mind?" I ask, realizing now the purpose of the new line of questioning. "Did she tell you I was fit for the job?"

He nods. "She did. I wanted to make sure before I sent you in. Look, I have no doubt you can do this, but it's a big commitment. One I hope you'll never have to repeat." My father stands up and pushes in his chair.

"It's gotten late," he says. "Why don't you take the night to think about it and we'll talk more in the morning." He leans down to kiss the top of my head, but I stare straight ahead, overwhelmed by my responsibility. I murmur a "good night" right after he walks out, and then look down at the file waiting on the kitchen table. Look at the life I'm about to finish.

After tossing my uneaten burrito in the trash, I grab my backpack and go upstairs. I take a quick shower to wash the red dye out of my hair, and then head to my room. When I walk in, I'm temporarily displaced by its familiarity. My tall queen bed—not made, never made—with dark wood frame. My pale pink walls dotted with a white and silver pattern that Deacon designed. I told him it looked like a flower—he told me it was a cricket. Either way, it's pretty cool. I set the file on my vanity table and cross to the walk-in closet, my backpack heavy on my shoulder. My jaw clicks when I yawn.

The closet is filled with everything I could need for an assignment. Wigs along the top shelf—different colors and lengths. An organizer with drawers for extensions and contacts cases. From the file picture, it looked like Catalina had short blond hair in a shade lighter than mine. I scan the wigs, thinking I'll have to adjust the length once I find the right color. I reach into my bag and pull out the hair extensions, combing my fingers through them to smooth them out. After I untangle them, I open the drawer and lay them next to the others, and drop my bag on the floor.

Again I yawn, my eyes too heavy to keep open much longer. I'll have to read through Catalina's file to see what sort of clothes she wore—what kind of makeup. Sometimes the photos are outdated, so each assignment takes a careful case study. But there's not much time for that. I click off the closet light and run my fingers along my wall, touching the raised pattern as I walk. I pull the first pair of pajamas I find out of my dresser drawer.

"Catalina Barnes," I murmur out loud. I wonder what her voice sounded like, if it'll be easy to mimic. If she had any quirks or interests that I can't master. I switch off the overhead light and lie in bed, staring up at the glow-in-the dark stars still stuck to my ceiling from a time I can't remember. Each blink lasts longer, and just before I close my eyes completely, I whisper, "What happened to you?"

I've never needed an alarm clock. I wake early every morning no matter what time I go to bed, like my body automatically dispenses a bucket of caffeine into my circulatory system. My internal clock is permanently set at seven a.m., no matter how much sleep I get the night before. Still, by afternoon I'll probably crash and end up napping.

My head feels thick and cloudy, and I climb out of bed to move around—let my brain catch up with my body. The house is quiet; my dad is probably wiped out from staying up late with me. I see my reflection in the vanity mirror and pause for a long moment. For a second, I don't recognize myself without the red hair. I don't recognize myself as Quinn.

The folder seizes my attention and the conversation with my father floods back. I'm going on assignment again—this time for two whole weeks. This is major. This is crazy. I pull out the small chair and sit down, resting my elbow on the vanity top. I open the file and find Catalina's picture.

She has small features and brown eyes and blond hair, although I can't tell if the color is natural or dyed. She doesn't have freckles, which means I'll have to cover mine. She wears more makeup than I normally would, but that actually helps when I'm trying to look like the subject. Her frame is similar to mine, but not as curvy. She's average in every way. And again I wonder: Why her?

I glance at the photo of her parents and then pick through her therapy notes. She's from Lake Oswego, a picturesque little town near Portland. I've had an assignment up there once before—Castle Dillon, twelve years old, drowning—but I don't remember much from those two or three days. Scratch that. I remember her brother. He was four and hung on to my leg when I got there, thinking I was actually his sister. The entire scene was a horrific mess, and it was decided that he didn't need to be involved in the closure process. He basically had to lose his sister twice.

I rub hard at my face, trying to rub away the icky uncertainty that comes along with these memories. If I got attached to the families, my job would become impossible. I respect them, their feelings, their lives—I don't become part of them. I don't love them. I'm not allowed to.

To distract myself, I dive back into the file. The death certificate is vague, and I wonder why it's in the file in the first place. Usually if the cause of death is of any importance, my father tells me what happened. I sift through, passing the picture of Isaac, and find a letter—a photocopy from a journal. Normally I'd get the entire book. I wonder where the rest of the pages are.

The handwriting is loopy and sweet, and I mentally compare it to my own—small and printed. The craving starts: a wish to mimic. That's the thing most people wouldn't understand: I like to copy people. I find it fascinating, observing them, studying them, and replicating them. I'm good at it.

Next to me on my dresser is a Disney cup filled with pens (a souvenir I might have lifted from Antonia Messner a few years ago), and I grab one.

I pick a piece of ripped paper out of my trash can. There's a random number scrawled across it, but I don't remember what it's from. Probably a telephone number that Deacon got but threw out here. His subtle reminder that I'm the most important girl in his life—even if he dates other people. I flip over the page and then examine Catalina's handwriting again.

This time we left before they threatened to lock the doors.

I set down the pen and pull the page in front of me, my interest piqued. Most of the assignments keep journals—it's a class we all have to take in high school, an extension of therapy. Once upon a time education was all about data and science and math. But society reassessed its goals. Now the schools here give us the basics, but they also help us identify our weaknesses, point out flaws in our mental health so that we can work toward managing it. Journaling was actually one of my favorite classes, even though turning over our personal journals to the teacher seemed like a bit of a missed point. They're not really our private thoughts if we have to let someone else read them. Then again, I'm a little more protective of my emotions because I know what happens to the information once we're dead. It ends up in a file.

This time we left before they threatened to lock the doors. Isaac pulled me along in the park and we were both laughing. Angie pretty much hates him now, but she sort of hates me too. What are little sisters for, right? Me and Isaac ended up on the baseball bleachers, kissing until someone beeped their horn in the parking lot. Isaac didn't want to leave, but his mother's face is hard to argue with. Especially when it's all scrunched up like that. We said good night, same way we do every time. I waited a minute longer to watch him leave, hoping he would look back. He didn't.

My eyes widen and I reread the journal entry, glancing at the date. It was written a few weeks before she died. Has my dad seen this? The therapists? Was the couple having problems? Like it's a marathon of a favorite TV show, I become obsessed. I spend the entire morning going through the file, studying the journal entries that were included and her parents' interviews. Turns out it's only two weeks until her eighteenth birthday and there was a party planned. A big bash that the mom can't seem to get past: *I already ordered the cake. It's chocolate raspberry—her favorite. What am I supposed to do with her cake? It'll still be her birthday.* The therapists thought it would provide the needed closure if I stayed until this party, let the parents say good-bye on their terms. It's a little morbid, but I guess I get it. I'll be out the door right after having a huge slice of chocolate raspberry cake.

There's nothing else out of the ordinary in Catalina's file, so I practice her smile until I get it right. I find the links to her different social media accounts, the passwords provided by the therapists. Before I can open up my laptop, though, my stomach growls, and I go downstairs to grab a bowl of cereal.

My father isn't in the kitchen, and I'm about to call for him when I realize that it's Thursday. He's probably at the hospital. My days are mixed up, and I'm only half aware of what I'm doing as I pull out the box of Frosted Flakes and the milk.

"I'm Quinlan McKee," I murmur, repeating Marie's words from last night. "I live at 2055 Seneca Place in Corvallis, Oregon. I'm seventeen and I drive a beat-up old Honda that my father won't replace." I sit at the table and stare down at my bowl. "I'm Quinlan McKee," I whisper.

CHAPTER FIVE

MY FATHER WORKS UNTIL NINE ON THURSDAYS, SO around six—after a well-deserved nap—I pull on the black Rolling Stones T-shirt and a pair of jeans to head over to Aaron's apartment. I'm feeling altogether miserable at the thought that this will be my last time hanging out for a while. It's hard for a noncloser to understand how difficult our lives can be. Tomorrow I give up my life for someone else's. The first time I'll talk to a friend will be when Aaron calls to check on me, and then again when he sets up my extraction. Aaron is supposed to be my first contact because we try not to change the variables of real life. These sorts of things always have to stay the same. Soon Quinlan McKee won't exist. That's my life—half the time I don't exist.

I grab my keys off the entry table and go outside to start

my car. When the check-engine light comes on, I sigh, and then back out of the driveway. The day after one of us returns, Aaron, Deacon, and I usually meet up to talk about anything other than our assignments. We eat and drink and act stupid to feel normal. Tonight I'm far too logical, but I'm willing to go through the motions. I do my best to put on my happy face when I park in front of Aaron's apartment complex. I toss my car keys into my bag and head up to the second floor.

On the open landing, I glance around. The sky is still bright, not even dusk. Right now it feels like I'm in an hourglass filling up with sand, waiting to be flipped over. I knock on the door before opening it and walking in.

"There she is," Deacon announces the minute I appear in the entry. He's on the couch in the living room, and he holds up an oversize blue plastic cup in cheers. He takes a sip, his eyes trained on me like he can already tell something's wrong. The girl next to him casts a curious look in my direction and then laughs and touches his thigh to get his attention. Deacon flinches, but turns to her and smiles—charming as ever. A little farther down the wall I find Aaron, his phone in his hand as Myra sits beside him, prattling on about something close to his ear. Aaron hits a button and music starts to play. He notices my shirt and snorts, and I offer him a sarcastic wave. Awesome—guess I'm fifth-wheeling it. Aaron could have told me Deacon had a girl tonight.

Without speaking out loud, I turn and stroll down the hallway toward the kitchen. There's a pizza box, empty except for two partially devoured crusts. Several two-liters of soda are open, along with a bottle of Jack Daniel's. I don't want to risk a hangover, so I don't bother with the alcohol. I pour some Sprite into a cup and take out my phone, check for any messages. I don't have any, of course. The only people who would call me are sitting in the other room.

This time last year, Deacon, Aaron, and I were at Deacon's, hanging out on his back porch. It was unseasonably warm, and Aaron busted out a small camping grill he'd picked up at the convenience store. It could only cook one hamburger and a few hot dogs at a time, but we didn't mind. There were cold drinks in the cooler, the smoky smell of fire signaling the upcoming summer. Deacon and I were dating then, and he was sitting on the stair below my feet, the side of his head resting on my thigh as we listened to Aaron talk about a new band he'd gone to see. That night seemed to last forever, the three of us hanging out and normal—or as close to normal as we could be. What I wouldn't give to have that back for even a second.

I take another sip of soda and then rest my hip against the granite counter. Normally I'd be in there with them, but right now I'm feeling a bit abandoned. I haven't been home twenty-four hours and I've already got another assignment. I'm not even fully me again.

"Hey, sad face," Deacon says from the doorway, startling me. I plan to roll my eyes or do something equally uninterested, but when I turn to him, he reads my misery too quickly. Deacon drains what's left in his cup and sets it on the counter before starting toward me. Tears sting my eyes, and I turn away so he won't see. *I don't want to go.*

Deacon wraps his arms around me from behind and rests his chin on the top of my head. He sways me to the awful song that Aaron's playing in the other room, soothing me by distraction. Deacon's body is warm, strong—a tether to my real life.

"What's all this about?" he asks, sounding worried. "You're home now."

"I wish," I murmur, putting my hands on his forearms to keep him close. "I have another assignment."

Deacon stills; both of us know the implications of taking back-to-back cases. He tightens his arms around me. "No," he says simply. "Your father can't send you out again. It's too dangerous. Tell him you need therapy instead."

"Not a chance," I respond. Deacon knows I would never volunteer for therapy. Closers covet their privacy, me especially. He also knows I've already made up my mind about this assignment or I wouldn't have told him in the first place. But there's no point in dwelling on tomorrow—this is my only night home. "Besides," I tell him in a lighter tone, "only the really screwed-up people go to therapy. Look how you turned out."

Deacon chuckles and starts to sway me again. "Aw, come on," he says, leaning down to brush his lips over my temple. "You afraid of what the counselors will find in the steel-trap brain of yours? You keeping secrets, Quinlan?"

The levity eases the heaviness I've been carrying since last night. "A few," I tell him. "But only the really sordid ones."

"That so?" he asks in a low voice. I close my eyes as his fingers skim over my hip. "Then maybe we should talk about them," he murmurs. "I'm an excellent listener."

The music from the other room cuts abruptly, and Aaron announces, "I think Deacon's in the bathroom, Shelly."

I open my eyes. Aaron's voice is a cold splash of water on my desire, sobering me up to reality. Deacon laughs at Aaron's obvious attempt to warn us that Deacon's date is looking for him. Not that we needed his cover; we weren't doing anything wrong. Not *really*.

I untangle myself from Deacon's arms, and he hums out his protest, holding on a second longer than necessary. When we're finally apart, he reaches past me to grab a bottle from the counter. Our proximity is still too close. Too connected. I move farther down the granite slab and change the subject.

"So Shelly seems nice," I tell him. "Been seeing her long?"

Deacon holds up the bottle to offer me a drink, but I shake my head no.

"Just met her tonight." He studies me for a moment, trying to guess my feelings on the subject. "She's awful handsy, isn't she?" he asks. "I feel so objectified."

I snort a laugh but secretly agree that she did seem to be all over him. In the hallway the echo of his date's approaching heels is ominous, and Deacon lifts his eyebrow like he's asking if we should make a run for it instead. I won't let him off that easy.

"He's in here, Shelly," I call, staring straight at him. He's made his bed. If Deacon doesn't like his date, that's his issue. I'm not going to be the excuse for him to get out of it.

"Cold," he mutters, and sips from his drink.

I pick up my Sprite and turn to leave. The girl appears in the doorway, her huge saucer eyes lighting up the minute she finds Deacon standing at the counter. I take that as my cue to exit the scene. Poor thing. This girl probably has no idea that she's hooking up with a closer. I doubt she'd be here if she did.

She smiles at me as I pass, unsure but polite out of habit. She's a bit more aggressive than his usual dates, but they're all fairly sweet. Deacon honest-to-God likes nice girls—it's one of his better qualities. Of course, once they learn what he does (or did) for a living, they're freaked out. The job isn't glamorous, and most people think we're terrifying—like we're somehow to blame for the deaths of the people we play. We make them confront their own mortality, and for the most part people don't enjoy being around someone who's great at impersonating the recently deceased.

When I reenter the living room, Aaron grins like he figures I owe him for warning us that Deacon's girl was looking for him. Just so he'll drop it, I mutter a "thanks" and take a seat on the couch closest to him and Myra.

Myra's sitting on the hardwood floor, her shoulders in between Aaron's knees while he twists tiny braids into her hair. She holds the comb, and with every new row Aaron brushes the teeth along her scalp to smooth down her curls. She flashes her heavily lined eyes in my direction.

"How are you?" she asks with little warmth.

I lower my head, not wanting to betray any emotion. "Fine."

"Don't look fine," she says. The room fills with a heavy silence, and I have to remind myself that I shouldn't feel this much disappointment. I can't be so selfish.

"That's because Quinn's got another assignment," Deacon announces, walking into the room. Shelly trails behind, pausing awkwardly when Deacon sits next to me. "Counselors are sending her in tomorrow," he tells Aaron and Myra.

"What?" Shelly asks from the doorway, looking around the room at all of us. The color drains from her cheeks, and she folds her thin arms over her chest. "You're *closers*?" But she spits the word like it's filthy. Myra groans because she knows what comes next, and Aaron and I exchange expectant looks.

"*I'm* not a closer," Deacon says earnestly, pointing to himself. "But she is." He hikes his thumb in my direction. I quickly slap it away. Deacon continues with his helpful explanation. "He's a total closer," he tells Shelly, motioning toward Aaron. He frowns at Myra. "But not her."

Shelly's shoulders relax slightly, eased by Deacon's tongue-in-cheek introductions. But then Deacon winces like he forgot to mention something. "Actually," he says apologetically, "I used to be a closer too. A really good one. Now I'm just the guy who hangs out with them. I have no other actual life skills."

Aaron positively busts up, covering his mouth and laying his head on the arm of his chair while his body shakes with laughter. Shelly is wide-eyed, trying to determine if Deacon is serious or not. When her gaze falls on me, my smile fades. All at once her judgment hits me square in the chest, a heavy weight on my already thin conscience.

"You take advantage of people's suffering," she says, staring me down like I'm dirt. "You take their money and lie to them, rewrite their lives. You're disgusting."

"Hey, hey," Deacon tells Shelly, holding out his hand. He looks between me and her, but I don't acknowledge him. I glare at Shelly, all of the humor in the room sucked away by her ignorance.

"I don't exploit people," I say evenly. "They come to me for comfort, for peace. I help them with their grief."

She scoffs. "Think what you want," she says. "But around here we know the truth. You're pariahs, a bunch of—"

"Okay," Myra calls out, her temper flared. "Enough of you, Little Miss Sunshine." Myra yanks the comb out of Aaron's hand and scrambles to her feet. Aaron quickly jumps up and wraps his arm around her waist to hold her back. Myra jabs the comb in Shelly's direction. "I suggest you take your noisy-ass shoes and walk them out my door before I let Quinlan beat the hell out of you."

I turn quickly to Myra, sure she knows I've never been in a fight in my life. Her braids are unfinished, springing up at the ends and making her look unhinged. Her bluff works, though; Shelly takes a step back.

"Go to hell," she tells all of us in a shaky voice. She stomps out the door and slams it shut behind her. The pictures on the wall rattle from the force, and Myra slowly works herself back down to the floor, holding up the comb to Aaron so he can finish her hair.

We're quiet. Deacon's staring straight ahead, looking sorry that he let the situation get out of hand. He's apologetic when he turns to me, but it's not his fault. We're used to people hating us.

"Well, she was a bitch," I say.

It takes a second, but then Deacon laughs. "Yeah, I think I missed the warning signs there," he says, rubbing his jaw.

"Bet she knew one of the assignments," Aaron comments, sitting back in the chair. "Friend from school, cousin, or something." He nods, agreeing with himself. "That was some visceral hatred."

He's right—she's probably lost someone in the past and it's colored her perception. People who aren't directly involved in the therapy have a different opinion of us, but it's because they don't understand. Her words leave a sting on my skin, though, but soon they're drowned out by my other worries.

Myra taps her braids and then pulls the rubber band from around her wrist. "Here," she tells Aaron, passing it up to him. "We'll finish later." Aaron ties off the ends, and Myra moves to sit next to him in the oversize chair. She looks at me, and when I meet her eyes, her expression softens.

"You've really got another assignment?" she asks. "I thought that wasn't allowed." She turns to Aaron with concern, maybe afraid he'll be sent away too. Aaron's face has gone ashen, his jaw tight as the reality hits him.

"It isn't really allowed," he says quietly to Myra. His dark eyes meet mine. "Who is the girl?"

I shrug. "Just a girl," I say. "There's nothing in her file that makes her special—it's a little more in-depth, sure, but not special." I think on it for a second. "Her death certificate was in there, but it said 'undetermined.'"

Deacon moves to the edge of the couch, his hands folded between his knees as he leans forward. "Her death certificate was in her file? What did your dad say about it?"

"Nothing. Said they were still waiting for the autopsy results. The girl's parents are his patients and he's afraid he can't help them. He said this is an emergency. They're sending me in for two weeks." Myra gasps and I hear Aaron curse under his breath.

"They should be in therapy," Deacon responds. "This breaks every protocol. I can't believe your father is seriously considering this. He shouldn't put you at risk to help them."

"The assignment's coming from Arthur Pritchard," I say, and his eyes widen. "Besides, I've already agreed. It's the right thing to do."

Deacon scoffs and sits back on the couch, grabbing his drink from the side table to take a long sip. He's only looking out for me, but my job is to provide closure. My dad's right—I save people.

A heavy silence fills the room, no one sure what to say next, especially when Deacon is clearly pissed off. But I haven't told them everything yet.

"I'll have a boyfriend," I say quietly, and take a sip from my Sprite. They all turn to me.

"What?" Aaron asks, exchanging a look with Deacon.

"Catalina has a boyfriend named Isaac," I say. "My dad wants him to be part of the closure."

"Tell him to fuck off," Deacon responds. "That's not allowed."

I shoot him a pointed look to remind him that he's talking about my dad. Deacon closes his eyes and I can actually see him try to gather his thoughts before speaking again.

"Sorry," he says in a controlled voice. "Politely tell your father no, Quinn. You're not a relationship counselor. If this dude needs closure, it's because he's still in love with his dead girlfriend. What if he transfers that to you? What if he falls in love with you instead? That's why this shit isn't allowed. And you're not going to be yourself—you'll be her." He says *her* like it annoys him, like she's already betrayed him. "What if you . . ." He stops and shakes his head out of aggravation.

"She's not going to hook up with him, Deacon," Myra says. "She knows the rules." I thank her for her vote of confidence and she nods to me. See—she's not always horrible. "Now," Myra continues, "it's been a long night already. Are we going to keep obsessing about Quinn's imaginary love life, or are we going to have fun? I spent ten dollars at the damn Redbox renting crappy movies with explosions. Yeah?" She looks around at us, and Aaron laughs—the sound deep and hearty in the sad little room.

"Yeah," he says, leaning over to kiss her. Deacon doesn't agree, but his hand brushes my hair as he wraps his arm around the back of the sofa and settles in. We don't mention Isaac again. We don't mention Shelly or assignments. We spend the next few hours watching mindless entertainment and pretending our lives are normal. We're always pretending.

Deacon yawns loudly from behind me while the credits roll across the screen. Aaron is braiding Myra's hair again, but they both look like they're about to fall asleep. I guess it's time to call it a night. Reluctantly (because I don't want to rush tomorrow), I climb up and stretch. When I turn, Deacon is smiling at me.

"What?" I ask.

"Can I have a lift home?" he asks sweetly. "My ride ran out of here in a blind rage, wishing me dead." Myra glances over curiously for my response.

"Yeah, fine. Grab your stuff," I tell him, waving my hand. He jumps up, grinning madly, and goes over to bump fists with Aaron and pick up his backpack in the corner. Myra lifts her eyebrows and I shake my head. "What?" I ask her. "He doesn't have a ride."

"Please, girl," she says with a laugh. "He was planning on leaving with you all along."

I look behind me and watch as Deacon slips on his sneakers, standing on one foot with surprising dexterity. "Either way," I tell Myra, "I still would have given him a ride home."

"I know." She comes over and pulls me into a lilac-scented hug. We stay like that a long second, both knowing this a real good-bye, at least for now. That's the thing about Myra—she may not be a closer, but she understands what the job takes and how it affects us. "We'll see you in a few weeks, okay?" she says quietly. She pulls back and I have to press my lips together to keep from blubbering like an idiot. I nod, and then hold up my hand in a wave to Aaron. He can barely even look at me but tries to smile anyway. I say good night, and then Deacon and I leave.

I pull into Deacon's driveway and he sets down the empty to-go cup we got from the drive-through. He caps the pen he grabbed from my console and then turns the cup in the holder so I can see his drawing. He draws on everything. "Look," he says. "It's us." I glance at the new school–style figures and respective . . . positions before lifting my gaze to Deacon's.

"Oh, yeah?" I ask. "And what exactly are we doing?"

Deacon chuckles and tosses the pen into the console before unclicking his seat belt. "Don't be gross—we're playing cricket, obviously." I tilt my head and realize that with a lot of creative license, that could be true. "So . . . ," he says with a devilish little smile. "Want to come in for a while?" Pinpricks race up my arms; there's a flutter in my stomach under his attention. This would be so much easier if I didn't find him completely adorable.

"Uh, no. I don't think so," I respond with a laugh, and look away.

"Come on," he says playfully. "Before you have a boyfriend."

"You sound jealous."

"I am," he says immediately. "I most definitely am."

"Oh, stop," I tell him. "He won't really be my boyfriend, you know."

"Yeah, I know," he says, and looks out the windshield toward his house. When he turns back to me, his smile softens. "We'll stay downstairs," he offers quietly. "Clothes on."

There's a pang in my chest, an impending loneliness. "And then what?" I ask. I'm making a point, but part of me wants an answer I know he can't give.

"And then I'll be really sweet," he says. All of the joking is gone from his expression, replaced with vulnerability—a look that tells me he'd do anything to be with me. Be close to me. But I've fallen for that look before, and it's always ended with regret.

Truth is, I don't know what Deacon wants anymore—it's not just physical. Whatever it is must scare him, though, and I'm the one who ends up getting hurt. So I make the concerted effort to resist his temptation, even if sometimes I'd like nothing more than to surround myself with his affection.

"I can't," I say quietly, putting my hand on his cheek, unable to keep myself from touching him. Deacon turns his face to kiss the heel of my palm, his lips warm and soft. His eyes steady on mine as my resolve wavers.

"But I really want you to," he murmurs against my skin.

My insides melt, but I don't let that sway me. Deacon knows exactly what to say and how to say it. But this is all because I have another assignment, our feelings heightened because I'm leaving. I know better than to think it's real.

"You're a really good friend," I tell him finally, ending our evening.

Despite the rejection, Deacon kisses my hand again and then leans in to quickly kiss my cheek. He grabs his bag from the floor, and I can't decide if I want him to argue or get out before I change my mind. I'm going to miss him like crazy. And I never miss him more than I do just before I'm gone. I may be a little nostalgic right now.

"Wait," I say. Deacon's breath catches, but before my comment can be misinterpreted, I work the extra car key off the ring in the ignition. "So you can use it while I'm gone," I tell him.

He smiles and holds out his hand, looking disappointed that I didn't have a different offer. Back when we were dating, I'd leave Deacon my Honda while I was on assignment so he could use it. My father wasn't thrilled with the arrangement, saying Deacon could afford his own car. But then Deacon would ask him how big his carbon footprint was and my father would laugh and tell him to go home.

I'll be gone for two weeks this time—longest assignment ever. Maybe I just don't want Deacon to forget me. I set the key in his hand and Deacon closes his fingers around mine, holding for a long moment before thanking me and saying he'll take good care of the car. I nod, knowing he will.

"Be safe, Quinlan," he says, opening the passenger door and getting out. He ducks down to look at me one last time. "And make sure you come back," he adds. If Deacon has a visible insecurity, it's me. All of his arrogance fades when I'm about to go on assignment, because he always worries I won't come back to Corvallis. I wouldn't be the first closer to jump ship without a trace. Deacon's afraid I'll tire of this life and pick another.

I smile at him, not admitting that I'll be at his door in two weeks, looking for comfort. Not admitting that seeing him with Shelly tonight annoyed me. Not admitting the way I still feel about him. Or maybe I'm just highly emotional right now and looking for any connection.

Deacon shuts the car door and heads to the front of his house. Just as he grabs the doorknob, he turns to look back at me, serious and solemn. And then he slips inside and disappears from my new life.

CHAPTER SIX

AT 6:59 A.M. I LIE FLAT ON MY BACK IN BED, STARING up at the stars on my ceiling, which have faded to a yellowish-green hue in the soft morning light. My room is stuffy because the heater kicks on full blast and neither my dad nor I have been able to figure out how to reset the timer. My hairline is damp with sweat, but I don't make any initial moves to get up. I'm drawing out my last moments, mentally saying good-bye to my room. I'm like a little kid trying to give thanks at a holiday meal, randomly naming objects. *Thank you for the lamp,* I think. *The stars on my ceiling. These itchy pajamas and my soft, fluffy sheets.*

I sniff a laugh and roll out of bed, pausing to glance around. I really do hate leaving my room, my life. And maybe that's why my thoughts turn to Deacon, and I wonder if he's lying in bed thinking of me.

"Quinlan," my father calls from downstairs. "You awake?"

"Yep," I say back automatically, and start toward the door. The folder is still sitting on my vanity, and I'll want to go over it several times more before we leave. After that, it's a matter of getting to the house and looking through Catalina's things. Smelling her perfume and trying on her clothes. I won't do this in front of the family, of course. I can't break the illusion. I'll show up with my hair back, hood up. I won't say too much at first—I won't want them to think of my voice. Instead, Marie will bring me inside and take me to the room. After that, she'll wait downstairs and have the initial consultation with the family. When they're ready, which can take anywhere from thirty minutes to several hours, I'll come in and meet them. At that point . . . I will be Catalina Barnes. I'll continue studying her family while there, but I won't break character if I can help it.

I don't know how I'll deal with her boyfriend, though. It's so out of my realm of expertise—I've never even been able to deal with my own boyfriend, although I'm not sure if mine and Deacon's relationship was ever exactly typical. What Catalina had with Isaac would be more normal. I furrow my brow, my worry once again spiked—I don't know what normal is. After another second of doubt, I push away the thoughts to steady myself. I'll have to lose these feelings of uncertainty if I hope to be successful. A confident closer is an effective closer.

I laugh to myself, walking out to the hall. I'm starting to sound like one of Marie's lectures. Every so often, we're brought into the offices to go over the rules, get recertified. We review the "person-centered" approach to what we do and how our role play frees up their minds to heal. Like tricking your brain out of its grief. People think it's a broken heart that hurts; maybe that sounds more romantic. But it's the brain, and it can be fooled.

"The closer must demonstrate empathy and understanding toward the clients, always maintaining a professional role, especially during the assignment," Marie would tell me in front of the panel observing us. "The goal is to use the client's own memories to help them close their loop of grief and accept their new life. The closer helps them find their place in a new world without their loved one, maintaining the delicate balance between denial and acceptance. This is achieved through nonjudgmental and careful guidance."

I always hate those reminders, as if I'd ever sit and judge the people I'm supposed to help. Or even act unprofessionally. I've been a closer most of my life—I'm more qualified than the experts on the panel. I think that should make me exempt from those horrible recert meetings.

I get it; I understand the need for our brand of role-playing therapy. More often than not, parents call us when they didn't get the chance to say good-bye, to say I love you or I'm sorry. This can lead to hurt and emotional trauma. The moms and dads I've met never considered a future without their child—they didn't want one. Part of my job is to show them that it's possible to be okay. Maybe not great, not right away. But they can get by.

I walk into the kitchen and find my dad waiting. There's toast on the table, and the smell of strong coffee is thick in the air. I say good morning and drop down on the hardwood chair while he pours me a cup. I rub my eyes, and my dad grabs the creamer from the fridge and sets both the coffee and the cream in front of me.

"Get much sleep?" he asks.

"I slept fine," I tell him. "Just . . . my head is a little cloudy. You know how it is on returning."

He nods and sits across from me, watching as I pour the cream into my coffee until it's almost white. I hate the bitterness but love the caffeine. The newspaper—a relic when it's so much easier to Google the news, I always joke—sits between us, and I see the headline talking about an uptick in noted side effects from the latest medication craze and the impending investigation. I grab a piece of dry toast and take a bite.

"Should we go over the rules?" my father asks, adjusting his glasses and looking far too tired for someone who didn't just get back from an assignment.

"I'd rather not," I say hopefully. I bring my mug to my lips and blow on the coffee before taking a tentative sip. When I peer over my cup at my dad, I see he's waiting for a different answer. "Maintain eye contact and keep facial expressions open and caring," I say, grabbing another piece of toast and talking between chews. "Be attentive and relaxed when speaking to the clients. Don't slouch or frown or look otherwise bored." I smile. "Even when I am."

"Good," my father says, reaching for his own toast. "Anything else?"

I hold out my hand and begin counting off points on my fingers, rapid-fire. "Keep my voice sympathetic, don't interrupt, don't rush, and most of all, let the client lead their recovery. Did I pass the interview?" I ask sarcastically.

"I just want you to keep things in perspective, Quinn," he says apologetically. "The clearer you are going in, the easier extraction will be later."

He's right, of course. I set my piece of toast on my plate, take another sip of coffee, and then exhale. "I'll monitor Mr. and Mrs. Barnes for physical reactions to their grief," I continue. "Change of appetite, trouble sleeping, memory problems, or erratic mood swings. Based on what I learn, I'll target the painful memories and help the family overwrite them with positive ones. In this case, I'll stay until the birthday party, turn eighteen, and let my family celebrate my life. That should help them with the unfinished business they've focused on." I pause, narrowing my eyes as I think. "But Dad, I have no idea what to do about the boyfriend. What does he want?"

"He won't say," my father says, leaning forward on his elbows. "But the signs are there and the therapists flagged him. The Barnes family is paying for his closure."

I furrow my brow. I hadn't thought about who was paying for his treatment. "That's awfully nice of them," I say.

"They were all very close," my father answers. "Apparently he's like a son to them."

My mind spins through the procedures and diagnoses. "They think if they keep him they'll still be connected to her,"

I offer. My father lifts one shoulder as if saying he's not sure but it's what he thinks too. Clients sometimes fixate on an object that reminds them of their lost loved one. I've seen family members fight over a key chain, a favorite blanket or stained T-shirt. Isaac may have become that object to them.

"I guess I'll see," I say, taking one last sip of coffee before standing. "I'll be in my room if you need me." The mention of Isaac is drawing me back to the file in the hope of finding more information about his and Catalina's relationship. Secrets that may be hidden in plain sight.

My father glances at the clock on the oven and reminds me that we're leaving shortly after lunch. I wave him off and walk out of the kitchen, heading straight for my room. I spend the next few hours checking and double-checking the file. I nearly memorize all of the journal entries, but they give me little insight into Isaac and Catalina's relationship. I just don't know what to expect, and I hate the uncertainty.

Just before eleven I glance around my room and close up the file. Time to get ready. I walk to the bathroom and turn the squeaky shower knob. As I undress, I try to drain away, be an emotional blank slate so that I can become Catalina later today. Numbness settles over me, and I adjust the water to scalding hot and step inside the tiled shower.

I'm wearing the jeans and T-shirt provided by Catalina's family, the style uncomfortably tight across my hips and chest, or at least tighter than I would normally wear. I have to adjust to my assignment's taste, so I grin and bear it, heaving my backpack onto my shoulder. I pull a zip-up hoodie off the hanger and fold it over my arm. Stuffed inside my backpack are my phone, a wig and makeup, and a second preapproved outfit of Catalina's. I'll sort through her closet when I get to the house.

I hesitate at the door of my room and then rush back to grab the Rolling Stones T-shirt I got from Emily Pinnacle's dad and the earrings that belonged to Susan Bell. I don't take anything significant from my life. I'm a patchwork of other people's memories, but somehow they feel truer than my own. Maybe it's because these items are tangible: I can touch them and know they're real. I don't keep souvenirs of home.

I toss one more look around the room, pausing at my reflection in the mirror. Although I've practiced Catalina's posed smile—perfected it—I'll need to study her a bit more to really get a handle on her behavior. Find out what makes her tick. Once I have access to her computer I'll go through the rest of her information. Normally this would have already been done, but the assignment is moving quicker than usual. Part of it will have to be on-the-job training. With a deep sigh I turn around, click off my light, and head downstairs.

Dad's waiting for me on the porch, and when we walk across the driveway past my car, I notice a note tucked under the windshield wiper and smile.

"I can just about guess," my father says in an uninterested voice. I tell him to hush and jog over to grab the paper. I unfold it and find a quick sketch of me, cartoon-style with outlined yellow hair and freckles, a picture of me with the word "Quinlan" underneath. It doesn't say what it means, but I already know it's from Deacon. It's so I can remember who I am. He used to do this all the time as a way for me to have a reminder of my real self. Plus he knows I think it's incredibly sweet. I trace the corner of the sketch until my father comes to peek over my shoulder. I quickly fold the note and shove it in my backpack.

"Don't be nosy," I tell him jokingly.

"Deacon?" he asks.

"Of course. Who else would make this much effort to annoy you?"

"Good point," he says, and adjusts his glasses in a fatherly way. He grabs my bag and opens up the trunk of his Cadillac to toss it in. I watch him, loneliness creeping over me. I'm going to miss him. I'm going to miss his half-assed dinners and his loud laugh. I'm going to miss being his daughter. My father slams the lid and catches sight of me. Without a word he rounds the car and gives me a big hug. He smells like laundry detergent and shaving cream, a smell that could only be described as Dad. I hold on a second longer, fighting back the scared-little-kid tears that threaten to fall. When I'm okay, I force a smile. He ruffles my hair in a movement I tell him I hate, but secretly enjoy. And then we get in the car and head to Marie's apartment.

"You're ten minutes late," Marie says when she meets us at the car. Her braids are tied up in a bun on the top of her head;

she has a heavy black bag over her shoulder. My dad is in the driver's seat, but I waited outside to greet her. Marie casts an uncomfortable glance at my father and then turns back to me. The second our eyes meet, her expression softens.

"I'm sorry, hon," she says, reaching out to put her hand on my upper arm. "I told him it was too soon, even if you are healthy enough."

A lump forms in my throat, and before I can even think about it, I jump forward to hug Marie. She drops her bag and squeezes me, the closest thing to my real mother that I can remember. After a long second she pulls back and looks at me seriously.

"Now's not the time for this," she says, smiling painfully. "You have to let it go. Leave Quinlan at my doorstep so we can be on our way."

"I thought I left her at my house," I say, forcing myself to be tougher. Harder. I pick up Marie's bag and open the back door to put it inside the car. Marie nods her thanks and climbs into the passenger seat. I walk around and sit behind my father.

There's an initial chill when Marie and my dad say their hellos, and my father drives toward the freeway. But Marie is right: Now is not the time to worry about my life—or how their relationship affects me. I need to focus on the assignment. I open the zipper on the black bag and take out the paperwork I need to sign off on before we get to the Barnes residence. I sign my life away and Marie adds her signature to the witness line. I sort through the bag, and at the bottom is a round blue hatbox. I shoot her a pointed look, and Marie shrugs and turns back around to face the windshield.

"You never pick the right color," she says conversationally. "Sometimes I think you're color-blind."

I laugh and pull off the lid to see a blond wig, the shade and length nearly right, the quality better than anything I own. Closers usually bring their own supplies, but Marie helps me out occasionally. She knows this business better than any of us. I think that might include my father.

There are a few more items—jewelry, more pictures—things that didn't get into the file. I clasp a necklace around my neck and tie my hair back. I bring my own bag onto my lap and take out my makeup. I smear a layer of foundation over my cheeks and nose, covering up my freckles. My dad glances at me in the rearview mirror, his face a portrait of concern, and Marie hums to herself with rigid posture as she looks anywhere but at him.

I grab my black zip-up hoodie and slide in my arms. I take the wig and flip my head over to pull it on, yanking it down on the sides. Oh yeah. This is much better than what I have. My wigs tend to feel like they're squeezing out my brains. This is almost comfortable—like wearing a beanie on a winter's day. I take it off and replace it in its box, and check the shade of the brown contacts. I get everything in order, and when I'm done, I pull up my hood and rest back in the seat. It'll be a while before we get there. When we do, Marie will say hello and I'll avoid eye contact with the family. And then they'll allow me to go into their daughter's bedroom, where I will become Catalina Barnes.

I must have dozed off, because my body jerks awake when the car pulls alongside the curb and stops. The space around me is painfully silent, and my eyes are itchy from sleep. I glance out the window and look at the expansive ranch-style home. Most of our clients are affluent. I mean, who else could afford a temporary replacement child? But this house in particular is spectacular. There's a wide driveway with a basketball hoop off to the side; a manicured lawn with slightly overgrown rosebushes. Massive windows frame the entire front of the house; Mount Hood is silhouetted in the background. Towering pines and bright green grass—I find it charming and grand all at once, especially compared to my neglected front yard in Corvallis.

Marie turns, studying me before she speaks in her confident voice—the one reserved for moments like this. "You sure you're ready?" she asks, as if I can just say no and walk away. I've never done that before, but she always acts like the possibility is still there.

I nod, and I meet my father's gaze in the rearview mirror. "See you in two weeks," I tell him with a catch in my throat. His eyes well up and a crushing sense of loss at losing him, losing my entire life for two weeks, presses in on me. My dad smiles sadly.

"Take care of yourself," he murmurs. We don't draw out our

good-byes, my safe return an unspoken promise. It's ironic—an entire department devoted to closure and yet we're terrible at it in our real lives. Marie glances over at him and then opens the passenger door while I gather the bags and climb out. My father waits in the car, because although he's met with the family before, seeing him now would only dredge up the reality of the situation. They've spoken to him about their real daughter, so Marie's job is to step in and become their new consultant, to make *me* the real Catalina.

Marie touches my elbow, and together we start up the walkway to the big double doors of the home. My heart pounds; knots tighten in my stomach. I've always hated this part, sort of like a performer before going onstage—only this is life and not a play, a grossly exaggerated form of method acting.

I pause for a moment, a sudden attack of fear closing in around me. I worry I'm not good enough for two weeks of this, that I won't be convincing. Marie halts and then comes back to stand next to me. She doesn't speak, only lets my mind work out what I have to do.

I exhale a cleansing breath, closing my eyes, and once again I hollow myself out to make room. And when all the fear has drained away, the worry and sadness, I open my eyes and stare straight ahead. A machine, a vessel, a replacement. And Marie and I walk together to the front door.

CHAPTER SEVEN

NO ONE ANSWERS WHEN WE RING THE BELL. MARIE and I stand, still as statues on the front porch, with her black bag next to me, my backpack on my shoulder. We wait a full minute, and then Marie outstretches her finger, sharp blood-red manicure, and presses the doorbell again. It seems louder, more impatient, even though it's just the same. *Perception colors everything,* I think. What's real to us anyway? Only our perception.

The door swings open suddenly, and I rock back on my heels. Before I can stop my curiosity, I look up at the man standing in the doorway. His entire face goes slack at the sight of me, and I realize my eyes are still blue—I haven't put in the colored contacts yet. Marie quickly steps up to divert his attention.

"Mr. Barnes," she says in her warm therapist tone. "I'm Marie Devoroux. It's a pleasure to meet you." I move to duck slightly behind her, keeping my gaze turned away.

"Miss Devoroux," the man says in greeting. His voice is thick with grief and despair, but I don't sympathize. Instead I adjust the strap of my backpack on my shoulder and glance back to where my father's Cadillac is parked. He doesn't smile or wave. He looks at me like I'm an employee, practically a stranger. It wasn't always like this. When I was little, there were occasions when Marie had to practically tear me from my father's arms, reassuring *him* that it would be all right. I wonder if that's why he shuts me out sometimes. Maybe he's given me away so often that the idea of me not existing has lost its effect.

What I wouldn't give to have him chase me down now and beg me not to go. Then again, neither of us would have a job if he did that.

Marie slips her arm around my shoulders, startling me from my thoughts, and I feel Mr. Barnes's heavy stare.

"May we come in?" Marie asks. After a long pause, Mr. Barnes steps aside, opening the door wider so that we can enter. "It's down the hall, second door on the left," he says. Even though there's a pull to look at him while I pass, I don't. It's too soon.

I'm not her yet.

Catalina's bedroom is exactly the same as it was the day she died. This is one of the instructions the grief counselors give parents when they sign up for closure. I imagine it's difficult to resist cleaning, making a bed, or hugging a pillow. Ignoring the clothes on the floor and pictures on a desk—a desire to make it perfect. Make it a shrine. But most of the time parents do exactly what Marie and my father tell them because for a few days they'll get their child back. At least some version of them.

I drop my bag on the bed and look around the room. The décor isn't exactly my style, but I take a moment to absorb the scene. The walls are bright blue with framed pictures—not random posters like most bedrooms. These photos are black-and-white, and after a moment I realize they're not professional. Did she take these herself? That's something to note for later—a small detail in her personality. Sure enough, I find a heavy-duty camera and tripod in her closet, tucked away and slightly dusty. I guess she's not into it anymore. That's probably why it wasn't in her file.

I continue searching the room, opening and closing dresser drawers, trying to get a feel for her personality. I pause at her desk and find a checkered wallet with a broken clasp. I open it and see Catalina's driver's license, credit card, and student ID. No pictures. I set it down and run my finger over her closed laptop. There are stickers—random graphics and ironic phrases—covering the outside. There's a red leather-bound journal on her desk, and I open it and recognize it's where the pages were photocopied from. I skim, finding more of the same until I get near the end.

There are pages missing, torn out. Interesting. I set the journal aside, pull out the chair, and sit before opening the computer. I type in the password that I've memorized by now. The wallpaper startles me at first: Catalina and Isaac, the same picture that was in her file. She's smiling and Isaac is watching her adoringly. There's a tug at my heart, and I quickly click on the Internet to fill the page with something else. I sign on to her social media pages and begin sorting through them. There are other pictures of Catalina's boyfriend, but none as telling as that wallpaper. I find images of Angie, Catalina's sister, both girls wearing sunglasses and laughing on the beach. Catalina's dad asleep in a recliner. Her mom wearing a visor on a golf course. The more I look through her albums, the more confused I am about the girl I'm about to become. By all accounts, she loved her family. She put their pictures on her profile page. It's so girl-next-door cute, it seems almost fake. I furrow my brow and switch to home videos, watching short clips of Catalina talking, laughing, and I practice mimicking her until I get it right. Once done, I click back to social media and find some of her interactions with Isaac.

Good morning, beautiful, he wrote two weeks ago. She liked the comment but didn't respond. Immediately after a death, the grief counselors shut down comments on an assignment's page, delete anything new, at least until I leave. Catalina is frozen in time.

For a moment I wonder what it's like to be in a relationship where you're *you* all the time. To have a past, present, and future you can share with someone. To have them love you completely. I'm envious of the freedom Catalina and Isaac had, the ease of their lives. Envious of the way he adores her. The her she got to be all the time.

"Shit," I mutter, quickly reminding myself that Catalina is dead and I'm an asshole for coveting her relationship. I take a second to compose my thoughts and then reach for her journal again. I start flipping pages, even though I've already read the passages that were included in her file. I find myself sucked in again, reading about a time Catalina and Angie had a party while their parents were out of town. A quiet *ding* sounds from the computer, and I turn back to it. There's a blinking icon at the bottom of the screen, and when I click it, a small box pops up.

Are you there?

It's from Isaac, or at least someone with his name and thumbnail picture. My stomach drops, and I don't know what to do. My heart starts racing, and my fingers hover over the keys. I think about responding with a simple yes, but then again, I'm not Catalina—he should know that. It occurs to me that he might not be trying to contact me at all. Maybe he does this, messages her, even though she's dead, hoping one day he'll get an answer. I've seen it before—parents calling a cell phone just to hear the voice-mail recording. Leaving messages as if their child will one day call them back. But they don't. They never will.

I start typing a *y* and then suddenly the small box changes and a blue line tells me that Isaac is no longer online. I'm surprised by the rush of loss I feel, and I wait, hoping he'll sign back on. But the minutes tick by and I have work to do, so I close the message box and return to Catalina's photo album.

The hours quickly pass, and when I feel prepared, at least prepared enough to begin the assignment, I walk to the mirror hanging on the closet door and apply the finishing touches on my makeup, accentuating certain features while downplaying others. The blond wig fits nicely and looks almost real, but I don't totally love it. I pin up one side like I've seen Catalina do in a few pictures, and then I turn my head to examine the effect. I find the contacts case and with skill, since I've done this a million times, I put in one brown contact and then the other. When I'm all together, I wait, still under the gaze of my unfamiliar reflection.

There's a soft knock on the door, and I turn as Marie enters alone. She presses her lips together and holds up her hands, bracelets jangling. "You ready?" she asks.

I close my eyes for a moment, and when I look at her again, I smile. "Sure," I say in a new voice, one I've learned from her videos. "Did my parents give you any wardrobe suggestions?"

Marie visibly stiffens, but then she nods toward the closet. "They did. For dinner they'd like you to wear your prom dress." I stare back at her, speechless. "I know it's a bizarre request," she says. "But you had a wonderful time that night, and they didn't get a chance to get pictures before you and Isaac left." She waves her hand. "Something about the camera battery being dead. Anyway, they'd love to see you in it now. We're going to accommodate that."

"Uh, okay," I respond. This isn't totally out of the question—I've been asked to wear favorite outfits before. The sweater Nana knitted for my birthday, footie pajamas on a mock Christmas morning. This will definitely be the first prom dress, though. I've never even tried one on before.

I quickly scan through my memory until I recall a picture of me and Isaac under a balloon archway. I walk into the closet, but it takes a little digging before I find the emerald-green dress. The fabric is flowy and satiny, and the minute I put it on, I'm grateful it isn't fitted. It's at least a size too small.

I shoot a panicked look at Marie, and she crosses the room to stand behind me as we both stare in the mirror. She adjusts the shoulder straps and then pulls a small pair of thread scissors and a clip from her bag to let out the seam a little. I feel ridiculous, embarrassed that I'll have to sit through the meal like this, but I want my parents to be happy so I let Marie fuss over the dress a little before she tells me I'm all set.

Marie turns to me, her cool hands resting on my shoulders, her eyes filled with the same concern they have every time she leaves. "You can still walk away from this," she says. "Or if it becomes too much, contact Aaron or me. My door is always open to you." Her intensity surpasses her usual good-bye talks, and my worry spikes. But before I can even delve into the reasoning behind it, Marie has me by the arm and is walking us toward the dining room. I'm barefoot in an emerald-green prom dress.

My feet pad along the shiny wood floor, and I'm impressed by the beauty of my house. The country-chic décor is straight out of a magazine—gorgeous and expensive, but also homey and welcoming. We round the corner, and I pause at the dining room entrance. It's obvious that my parents have gone to a lot of trouble to welcome me home. The minute I come into view, my mother jumps up, twisting her hands nervously in front of her. She's overdressed. Her hair is set in curls, stiff with spray, bright lipstick on her thin lips and too much blush on the apples of her cheeks. Her sleeveless black dress is cinched with a belt, and her jewelry is bulky and out of place in our dining room. Her mouth pulls into an anxious smile, and she shoots an expectant look at Marie, waiting for the introduction. My father doesn't turn toward me; his chin rests on his folded hands, his elbows on the table. I can see his grief, see it radiating from his skin, and I make a mental note to check his emotional state after dinner.

"Good evening, Mrs. Barnes," Marie says warmly. The advisor turns to me graciously and motions toward the table. "Please sit, Catalina," she says without missing a beat. From the corner of my eye, I see my mother flinch at the sound of my name. Feeling vulnerable and on display, I make my way around the table to a seat with a bowl of salad already waiting. Marie follows and sits next to me, black coffee already set out in front of her. Marie doesn't change her habits, even if she's grown tired of the taste of coffee by now. It's important to have some steady touchstones. I nod at my mother and take my spot at the table.

Visibly shaking, my mother moves to stand next to her husband, who looks like he'd rather be anywhere but here.

"I've made your favorite," my mother says, wiping a tear that has found its way onto her cheek. It leaves a flesh-colored trail through her makeup. "Spaghetti with extra meatballs," she says, her expression hopeful. To be honest, I've never been a fan of pasta, but I smile eagerly anyway.

"Great," I say. "Thanks, Mom."

Her face goes slack and my father flinches and immediately looks at me. We're all silent for a moment as they soak it in. My voice is so familiar to them; I know it hurts. But it's part of the process. I'm suddenly self-conscious of my wig, wondering if it's the right shade after all. Marie calmly sips from her coffee, letting the quiet tick on.

After what feels like an eternity, my mother swallows hard. "I'll go get the food," she says, and quickly leaves the room. I don't react, caught in my father's gaze as he studies me. He's built like a football coach, burly and massive. I watch his green eyes well up until tears slip down his face. He makes no move to wipe them.

I can see his intense longing, his deep sadness, his inability to trust—all classic symptoms of complicated grief. If I monitor a bit longer, I'm sure I'll find that he's lost interest in his daily life, maybe even in life in general. He can't find meaning without me. He's lost in his emotions. He loves me, present tense. It won't be easy for him to trust enough to heal.

Marie's cup clinks against the saucer, and she sighs quietly when my mother returns, holding a large serving bowl filled with bright red strands of spaghetti, a mountain of meatballs on top. The initial awkwardness begins to fade when we start to eat. As far as Italian food goes, this is pretty good. Something about the texture of spaghetti has always bothered me, though, and the dough acts to bind my teeth together.

"I'm sorry that Angie's not here," my mother says, tapping her napkin on the corners of her mouth. "She's staying at Aunt Margot's for a few weeks to be closer to school. You know how busy she gets."

What I know is that my sister doesn't want to be a part of the closure. There's an empty place set on the other side of me, and I wonder if my parents hoped she'd show up for dinner anyway.

"And I was thinking," my mother adds, "that tomorrow we could go out. We can grab lunch and then we can stop by the salon."

"I could get a pedicure," I offer in a high, positive lilt. She smiles, shaky and unsure, but ultimately encouraged.

"Wonderful," she says, pleased. "I'll call and set it up."

Marie flips her over her wrist and checks the time on her delicate gold watch. We exchange a glance and I can see her impatience growing. She's not eating; she never eats. Just drinks coffee. She's here to monitor, to make sure I'm in a safe environment, and to determine if my parents are ready for this therapy. Since she hasn't removed me, I'm guessing she's approved this assignment.

I take another bite of food, chewing while I feel the stares of my parents. Occasionally I glance up and smile at them politely, and my mother smiles back, relieved I'm still here. My father hasn't touched his food, but at least he's not crying anymore.

There's a knock on the door, and we all turn. Marie sets down her cup hastily, rattled by the unexpected interruption. Personally, I'm grateful for the distraction. I lay my fork on my plate with spaghetti still twirled around the prongs. No one moves, and I wonder if I'm the one who usually answers the door. I start to stand, when my father jumps up and motions for me to stay.

"I'll get it," he says, giving me a once-over as he adjusts to my presence again.

My mother smiles nervously, glancing at Marie. "Perhaps Angie decided to join us after all." I see the irritation in Marie's posture, but it would be imperceptible to a client. I just know her too well.

"We want to do our best to maintain the control group, Mrs. Barnes," Marie says. "It's conducive for therapy."

I watch my mother to gauge her reaction, still learning. "I understand," she says. "But Angie's her sister. They're best friends."

She's blocking out the actual fact of my death, and reimagining our lives. I haven't found any mentions of me being best friends with my sister. We loved each other, sure. But my mother is making more of the relationship to build me up. Build up the family. It's another sign of her complicated grief and denial.

Voices filter in from the foyer, both male, and my mother smiles gently and then lowers her eyes to her plate. "Guess it's not Angela," she says, sounding disappointed, and begins to spin the spaghetti around her fork.

My new father's voice is deep and tainted with a gruff sort of grief. "She's in here," he says. My heart begins to race, and I grab the napkin to wipe my mouth. He's introducing a new variable, deviating from the expected dinner introduction. I shoot a panicked look at Marie and she holds out her hand to tell me to be steady. This is not a time to break character, especially so early in the assignment. My gut just about hits the floor when the two men stop at the entrance of the dining room, both staring straight at me, cold and uninvested in my existence.

CHAPTER EIGHT

"ISAAC," I BREATHE OUT BEFORE I THINK BETTER OF it. His lips part and he steps back, inadvertently putting his hand over his heart. Marie turns to me immediately, but I'm too caught up in the presence of this boy—this person who loved me so much. His eyes slowly rake over my prom dress, my necklace, my hair, and my face.

His breathing is uneven, shaking his entire frame. I stand slowly, letting him take in my appearance, completely vulnerable to his reaction. I use the moment to assess his emotional state. I notice the dark circles ringing his eyes, the drawn pull of his face. His jaw is shadowed, and his tan skin has red patches like he's been crying. I can't remember the last time I've seen someone look so hollowed out. So broken. Isaac's tall and thin, and I know from my journal that he's a shortstop for the high school baseball team. I know that he has a birthmark on his right hip and a scar across his knee. What I don't know is what he's thinking right now.

"Isaac," my mother says with a hint of scolding. "Don't be rude. Catalina's come down for dinner. Would you like to join us?"

His head snaps in her direction, and I see immediately from his disgust that he is not open to this therapy. A knot forms in my throat, and Marie reaches out to take my hand, reminding me of my job.

"Are you fucking kidding me?" Isaac calls out. My father tsks and steps in front of Isaac, pushing him back a step. My dad may not have welcomed me with open arms, but he loves his wife and won't let her be disrespected. He hasn't forgotten that. Isaac gives him a betrayed look. "What are you doing, Barrett?" Isaac demands. "How could you do this? How could you bring that thing in here?"

I sway back, my knees hitting my seat and dropping me into it. I feel like I've been punched, and in an attempt to correct the situation, Marie stands—strong yet supportive—and shields me from his view.

"Mr. Perez," she says. "I'm Marie Dev—"

"Look, lady," Isaac says, waving his hand wildly. "I don't give a shit who you are. *That* is not Catalina." He cranes his neck and stares at me. The anger in his expression turns to utter and inconsolable grief. "You're not her," he barely gets out between hitched breaths. "You're not my Catalina. You're an impostor."

"Mr. Perez, please," Marie pushes on. Isaac tears his gaze

away from me, openly sobbing before he puts his hands over his face, shaking his head. My father and mother begin to cry too, and this entire evening ruptures from his emotional napalm. I don't know what to do.

"No, no, no," Isaac murmurs until my father wraps him in a hug, each holding the other up. Isaac buries his face in my father's shoulder, completely torn down. But it's only a moment before he pushes back, looks accusingly around the room. "I won't agree to this," he says. "I won't be a part of this."

"I understand your hesitance," Marie says. She turns to look down at me sternly as if trying to snap me back to protocol. I'm so distraught; it takes me a moment before it clicks together. "But this therapy is very effective," she says, turning to Isaac. "We want to help you overcome your loss, Isaac. All of our doctors determined you are suffering greatly. They're worried about you."

"You can get closure," I say in a soft, familiar voice, making the entire room fall silent. "You can tell me everything you never got the chance to. I can hear you and react. I can make you stop longing and hurting and suffering. It's all part of the process." I'm not immune to the weight of my words; I know from the outside they can appear cruel or delusional. But this therapy has been tried and tested—it works. And right now, my heart aches for this boy in front of me. I understand why he's been flagged by the grief department. He's a risk to himself. If I can't help him . . . I'm not sure what will become of him.

My words play across Isaac's features—a flinch of love, of hate, of disbelief. He wants to pull me into his arms and never let me go. He wants to shove me away and tell me to never come back. He's so conflicted I'm not sure there's much I can do to bring him peace. I want to cross to him and wipe away his tears, stitch together his pieces. That's what I would have done before. But right now I'm not the remedy for his breaking heart. I'm the cause.

When he doesn't answer, I try a different path. "We can talk online instead," I offer. "That's easier sometimes."

He blinks, his movements slow and exhausted. If my dad wasn't holding him up, I'm afraid he would fall. Isaac examines me again, taking a long time on the prom dress. His expression empties, as if all of his emotions have drained away.

"No," he says simply. "I want nothing to do with you."

Both of my parents react as if he's really just broken up with me. As if I'm not dead and this is my future husband telling me it's over. In truth, it does hurt. Isaac is a huge part of my history, my personality. We've shared so much—I'm not sure he can handle this loss either.

"Please," my mother pleads. "The party is in two weeks, Isaac. Can't you just make this perfect for two weeks?"

Isaac laughs softly, sadly. "I'm sorry, Eva," he tells her. "But I can't do that." He moves past my dad, patting his upper arm as he does. Without even a curious glance back at me, Isaac exits the room and leaves the therapy behind. Leaves us in his emotional wake.

The rest of dinner is solemn and uneventful. My prom dress, maybe at first nostalgic, feels garish and silly now that Isaac has shattered the illusion. I stay in character, though, and Marie directs the conversation with a friendly set of questions meant to offer comfort as my parents reminisce about our lives. My dad doesn't participate much, although he sits through the entire meal. I offer to clear the plates, and my mother chuckles and tells me not to worry about it tonight.

"Chores can start again tomorrow," she says good-naturedly, slipping back into her denial. My mother takes my plate, but pauses next to me. She's surrounded in the soft scent of detergent and flowery perfume, both subtle and comforting. When I look up, she brushes her hand over my hair adoringly. Her eyes are the same color as my contacts. Then she takes my dirty dish to the kitchen.

"I think we're done for the evening," my father says to Marie. She nods, and they both stand. For a moment I wonder if this means he wants me to leave, and I'm truly afraid of failure. "Thank you for bringing her," he tells Marie, and presses his mouth into a closed-lip smile. I'm awash with relief.

"Of course," she murmurs. "Now, Catalina," she says, turning to me, "would you mind walking me to the door?"

I get up and follow her out of the room, wilting slightly under my father's study. He doesn't trust me, but something about the evening has made him at least willing to give therapy a shot. For that I'm grateful, because it's obvious how much the family needs help.

By the time we get to the foyer, I'm already missing Marie—the jangling of her bracelets, the smell of her lotion. I don't tap into those feelings, though; it's best to keep them away when I'm on assignment. I blow out a cleansing breath, and Marie and I take a second to look each other over. She tilts her head as if giving my appearance her final approval.

"Aaron will be in touch," she says. "Tell him everything so I can be aware of your situation and monitor it for any changes. And as I said before, you can contact me directly if you need to. You have your phone?"

I think about my cell phone tucked in my backpack upstairs, and nod, afraid that if I try to talk, my voice will crack and give away my emotions. I'm about to be abandoned in this new life. This part is always a bit unsettling.

"Good," she says. "Only use it for contact and extraction. No social calls." She smiles. "At this point I want you to focus on your parents, and we'll figure out how to deal with Isaac after I consult with the other therapists. You can reach out to him online, but don't engage him in person. He's unpredictable right now, so be careful."

"I will," I say faintly.

Marie pauses. "And stay away from Deacon," she adds. "He distracts you."

"I'm sure he'd love to hear that."

Marie laughs and then reaches to pull me into a hug. I close my eyes, drinking her in, and when she lets go, I don't allow myself to look at her again. In complete silence she walks out the door, and I close it, locking the dead bolt behind her.

* * *

After dinner, my family and I retire to the living room, where we watch my favorite show, one I've never seen before, and eat popcorn. They asked me to change out of my prom dress, so sitting on the couch in sweats and a T-shirt is actually relaxing, maybe even a little fun, as the three of us laugh at a few one-liners on the television. Although it's full immersion, my father is still resistant and finds it impossible to say my name. We'll have to work on that.

After telling them good night, I head to my room, drained from all the smiling and ready to think over my next steps for therapy. My room is starting to feel a bit more like mine, but I pause when I notice my computer on the desk.

I fidget, but then walk over to it and sit down. I open the screen, and sign in to my e-mail, checking for a message. My heart sinks when there's no new note from Isaac, and I suppress my guilt and allow myself to think selfishly for a moment. Whether I truly know him or not, that picture of Isaac staring at me, that adoration . . . I want that. I want to know what it feels like to be someone's world. And the devastated look in his eyes tonight, I want to know more about that, too. I want to know how to fix it.

I'm curious and anxious and inexplicably drawn to Isaac. And not just because of who I've become. I believe I can help him—save him, even. He can be my own personal case study. Closers have never dealt with a relationship like this, not that I know of. I'll be the one to find out if role-play therapy can work. No, I'll *prove* that it can. I don't want to see Isaac locked away. I want to bring back his smile, show him he can have a full life, even after his loss. And maybe in exchange he can give me a look into what it's like to be normal, to have a normal and perfectly average life.

Resolved, I consider contacting him. But it's late, and I think it would be crossing a line, especially when he was so outspoken about not being involved in the therapy. Those seeking help approach us. We don't chase them. I'll have to give him time to come around. I believe he will.

I wait a minute longer, but without any word from him I close the screen. I take off my wig and brush it out, and then remove my contacts. When I'm stripped down to the studs, I click off the overhead light and climb into bed.

The ceiling fan swirls above me, the dangling string ticking against the glass. The grief-stricken sound of my father's voice, the attentive manner of my mother, the entire night plays over in my head. And then there was Isaac. My existence disturbed him, upset him so much he left; he couldn't bear the sight of me. *How could you bring that thing in here?*

Crushing loneliness spreads over me. I curl up on my side, hands tucked under my cheek. I hate this feeling. Closers rarely talk about their emotions; I guess we repress most of them. And we definitely don't discuss the way people react to us. Imagine the confusion for the clients. Their reactions can switch from love to agony to hatred in a matter of moments. We're everything they want and everything they hate to be reminded of. We're a paradox.

And then there's the backlash. People are afraid of us—I saw it in Isaac's eyes tonight. I'm unrelatable and untouchable. I'm an abomination to them. A thing.

Right now, my soul feels paper thin. I'd give anything to talk to my dad, or Deacon, or Aaron. Hell, even Myra. But I'm alone in this. I close my eyes and search out a memory that will bring me comfort, make me feel loved.

I think of Anna Granger, my best friend all through junior high. We did everything together: shared classes and secrets. We even got our periods at the same time. I smile, thinking of the ridiculous picture of us at our ninth-grade semiformal, our dates in oversized suits and Anna and me with terribly cut bangs. We bailed before the end of the night and had our parents bring us to IHOP for pancakes. Anna and I were close enough to be sisters, and I miss her. I miss the thought of her.

Because I've never met Anna Granger. She belonged to someone else's life.

CHAPTER NINE

I BLINK MYSELF AWAKE. THE BLINDS ARE OPEN, letting in huge patches of unfiltered sunlight that fall across my bed. I turn to the clock on the side table, not surprised to find out it's barely seven a.m. I open and close my jaw a few times, the muscles sore from smiling the night before. I can hear the kitchen sink running, the low murmur of a television. Seems my parents are early risers too.

I'm not quite ready to see them yet this morning, so I stand, moaning with my sleepy muscles. The wig is on my desk next to my computer, and I pick it up and brush my fingers through it again. Marie did a great job, but it still doesn't feel right.

I drop the wig back onto the table and sit at the computer. The wallpaper startles me, the adoring picture with Isaac—so different from the way he treated me last night. I click open my e-mail and scan the messages. They're mostly spam or people who don't know I've died yet. They're not part of this closure, so I don't respond. They'll find out sooner or later, I guess.

My computer dings, and my body tenses as I search for the blinking icon. Anxiety twists inside me the second I pull up the small screen and see Isaac's image. He's reaching out. There's a short message: I DIDN'T SLEEP LAST NIGHT, he writes. Then a moment later: IT FEELS LIKE I'LL NEVER SLEEP AGAIN.

My brain notes *difficulty sleeping*, but my heart swells because he's asking for help. I study his thumbnail image, the vibrant ideal of the boy I met last night. I swallow nervously, and then type back.

IT WON'T ALWAYS FEEL LIKE THIS, I tell him, immediately biting my nail after I hit send. He's typing. Then stops. Starts typing again.

I MISS HER.

I lower my arm, welling up with sadness as I imagine him sitting at his computer, frayed from lack of sleep and overwhelmed by his loss. I KNOW, I respond. I'M SORRY. The cursor blinks, neither of us writing. My training is trying to eclipse my sympathy.

I CAN HELP, I write. IF YOU LET ME.

HOW?

TALKING. WE'LL JUST TALK, ISAAC. I CAN HELP YOU FIND A WAY TO DEAL WITH THIS. HELP YOU GET OVER IT. I'm starting to sound clinical, and I immediately regret mentioning him "getting over" the love of his life. I should have just listened. Right now he needs someone to listen to him—any therapist could have told me that.

YEAH, NO THANKS, he responds, and I can taste his bitterness. I expect him to log off, but he doesn't. We're both sitting at the computer, waiting.

OR MAYBE YOU CAN WRITE AND I WON'T RESPOND WITH SOME HORRIBLE THERAPY-LIKE ANSWER. I try a new approach, hoping to gain his trust with a little bit of humor.

YOU'RE NOT EVEN A REAL PERSON, he responds. YOU'RE JUST A REPLACEMENT. HOW CAN I POSSIBLY TALK TO YOU?

Sickness sweeps over me. He's not entirely wrong, but I'm insulted anyway. Each second that passes echoes his sentiment, deafeningly loud in my head. This is how some of the public sees us—cold and empty. Closers are nonpeople to them. We're a threat.

I HAVE FEELINGS, YOU KNOW, I write back, without considering what Marie would think of me engaging. But Isaac's words have brought tears to my eyes, an ache in my chest. *Try living your entire life as different people,* I think. *How would you fucking feel? Having to watch families lose everything, losing it with them over and over and over. I have no more grief, Isaac, but I can still hurt like a real person. I hurt all the time.*

Warm tears rush down my cheeks, and I slam the computer screen shut. I am real. I just lost my parents a few days ago. I lost my other parents not even two months ago. I lose *everyone.* Everything.

I curse and swipe my hands roughly over my cheeks, my mind spinning. When I look down, there's a smear of foundation across my fingers. I stare for a moment, realizing I didn't wash off the makeup from last night. *Last night?* Confused, I glance around the room, a mix of complicated memories flooding my head. I'm Catalina Barnes. But then there's also Emily Pinnacle and Rosemund Harris. There's my mother with dark hair lying in a hospital bed.

A headache starts behind my eyes, and I grind the heels of my palms into them. I get up from the desk, accidentally knocking my chair to the floor. I'm searching for Quinlan McKee, but I can't be certain of my memories. I'm adrift in my mind, trying to ascertain which thoughts are mine. It was too soon. I need a tether.

An image pops in my mind, and I rush to the closet to find the backpack I came in with. I drop to my knees next to it, rummaging through until I turn it over and dump all of its contents onto the floor. Then I find it: the folded and slightly crumpled piece of paper. I fall back against the wall and slowly open it, smiling my relief as I examine the picture of me that Deacon drew. *Quinlan.* With a shaky finger, I trace the lines of my cartoonlike features, relieved that I can find myself through his eyes when I can't find me on my own. That's why Deacon was a great partner; he anticipated what I needed. He knew me better than anyone. I stare at my name, and slowly my life floods back.

* * *

The first time I met Deacon Hatcher, he was sitting at my kitchen table, eating pancakes and talking with my father. I thought I'd walked in on the wrong family, and I stood in the doorway—wearing pj's and bed-dreads—staring at them. Deacon looked up first, paused midchew, and then stabbed another bite of pancake without a word and continued eating.

"Dad?" I said, making my father turn around.

"Oh," he replied good-naturedly. He jumped up from the table and joined me in the doorway to observe the random teenager he'd brought home. "Glad you're up," my father said. "I want you to meet someone."

"Clearly," I responded. For his part, Deacon continued to eat as if we weren't talking about him at all. I have to admit, I sort of liked how blasé he was about the whole thing. I turned back to my father. "But first maybe I could . . ." I motioned to my clothes, proving that I was still in my pajamas.

"It's fine," my father said with a shake of his head. "Deacon, this is my daughter," he told the stranger first. Deacon held up his fork in greeting and then smiled, acknowledging in his subtle way that yes, this was weird. And yes, I was definitely still in my pajamas.

I was a little charmed. "Well, it's certainly nice to meet you, Deacon," I responded with sarcastic politeness, and then spun to my father. "Can I go now?"

My father tsked, and took my shoulders to turn me toward the stranger again. "Quinn, this is Deacon Hatcher. He's our newest closer, but more important, he's your partner."

My stomach dropped. "What?" I demanded. "What about Marie?"

"Marie will continue on as your advisor, but a new safeguard has been put into place," my father explained. "Deacon will check in with you throughout your assignment, find out any info you need. Extract you and then assimilate you when the assignment is up. You'll do the same for him."

I looked at the stranger sitting at the table, imagining all the secrets of my life that he'd now be privy to. This was a complete violation of my trust. Deacon shrugged, acknowledging he thought this was pretty crazy too. I turned back to my dad. "I don't even know this guy," I said. "What if he sucks?"

Deacon snorted from behind me.

My father shot him a pointed look, and then steadied his gaze on me. "I assure you," he said in a slightly patronizing tone, "Deacon is well trained. I wouldn't trust your safety with just anyone. He's been on several assignments already. Glowing reviews."

His comment didn't alleviate any of my worries. "No," I said definitively. And then to Deacon, just in case he didn't get the message: "Absolutely not. I don't need a partner." And with that I stormed back to my room, slamming my door.

Deacon was the one who picked me up from my assignment a week later. He became my most trusted ally. And now, at the thought of him, I've brought myself back.

I stay in my closet for a while, leaning against the wall with the sketch. My pulse is still racing, but I've found my tether to the real world. I close my eyes and think that Deacon was exactly right about something I already knew: It was too soon for a new assignment.

I shower and change into the softest T-shirt I can find, and leave my room. I'm craving comfort after this morning's emotional outburst, debating whether or not I should call it in to Aaron. Ultimately, I decide I don't want my brain picked over by a counselor. I can handle this. And in a way, I'm glad I broke down. I feel cleansed. First nights are always tough, like sleepaway-camp homesickness—only I have lifesickness.

I enter the kitchen and find my mother at the stove, stirring a batch of scrambled eggs. Her eyes widen at the sight of me, and I wilt, self-conscious under her attention. My mother's face relaxes and she motions to the kitchen table.

"You're up earlier than usual," she says. "And good thing. I *was* making breakfast for your father, but he's not hungry. Hope you are." She glances back at me and I nod. "I'm excited to spend the afternoon together," she adds. "We can buy you some new clothes."

I smile politely, thinking more clothes would be a great idea. Other than the outfits I brought and a few T-shirts, most of Catalina's clothes are uncomfortable, tighter than I like to wear—especially over my curves. "Sounds great," I tell her, settling back in my seat. "Where's Dad?" I ask when she sets a cup of orange juice in front of me. Her mouth tightens.

"He went back to bed. He's very tired," she says, although I detect the lie in her voice. I guess he's avoiding me, but that's not unusual. I sip my juice.

"Anyhow," she says, walking over to grab the pan and a spatula, "I'm really looking forward to today. It'll be nice for it to be just us. It's been a long time since you've wanted to have a day with me." My mother piles food on my plate, and I consider her statement, wonder about the difference between the pictures on my computer showing my family together and the truth that I hadn't been spending time with her. I thought we were happy and perfect. Nothing is ever perfect, though.

"Well, I'm here now," I tell her warmly, and shove a forkful of eggs into my mouth. "We can have whatever day you like." She smiles at the statement and then goes back to the sink to wash the pan.

As I eat, I'm thinking about the pictures I saw online, what they mean, what they represent. I can't help but think I'm missing something, like I'm keeping a secret from myself. I furrow my brow, but then my mother is there, chatting about her friend Maryanne, who just got divorced, and maybe we could stop by and bring her some groceries. I don't think my mother quite understands the concept of closure—I'm not a replacement daughter to build new memories with, just a substitute to help her right the past and find a way to move on.

I nod along and don't correct her, even though I know I should. This is comfortable, so I let her dote on me. I enjoy the attention and praise. For a second I wish this was all real, which

I can see in her eyes too, but a nagging voice pulls me out.

Don't get attached, Marie warns. *It's the worst thing a closer can ever do.*

I finish my breakfast and help my mother clean up. The minute I'm back in my room, I throw open the window and let in the fresh air. I stand for a moment in the breeze and close my eyes. The weather is morning crisp, alive. My skin chills, and I walk to the closet and grab my zip-up hoodie.

I go to the computer and start clicking through the different social media outlets, trying to find something new I can think about. Instead, I'm scanning Isaac's page, noticing the girls who have commented about his loss. Offering their condolences. I don't personally have any accounts, any wall that people can write on. I see it as public spying, throwing your identity out there for the world to take what they want. For people to mimic. None of the closers participate, because we know how the information can be used. I rest my elbow on the desktop, wishing I at least had a few pictures of my own—something of Deacon, maybe. I smile, imagining that any picture he would put online would be completely indecent.

A reminder message pops up on my calendar, and I click it. BASEBALL PRACTICE—10 A.M. is highlighted. I stare a moment, and then I shake my head to clear it. I was slipping back into my real life when I should have been concentrating on my assignment. Marie was right: Deacon is distracting.

I grab a purse and stuff in a few essentials, and then head out into the hallway. Why is Isaac's practice on my calendar?

And why am I even considering going? He was clear that he didn't want anything to do with this therapy. Then again, he showed up here last night, reached out to me in that message. Sure, he was a jerk, but at least he opened up a little. Marie said not to engage him in person, but what if I'm only observing him? That doesn't totally count as breaking her rules. Especially not if I can help him.

I enter the family room, searching for my mother, and find her sitting on the couch alone, an album opened on her lap. She jumps when she realizes I'm there, and I feel a tug of sympathy at the sadness in her expression.

"Hi," she says brightly, wiping tears quickly off her cheeks. She sees my hoodie and purse. "Are you going somewhere?" She sounds worried, but not because she's afraid people will see me; she's afraid I won't come back.

"I . . ." Now I'm torn about leaving her. I motion to the outside. "There's a baseball practice?" I phrase it as a question, because I'm not sure if I would actually go to see Isaac. Maybe I just kept tabs on him.

"Oh," my mother says with a small laugh. "That's right. It's Saturday. How could I forget?"

I shrug because I don't know what she means by *Saturday*. I want her to clarify, but I'm afraid to ask. I have to be careful how I phrase things, or I could pull her out of the illusion of me. I fidget with the zipper on my hoodie, nervous as if I'm actually asking permission to go out.

We're quiet for a moment before my mother closes the book,

a family photo album, and sets it aside on the couch. She seems to realize my hesitance, and points to the sofa table, where the car keys lie in a small wicker basket. "You can use the Jetta," she says. "It's yours. On Saturdays you normally watch Isaac's practices. Although sometimes you go out with Virginia instead."

My lips part in surprise. Virginia—I didn't know about her. She's not in the file. She's not anywhere on my social media pages. Pinpricks race up my arms because, once again, I've been keeping secrets.

"I think it's a great idea, Catalina," she adds, standing and brushing off her beige skirt. "Your father needs a little time alone, and I'm sure Isaac would want you there today. You never miss a practice. At least . . . you never used to." My mother crosses the room and pauses in front of me, studying my every feature as if trying to memorize the new me. I want to hug her, but I resist.

She smiles gently and reaches her finger to smooth the crease between my eyebrows, startling me with the kindness of her touch. "Don't look so worried," she says. "He'll come around." She pats my arm before turning to walk toward the bedrooms, leaving me wondering if she's talking about Isaac or my father.

CHAPTER TEN

A WARM BREEZE BLOWS THROUGH MY HAIR, TICKling the back of my neck. I'm not used to wearing my hair so short. I slam the car door and tug up the zipper of my hoodie, wishing that I'd changed into something a little more appealing before leaving the house. After talking with my mother, I almost didn't come at all. But her words echoed in my head, telling me I wouldn't normally miss a practice, that Isaac would appreciate seeing me. In hindsight, I'm pretty sure this is the opposite of how Marie wanted me to handle this. But if I'm going to help him, I need more information.

My phone is set to vibrate in my back pocket in case Aaron calls. I sent him a message earlier, asking him to check into a girl named Virginia. When I get back home, I'll read through the journal again—look for clues. For now I start down the side of the field, combing my fingers through my wig to keep it looking natural. The baseball team practices on my left, and I squint against the sun toward the metal bleachers on my right, relieved to find them mostly empty.

There is a low murmur from the girls sitting on the bottom row, but I keep my eyes downcast and climb up to the very top. My nerves start to take over, and I consider running off before anyone else notices me, but I don't want to walk past those girls again so soon. I sit down, feeling the warmth of the sun-heated metal through my jeans. The red-headed girl from the front row glances over her shoulder at me, but I pretend not to notice. I stare past her, scanning the field for Isaac.

In uniform all the guys look the same, but my gaze eventually finds the shortstop. Isaac's biceps stretch the sleeves of his jersey; the tight pin-striped pants accentuate his lean frame. As if sensing my stare, Isaac turns his head in the direction of the bleachers. He adjusts the brim of his hat, and when I see a flash of his dark eyes, I lift my hand in a self-conscious wave. He stills, his reaction completely unreadable, and I'm sure I've made a mistake in coming here. He's not ready. But then, just as awkwardly, Isaac raises his hand in return.

There's the crack of ball against bat, and his attention is torn away and back to the game. I smile and look down at my lap, deciding I can stay a little longer. It's not like I'm interacting with him in person—not really. I'm studying him. It's no different from how I studied my videos. This is all part of the process.

"You're sick, you know," a voice calls. I jump and see one of the girls from the front row turned around and glaring at me. My gut hits the ground when I realize who she is. Angie—my sister. "Yeah," she continues with a vicious nod, "I know who you are. And I think what you do is disgusting. Both you and my parents are twisted. I would never do that to someone I love. I could never replace them."

"I hope you never have to," I respond in an even voice. Whether it's my words or my tone, Angie's expression flips to uncertainty, a little bit of fear. Her friend reaches to tug the sleeve of her sweatshirt

"Ang," she says in a hushed voice. My sister doesn't acknowledge her, holding me fast with her glare instead. The other girl squirms in discomfort, the idea of being this near to a closer clearly unsettling her. "Please," she mumbles to Angie, her eyes trained on the ground.

My sister looks at her and nods, reluctantly giving in to her friend's request. But before they can walk away, Angie turns back to me.

"I hate you," she calls. "I hate everything you stand for. You should be the one who's dead"—her voice cracks—"not my sister." My eyes well up as I watch Angie fall apart, cry so hard that her friend has to put her arm around her and lead her away. I know Angela's venom was misdirected at me and that her words came from her grief and anger. I don't believe she wants me actually dead. Still, I'm sorry for her pain. She may not be my real sister, but I care about her nonetheless.

I watch Angie and her friend walk away, wishing I wasn't the reason that they left. It was clear how uncomfortable I made the other girl, but I understand. In a different situation, I could end up *being* her. The thought of me must have terrified her. And Angie, seeing me again without warning, seeing her dead sister . . . it's almost cruel. Guilt-ridden, I slump in the bleacher, resting against the back fence to watch practice for a little longer. Alone.

The sun has shifted out of my eyes as practice winds down. I consider leaving before Isaac can confront me, but ultimately I stay to see how he'll react. Take mental notes on his behavior. Isaac casts a few glances in my direction as the team meets on the mound, and I'm glad the others haven't noticed me. Not like Angie did. There's a twist in my stomach when I think about the pain in her expression. How betrayed she must feel by our parents. I push it out of my mind, though—she's not part of this assignment. I refocus on Isaac. I have to get him to trust me if I hope to give him closure. But I can't force it, act like a deranged lunatic and scare him away. Being a closer is about subtlety, about letting the client lead the course of their treatment.

As the players head to the dugout, Isaac turns toward me, his eyes shaded by his hat. Seeming truly torn, he starts in my direction, and I stand, unsure of what to do now that he's on his way over. Slowly, I make my way down the stairs and meet him just as he gets to the fence. I wish I could see his eyes.

"Where'd Angie go?" he asks, looking behind me. His voice is a raspy sort of whisper, different from last night. It's boyish and cute. He sounds like a baseball player.

"Not sure," I tell him. "She left about twenty minutes ago." The familiarity of my voice must startle him, and Isaac looks up, alarm and pain in his eyes. He takes in my appearance, my hair and clothes. I must look enough like her, because his resolve to distrust me weakens slightly.

"And what are you doing here?" he asks quietly, but not unkindly.

"I never miss a practice," I say, and try to smile. "I thought we could—"

"Don't do that," he says, shaking his head. "Don't talk like her."

I swallow hard. "I have to, Isaac. It's why I'm here. You weren't connecting with the other therapists. You wouldn't let them in. They think this is a better way. I want to help you."

He adjusts his hat roughly, and turns away. "Stop," he says, his face growing redder. "I don't want you here. I don't want the reminder. Just . . . fuck. Just go away." He pushes hard against the fence, making the metal rattle, and then walks across the field, heading to the dugout.

"Isaac, wait!" I call, but he hunches his shoulders, blocking me out. I've hurt him again. I shouldn't have come here, or at the very least I should have left earlier. I take a step back, absorbing my regret.

I watch as Isaac disappears into the dugout, going to the

locker room. In the cool breeze I shiver, vowing to do better, to find a way inside the relationship to get him to trust me. Get my father, and maybe even my sister, to accept me.

I'm failing, I think, imagining returning early from this assignment. Heading back to my life to deal with my real father's disappointment. He thought I could do this, but I'm screwing it up. I have to be better, smarter. I haven't been committed enough to this role—I've been holding it at a distance, always trying to keep one foot in reality. If I want to help these people, truly help them, I need to be fully immersed. I need to *be* Catalina. I have to try harder.

I'm a bit lost when I walk into my house a while later, Isaac's rejection coupled with Angie's hatred enough to wear me down, eat away at my self-esteem. More than anything, I hate failure. The sensation winds its way from my gut to my heart, hollows me out.

I'm startled to find my mother waiting in the entryway for me, purse in hand. She's thrilled to see me, and the juxtaposition with how unwanted I felt only minutes before fills up my empty soul.

Before I can even check on my father, my mother takes my elbow and we're back in the car, heading to the mall, of all dreaded places. Although it's not ideal, I'm happy not to be alone right now. She and I will be out in public together as mother and daughter, possibly seeing people who will know that I'm a closer. This is allowed, but I'll have to steel myself against the public reaction. Remind myself that other people don't really hate me. They just miss who I used to be.

I have two heavy bags, one from Gap and one from H&M. Although I've researched enough to know the right clothes to buy, I let my mother pick them out, mostly because it was fun for her. We stop in the food court and I get a slice of white pizza with veggies while my mother nibbles on a Caesar salad. The mall is bustling around us, but so far no one has thrown me a strange look or noticed me in any significant way. I'm anonymous; we're just a typical mother and daughter, sharing a day out together. Can't say I've ever had that before.

"There's something I have to tell you," my mother says quietly from across the table. I lift my head, worried that I've overstepped. I haven't been paying attention to my words, enjoying myself instead. I set down my pizza and watch her. She stares back, silent at first, and I can see a million thoughts playing over her features.

"I'm angry with you," she says simply. "I'm angry that you died."

I blow out a breath, hit with a sentiment I wasn't expecting. Weighed down by the heaviness of her grief. I reach across the table to take her hand. "I'm sorry," I respond sincerely.

My mother purses her lips, still thinking. "But it's not just that," she adds miserably, squeezing my fingers. "You'd left me months before. Even Isaac saw that. You withdrew from all of us. Why?"

"I don't know."

"We loved you so much, Catalina. We'd have done anything to help you. Why didn't you come to us?" Her voice is clicking up in volume, and a couple at the table next to us glances over.

"I don't know," I repeat in a hushed voice. My mother seems unaware of the attention she's garnering, and she shakes her head like I'm not giving her the right answers. But now I have a question of my own.

"Mom, how did I die?" I ask, leaning into the table. "What happened to me?" I hear the couple next to us gasp, and then they disappear from my peripheral vision. My mother closes her eyes, letting go of my hand. When she looks at me again, her pain is lost somewhere behind her denial.

"Doctors say I shouldn't fixate on that," she says. "It doesn't matter now, does it? You're back to make things right. We should stop dwelling and enjoy our time together." She sniffles hard and looks around, as if just noticing there are other people. I'm overwhelmed with disappointment, almost desperate to know the truth about myself. My mother motions to my food. "Do you want another slice?" she asks kindly.

I shake my head no. I'm not very hungry anymore.

"I called ahead and booked us nail appointments," my mother says, leading the way into the salon. "I know you can't . . ." She pauses, shrugging nervously. "I know you can't get your hair done now, but you love this salon. Ty is the only person you let near you with scissors."

I nod politely and walk with her to the reception stand, glancing around the expansive room. I'm amazed that one, a salon this nice is in a mall, and two, that I can't remember the last time I've been to a professional. Usually Myra cuts my hair for me.

The scent of peroxide hangs in the air, mixed with vanilla and shampoo. The girl at the desk has perfect red ringlets and a stylish black colorist's apron. She says hi to my mom, but when her eyes fall on me, her expression falters. She quickly looks away.

"I'll let the nail tech know you're here," she tells my mother, and quickly flees toward the back. My mother sits down and beckons me to join her, but my stomach is knotted up. They obviously know me here. I realize now what a terrible idea this was.

"Mom," I say, leaning closer to her. "I don't think—"

"Eva," a guy says, strolling in from the main room. He's tall and broad with short dreads he has pulled into a half ponytail. He and my mother embrace for a moment, and Ty whispers his condolences for her loss. When he pulls back, he doesn't even acknowledge I'm standing here, like I'm invisible. He touches the ends of my mother's hair, turning them over. "I didn't know you were coming in today. What are we doing?" he asks.

"Sorry I haven't been by," she says, smiling. "Just nails, though." She wiggles her fingers to prove her polish is chipped. Ty shushes her.

"Eva, you need a root touch-up and a trim," he says with his right eyebrow hitched high. “No self-respecting stylist would let you walk around like this. Now grab a chair.”

She laughs, tapping sheepishly at her scalp. “Ty,” she says when they start across the room, “maybe you could . . . something for my daughter?” She motions to me, and slowly the stylist turns.

I have to give Ty credit because rather than call my mother out, call her crazy or selfish, he runs his eyes over me like he’s actually considering my hair situation.

“Yes,” he agrees, turning back to my mother. “A trim would be good. Just like before.” He winks at her and she smiles broadly, obviously relieved that he’ll play along. I, on the other hand, am slightly disturbed. I’m not used to being out in public with my clients, not like this. This is a different level of acting.

Ty has my mother sit at his station and he places me near the back, turned away from the other clients. I sit there and wait, listening as he chats with my mother, helps others. At one point he comes over, pausing behind me and staring at my reflection.

“It’s uncanny,” he says. “Even with this wig, you look a lot like her. I’ve never seen one of you in person before.”

One of you.

“I can trim the ends,” he offers quietly. “Catalina wore it a little shorter than this in her last few weeks. She had the bone structure for it.” He pauses a minute, and then reaches to turn my head, examining my face. “To be honest,” he says, pursing his lips, “you do too. If you want to cut it for real, I think it’d be very flattering. And the color would go well with your skin tone. Then you wouldn't have to wear this nasty-ass wig." He smiles and tugs gently at the lower strands. "Think about it."

I smile in return, relieved that he didn't say something cruel. That he actually cared enough to make a suggestion. I thank him, and then Ty leaves and directs my mother to the back to have her hair washed. Before she goes, my mother beams at me like she's having the time of her life—proud to show off her daughter. Ty goes to the chair of another client and I lower my eyes into my lap, considering his suggestions. I've cut and dyed my hair like my assignments before; it wouldn't be completely unheard of. I haven't cut it lately because most of the dead girls have had longer hair.

I study my reflection again, trying to remember what I look like without the wig. The only image that comes to mind is the picture Deacon drew; my hair wild in comparison to this sleek bob. I glance behind my reflection; the salon is alive and vivid. The people are all genuine, and I'm hidden in the back like a horrible secret. I run my fingers through the strands of my wig, remembering a video I watched of me and Isaac—a quick clip where he kissed the top of my head and brushed his fingers through my hair, whispering how adorable I was. He couldn't do that now. He'd see I'm not real, and it would break him all over again.

I'm not making progress, not like I hoped. My mother is in denial, my father in avoidance. My sister hates me and my boyfriend is terrified of letting me too close. This could be my chance to change things. To save them. To know them. To be a part of their lives and give them closure.

And I'd be lying if I didn't admit how much I want them to accept me. To know, for even a minute, what it would be like to have a family. Something more than just my father and a few coworkers. I want to know what it's like to be normal.

"Ty," I call, checking first to make sure my mother's still gone. Ty turns to look over his shoulder at my reflection. I swivel in the chair to face him, and then grip the end of my wig and pull it off, making several people whisper around him. But my hairdresser doesn't say a word. Instead his mouth twitches with a smile.

Ty abandons the other station and walks over, stopping in front of me and pulling scissors from the front pocket of his apron. He reaches over to pluck the wig out of my hands, staring at it before tossing it in the trash. "Thank God," he says, and turns me in the chair, swishing my hair back and forth to examine the color and texture. When his eyes meet mine in the mirror, he lifts his eyebrow again, questioning me.

My heartbeat is so loud in my ears, I barely hear myself when I respond: "Make me real."

PART II

YOU CAN ALWAYS GET WHAT YOU WANT

CHAPTER ONE

SOMEWHERE AROUND MY THIRTEENTH BIRTHDAY, my real thirteenth birthday, I was on an assignment where a girl had been run over in her driveway by her own mother. The girl had been fixing the chain on her bike when the mom backed up, killing her instantly. In hindsight, I think the client needed more than a thirteen-year-old girl to bring her closure. The guilt and self-loathing went far beyond grief.

The first day I showed up there, my mother lay on the floor at my feet, sobbing. Marie had to pull her away, calm her down with the help of a strong sedative. The father had left years earlier for a new marriage, and Donna Royale had made me her entire life. My death was a careless mistake. It was an accident.

Marie stayed with me the entire two days, worried the mother would dissolve again. She kept her medicated, dreamy.

In the end, what my mother needed to hear was that I forgave her for killing me. That I would see her again someday. She let us leave after that, seeming more at peace. I'd never thought to look her up, find out if the remedy took. Basically Donna Royale disappeared from my life, and I never thought of her again. I'm not sure why she's in my head now, why I'm worrying about her all these years later. Maybe it's because my new mother reminds me of her in a way. This burden of guilt hanging around her that I can't quite place.

"I love your hair so much," my mother says for the third time, startling me from my thoughts. She gazes over from the driver's seat as we take the turn into the circular driveway. Her brown eyes are kind, but lost. Loving, longing, desperate. I smile at her, close-mouthed, and then turn to face the house as we park next to my father's car.

"Don't you love it?" my mother asks, turning off the ignition. I nod, and flip down the mirror again to check it before we go inside. I'm shocked by my appearance, but in a good way. I brush my fingers through the blond hair, the shade tinted lighter to make it an exact match. I push the strands this way and that, enjoying it from every angle. *I'll keep this,* I think. *It really does suit me.*

"I do," I tell my mother, and she bites her lip, beaming with adoration. I've made her happy, and in turn my heart hurts with the idea that this will all crash back on her later today. One step forward, two steps back. That's usually how the first full day goes. Her guilt will deepen because she'll feel a connection with me, and she'll wonder if she's betraying her daughter's memory. It will eat away at her, keep her from sleeping, but in the morning she'll see me, and her anxiety will fade.

That's one of the toughest things about this job: Seeing the heartbreak is never easy, but watching them accept me is almost worse. Seeing how they miss their child so much that they'll love a stranger in her place just to feel close to her a minute longer. They don't care if it's real. They're too broken to care.

"Where'd you go?" my mother asks softly, reaching out to touch my arm. I blink rapidly and focus on her, seeing that she's concerned.

"Sorry," I say. "I was just . . . thinking about Isaac," I lie. My mother nods knowingly.

"I'm guessing he wasn't happy to see you today?" she asks.

Would she understand how Isaac's rejection made me feel? Is it improper to ask her advice?

"It's okay," my mother says, reading my hesitance. "You can tell me." Around us the temperature in the car has risen now that the engine is off. Beads of sweat form in my hairline, under my bra strap. At the same time, the warmth is comforting. Suffocating my doubts. "We used to talk about him a lot," my mother adds. "Especially in the beginning."

"He's suffering," I say, letting down my guard. "I see it and I'm frustrated because he won't let me help him. How can I get through to him?"

My mother tilts her head from side to side as if saying there isn't an easy answer. "Isaac doesn't put himself out there. He never has. He's a reserved boy, kind of like your father. That's why it feels so special when people like them give you their love. Like you're the only person in the world who matters."

I think again about the picture of me and Isaac, wondering if that's how it felt for him to love me. Like I was the only thing that mattered, inhabiting a place that was just ours. I know Deacon cares about me, but our relationship is too hard. Too painful. With Isaac it'd be different.

I reach to run my hand across my forehead, wiping away a bead of sweat. My mind has spun out, and I quickly try to reel it back in. "I'm just so confused," I admit. My mother laughs softly.

"It was like that in the beginning, too. You weren't sure how you felt about Isaac. Then suddenly you loved him like crazy. Couldn't be without him. But then . . ." Her expression falters slightly.

"Then what?" I ask, my heart rate picking up. "Did things change?"

My mother's face settles into a calm, resigned expression. All at once, I don't feel like her daughter anymore. I feel like a stranger.

"Yes," she says sadly. "Yes, everything changed." She turns to look at the house. "Everything good, at least." Without a backward glance at me, she grabs her purse and climbs out of the car. I'm stunned, rooted in place until I see her nearly at the front door. I quickly get out and grab the bags from the backseat. My mother doesn't wait for me before she goes inside.

I scold myself for pushing too hard, pushing for selfish reasons. I'd promised to be better—this was not the way. I think I need to talk to Marie, find out what exactly was going on in Catalina's life. These pieces are not adding up to what I've seen online and in her journal. They're not matching the information provided—but do I have all the information? Or is someone purposely hiding facts? If so, why would they hide them from me? I'm here to help, not judge.

I stop on the front porch, the shopping bags hanging on either side of me, heavy in my hands. I stare into the house at my mother, watching as she drops her keys into the bowl on the entry table. The false world fades around me. This assignment required more research; I have no idea who I was before I died. My job may not include solving mysteries the deceased left behind, but if my parents and the grief department want me to fix this, to cure this, I need the information.

I walk inside the house and shut the door behind me.

My mother decides to lie down for a while before starting dinner. I offer to help with the meal, and she agrees, although I can see her mind is elsewhere. As she disappears down the hall, I go to the kitchen to grab a drink. I fish out my phone and check for any messages from Aaron about Virginia. I meant to casually ask my mother about her, but there never seemed to be the right moment. Prying into my past would only pull my mother out of the role play. I'll have to try old-fashioned research first. Besides, parent information is sometimes unreliable.

I hear a hollow crack from outside, and I spin quickly to the sliding glass doors. I'm surprised when I find my father in the yard, a metal bat in his hand. He tosses up another baseball and swings, smacking it through the air and beyond our back fence into the woods. At his feet there are at least a dozen more balls, and I wonder how long he's been at this. I watch for a moment, taking a sip from my soda as I debate what to do. I slide my phone into my pocket.

My father doesn't want to talk; he's been avoiding me. From my journal, I know we were close. I was Daddy's little girl while my sister was my mother's protégé, at least until recently. My sympathy peaks as I watch this huge man roll his shoulders, obviously tired. Overwhelmed with pain he has nowhere to place. No way to work out the kinks in his heart. I have a muddy sense of homesickness, reminded of a time with my own father. We had been mini-golfing when he got the call that one of his patients had died. He didn't react at first; we finished the game and he let me win. But at home that night, after I'd gone to bed, I heard him crying in the living room. I snuck downstairs and found him with files spread all over the coffee table, a bottle of rum on the carpet near to where he sat. I didn't interrupt him. It was his grief to process.

But after he fell asleep, I cleaned up the papers and covered him with a blanket from the couch. We didn't talk about it the next day, but I could tell he was glad I was there. Some people don't want to be confronted with their grief. They just want to know they're not alone.

I take one last swig from my soda and set it down, watching my father through the glass. I brush my hair to the side, self-conscious of how he might react to my change. I build myself up to approach him, running through several possible starting points in the conversation.

Can I play?

Do you want some company?

I saw Isaac today. Oh, and by the way, my sister hates me. She's pretty pissed at you, too.

Before I've committed to a course of action, I'm sliding open the heavy glass door and stepping out into the sunshine. My father glances back, at first disinterested, but then he bristles as he takes in my appearance. Running his gaze slowly over my hair. My clothes. He sways, but then sniffles hard and grabs a ball from the ground and hits it so hard, the crack of the bat against it makes me jump. Nothing I can say would reach him, I decide. I walk past the house to where a few bats lie in a pile on the ground next to the shed. I pick one up and test its weight, and then decide on the biggest one. Without a word, I walk over to where my father's standing, looking into the trees beyond our yard like I'm measuring the distance. I feel him turn to me, watch as I lean down to pick up a ball.

I blow out a breath and then toss the ball in the air, swinging with all my might. I miss. My arms continue through the swing, spinning me in my shoes. *Ouch.* That can't be good for my shoulder. There's a snort, and I look over to see my father covering his mouth with his hand. I fight back my own embarrassed smile.

"That looked really stupid, huh?" I ask.

"It was quite possibly the worst swing I've ever seen," he says, trying to stay straight-faced. "You nearly screwed yourself into the dirt."

I laugh and bend to pick up the ball. I narrow my eyes, looking at the trees, my lips pressed tight together while I concentrate. And then I try it again and barely get a piece of the ball, making it land *behind* me.

"That was actually negative progress," I say, glancing sideways at my dad. "Good thing we're not keeping score."

"Good thing for you," he says. He picks up a ball and smacks it beyond the fence with what looks like little effort.

"Show-off," I mumble, and then try again. He doesn't offer advice or show me how to choke up on the bat. He's clear on the difference between me and his daughter, still keeping his distance. But the fact that he's letting me be here at all is a step forward.

It takes me five tries before I hit the ball in any measurable way.

"There you go," my father says, mopping his forehead with a handkerchief from his back pocket. Sweat rings his underarms and patterns a V across his chest. We take a few more swings, my arms and back already aching, and I look longingly at the patio set.

"Let's take a break," my father says, reaching for my bat.

He doesn't meet my eyes, but I appreciate the gesture and give him the metal bat before following behind him to the table. I sit down first, and he takes a spot across from me, looking over my head at the woods. I'm thirsty, but I don't want to interrupt our moment by going inside.

Birds are chirping and a slight wind picks up. The sun fades behind a few scattered clouds. My father exhales heavily and meets my eyes from across the table.

"How long have you been doing this for?" he asks. His question startles me, breaks me from my role play.

"Since I was six," I tell him, still using his daughter's voice. His eyebrows pull together, whether in sympathy or disbelief, I'm not sure. "I've been well trained," I assure him. "I'm the best." He smiles softly at this, but sadness overwhelms his expression.

"Have you ever lost anyone?" he asks.

"I lose someone every time I have an assignment," I say. He shakes his head.

"I mean in the real world. Have you ever lost anyone close to you?"

Tiny pricks of grief that I can't quite place break over my skin. "Yeah," I tell him, my face growing hot. "My mother."

He swallows hard, looking apologetic for bringing it up. He leans forward, his elbows on the table.

"How did you get over it?" he asks. "How did you learn to do that?"

"I don't know," I say, my shoulders hunching. "I don't

remember anything about her." I look up and meet his eyes. "I've forgotten her completely."

My father's lips part in surprise, and he watches me for a long moment. "Well, that's almost worse, isn't it?" he asks quietly.

"Yeah. Yeah, I guess it is."

He looks back at the trees, but his eyes have glassed over. He feels sorry for me, and all at once I'm the vulnerable one. I lower my head, staring down at my hands on my lap. "I still miss her, though," I say. "It's just . . . a gnawing sense of loss. One that isn't attached to an actual memory. An ache that never goes away." When my father doesn't respond, I look up to find him staring at me sadly. I shrug, trying to lighten this heavy moment I've brought down around us.

"I'm sorry," he tells me sincerely. "You don't deserve that. You're . . . you're just a kid."

"Who deserves pain, then?" I ask. "Not you or your wife. Not Isaac or Angie. No one deserves what's happened to your family. If I can make that go away . . ." I pause. "It's worth it."

My father stills, a million different thoughts playing across his features. "Do you really think you can help?" he asks, sounding hopeful but cautious.

This burly man with the bushy mustache is holding on to the idea of me, his daughter. He doesn't want to let me go, although everything around him tells him he should. In this moment, I would do anything to bring him peace. I would give up the real me for that.

"Yes," I say simply. "I can help."

Tears fill his eyes until they brim over and run down his cheeks. He draws an unsteady breath, and then this formidable man covers his face and sobs at his backyard patio table. My nose burns with the heat of my sympathy tears. My father's shoulders shake with his cries; a broken sound like a wounded animal escapes from behind his hands. A broken man.

I stand up, trying to push away my own feelings so I can focus on what to say. Instead I find myself rounding the table and standing by my father's side. I put my hand on his shoulder, and all at once he turns and wraps his arms around me, his face at my hip as he holds me tight and cries.

"It's okay, Dad," I say quietly, putting my palm protectively on the back of his head. "I'm here now."

"I miss you," he breathes out. "I miss you so much, Catalina. Don't ever leave me. Don't ever."

Warm tears roll down my face as I stare into the trees, brushing my father's thinning hair. Absorbing his grief as my own. "I'm here now," I say again, until his pain fills me up.

CHAPTER TWO

THE HOUSE IS QUIET WHEN I RETURN INSIDE, MY father opting to hit a few more baseballs before dinner. I give him his space. We had a moment, a small breakthrough. Pushing him now could make him distrust me again. I grab a soda and wander to my room, glancing around the unfamiliar space before dropping down at my desk. I roll my shoulder once to stretch it out, wondering how much pain I'll be in later.

I check my phone again, surprised I still haven't heard from Aaron. He's usually really quick on the research end, but maybe he's having trouble finding anything on a "Virginia." Now that I think about it, it's possible she's a complete figment I made up to spend more time with Isaac. I groan. "Which doesn't make sense," I scold myself, taking a swig of my Coke. My parents love Isaac—I don't think they would have minded us spending time together.

With a deep sigh, I set my phone aside on the desk and open up my computer. I click on the search and type in "Virginia" to see if I have any documents with her name in it. All that come up are a few history-class papers. Not the right Virginia. Next I check e-mails and again type in her name. Not one mention. Not from me or her or any of my friends. It's like she doesn't exist.

"Probably why Aaron's not calling me back," I murmur to myself.

Next I try all the different social media sites, and when I find nothing again, I start studying my pictures. I pause on a picture of me and Isaac—happy and beaming. It was from last year, at the lake. Isaac's family has a house near Crater Lake, and we'd head there a couple of times during the summer to go boating, swim, sit around the fire pit and talk all night. Isaac's mom got the house in her divorce settlement, and she would let Isaac go whenever he wanted. She didn't really consider that he'd bring me every time. She might have changed her mind about letting him go.

There's a flashing message on the bottom of my screen, signaling a new e-mail. I click on it and pull up my account, initially surprised to see it's part of an e-mail chain. Someone must have forgotten to delete my account from their address book.

WAREHOUSE—TONIGHT AT 11!

I furrow my brow, trying to recall if I've read anything about a warehouse, but nothing comes to mind. I search for an earlier mention in my messages, and find an initial e-mail from Conner Fairhaven from last month.

WHERE WERE YOU TODAY? YOUR MAN TOLD ME YOU'RE BOTH IN. WAREHOUSE ON MAY 18TH! BOUNCER SAYS WE'RE GOLDEN.

Conner didn't mention Isaac by name, which is why this didn't pull up in my earlier searches. I click back to the original group e-mail and find Isaac and Angie among the recipients.

The page shifts as a new e-mail comes in, and my heart seizes when I see it's from Angie. She tells them she'll be there tonight. Immediately a slew of apologies soon follow, condolences on my death. Tension tightens my shoulders, and I hate how everyone is patronizing her. I wonder how often Angie has to hear about my death—as if it's the only thing people can talk to her about anymore.

There is a *ding*, the sound of my instant messaging, and I quickly pull up the screen. I'm stunned to see my sister's name and image. Her lips are puckered, her red hair in stylish low pigtails. A picture taken in a happier time, I'm sure. I'm scared of what she has to say, and I quickly try to flip into therapy mode before reading the message.

I CAN SEE YOU'RE ONLINE, she writes. There's a yellow circle above my name, signifying that I'm here. I should have switched it to invisible.

I sit back in the chair and wring my hands, my heart thumping. Angie isn't a client, but I know our mother misses her. Maybe if my sister could get involved somehow, spend time with our parents, make them see that life will go on, even without me, it could help.

This is a terrible idea, I shouldn't reach out, but she's already part of this. I'M HERE TO HELP, I type, deciding to follow my gut. YOUR SUPPORT COULD ONLY ASSIST IN YOUR PARENTS' RECOVERY PROCESS.

DROP DEAD.

She signs off, and I'm left with a sting as if she slapped me. I look around my room, humbled, but then my temper flares. Angie doesn't mean it, but there comes a point when you have to stop making excuses for people. The fact is, Angie isn't just lashing out at me; she's being cruel to our parents. I know my mother has been trying to call her, but she won't answer. Angie isn't part of this assignment, and I think that was a mistake. She may have accepted her loss, but to what end? She's closed off and angry. If she doesn't get some kind of help, this could lead to destructive and dangerous behavior. I've seen it. And our parents need her. I have to make her understand that.

I glance at the computer screen, noticing the original e-mail again. A crazy and completely deranged idea pops into my head. I have to see her, and both she and Isaac will be at that place tonight. Maybe I could be there too. I'd keep my distance, but I could observe them with their friends, use that to figure out how to get inside their heads. It's not lost on me that my sister was right: Closers do manipulate people. Going to the Warehouse would be totally wrong.

Which is why I can't tell Aaron. Even if he doesn't report me, who's to say it won't come out when Marie debriefs us later? I can't trust him with this—even if he's my partner. I bite my lip, reading over the e-mail again, nervousness bubbling up. Can I really spy on my sister, involve her in this assignment, without Marie's permission?

I run my fingers through my short hair, and take out my phone. I NEED YOU TONIGHT, I text. My phone rings immediately.

"Well, this escalated quickly," Deacon says, sounding amused. I laugh, comforted by his voice. Normally I wouldn't talk to him while I'm on assignment—it certainly pulls me out of my role—but he's the perfect person to ask for help. Since we're no longer partners, Deacon won't be subjected to an interview after this assignment. There's no reason for Marie to find out we interacted at all. And if anyone knows how to manipulate a situation, it's certainly my ex-boyfriend.

"There's a meet-up at place called the Warehouse," I tell him. "Know it?"

"Yeah," he answers. "It's a bar in Portland. Why?"

I pull up my knees and hug them to my chest. "Don't judge me," I start, making him chuckle. "But this assignment has gotten complicated. I need your help figuring some things out." Deacon's good at digging, seeing the small details others miss. We've collaborated before, especially when we worked together. He was always able to help.

"Of course," he says. "But I have to point out that you're asking me to drive up to Lake Oswego to take you to some sketchy dive bar in the city. What's going on?"

"Hey, I thought you weren't going to judge!"

"Didn't agree to that," he says quickly. "But let's just call this curiosity if it makes you feel better. Why do you want to go there?"

I sigh, knowing there's no way to dodge his question again. "I'm going to observe a nonclient. Which is why this is off the record."

The line is silent for a moment, and I don't provide more details. If Deacon wants to know the rest, he'll have to come here. When the quiet goes on too long, I groan. "Deacon, are you in or not? I can just call Aaron."

"No you can't," he says. "Aaron's out of town. Besides, he's already got me researching something, so he's a little tied up. And Jesus, Quinn. When have I ever told you no?"

"Wait." I drop my feet to the floor. "What do you mean Aaron's out of town? Since when?"

Deacon blows out a breath. "Don't know. Since you left, I guess. He told me yesterday morning he'd be out of touch for a while. Didn't want to talk about it."

"Seriously?" I sit back against the chair, a bit stunned. Aaron didn't tell me he was going anywhere. Why wouldn't he have mentioned that? What if I need him? "Does Marie know?" I ask Deacon.

"Not sure."

This is crazy. Aaron has never abandoned me on assignment, not even when he was deep in his own role-play. I think a minute, running over my conversation with my father. This assignment was an emergency, a last-minute case that Arthur Pritchard sanctioned. What if they asked the same of Aaron?

"Do you think this has anything to do with Arthur Pritchard?" I ask Deacon.

"Naw," he responds. "Aaron's probably just taking a breather with Myra. Don't worry, Quinn. I've got your back. What do you need from me, other than a ride?" he adds.

I'm not comfortable with the idea of Aaron being MIA, but I notice the time on my computer and force myself to focus on my assignment again. "Will you come with me tonight?" I ask.

"Sounds super-not-fun, but yes."

"Thanks," I say, smiling. "I'll text you my address. Meet me here at about eleven? I'll have to sneak out."

"Wow, you're full of bad ideas," he says. When I tsk, he apologizes. "Yes, I'll be there."

"Actually . . . ," I add. "Can you check into someone for me? I asked Aaron, but obviously he hasn't responded."

"Who?"

"A girl named Virginia. My mother says I hang out with her, but I can't turn anything up. I'm not entirely sure she's real."

"No last name?" he asks, his interest piqued by a true mystery.

"Nope. Only said I sometimes meet her on Saturdays. Let me know if you find anything."

"Absolutely. Okay, I'm going to get pretty," Deacon says. "Meet you outside your window at eleven."

I smile. "Just like old times."

"Right?" he says. "We always were good partners."

"We were terrible partners," I tell him. That's not true, but I like to torture him every so often with my denial.

"Liar," he returns immediately. "We were good partners in every way possible." A sense of warmth rushes over me, settling in so that my face grows hot. Deacon's not just talking about being closers. And it's not even about our relationship. It's the simple fact that Deacon and I are completely and helplessly intertwined in each other's lives. Even though he pushes me away sometimes, he pulls me in twice as hard.

"See you later," I say, not willing to prolong the flirtation. He takes the hint and we say good-bye. I text him my address and the passwords to my accounts so he can research Virginia. Afterward, I set my phone facedown on the desk. My heart is still beating quickly, and I turn to gaze out the window. Watch the trees sway in the breeze as I get lost in a memory.

It was a week after I first met Deacon at my kitchen table that he pulled up in my father's shiny black Cadillac, easing to the curb a few feet in front of me. He'd only gotten his permit the day I left for my assignment, but already my father was handing over the keys. I planned to reiterate the driving laws to him when I got home. Here was Deacon, perfectly on time, which annoyed me because I hadn't quite lost the mind-set of Annabeth Trayner yet. I could have used an extra moment or two.

I tossed my bag onto the backseat and climbed in the passenger side before yanking off my wig. Although Deacon had called earlier that day to set up the extraction from my assignment, I'd hoped Marie would be the one to pick me up. I felt a little betrayed.

I grabbed my seat belt, and as I clicked it, I glanced over to find Deacon studying me, drinking me in like he'd never seen me before. When his eyes leveled on mine, there was a flutter in my chest—a feeling of being completely known, seen, memorized. Of being totally exposed.

"I brought you a candy bar," he said simply. I stared at him, slightly confused when his mouth twitched with a smile. He nodded down at the center console to a Snickers bar, crooked and slightly melted.

"I don't eat peanuts," I told him.

"Noted." He shifted the car into gear, and pulled out into the street. Despite his calm exterior, I could tell by the way he constantly checked his mirrors that he was nervous driving. I liked that quick peek into his personality, his temperament. I continued watching him, waiting for him to ask me about the assignment, but he didn't. He didn't say anything. My father thought Deacon would be a great partner, but so far he'd done nothing to assess my state of mind. That was neglectful.

"Aren't you going to ask me any questions?" I finally blurted out.

"Like what? I already offered you a candy bar." He looked over and smiled. "But you don't like peanuts."

"True," I said. "But I'm talking about the assignment. The family."

Deacon shrugged, slowing us to a stop at a red light. "Do you want to talk about it?" he asked. "Because you looked like you were still processing to me. Seemed unproductive to force you to discuss it before I take you somewhere where you'll be forced to discuss it, you know?"

"What if I needed help?" I asked.

"Then I would help you."

He said it like it was the only answer. It offered me a degree of comfort, his confidence and determination. It was a quality I admired, especially in my line of work. And so I rested back in the seat, watching him curiously as the light changed and we drove toward Marie's apartment.

The next time he picked me up from an assignment, he was five minutes late, and in the console was a bag of Skittles.

Now I can see that Deacon had me figured out from the start. He's brilliant that way. He can read anybody. My phone buzzes, startling me out of my thoughts, and I check the message. Deacon sent a thanks for the passwords, and I set my phone down, reminded that my real partner is out of town. Aaron ditched me. Not only is this unusual; it's dangerous. I mean, I could contact Marie—but no one wants to bring in their advisor unless it's an emergency. How could he abandon me like this?

I stand up from the computer and walk over to the bags of clothes I brought home from the mall. My real life is growing just as confusing as this assignment, and I hope to distract myself by trying on clothes. Ultimately, I decide I don't love any of them. I grab the outfit my mother liked the most and slip it on before heading out to help her with dinner.

My nerves are ratcheted up at the thought of sneaking out, breaking my parents' trust. But, ultimately, talking with Angie can help me figure out how to bring our family closure. And if I get caught, I'll manage a believable cover story. Convincing my parents would be easy. Marie not so much. But I'd be able to explain.

I just really hope I don't have to.

CHAPTER THREE

DINNER WITH MY PARENTS IS ACTUALLY NICE. MY father even smiles at me once when I mention how much my arm hurts, but that I'm pretty sure my draft letter to the MLB will arrive within the week. We have roasted chicken and mashed potatoes. My mother talks about her friend Maryanne again, and my dad tells us about a new project he'll be starting at work on Monday. For an entire hour, I forget I'm on assignment. For an entire hour, I have a family—a mother and a father who share a meal with me. Me and my real dad never do that. We never have time.

My parents say good night around ten, but by now my anxiety has reasserted itself. When I finally get to my room, I stuff a pillow under my covers. I'm pretty sure that's never worked in fooling a parent, not ever, but I'm not sure what else to do. Locking the door would be a dead giveaway.

I pull on a pair of soft jeans and do a couple of lunges to loosen them up. My T-shirt from this morning is over the back of my desk chair, and I slip it over my head and spritz on some body spray. There's a still a little time before Deacon's supposed to arrive, so I check my e-mails and am disappointed to find I was indeed taken off the e-mail chain. There's a vague sense of being left out, but I quickly remind myself that I was never really invited in the first place. I close the computer and take out my phone. I click through to find Aaron's last message.

CALL ME, I type. I don't ask Aaron where the hell he is, or why he didn't tell me, just in case someone else is monitoring his line. I wouldn't want to get him in trouble. When he doesn't respond, I tuck my phone away and shut off my overhead light. I ease open my window and sit on the sill, watching the street for Deacon.

I'm scared about tonight. Afraid I'm making a mistake. But there have been too many anomalies with this case already. I need actual research. Answers. It's like everyone keeps telling me lies—starting with why Arthur Pritchard sent me on this assignment in the first place.

The minutes slowly tick by, and I listen for any sound coming from the hallway. Both my parents have gone to bed, and I don't hear anything beyond the humming of the refrigerator in the kitchen. Finally a car drives up and parks in the shadows between lampposts before clicking off its lights. I quickly grab the hoodie from my desk chair and look at the doorway, listening. When I hear nothing, I push open my window the rest of the way and climb through. I ease it down, but not entirely, and then dash across the lawn toward the car.

I climb in the passenger side of my Honda, and then Deacon pulls away from the curb quickly in case one of my parents happens to look out the window. He doesn't turn the headlights on until we round the corner and are out of view. The minute he does, we both exhale and look at each other.

It's been a long time since I've seen Deacon while on assignment—not since we were partners. His eyes rake over me, pausing at my hair before he turns to face the windshield once again.

"You cut your hair," he says.

I pull at the strands in the back of my hair, embarrassed of the change, which must seem extreme. It feels extreme now that I'm away from my assignment. "Yeah . . . it was just easier."

He darts a look between me and the road. "Looks nice," he says simply. I wait for him to go on, but he doesn't. The moment fades, and then it's just us in the car, all of our baggage stowed away.

"Now, who exactly are we observing tonight?" he asks, taking a turn onto the freeway. Outside, the dark sky has a hint of gray from cloud cover; the first ominous drops of rain hit the windshield.

"My sister," I tell him. "Her name's Angie."

Deacon turns to me. "What? You didn't mention there would be a sister."

"That's because she's not part of this assignment." I look at him seriously. "But she should have been. I'm not sure why the counselors didn't flag her, or at least ask her to remain in the house to support her parents. How am I supposed to position their lives without all the pieces?" I ask. "The minute Angie comes home, *if* she comes home, the family dynamics will change. That could throw off the entire recovery process."

"Reasonable argument," Deacon says slowly, thinking it over. "And you've talked to this girl?"

"Sort of," I say. "She hates me, wishes I was dead instead of her sister."

"So you've made progress."

I laugh, and when I look down, I notice a bag of Skittles in the center cup holder. Deacon smiles when I turn to him. "Like old times," he says.

I'm not expecting his comment to hit me the way it does: a mix of nostalgia and longing around the thought of Deacon. Then again, maybe I'm just craving a connection. "Have you turned up anything on Virginia yet?" I ask, trying to refocus on the assignment.

"No, but I just started looking," Deacon says. "If she exists, I'll find her."

We spend the rest of the drive going over my assignment so far. I tell him about the haircut with my mother and playing baseball with my dad. I even reenact the confrontation with my sister. Neither of us mentions Isaac.

On Mississippi Avenue, I see a small brick building with the word WAREHOUSE embossed in iron above its door. People are standing around outside, smoking and hanging out under the awning. The rain has softened into a drizzle as Deacon pulls into the back lot and finds a spot near the chain-link fence. He was right—this place is kind of seedy. When Deacon looks at me, I smile. It also looks kind of fun.

"All right, trouble," he says with a laugh, "we need a plan. There will be a least a few people at the bar who'll recognize you," he says. "How do you want to play that?'

I look uncertainly at the building, adrenaline rushing through my system. I've done some crazy things before, mostly with Deacon, but never on assignment. Not when I'm supposed to be professional. Doubt sinks in.

"Is this unethical?" I ask. The light from the streetlamp falls across Deacon's face, clouding his expression with shadows.

"Sometimes the ends justify the means," he says solemnly. "And those times, we have to be the ones to decide what's worth losing." His voice is far more serious than I expected, and I can't help but think there's more behind it. "Is it worth your sister losing her privacy?"

I sit back, thinking over the question. Ultimately, this isn't just about Angie. It has larger implications for the entire family. "I think so," I say, looking at Deacon. He presses his lips into a sad smile.

"Then we go inside."

Deacon doesn't think this is a good idea, but like me, he understands it. The most troubling part about tonight is that if I see something concerning, something I can't ignore, I'll have to report it. I'll have to flag Angie for the therapists. I'm not sure I'd want someone watching me that closely in my real life.

Both Deacon and I get out of the car, and the night is cold on my face. I zip up my hoodie a little higher, shivering. My nerves are frayed, and Deacon comes around the car and meets me to walk across the parking lot toward the building.

Deacon has a fake ID, but I'm relying on the bouncer being "golden" like the e-mail said. I hope he doesn't know that I'm dead. We walk through the drizzle, and I pull my hood over my hair. Deacon takes my hand, intertwining his fingers with mine, and when I look at him questioningly, he shrugs as if saying, *What? Friends can hold hands.* I snort a laugh, and turn away to focus on the mission.

We weave through the crowd, and I'm careful to scan their faces in search of my sister without being obvious. No one pays attention to us, and I'm grateful. But that's a skill we've learned over the years, how to blend in. How to hold ourselves in a way that doesn't bring attention to our features. It comes in handy when trying to assume the identities of other people.

Deacon stops in front of me, dropping my hand, and I lower my hood now that we're under the awning. Smoke drifts over from the group behind us, and I swallow hard and watch Deacon flash his ID, looking past the bouncer into the bar. The guy checks it quickly, not paying attention because Deacon's mannerisms are confident, older. The bouncer waves him in and turns to me. Deacon goes to wait just inside the door, but I'm scared. It wouldn't be the end of the world if I got turned away, but it would be the end of tonight's adventure.

I hold out the ID I took from the wallet on my desk, which reads *Catalina Barnes* and identifies me as completely underage. The bouncer looks at the picture, and then at me. He winks. "Tell Isaac he owes me," he says, and nods me through. I tense at the mention of my boyfriend's name, but smile as though I'm not the least bit fazed.

"I will," I say, touching the bouncer's arm, and glide past him to meet Deacon in the doorway. When I look sideways at him, Deacon's face is a little colder and his eyes scan the crowd inside. I have a slight twinge of guilt but then remind myself I haven't done anything wrong. Any jealousy he may have is totally on him.

"We should grab a spot in the corner. The light's not hitting it." He motions to an empty space near the bar that's almost completely lost in darkness. I agree, and we walk toward it, my eyes trained on every face, flipping from one smiling or scowling expression to another. The bar is packed; in the back room a band is setting up their equipment on the stage, and people have already flocked to take their positions in the crowd in front of them.

Zigzagging through the people proves difficult, and I lose Deacon at one point since I'm not tall enough to see over the shoulders of the guys in front of me. By the time I make it to the corner, Deacon has already taken off his sweater, and he's resting casually against the wall.

"Was about to send out a search party," he says, smiling now that we're alone in the crowded room. I unzip my hoodie; the air is warm from all the bodies packed together. Deacon looks past me. "This is going to be a little more difficult than you thought, isn't it?"

I take up space next to him on the wall and check over the crowd. "Definitely didn't expect it to be this busy."

"It's a good band tonight," Deacon says, taking out his phone and checking for messages. "And this place never charges a cover, so they pack them in. Hey, do you want a drink?" he asks.

"No," I say shaking my head. "I need to stay clear." I continue checking the crowd, worried that my sister may not have come here at all.

"You know," Deacon says, not looking at me, "if she's not here, we could just hang. Dance, even." I watch him a minute, trying to guess his intentions, but he's unreadable. Although a night out, a normal night out, sounds amazing right now, it's not my reality. I don't belong here with Deacon—I'm breaking character.

"Not tonight," I say quietly, and turn away. There's a sting, that familiar ache I get when I know I've hurt his feelings. But I chalk it up to the pinch of a needle when you get an inoculation. It hurts for a moment, but it prevents a much bigger problem down the line. Deacon shifts next to me but doesn't say anything else. He slides his phone back into his pocket and asks me to describe my sister once again.

The band finishes setting up, and when they start to play,

Deacon takes a walk through the crowd, closer to the stage, so that he can look around. I wait, fading into the background so I can observe without being noticed. About halfway through the band's first song, I find Angie.

She looks unsteady as she runs her hand along the brick wall, making her way toward the music. Her behavior garners looks, and a few people whisper as she passes.

She's alone, I note. In her posture and expression, I can see she's alone in every sense of the word. Even her broad smile at a passing guy is a mask. Her eyes are darker, her skin sallow in the places that makeup doesn't cover. She looks unwell.

I bite on my thumbnail and look around for Deacon, hoping he'll get back here before she disappears into the crowd again. Instead my gaze falls on Isaac, sitting on a stool at the bar. People are reaching around him, holding out money for the bartender, taking drinks before a new crush of people filters in. But Isaac's in slow motion, stagnant in the madness around him. He sips a cup of ice water, staring at nothing. Sympathy floods my chest. Without thinking, I take a step forward into the light so I can watch him a little more closely. Watch him ignore the entire world as he drowns in his grief.

"What the hell are you doing here?" a voice calls sharply, cruelly. Startled, I spin and find my sister a few steps in front of me. Her eyes are blazing; red flares on her cheeks. Her body sways with anger, and I try to move back, but it's too late for me to fade away now.

"Angela, I—"

"How *dare* you come here!" she says, her tone unhinged. "How dare you!" Her mouth is pulled tight in an ugly scowl. Several people around her have turned to stare, but I don't acknowledge them; I don't even turn to see if Isaac has noticed. I have to defuse this situation. The crowd in this room has quieted, and the echoing music from the band is hollow around me.

"I'm sorry," I say, my voice not nearly as close to her sister's now. I'm trying to calm her, and to do that, I need to be less aggressive. "I just wanted to talk to you."

She laughs, a sad laugh of disbelief. "You're playing my dead sister," she says, earning even more looks. "What makes you think I'd have anything to do with you? You're a monster."

Heat crawls over my cheeks, but I try to exude calm. "I know you're upset," I say, holding up my hands in surrender. "But if I could just talk to you about your parents. I really want—"

"I don't give a shit what you want!" she shouts, and now it feels like the entire bar is watching us. Where the hell is Deacon?

"Maybe if we go outside," I start, but before I finish my thought, there is a blur of movement. Angie grabs the drink from the guy nearest her and then hurls the liquid at me, splashing my face and clothes in cold, red liquid. I scream and fall back a step, completely shocked and dazed. I swipe my hands over my eyes, the alcohol burning my skin.

"I don't want your help," my sister growls. "I don't ever want to see you again." She turns and walks away, the guy calling after her that she owes him a drink. There is laughter, a couple of curses about how they shouldn't let underage people in the bar because they always ruin the night. But mostly it's the judgmental stares of the people who know what I do now. They know I'm a closer; they've put together why I'm here. And they hate me for it.

Sickness washes over me, and I try to back into the corner, shivering and sticky. Then suddenly, out of the crowd, Deacon appears, his posture hardened. He reaches past a couple of guys at the bar and grabs the stack of napkins without missing a step. When he reaches me, he takes my arm, not saying a word, and turns us toward the door.

I can feel the bouncer's stare as we walk past him, and I'm not even out from under the awning when I start to cry. Humiliated, degraded, I take Deacon's hand and let him lead me back to the car.

CHAPTER FOUR

DEACON DOESN'T ACKNOWLEDGE MY TEARS. THE rain has picked up, but I don't flip my hood. I let it wash over me, wash off the drink my sister threw in my face, wash off my shame. When we get to the car, Deacon hands me the damp napkins and unlocks the passenger side, helping me in. He closes the door, and pauses to look back at the building, as if he's considering going back in to fight for me. But there's no one to fight. He rounds the car, tossing a concerned glance at me through the windshield, before climbing in and slamming his door.

We sit quietly with the sound of rain splattering on the glass. Deacon doesn't start the car, even though it's cold. He doesn't do anything. Which is exactly what I need him to do in this moment.

Back when we were partners, I was slow to let Deacon

in—at least on a personal level. I may have liked him, but I didn't let him know. I definitely didn't want him to like me, either. It seemed like it'd make things more complicated. Then one night, we found ourselves parked outside the house of his assignment. He would do that sometimes: convince the clients to go out, to reconnect. I think it was more so that he could get a break from them. Get a break from the job.

This one night, he asked me to bring him food. He complained the family was vegetarian and that if he didn't get a hamburger soon, he might die from starvation. I had nothing better to do, so I agreed. I picked up takeout and met him outside the house, surprised when he got in instead of taking the bag back inside. He said he wanted the company.

We were there for about ten minutes, and I watched him tear through two cheeseburgers and a handful of fries. I guessed he hadn't been joking when he'd said he was starving. At one point, he turned to me, his brown eyes curious, flashing with mischief. "Do you have a boyfriend?" he asked, midchew.

I gave him a scathing *It's none of your business* look.

"Oh, come on," he said with a smile. "There's no *special someone* in your life?"

"Shut up." I laughed, looking out the window. The air from the heater made me entirely too warm, so I turned the directional away from me. It didn't lessen the heat on my face, though. Deacon and I were quiet for a painfully long time, until I finally sighed and turned to him. "No," I said. "No boyfriend."

"Yeah. I can believe that."

"Hey!" I called. "What's that supposed to mean?"

"It's not because you're horrible or anything," he said, like I'd totally twisted his words.

"Oh, thank you." I narrowed my eyes at him.

"Listen, it's cool," he said. "I'm not dating anyone seriously either. I'm just saying, people like us, we can have commitment issues, wouldn't you agree?"

I smiled. "I think maybe you just have asshole issues."

"Nice," he responded with a laugh. "You totally called it." He grabbed the soda from the cup holder, smiling as he sipped from the straw. I couldn't help it—I found him completely disarming. And even though I didn't say it, I was happy to know he didn't have a girlfriend.

No one's asked me that since him. No one's cared about the answer. I look down at my lap, shivering uncontrollably in the car. My teeth chatter as my wet hair clings to the side of my face. "Everyone hates me," I murmur.

"I don't hate you."

I'm so cold, both inside and out. I'm lonely and scared that nothing will ever be okay. I want a life—I want my life. I let the napkins fall to the floor. I'm sick of living on the fringes of society. And maybe I don't want to admit that the idea of coming out tonight, it wasn't totally about Angie. I liked the idea of being invited—even if I wasn't really.

"Quinn," Deacon says softly, reaching to take my hand. He squeezes it, his skin hot in comparison to mine. "Tell them you can't finish this assignment," he says. "Tell them it was too soon."

"My father—"

"I don't care about your father," he interrupts. "I don't give a shit about Arthur Pritchard, either. Every time you go on assignment, you come back a little different. You should end your contract. Who cares about money? I'll give you mine. I just . . . I don't want you to lose yourself."

"It's not about the money," I say, looking up at him. "It's never been about that." I pause, thinking over my decision to take this assignment, even though I was so tired. "I'm doing this for my father," I say. "He counts on me, Deacon. I'm supposed to be good at this. Do you know what it would do to him if I failed? This is his life's work. He believes in me." My voice cracks. "I . . . I can't disappoint him."

"He's disappointing you." Deacon's stare holds me fast, fiercely protective. For a minute I wonder what it would be like to give it all up, be free like Deacon. But then I realize that my father would never forgive me, just like he's never forgiven Deacon for failing him. I can't do that. I can't give up everything I've worked for. My father's the only family I have left—he's the only person who's never left me.

Deacon looks like he's waiting for an answer, but then his eyes follow something beyond my shoulder, and he adjusts his position to get a closer look. "Isn't that your sister?" he asks.

I turn immediately, wiping away my tears as my training floods back and washes me away. I'm dismayed to see Angie stumbling out from the back entrance of the bar, talking loudly into her phone. Although she would have been troubled tonight anyway, the confrontation with me has sent her on a destructive path. I can see from her mannerisms, her wild look, that she doesn't care what happens to her tonight. She doesn't care about anything.

"She's drunk," I say. My worry spikes, and I turn to Deacon. "What should I do?"

He leans forward, draping his arms over the steering wheel as he watches the scene unfolding outside the windshield. "I don't know," he says, watching her carefully. "It's a tough call. If you confront her again, who knows how she'll react. She already threw—" He stops and looks over at me apologetically for bringing up the drink incident.

He's got a point, but I don't care about what happened inside the bar. She's my sister, and I should have been looking out for her. Now the situation has gotten out of control.

Angie leaves the parking lot, heading toward the street. She kicks off her shoes into the bushes along the sidewalk and laughs. She pauses and takes the phone from her ear, staring down at it. I wonder if whoever she was talking to hung up. She opens her palm and lets her phone smash on the pavement, and then sways. She drops into a sitting position in the middle of the sidewalk.

Deacon curses, recognizing that we have to intervene in some way. I wonder where Angie's friends are. How could they leave her alone when she's obviously a mess?

My sister splays out on the pavement, her head falling into the edge of the grass in front of a beat-up old house. She stares up at the sky, letting the rain run over her face. God, is she going to pass out like this?

Deacon and I wait another minute, but no one comes for her. Whether Angie's isolated herself or she's always been this alone, I'm not sure. All I know is that I feel incredibly sorry for her. With a sore heart, I turn to Deacon.

He lifts one shoulder in a shrug, and nods out the window. "I can go," he offers. I consider it. Deacon's a stranger, and he can try to help her get back inside. Then again, my sister doesn't exactly look up to walking. She might cause another scene, and the cops might get called. Deacon can't be involved if that happens. He's not supposed to even see me when I'm on assignment.

"No," I tell him. "She's my responsibility. I'll bring her back to the bar." I don't mention that Isaac is inside and that part of me doesn't want Deacon to see him.

Deacon weighs it out and then agrees, acknowledging it's a bad situation all around. But he also knows helping her is the right thing to do. I smile, once again reminded of how well Deacon knows me. How deep our connection runs. I lean in and hug him, our bodies pressed together, my cheek against his neck. His skin is burning hot in the cold air, and longing sweeps over me. Invades me. I pull back slowly, our eyes locked like this moment can last if we want it to. If we let it.

He smiles slightly, acknowledging that he feels it too. His

fingers brush my thigh as I move away. Lights from a passing car illuminate the space around us, highlighting the passion in his eyes. I could get lost in here forever.

"I'll be right back," I mumble, quickly opening the door and climbing out into the rain. The cold night air hits my damp face, sobering up the crazy I just indulged in. Another minute and we might have ended up in the backseat. But Deacon and I are just friends, that's it. It's too dangerous to be anything else.

I wrap my arms around myself, heading toward the sidewalk. My sister laughs from where she's lying on the pavement, and I start jogging in her direction. I pull up my hood, hoping that with a bit of cover I won't elicit such a violent reaction from her. I slow down when I get close, and come to pause far enough away so I won't startle her.

"Angie," I say softly. She turns her head in the wet grass, a bit of dirt smudged on her cheek. She runs her eyes over me and then scoffs.

"Go away, impostor," she calls. Her arms are bare, her pale skin glowing in the streetlight. I sit on the pavement next to her, folding my legs under me, and settle in. I won't leave her like this.

"Can I at least help you back inside to your friends?" I ask, using my natural voice. Angie doesn't want to know me as Catalina. I can spare her that pain since she's not technically part of the assignment. At least until I know more about what she needs.

"I don't have any friends," she tells me, staring at the sky. "I don't want any."

At baseball practice she was with another girl, so I assume she has at least one friend, but she doesn't want to think about that. She wants to feel sorry for herself, hate herself so she'll have to reason to withdraw. She's sad. She's so deeply sad that I can't believe she's gotten this far without anyone noticing.

"Does your mother know how you feel?" I ask, keeping my voice steady but quiet. Angie winces at the mention of her mother.

"Of course not," she says bitterly. "Only thing anybody sees is Catalina. 'Catalina's depressed,'" she mimics in her mother's voice. "'Catalina's fighting with Isaac. What's wrong with *Catalina*?'"

As I listen, my heart rate speeds up, finally about to get some answers to this assignment. There was nothing in the file about a change in Catalina's state of mind. "And then what happened?" I ask.

Angie turns to me, her mascara bleeding black over her cheeks. "Then she died," she says coldly. "She died right in front of me."

I take in a sharp breath, the answer completely unexpected. This should have been in the file. This most definitely should have been in the file. "How did she die?" I ask, getting up on my knees.

For a moment I think she's going to tell me everything. I watch pain cross her expression, pull and distort her features. But rather than answer, Angie turns away, staring straight up into the sky, hitching in uneven breaths like she's about to break down. "She just died," she says.

I start to move closer when I hear a shout from the bar. I look over my shoulder; my body exploding in panic as I see

Isaac running toward us, his shoes sloshing in the puddles on the wet pavement. "Angela," he yells.

"Oh, shit," I mutter, and quickly get to my feet. I can't talk to Isaac right now. I'm completely out of character, and my makeup has probably run off. I turn back to the car, where Deacon looks equally concerned. But just as Marie would, he holds up his hand and tells me to be steady.

Isaac runs right past me to where Angie is crumpled on the ground, and he helps her sit up. For a moment I watch them, wondering if I could hurry back to the car, cut my losses, and start again tomorrow. But before I can make the decision, Isaac looks back at me and stills. He didn't know I was the person waiting here with Angie.

"You," he breathes out.

The rain has soaked through my clothes, chilled my body. It's almost impossible for me to flip back; I've been out of character for too long now. But before I answer him, I mentally review the file. Scan all the pictures and videos. Remind myself of an entire life. When I speak to Isaac, my voice has changed.

"She needs help," I say. "I was leaving and saw her sit down on the sidewalk. No one came out after her. . . ." I trail off, caught up in the disbelieving way Isaac is staring at me. I bury my hands in the pockets of my sweater, feeling exposed.

"I heard she threw her drink on you," he says after a long silence.

"Technically it wasn't her drink," I respond, darting a look at my sister. She's not paying attention. Her head hangs as she

sits with her knees up, her pose signifying that she might barf at any second. When I look back at Isaac, there's a hint of a smile on his lips.

"I hadn't heard that part. Seems like I owe someone a cocktail," he says.

"Well, not her." I point to Angie and she murmurs something unintelligible. Isaac turns to talk to her, quietly brushing her hair back from her face. I take the moment to observe him. His brown hair is matted down from the rain, and every so often he slides his fingers through it to keep the water from running down his face. His salmon-colored T-shirt is soaked through, nearly red now as it clings to his body. He looks at me, catching me staring, and I smile politely trying to play it off.

"We should take her home," he says, standing. "Let's get her on her feet."

I'm surprised by how easily he's talking to me, and I jump at the chance to participate. I get on the other side of my sister, careful not to say too much now that I'm back on assignment. I don't want her to freak again, point out to Isaac how untrue this all is. The minute I put my hand on her arm, she rips it away, dashing any hopes I had of her going quietly.

"Don't touch me," she says.

"Calm down," Isaac soothes. "We're just getting you out of here before the cops pick you up." He reaches his arm around her waist and props her unsteady body against his hip. "Where's your car?" he asks me. I freeze, wanting to look at the lot but afraid of drawing attention to Deacon.

"I took a cab," I lie. Isaac swears to himself, and then glances around.

"Well," he says. "You're going for a ride, Angela." He dips down and puts his arm behind her knees and then lifts her easily, resting her head against his chest. "I'm parked down the block," he says, starting down the sidewalk.

I watch after them, noting the bits of behavior I've seen throughout the night. But then Isaac stops and looks back at me. "Come on," he says with a shake of his head. "I'll give you a ride too."

My mouth opens in surprise, but at first nothing comes out. Then, just: "You will?"

"I'm not going to leave you in the rain," he says. Uncertainty flips through his eyes, but then he starts walking again, expecting that I'll follow. I turn back to where Deacon is waiting in my car.

He stares at me, but now the car is running, warmed up for me. I could walk to him, walk away from everything: that's exactly what his expression is asking me to do. I don't know if it's fear of failure, desire to do the right thing, or terror at the thought of falling back in love with Deacon—but I motion down the street toward Isaac and my sister.

Deacon waits a beat and then mouths *Okay* in a simple surrender. My conscience hurts for a moment, but I turn and jog after my sister and my boyfriend, unsure of where this night will lead.

CHAPTER FIVE

ISAAC STOPS IN FRONT OF A WHITE FORD F-150 WITH the extended cab for a backseat. He tries to balance Angie while getting out his keys, and at one point when he looks at me, there's an awkward moment where I think he's going to ask me to fish them out for him. He doesn't. He finally gets them in his hand and clicks the locks, nodding for me to open the doors.

Getting my sister's rag-doll body into the back proves difficult, and eventually I have to climb in first to help drag her onto the seat. When she's propped up, she stares at me for a moment like she wants to call me Catalina. But then, without talking, she moves to lie down, and I climb over into the passenger seat.

Isaac gets behind the wheel and turns to me, the interior of the cab bright from the overhead light. His eyes travel over me, taking stock of my entire person. Each second that passes seems to hurt him more, and just before I tell him he shouldn't look too closely, he licks his lips to talk.

"You're not her," he says in a quiet voice. "Not up close."

His comment doesn't warrant a response, so I sit there under his scrutiny as he tilts his head, memorizing my face. "You have freckles," he says. "A different mouth. When I look at you, I know you're not her." He turns away, sadness darkening his mood, and he starts the engine. "No matter how much I want you to be."

Music blasts through the radio, left on from the last time he was in the truck. I jump, startled from the melancholy moment, and Isaac reaches quickly to turn off the radio. He pulls into the road and I look back to where Deacon is parked, but the car is lost from this angle. I hate that I just ditched him, but what choice did I have? Tell Isaac I was here with my ex-boyfriend? *A closer?* That might not have been very effective in getting him to trust me. Still . . . Deacon is going to be pissed. I'll have to apologize to him later.

The wipers scrape along the window and send streams of rain down the sides. I wish the rain would let up, show some sign of summer. Marie always says that the minute the sunshine hits Oregon, we forget about the all the months of rain, like we're reborn. Like we're flowers blooming. Right now, I'm sopping wet and cold and so far from feeling like a rose it isn't funny.

"Angie's staying at our aunt's house," I say quietly, afraid to look at Isaac. I debate dropping the act, but ultimately it's not confronting Catalina that is bringing him misery. That's the part that has to be fixed. I'm the demon he has to face.

"She told me," he says. "She wanted to leave before you showed up."

I worry he's about to go on a tirade about how terrible I am for being a closer. I pray he doesn't. I don't think my heart can take any more tonight. I just want one minute of everyone being okay. Of me not being the source of their pain. Of not being hated.

"When I first saw you outside," he says, "I was overcome. I . . . I thought you were her. For one fleeting moment, you looked at me just like she used to. And when I realized it was all a lie . . ." He glances over, tears in his eyes. "It fucking hurt."

I bite down on my lip, holding back my sympathies. I don't want to patronize him, but I'm not sure how anyone can observe this and not have it affect them too. *Be patient,* Marie's voice tells me. *Let him lead his recovery.*

"I'm sorry," Isaac says, turning back to the road. "I've been an asshole to you, and I don't mean to be. Honest. It's just . . . seeing you breaks my heart." He takes a shaky breath and then exhales to keep from crying. When he looks at me, I see it didn't help. "Can you fix that?" he asks, his voice choked off.

"I want to," I say. "But I'm not the cure for a broken heart. You're the only one who can mend that."

He sniffles, nodding as if he understands. He seems more

wilted than before, and we drive quietly the rest of the way to Lake Oswego. The only sound inside the truck is the sound of my sister snoring.

Isaac tells me to wait in the truck as he fishes Angie out of the backseat. He says it'll be easier for my aunt to accept him dropping her off instead of her dead niece's doppelgänger. He even asks me to duck down while in the driveway, which stings my pride a little. But I take off my seat belt and do as he asks.

I hear voices at the door of the small ranch, and wait for what seems like forever, crouched low in the front seat. I glance around the cramped space, looking for something to focus on to pass the time. Out of boredom, I open the glove compartment. The entire box falls out, heavy from the pile of papers stuffed inside. I curse, and quickly try to gather them up, shoving them in before Isaac returns and busts me for spying. I fit the glove box back in its slot, but before I close it, I notice what's hidden among the usual registration and proof of insurance. There's a bunch of crumpled notebook paper. I take one out and unfold it to see a dark spiral drawn in the center in black ink. I furrow my brow, and pull out another and another, finding more of the same.

Although I have no idea what these papers mean, they set my teeth on edge; the fact that there are so many of them—all the same—creeps me out. Are they Isaac's? Why is he drawing them?

There's the sound of a screen door slamming, and I quickly

stuff in the rest of the papers and snap the glove compartment shut. It doesn't close at first, but after three more tries it sticks. I barely get in a breath before the door opens and Isaac hops inside the cab.

"Well that was a shit show," he mutters, and looks over to the passenger seat. He finds me on the floor and stifles a laugh. "I didn't mean that low," he says. He turns over the engine and then puts his arm over the seat to back us out of the driveway. Once we're in the road, I sit up, slightly embarrassed, and put on my seat belt.

"Aunt Margot's not thrilled," Isaac says. "I don't suspect Angie will be leaving the house anytime soon. Which, between us"—he looks over—"is probably a good thing."

I feel a twinge of affection for Isaac; the fact that he's concerned about her is a bit endearing. They're both a total mess, but I like that he cares. I kind of like him.

"Has she done this a lot since . . ." I trail off, deciding not to finish that thought.

Isaac swallows hard, but continues like he doesn't know how that sentence ends. "Yeah," he says. "Couple of her friends came to me worried, but it's not like she listens to me. All I can do is treat her like I usually would. People get sick of hearing *sorry*, you know? I'm sick of it," he says.

I'm afraid if I ask him questions, my clinical approach will put him off. Besides, right now he's content here with me, and it's the first step toward trust. Then we can start working through his unresolved issues.

My house comes up sooner than I want, and Isaac pulls into the driveway and kills the lights. It was nice, riding in comfortable silence for a few miles—like we were two regular people coming home from a night out. I decide I enjoy his company, his quiet courage. He is definitely someone I won't forget after this assignment is over.

I zip up my hoodie, smiling my good-bye, and then reach for the handle of the door.

Isaac shifts in his seat. "Wait," he calls softly. Surprised, I look back, wondering if I forgot something, but instead I find him with his posture stooped, staring down at the steering wheel.

"Do you actually think this will help?" he asks. "Therapy?"

"Yes." If I were him, I would doubt the methods too. But I've seen the role play work. I've seen families be able to move on.

"But . . ." His eyebrows knit together. "You can't give someone closure in a few days. You can't just take the pain away."

"You're right," I agree, turning in the seat to face him. I note how near we are, closer than I normally talk to my clients. "The grief doesn't disappear," I continue. "I don't have that kind of power. This therapy helps people see a bigger picture. Let go of unrealistic expectations of a deceased loved one. Once they've told me what they need to, they accept the death. It still hurts—I'm sure it hurts like hell. But it's the pain of moving on. After I'm done, clients realize that they can't 'fix' this. They can't bring anyone back. They can't build any new memories. They can only keep living and enjoying the memories they have."

He listens, letting me continue.

"I reset them on a new path," I say, trying not to sound like a therapist. Trying to sound like the girl he loves. "A path with less guilt or longing. You can't imagine the degree of comfort that comes with saying good-bye. Our brains accept that, accept that it's over. That it's okay for it to be over. I don't cure people," I say sadly. "I just take away some of the sting."

Isaac puts his hands on the wheel, gripping the rubber. Finally he turns to me, his handsome face weakened with grief. "I'm having a bad time with this," he murmurs.

My heart aches. "I know," I say. "That's why I'm here."

He bites down on his lip, pulling it through his teeth. He shakes his head as a thought occurs to him. "Why do you do this?" he asks. "Why put yourself through this?"

I'm taken aback at the question. I debate how to answer; discussing my real life would certainly pull him from the therapy. But I also don't want to dodge his questions. Maybe if he trusts me to tell the truth, he'll trust me with his therapy later. "Because I can help people," I answer.

He smiles a little, seeming to appreciate that I'm willing to talk out of character. "No." He narrows his eyes like he can figure me out. "No one is that selfless. Why do you really do this?"

"I'm good at it. I close out people's lives because I can." I pause. "And because my father asks me to." I didn't intend to be this honest, but here in the dark and warm cab of Isaac's truck,

I let my defenses down. "People . . . people are kind of terrible to me because of what I do. Being a closer, it's who I am . . . but I don't ruin people's lives. I'm trying to make them better. Instead people hate me, fear me. I've devoted myself to this, but I don't always love it. Like I told you that first night, I hurt too."

"Don't you want your own life?" he asks. "Believe me when I say that Catalina's was far from perfect."

"This life seems pretty great to me," I say, lowering my eyes to my lap. "Her family. You. I wouldn't even know what to do with that much love."

"Doesn't anybody love you?" he asks. I look up at him, his dark eyes glistening in the low light. Curious and kind.

"No," I say. "Not that way." My own words destroy me, the truth in them ringing through my ears. My father loves me, but not like a regular dad. Not the way Catalina's dad loved her—endlessly and unconditionally. With my dad there are expectations. Then there's Deacon, but his hot-and-cold love tears me down sometimes. We're just too . . . complicated.

The vision of the dark-haired woman in the hospital bed fills my mind. *She loved me,* I think. *Whoever she was, she loved me.* That might mean that the only time I've ever been truly loved was when I was playing someone else.

I feel tears coming on, and the burn makes me conscious of where I am, who I'm with. "I should go," I say quickly, and open the door. "Thanks for the ride, and thanks for helping Angie."

"Of course," Isaac says, sitting up like he's disappointed

that I'm leaving. He doesn't call for me to wait again. Maybe his curiosity has been satisfied, or maybe he's remembered that he thinks I'm a "thing." I get out and hurry toward my house, ashamed of what I said to him. Of having exposed myself like that. I know better than to break character. I was being selfish.

I stop just under my bedroom window and look back; Isaac waits at the curb. He holds up his hand in a wave, and I return it, unsure of what this means in his recovery. But, more alarmingly, what it means for my assignment.

CHAPTER SIX

I SOON REALIZE THAT GETTING OUT OF MY BEDROOM window was a lot easier than getting back in. The sill comes up to my chin, so pushing the pane the rest of the way open proves difficult, even on my tiptoes. But I grunt and stretch and get it far enough that I think I'll be able to shimmy through.

I put one sneaker on the siding and grip the sill with my hands before hoisting myself up. I'm not strong enough, and the toe of my shoe slips, trying to find purchase against the house. God, if I end up having to ring the doorbell I'll kill Deacon for letting me do this in the first place. But finally I'm able to get my elbow over the other side, and I pull myself the rest of the way up. I adjust the glass and slide in, nearly falling on the wood floor before flipping my legs around to catch myself.

I stand up in my darkened room, out of breath and with sore

arms. *Well, I won't be doing that again.* I look toward the door and see that it's still closed; my pillow is still tucked under the sheet like a sitcom setup. My hoodie is wet, and it feels great to peel it off my skin, lay it over my desk chair to dry. Now, in the quiet of my room, the end of the night settles over me. But mostly the final moments I shared with Isaac. Using the dim light from outside the window, I find and change into my pajamas, thinking about Isaac. I wonder if his idea of me is altered after tonight.

I'm still wired from the night out, and I know I should wash up before getting in bed, but I'm afraid the noise will wake my parents. So I grab a couple of makeup remover wipes and rub them over my face. My hair will dry crunchy from the drink my sister threw at me, but hopefully the rain washed most of it out. I check my phone, but it's dead, so I plug it in and grab my laptop from the desk before climbing into bed to get under the covers.

In a moment I'm toasty warm. On a soft mattress with overstuffed pillows, surrounded by a nicely decorated room that smells like fresh laundry. I'm comfortable, and I consider the difference between this house and my own. This room feels permanent, and not because it's not allowed to be changed, like my room. A person lived here, lives here. This is a home.

I open my computer and click around the different sites, checking in on what I've missed. I want to send Deacon an apology message, but he's not much into e-mail. And the situation is too complicated to explain via text. I'll have to call him in the morning.

A message flashes on the bottom of my screen, followed by

the quiet *ding*. I click it, sending the message up to the middle of my screen. I let out a held breath when I see it's Isaac.

I REALLY AM SORRY FOR THE WAY I'VE TREATED YOU, he writes. His words repair the small hole torn in my soul tonight, and I smile with the relief.

THANK YOU, I return. THAT REALLY MEANS A LOT. I should say more, but I'm afraid of ruining the moment. The screen tells me he's writing, and then another message pops up.

I'VE BEEN REALLY LONELY, he writes. NO ONE UNDERSTANDS. THEY THINK I SHOULD BE OVER IT ALREADY, OR THEY WANT TO TALK ABOUT IT ENDLESSLY. I DON'T WANT EITHER OF THOSE THINGS. BUT TONIGHT, YOU MADE ME SEE HOW ALONE I AM.

I PROMISE YOU—IT WILL GET BETTER. TIME WILL MAKE IT BETTER.

YOU MADE IT A LITTLE BETTER.

My breath catches, and I glance around the dark room as if worried someone is watching. They're not, of course—the only sign of life coming from the glow of my computer screen. But I feel guilty nonetheless. My fingers are poised over the keys, but I have no idea how to respond to his statement. I don't want to give him the wrong idea. I'm not his replacement girlfriend. I have to answer, though.

I'M GLAD, I write. Good thing this isn't my everyday life or he would think I'm completely boring. *I'm glad.* Really? I exhale, figuring we're done for the night. But he sends another message, and this one makes my heart soar.

DO YOU WANT TO HAVE LUNCH TOMORROW? he asks. I CAN PICK YOU UP AT NOON.

I rest back against my pillows, torn on how to proceed. *This is therapy,* I remind myself. *There's nothing to feel bad about.* But I call myself out on my bullshit. I'm happy that he asked me, and I want to go. To be perfectly honest, I just want to be around him. I liked how it felt tonight. I even liked being honest.

OKAY, I answer, heat immediately flooding my cheeks. SEE YOU THEN. I click off the screen and slam my computer shut, my body pulsing with electricity. I set the computer on my nightstand and slide back under the covers in the dark. I curl up on my side, my hands folded under my cheek. Normally I don't let myself fantasize on assignment; I keep my imagination reined in. But tonight I let my mind wander.

I imagine a different time, a different person. Isaac is there. He murmurs how much he loves me, leans in to kiss my lips softly. My fingers trail over his skin, and I stretch my leg over his thigh to press us closer.

I ache for him. Ache for him to love me like he loved her.

I have no more thoughts of closers and assignments. I drift off to sleep dreaming that I'm Catalina Barnes, lost in love with Isaac Perez.

"Catalina?" a soft voice calls from somewhere far away. My eyelids are heavy, and it takes me a moment to get them to stay open. My mother's voice calls me again from the hallway.

"I'm awake," I mumble, hopefully loud enough for her to hear.

"Breakfast, honey," she says cheerfully, followed by the sound of her footsteps echoing down the hall.

Confused, I glance toward my alarm clock, surprised to see that it's after nine a.m. I can't remember the last time I slept through my internal alarm. I roll over, still tempted by the comfort of my sheets. I lie there a minute, and then I remember what I was thinking about before I fell asleep. Sure enough, in the light of day I'm ashamed. There has to be a rule about coveting your assignment's boyfriend. Hell, coveting her life. I sit up and throw off my sheets.

A morning chill runs over my arms, and I rub my skin with my palms. Now's not the time to psychoanalyze myself, so I get dressed. I grab a sweatshirt from the closet and I pull it over my head. I didn't take out my contacts last night, and my eyes are itchy, but I don't have time to clean them now. Instead I grab a small tube of eye drops and drip liquid into each eye.

"Oh God," I say, blinking away the artificial tears as a new worry sets in. I agreed to go out to lunch with Isaac today. I didn't consider the implications, think about what I'd tell my parents. Maybe there's still time to cancel. I turn around, lean against the desk. My mind is swirling so fast, I can't make sense of anything. I put my hand over my forehead and squeeze my eyes shut.

This is progress, I think. *He wants to talk. He wants to meet. That's your job.*

But then: *He's projecting. He's using you as a stand-in for his girlfriend. He can't heal if he won't let go.*

And finally: *This would be totally acceptable if you weren't interested in him.*

My mother calls my name again, and I straighten, preparing myself to face the day. I will go with Isaac today, but I will be a total professional. I'll let him lead his therapy, but I'll guide it more closely. I can do this.

I go to leave the room but pause to grab my phone. I don't have any messages or missed calls. I pull up Aaron's name and type WHAT. THE. HELL. and hit send. I'll continue to text him, and if I don't hear back soon, I'm calling Marie. This is dangerous. Maybe if Aaron had been around yesterday, things wouldn't have gotten so out of control.

I slip the phone into my pocket. Deacon will be expecting me to call him today, and really, I do owe him an apology for leaving him behind at the Warehouse. I just hope he doesn't ask what I did after. I can't lie to him. Even if I wanted to, he'd see right through it. And this is definitely something I don't want him to see.

I open my bedroom door, immediately hit with the smell of bacon, and then head toward the kitchen where my mother is waiting with breakfast.

"Well, good morning," my mother says when I enter the sunny kitchen. My father's seated at the table, and he looks up from his coffee. Although he doesn't smile, I can see his relief at my continued presence. I nod to him, and sit down just as my mother sets a glass of juice in front of me.

"I'm making breakfast," she adds, and goes back to the stove, where she continues stirring a steaming batch of liquid eggs. There's a pile of bacon in the center of the table, and I reach to grab a slice. Now that I'm moving around, I have a slight headache, a dull throb behind my eyes. Hopefully a bit of food will relieve that.

"You okay?" my father asks. I turn to him in time to see him exchange a concerned glance with my mother.

"Yeah," I say. "Just a headache."

My mother goes over to her purse and takes out a white bottle. "Here," she says, trying to sound calm, but her voice is rushed. "Take two of these." I hold out my hand and she shakes out two pills into my palm. I thank her and toss them into my mouth, wash them down with juice.

When the eggs are ready, my mother comes over with the hot pan and a spatula, dishing them onto mine and my father's plates. She only puts a small bit on her own. *Lack of appetite,* I notice, filing it away for later.

My mother joins us, but she barely picks at her food. I'm starving and shovel in eggs and three strips of bacon. My mother gazes at me affectionately, and it makes eating sort of uncomfortable, so I slow down.

"Your sister called today," she says. Panic sets in. Did Angie tell her that she saw me last night? Does my mother know I snuck out?

"How is she?" I ask, giving no indication of my anxiety.

My mother puts her elbow on the table and leans forward. "She's . . . good, actually." She smiles. "She was calling to check up on me and your dad." She turns to her husband, and he nods at her, seeming heartened by her improved mood. My mother wraps her hands around her coffee cup. "She's been worried about us. She thought maybe she could come home for the party."

"Oh," I say, surprised but thrilled. Although my sister can't stand me, something I said last night must have resonated. That will give me a chance to include Angie in the final meeting. I honestly couldn't have hoped for better news this morning. "Well, that's great," I tell them both.

I go back to my food, and my mother ends up making another batch of eggs and dumping them on my plate. I tell them about my lunch date with Isaac, and my mother seems thrilled at the idea. She starts talking about her friend, getting my father's opinions although he doesn't look too invested.

After a time, my head starts to swim. My ears feel plugged up with cotton—but it's comforting. Insulating me from the world. I look dreamily from my father to my mother, listening to them talk. I leisurely have a bite of bacon, savoring the flavor. My mother smiles at me.

But my happiness starts to dim. I look back down at my plate, knowing something isn't right. I don't feel right.

"Then Maryanne told me that the butcher from the grocery store—"

"What was in those pills?" I interrupt, my voice sounding faraway. My mother's mouth opens, then shuts while she considers her words. Her hesitation sets off an alarm bell.

"They're from Dr. McKee," my father says when my mother

doesn't supply a fast answer. Still underwater, I turn, sure I didn't hear that right.

"What?"

"Dr. McKee said that in long-term . . . assignments"—he stumbles over the word—"your kind tend to get stressed. Get headaches. He advised us to give you a dose to help. I . . ." He looks at his wife, concerned, and then back at me. "I thought you knew."

I rub my eyes, trying to clear my vision. Fight off the impending sleep. "Yeah," I say, agreeing. "I just forgot. Thank you . . . for reminding me." My body has slipped into panic as my mind tries to keep submerged. I stand up from the table and smile at my parents, although I'm not sure my muscles are working correctly.

"Is it okay if I go back to bed for a while?" I ask. "I'd love to sleep off this headache and be fresh for the day."

My mother nods, seeming to think that's a good idea. "Of course, honey," she says. "You have some time before Isaac comes. Can I get you anything else?" She looks worried.

"No," I tell her. "I'm good. See you in a bit." This forced happiness is leaving a terrible taste in my mouth, but I take the extra step to put my dish in the sink and head back toward my bedroom. My hands are shaking.

The minute I close my door, I scramble to get my phone out of my pocket. I'm growing disoriented and I am *pissed.*

"Quinlan," my father says immediately upon answering. "Are you okay? You know calling me is against protocol."

"Did you advise Mr. and Mrs. Barnes to drug me?" I demand. He sighs, and I can imagine him in his leather chair, annoyed that I'm asking questions because he thinks he knows what's best for me.

"Are you under the influence now?" he asks parentally.

"Are you fucking kidding me?"

"Quinlan," he warns.

"Don't even," I say, shaking my head. "They thought I knew that the *doctor* had prescribed me something to help with my anxiety. Guess what, Dad. You must have forgotten to mention it."

"I understand you're upset," he says in his therapist voice. "And we can talk about it. But let me first explain that this a safety measure due to the length of the assignment. I see now that I should have given you the pills directly, but I anticipated you not taking them, even if you were in trouble. Please, Quinn. You know I'm looking out for you."

I groan, running my hand through my hair. The world has soft edges, fraying and growing fuzzy. "You should have told me," I say, and sit on my bed. The blanket is warm and inviting. "This assignment is a mess, Dad." I lie back against the pillow, the phone resting on my cheek. Normally I wouldn't tell my father that I'm having trouble, but the pills have made me a little more pliable.

"I know," he says sympathetically.

I laugh. "How could you know? You're not here. Nobody's here but me." I let my eyes close, and find it's tough to reopen them. "All you ever do is send me away, Dad," I murmur. "Sometimes I'm not even sure if you love me anymore."

"What?" he snaps. "Of course I do. Don't ever question that. I have and will do anything for you."

I smile, comforted by the validation I would never ask for under normal circumstances.

"It's just that you don't always know what's best for you," he continues in a quieter voice. "I want to protect you. Make you the best closer possible."

My stomach turns as his comforting words turn toward work once again. Always reminding me of any responsibilities. I roll onto my side, the phone pressed to my ear.

"You know, Dad," I say, my voice trailing off. "Sometimes you're a real asshole."

He sniffs a laugh, probably realizing that I'm drugged, and also realizing I'm kind of right. "I'm proud of you, Quinlan," he says softly. And then the line goes dead.

CHAPTER SEVEN

THERE'S A VIBRATION CLOSE TO MY FACE. I TRY TO swat it away, but reality crashes in on me and I sit up, looking around the room. I'm a bit hazy, but the drugs have worn off enough for me to focus. I think I called my father an asshole.

I look down and see my phone ringing, and when I turn it over, I find Aaron's number on the caller ID. It's about damn time.

"I'm going to murder you," I say the minute I answer. Aaron chuckles in response, and I'm already grinning and hating him at the same time.

"Dang, girl," he says, sounding amused. "You knew I was gonna call you back."

"How could you leave without telling me?" I ask, and then check around when I realize how loudly I'm talking. "Seriously,

Aaron." I lower my voice. "What if Marie found out?"

"Who do you think sent me away?" he asks.

"What?"

"Yeah. I'm on assignment. Something crazy—just like what happened to you. Your dad called me in, said it was an emergency from Arthur Pritchard. Look, I'm in Lake Oswego too."

"Speaking of my dad," I say, climbing out of bed. "I just found out my father drugged me."

"Whoa, what?" Aaron asks, incredulous.

"Yeah. He gave the family pills and told them to give them to me if I acted stressed out. Isn't that nuts?"

"Uh, yes," he says. "Did they give you one?"

"They gave me two. Really messed me up."

"Are you stressed?"

"Of course I'm stressed. This entire assignment is a disaster. I've had a few small breakthroughs, but nothing like I usually do. Everyone's acting weird. That's why I need you." I stop, realizing I've been ranting, ignoring the fact that Aaron is just as screwed as I am. "Damn," I say apologetically. "They sent you out too? I mean, what's going at the grief department? Two closers on back-to-back assignments? I've never heard of that."

"Me neither," he says. "And girl, you should have seen Myra. She's been hysterical, saying I'm going to lose myself. That I'm gonna skip town without her."

"Couldn't you tell my father no?" I ask him. Aaron has the advantage of not actually being related to his boss.

"Wasn't really an option."

I turn and rest my back against the wall, my mind spinning with scenarios. "What's your situation?" I ask.

"It's a shorter assignment," he says. "But it's got me thinking there must be something else going on. A change in the system? Change in the environment? I don't know, but I got Deacon looking into it."

"Yeah, he said he was researching something for you. He's investigating for me, too." I smile. "He really should be on the payroll," I add.

"Right?" Aaron laughs. "Well, don't worry. I've got you covered. That Virginia person, right?"

My stomach drops, and I straighten up away from the wall. "You found something?"

"Hell yeah. There were some deleted messages, but they were coded. Luckily, I'm super dope at this spy shit, so I plan to have it figured by the end of the day."

"You're amazing."

"I know." He chuckles. "And don't worry—I'm on it. I'll find her."

"I'm just glad she's real," I say, feeling relieved. "At least my mother wasn't lying about that."

"What do you mean?" he asks. "What else is going on there?"

"It's just . . . weird inconsistencies. It's like everybody's keeping secrets. Especially the girl I used to be."

"Check your journal."

"I did, but it's total Pollyanna. I loved my family. Loved my life. I can't find one bad thing about me, and yet it seems like everyone was walking on eggshells or handling me with kid gloves. I can't explain it."

"Think about it," Aaron says. "If you were into some bad shit, you wouldn't have kept it out in the open for counselors, right? You'd probably hide it."

"You have a point," I say. "And come to think of it, there were some missing pages, but I didn't look for them. I've been . . . distracted."

He laughs. "You didn't search the room yet? I thought you knew better."

"I did a basic sweep, but no—I didn't turn the place over. I didn't think I'd have to." I wonder briefly if my parents are still in the kitchen, buying me time to search this room properly. "Aaron," I say. "You mentioned that your assignment was like mine. What did you mean by that?"

"Emergency situation," he says, like he's thinking. "Death certificate in the file. Long-term—"

"Wait. Did you read the death certificate?" I ask.

"Sure. But it was 'undetermined.'"

"So was mine. What the hell do you think that means?"

"To be honest, I'd normally say it was a coincidence, but your dad was acting pretty shady. He even asked if I thought Deacon would consider returning to the department."

"Well, shit," I say. "Then something is definitely wrong." The sink in the kitchen turns on, and I realize I'm running out of private time. "Look, Aaron, I've got to go. Let me know when you turn up something on Virginia. Otherwise I'll check in with you tomorrow."

"Be safe," he says, and we hang up.

I set my phone on the desk and exhale, looking around the room. Aaron's right—if I were keeping secrets, I wouldn't leave them in a journal that someone would read. There were pages missing. Question is: Did I keep them?

I pace the length of the room, looking at it from every angle. Trying to see it in a different light. Nothing sticks out, so I open the dresser drawers and run my hands along the bottom. Nothing. I look underneath in case I got all covert, but nothing is taped there.

My closet is small, so it doesn't take me much time to thoroughly check it. Still nothing. The bedside table, the desk—I even check behind the framed photos on the wall.

This is frustrating, but Aaron totally called it. I should have done this the first day. I glance at the time and see it's nearly noon. Isaac will be here any second. "Damn it," I say, running my hand through my hair. My fingers get stuck in the tangles and I groan. I'll have to set my mission aside and take a quick shower. I want to feel human again, or at the very least have clean hair when I see Isaac. Before I lose any more time, I grab a fresh set of clothes and head to the bathroom.

Fifteen minutes later I'm running a comb through my short hair, grateful for how fast it dries now. I walk back into my room and survey the scene. Where would I have hidden journal pages? I wander around until I come to pause at the edge of my bed. I duck down to check underneath, but there are only a few dust bunnies and a plastic aerobic step. I straighten, defeated. Hmm . . . I tilt my head, examining the bed frame.

"No way," I say, making my way to the other side. I get down on my knees and slip my hand in between the box spring and the mattress. Something scratches me, and I wince, yanking out my hand. There's a small scrape near my knuckle.

There's something hidden in my mattress. *Are you kidding me? The most clichéd hiding spot in the world, and that's where I put things I didn't want anyone to find?* I can't decide if it's genius or pure stupidity. I shake off the sting on my hand and push up on the mattress, balancing it on my shoulder while I peek underneath. There's a small square of folded papers. I found them.

I grab the journal pages and drop the mattress back onto the bed. I breathe an exhausted breath and sit down. I smooth out the papers and find there are about a dozen or so. But the last few are only dark black spirals scratched onto a page. They're the same pages I found in Isaac's glove compartment. They must have been mine. I check them over for a minute longer, and they fill me with a sense of dread. Then I find the first page, noting that the date is earlier this year. I scan the first few lines.

Isaac is at baseball camp and I miss him. I hate that they won't *let him call. I told him I'd write, but decided what I really wanted was to read our story. I figure I'll start from the beginning. Who knows—maybe I'll even show him when he gets back.*

The doorbell rings, and I glance at the clock, my heart rate spiking. I hear my father's voice, naturally loud enough to travel the length of the house and back. Isaac must be here. I stand up, temporarily displaced in the room. I should put on lip gloss. Some perfume, maybe. I'm . . . nervous. I'm nervous he won't like me today—not like last night.

My mother calls my name, and I hear her footsteps heading in my direction. The pages are still in my hand, and I bend quickly to stuff them under my mattress. I barely get them in when my door opens. I stand and pretend to adjust my covers.

"Hi, Mom," I say casually. She beams at me.

"Isaac's here to pick you up," she says. The hopefulness in her expression is a bit heartbreaking. Somewhere, she must know that this is all an act, that I'm not really her daughter. But she's buried that part of her. All she knows now is that her daughter has a date, a perfectly average occurrence for a Sunday afternoon. And it's in the average moments that we live life. Right now, this makes me alive to her. It renews my purpose here, crashing me back to reality.

"Mom," I start in a steady voice. "When I get back, I was hoping to talk with you and Dad. I'd like to go over some of our memories together. Would that be okay?"

Her mouth flinches, but she nods. "Of course, honey. We can talk over dinner."

I thank her, and she turns and walks out, a little stiffer, a little sadder. She didn't want the reminder that this is therapy, but it was necessary. And tonight, we'll sift through some of the good memories, easing slightly into the ones that are bothering them. They need to work through their grief. I'm a Band-Aid, not a permanent solution.

Left alone for the moment, I look longingly at my bed, wishing I could read more of the journal pages. But my job isn't to spy on my old life. I have a client to work with, and he's waiting in the other room.

Before leaving, I stop at my dresser and dab a bit of perfume on my wrist, slide a lick of strawberry gloss over my lips. I smooth down my hair and notice that my freckles are still visible. I quickly dab some foundation over my nose and cheeks, hiding them. Hiding me.

I smile at the result, thinking I look very pretty today, and hoping that Isaac notices. With that I turn and leave my room, closing my door behind me.

When I enter the living room, I find Isaac and my dad on the couch, talking quietly. Their expressions are solemn, like seeing each other reminds them of the horrible truth. Isaac

isn't wearing his baseball hat, and I take the moment to look him over in the sunlight filtering in through the windows. The line of his jaw, his slight underbite. The way he licks his lower lip before he talks. There's a dash of attraction, and I quickly pull myself out of it and pretend that I've only just walked in the room, making a wide gesture so they'll notice me.

Isaac glances over, and his eyes widen. He's overcome by my presence, and he visibly sways in his seat. My father puts his hand on Isaac's shoulder, and then gets up.

"Have a good time," he tells me, sounding parental. I smile and I tell him I will, and watch him leave the room.

When I look back at Isaac, he's gotten to his feet. He rubs his chest over his heart like it aches. He hasn't thought this through, I realize. He forgot how much it hurts to see me.

"Hi," I say when the quiet goes on too long. I want to tell him that we don't have to do this, we can try a different way. But I don't want to give him that out. I want him to interact with me, face me.

Isaac stares down at his feet, gathering his thoughts. "You," he starts in a raspy voice. "You look nice." He lifts his head, and we're both caught in a gaze—a magnet between us.

"Thanks," I say, and smile, trying to lighten the mood. "So do you."

He laughs and brushes his hair. I think the trick with Isaac is to never let him get too self-analytical. When he lets his guard down, he also lets me in. So today I'll keep it light and fun. I'll

plant seeds in his consciousness that he can turn over later. For now I just want him to be happy.

"You ready?" I ask.

His dark eyes travel over my face, and he's a little breathless when he says, "Yes."

CHAPTER EIGHT

ISAAC ASKS WHERE I WANT TO EAT AND I RECALL pictures of us at a place called Pizza Buono. He smiles when I mention it, and turns on the radio as we drive there. I can tell from his movements that he's nervous, but it's an excited sort of feeling—not one of dread.

The sun continues to peek out from the clouds, and I suggest we sit outside to take advantage of the weather while it lasts. We grab a table that falls in a ray of sunlight, the entire scene looking hopeful. We sit and a server comes over to take our drink order. I can feel Isaac watching me while I ask for Coke, but when I turn back, he's staring down at his menu.

I put my elbows on the table, leaning toward him. "Thanks for taking me out today," I say. "I'm glad you suggested it."

"Me too."

The server returns with our drinks, and we ask for more time to look over the menu. Now that I'm here, I'm not very hungry. The girl leaves, and just then the sun dips behind the clouds. Isaac looks up at the sky, frowning.

"I hope it doesn't rain," he says. "I checked the forecast and it promised sunshine—at least until later in the day."

"You checked the forecast?" I ask.

He licks his bottom lip. "Well, yeah," he responds. "It'd be a mess to get caught in the rain somewhere—especially after last night. I wanted it to be perfect."

My body warms at his consideration. "That's sweet," I say quietly. I almost ask him if he's always this sweet to me, but I catch myself before I do. I steer us away from flirtation and toward safer topics.

"Remind me," I say. "What are your plans for after graduation?"

Isaac sips from his soda, and then leans in. I note how much closer we're sitting to each other now. "Scholarship to UCLA," he says, trying to be humble but I can see how proud he is. "Right now I'm debating whether I want to major in business or photography."

"Photography?" I say, honestly surprised. "And wow—those are two very different life plans."

He laughs. "Yeah, well, one is my mother's idea, and one . . ." He pauses a moment. "And one is your idea, actually."

"Oh," I say, looking down. I put my finger on my cold glass, tracing a line in the condensation. "Those are your pictures on my wall, aren't they?" I ask softly. I meet Isaac's gaze, and he nods.

"You liked to find things for me to shoot," he says. "Those were all places and objects you picked out. I took them for you."

He loves me so much. Every inch of him reaches for me, wants to wrap me up. It's overwhelming.

The sun comes out again, and I close my eyes and lift my face toward it, letting it warm my cheeks. *He took pictures for me,* I think. I should have known he did that. I should have found the journal pages earlier. When I get back home, I'll read everything. I want to know more about him. It's important. For his recovery.

When the server returns, Isaac orders "my favorite." Luckily, when the patchwork pizza arrives, it's covered in cheese and vegetables, and it's something I actually like. The breeze picks up, tickling my cheek with the short strands of my hair.

"I know I only asked you to lunch," Isaac says between bites of food. "But do you want to go somewhere after this? To the river, or even a movie?" He pauses, scrunching his nose. "I know you hate the movies, but you like popcorn." He smiles, adorable in his nervousness.

I'm about to tell him that I'd love to, when someone enters my peripheral vision and walks past us to take the table just behind Isaac. When the guy lifts his head, I gasp audibly. Aaron winks behind a pair of black hipster glasses, his face smooth and beard-free. How did he even find me?

Isaac turns around to glance at Aaron, but with ease my friend is examining his menu like he has no idea we even exist. Isaac looks at me, and I smile politely.

I pick up my drink, but my hand slips and the glass falls and hits the table. A wave of soda and small cubes of crushed ice splash across the white cloth. Both Isaac and I jump up, trying to dodge the river of liquid, but it's already dribbled onto my lap.

"I'm so sorry," I say, brushing the liquid off my jeans.

Isaac grabs his napkin and rounds the table. He uses the fabric as a dam at the edge of the table. "Here." He shakes out my napkin and hands it to me. "I'll get the waitress."

He touches my arm as if assuring me it's no big deal, but we both freeze at his touch. He doesn't pull away immediately, and my stomach flutters as his fingers slide down my arm, touching my hand before letting go. He apologizes quietly, whether for touching me or for letting go, I'm not sure. Without another glance, he goes inside to get the server.

The minute the door closes behind him, I turn abruptly to Aaron. "What the hell?" I say.

Aaron laughs. "I have to admit, you're freaking smooth, Quinlan. I almost believed that was an accident."

"Har, har," I say, walking over to pause at the end of his table. "How did you even find me here?"

"Tracking app on your phone," he says, like it's completely normal. My hand immediately goes to my pocket, but Aaron brushes off my concern.

"Don't be paranoid," he says. "We all have them. Standard issue. What I want to know," he says, sitting back and crossing his ankle over his knee, "is what you're doing on a date."

"I'm on assignment," I correct. "And he can't see you here"—I look toward the door—"so this had better be good."

Aaron smiles broadly. "Oh, it is. Remember Virginia?"

My body tenses. "Yeah?"

"I found out who she is, and you are not going to believe it."

I take a worried look at the door, expecting Isaac any moment. "Spit it out," I tell Aaron, putting my hand on my hip to show him my impatience.

"Her name is Virginia Pritchard," Aaron says. "And Arthur Pritchard is her father. The same Arthur Pritchard who created the remedy. Now how the fuck do you explain that coincidence?"

I rock back on my heels. "His daughter?" I repeat. "That means . . . he's involved in this case somehow. Why would he keep that a secret? Why—" I hear the door of the restaurant opening behind me, and Aaron flicks his glance in that direction. Without missing a beat, I snatch a napkin off his table.

"Thanks," I call out to him, like he's a stranger, and then turn to find Isaac walking toward me with the server. I hold up the napkin to prove why I was talking to the guy at the table. "I'm a walking disaster today," I tell Isaac. "I'm sorry."

Isaac laughs. "It's fine." We stand aside while the server moves us to a new table, beyond Aaron's judgy stare, and the busser comes out to clean up my mess. I apologize profusely, but the server tells me not to worry about it. I don't look at Aaron, and I compartmentalize what he told me about Virginia. I can't think about that now. I store it away for later.

Isaac pulls out my chair, and I sit, watching him as he moves to take the spot next to me rather than across from me. "I think I like this table better anyway," he says. His knee is close to mine, his energy radiating to my skin. We both look down at our plates, helplessly trying to avoid the awkwardness. After a minute or two, I feel him look at me.

"Is it okay?" he starts in a quiet voice. "Is it okay if I pretend you're her? Does that make me a terrible human being?"

"No," I say, looking straight at him. "Not at all. It's part of the process."

"It just . . ." His eyes drift over me. "It feels good, you know? Filling this emptiness." He sniffles, and shakes his head like he's angry for thinking this way. He's made so much progress, though; I don't want him to doubt himself now.

I reach out and put my hand over his, the movement making him take in a sharp breath. "Isaac," I whisper, leaning in to get his attention. "Let me help you."

He looks down at our hands, and he's lost in his head, trying to decide if what we're doing is wrong. Immoral. Slowly he turns his hand over, our palms pressed together. He slides his fingers between mine, sending a shiver down my spine. It's intimate. Too intimate, and I have to pull away.

I dart a worried look at Aaron, but he's pretending not to have seen. I know he has. Guilt rushes over me, the idea that I'm not only getting too attached, but that I've wronged Deacon in some way. Not technically—we're not dating. Even if those lines are sometimes blurred.

Isaac apologizes for trying to hold my hand, but I quickly wave off the apology.

"It wasn't that," I lie. "I just remembered that I told my parents I'd come straight home after lunch." Isaac bristles at "my parents." That combined with my rejection reminds him that I'm not his real girlfriend. But he takes a moment, trying to push away his rational thoughts.

"Maybe another time, then," he suggests, and takes a sip of his soda, preparing to leave. I hate seeing him so dejected. I don't want him to think about the truth. He *wants* me to play this role. He asked me to.

"Maybe tomorrow," I suggest quickly.

He turns to me, his knee brushing against my thigh. "What about tonight?" he asks. "A friend of mine, an old friend who doesn't know about . . ." He trails off, not wanting to bring up my death. "Anyway, he's having a party tonight. I could—you could—"

"Sneak out?" I ask with a flirtatious grin.

"You used to call your window the emergency exit," he says. "You'd hide a plastic step in the bushes when you went out so you could get back in."

That's how I did it, I think, remembering the aerobic step I'd seen under my bed. Isaac shifts in his seat, and I'm suddenly aware of how close we are. I grow breathless.

"I'll go," I say, my heart starting to race. "What time?" I want to put my hand on his leg, move in closer, and brush my cheek against his. Smell his cologne, feel his touch. No one has touched me in that way since Deacon. And not before him either.

"Let's say midnight," Isaac offers, and I can see the desire in his expression.

Attraction can be a dangerous thing, I think. *Makes people act in ways they normally wouldn't. Clouds their judgment.*

Before this moment goes on any longer, I jump up from the seat, clearing my throat and reaching into my pocket for money.

"It's okay," he says, standing. "I've got it, Catalina." This time he doesn't flinch at my name. In fact, he doesn't even seem to notice that he said it. He tosses a few bills down on the table, looking content with our plan, and puts his hand on the small of my back to lead us to his truck.

I walk with him, hyperaware of Aaron watching us, but that fades when we get out onto the street. Instead I look sideways at Isaac, thinking again about our attraction. And how good it feels.

CHAPTER NINE

MY MOTHER'S SURPRISED TO SEE ME WHEN ISAAC drops me off ten minutes later. She waves to him from where she's in the front yard, gardening. When he drives off, I'm on a bit of a high—still tingling from the way his fingers felt next to mine.

"You're back early," my mother says. "Everything okay?"

"Isaac's doing great," I assure her. "Really great."

She smiles broadly, looking relieved. "I'm so glad to hear that," she responds, choking up slightly. She glances around the garden, and then turns to me eagerly. "I'm just cleaning up the rose beds. Would you like to help me?"

"Uh . . ." What I need to do is go inside and read the journal pages, try to figure how Virginia fits into this story. Find out more about Isaac so I can complete this therapy. But my mother stares at me with her wide, brown eyes, needing me to be with her. I smile. "Sure."

She opens the plastic tub near the house and hands me a pair of gloves and some shears. We make our way around the side, where there are at least a dozen red rosebushes. They're breathtaking.

My mother hands me a kneeling mat, and I take a place at a bush close to where she's working. I watch how she trims, cutting back the branches that have grown too long. I mimic her, and at one point she looks over to tell me my roses are perfect. My entire demeanor brightens under her praise. We continue on down the row.

Twenty minutes later, I swipe my gloved hand across my forehead. My back aches from bending around the roses, and I remember now why my house in Corvallis is overgrown and untamed. Gardening is hard.

"These really are beautiful," I tell her. She takes a look for herself as if seeing them for the first time, and nods.

"You know, I planted yellow once," she says. "Lemon-yellow roses. They died after the first freeze of the year and wouldn't grow again. I thought the color would be cheerful, but it had the opposite effect."

"Weird." I wince, pricking my finger on a thorn. "Ow." I pull off the glove and shake out the sting in my skin. "It got me through the fabric."

"Those little suckers are nasty," she tells me, peeking over to make sure I'm not bleeding to death. She kneels down next to me and reaches into her gardening apron. She pulls out a Band-Aid, and I watch as she takes my finger and examines the small puncture. She tsks, and pulls off the wrapper on the bandage. Lovingly, she winds the adhesive tape around my finger, taking special care not to hurt me. When she's done, she looks at me and smiles. "There," she murmurs, and reaches to brush a strand of hair behind my ear.

My entire body aches with loss. I feel the tears gather in my eyes: This sense of being taken care of—it's completely enveloping. It's warmth and comfort. For a moment I'm sure it's everything I've ever wanted.

She must read my expression, because she presses her lips into a smile and then goes to tidy up my rosebush. "You know," she says quietly, considering her words before she continues, "if you wanted to stay, live here while you go to college, save some money—you can. You can stay as long as you want."

My stomach sinks, but not because I hate the idea. I actually love the thought of sticking around longer. I love the idea of being part of this family. My training tells me I should redirect her, make it clear immediately that this is a temporary situation. There's no way the department would let that happen, no matter how much I wanted to stay. I look over at her and smile—a moment passing between us without words. Without a no.

It's enough for her to go back to gardening, humming a tune that sounds like a lullaby, one I'm sure I enjoyed when I was a baby. We dig in the dirt in front of a big white house, letting the sun warm our faces, happy in the idea of being together just a little longer.

I've forgotten most of my worries when we come back in the house, slightly achy but in that rewarding hard-work sort of way. My dad is in the kitchen, adding pieces of bread to the toaster. Sliced tomatoes and lettuce are on the table next to the leftover bacon from this morning.

"Thought we'd have some BLTs," he says, smiling beneath his bushy mustache.

"Barrett," my mother scolds, although it's more playful than scoldy. "You'll ruin dinner."

"We'll be hungry again in a few hours," he says. When she sighs, he comes over and kisses her cheek as an apology. My mother laughs, shooing him away. I feel my cheeks blush; their flirting is a little embarrassing, but also completely adorable at the same time. I can honestly say that I don't think any of my other parents liked each other this much.

My phone vibrates in my pocket, startling me. While my parents work together to make sandwiches for us, I glance down and see it's a message from Deacon.

FOR ALL YOU KNOW I COULD HAVE DIED FROM EXPOSURE IN THE PARKING LOT OF THAT BAR LAST NIGHT. THIS IS TO ASSURE YOU THAT I DIDN'T.

I wince. I forgot to call him today and apologize. Before I can send a pathetic I'M SORRY, another message pops up.

AARON WANTED ME TO TELL YOU THAT HE WOULDN'T KNOW MORE ABOUT THE VIRGINIA SITUATION FOR A FEW DAYS, BUT TO HANG TIGHT. HE ALSO TOLD ME HE SAW YOU TODAY. HOPE IT WAS A NICE LUNCH.

I glance at my parents, and when I see they're still busy, I quickly type out: I'M ON ASSIGNMENT. THAT'S IT.

He waits a painfully long time to answer. YOU'RE QUINLAN MCKEE, he writes simply. There's a sting on my face, a cold slap of reality. I slip my phone back into my pocket and begin to gnaw on my lip.

I know who I am, Deacon, I think, unnerved by his text. *I do still know that.*

My parents are talking, laughing, occasionally looking back at me to grin out an *Isn't this fun?* I nod encouragingly, a little rattled from Deacon's message, but glad to hear that Aaron should have more information for me later this week.

The house phone rings, startling me. I have this irrational thought that it's Deacon, and when my mother clicks the button and says hello, my heart is in my throat. She smiles, and touches my father's arm to get his attention.

"Hi, Angie," she says, tears gathering in her eyes. Both of my parents hover around the phone, turned away from me as they ask how she is, tell her they're doing well and missing her. I'm cut out of the family circle then, a stranger in their house. Without a word I slip away, back to my bedroom, my heart feeling heavy and a bit left out.

When I get into my room, I lie on my stomach across the middle of my bed. I think about what my mother said, about how I could stay here while I go to college. Although I know that was only her grief talking, I imagine for a moment it could be true. What it would be like to have a family like this. To eat dinner together and laugh and even garden. To feel safe.

At this moment, if anyone asked me what I wanted . . . I think this would be it. I would want to be part of this family, this life. I close my eyes, feeling guilty for betraying my real father. I do love him; I would never abandon him. Besides, people like me aren't meant to have normal lives. But . . . if I had started this way, I wouldn't have ended up a closer.

I dwell a bit longer on the family, happy that my sister seems to be coming around. It may be caused by my presence, or maybe she always would have; either way, it's good for the recovery. I get up and go to my desk, open up my laptop to write an e-mail. I get my sister's address and type out a short message.

THANK YOU FOR CONTACTING YOUR PARENTS. YOU'VE MADE THEM VERY HAPPY.

I leave it short and sweet, not wanting to give her much to argue with if the message finds her when she's feeling particularly murderous. I click around on the Internet for another minute when the e-mail pings back to me. My heart stops.

GO TO HELL.

I stare at the words until my eyes go blurry, and then shut the laptop without exiting the program. I'm tired—I'm tired of being feared, hated. Right now, all I want is some comfort, but I can't find it with the strangers in the kitchen.

My shoulders slumped, I head back to bed and lie down. I retreat into my memories, finding one that I can wrap around myself. This time I come back to one of me and Deacon, sitting on the back porch of his house shortly after he bought it. We were broken up, but there we were on the steps, me leaning against him as we watched the rain fall over the trees. A cold breeze blew my hair across my face, and Deacon reached to brush it back, leaning his temple on the top of my head.

"Christ, it never stops raining," he says. We had planned to go hiking; the forecast swore it would be clear skies. Of course, we all know never to trust the Oregon weather forecast. Now we were stuck on the porch in hiking boots with a backpack full of bottled water and trail mix.

I sighed. "I'm leaving on Wednesday," I said quietly. "Assignment down near Grants Pass. Drowning, I think. Anyway, mother and stepfather—Dad says they're a wreck."

Deacon was quiet for a long moment, and then moved to wrap his arms around me like a jacket. We settled in together, absorbing each other.

"One more year, Quinlan," he said. "One more year of someone else's life, and then you're done." He looked at me. "And you will be done."

"That's the plan," I said. "But we both know how persuasive my father can be."

"Funny," Deacon said, "I told him to fuck off easily enough."

I slapped his leg and he laughed, admitting that he didn't

really cuss my father out, just imagined it in full detail. We fell into a comfortable silence, broken only by the clap of thunder above us that made the windows rattle. I jumped in Deacon's arms, and he held me closer, his fingers trailing over my skin in a way that brought me to a new realization. A sudden awareness of his body against mine.

"We should go inside," Deacon said in a quiet voice, the rain falling harder around us. I hummed out agreement, but didn't move. Didn't want to break the spell. Deacon brushed his lips over my cheek. My jaw. "I miss you," he murmured as his mouth touched my neck. "It's fucking killing me how much I miss you."

I was lost then—lost in my desire for him. I ended up staying the night, and we were romantic and sad at the same time. Our passion was reckless and panicked, but it felt good. It felt like love. Like everything had been set right again.

When I woke up the next morning, Deacon was gone. No text. No note. I left his house and I didn't see him again until my assignment was over. It was like our night together had never happened. He didn't mention it, didn't act any differently. But I wanted things to be different. I wanted commitment. I swore I wouldn't give him another chance to hurt me after that.

In all of our time together, Deacon's never said the one thing I needed to hear. He has never, ever said he loved me. And yet if he were here now, Deacon would be wrapped around me, telling me that even if the entire world hated me, he'd still be on my side. He'd threaten to kick all of their asses. He'd promise to do anything for me. But I guess promises only go so far.

I roll over in bed and take out my phone. I scroll through to see if I have any other messages, but there's nothing. Disappointment burrows itself into my consciousness, and I wish I'd talked to Deacon sooner. Apologized for ditching him at the bar. I wish I could be on his back porch right now, letting him whisper into my hair about how shitty the rain is.

I allow myself another moment of dwelling, and then make the decision to put away all thoughts of my life to focus on my assignment. Boredom soon follows, but it's not entirely unusual. When I'm working, I can't go out with friends or do my normal activities—I'm quarantined in a life with as little of my own as possible. I'm sick of the Internet, of depressing news. I'm sick of feeling bad about everything.

I remember the journal pages. Of course.

The crumpled pages are just where I left them between the mattress and the box spring, and I'm all nerves and anticipation when I pull them onto my lap. I turn toward the doorway, trying to gauge the position of my family members, and hear my mother still talking on the phone with my sister. That should keep her distracted for a while. I wouldn't want her to walk in on me reading them, especially if she didn't know they existed. A better person would have turned the pages over, or at least alerted Marie. Luckily, I'm only average in the good-person department.

I begin, skimming and finding that all of the pages are about Isaac—like a love letter, a retelling of our relationship. I'm riveted, completely invested in learning everything. I read about how we met, our first kiss, and then I stop and go back to the start so I can absorb more.

Kyle first told me she wanted me to date Isaac at the end of homeroom. I laughed, because, yuck—he was a total jock. But mostly because he'd just dumped Alexis Culverson. That was a serious douche alarm. Alexis was awesome.

I stifle a laugh, and turn the page, beginning to chew on my thumbnail.

Kyle was a total idiot. If I didn't love her, I would have killed her to death and then killed her again. After school we went to eat at Off Campus, like we do every day. While I was mid-bite into my cheeseburger, Kyle called for Isaac and Nando to come sit with us. I gave her the death glare, which she completely ignored, and slid over for Nando to sit next to me. He and Kyle laughed about some stupid test, and it was painfully obvious to me and Isaac that we were supposed to talk too.

He looked up. I looked down. And thankfully the entire awkward exchange only lasted long enough for Kyle to get an invite to Nando's party the next weekend. The guys got up, and I halfheartedly waved, thinking that was the end of it. But then, right next to my seat, Isaac looked sideways at me. He smiled, sort of sweet. Sort of shy. And then he left.

I didn't admit it to Kyle—screw her—but once I looked at him, I realized Isaac Perez was kind of smoking hot. Even if he probably sucked as a person.

I lay the pages across my chest and stare out the window, smiling to myself. How much fun it must have been, being so carefree. Going to school and hanging out with friends. Meeting boys and making plans. I've never had that. I never will.

What I wouldn't give to be Catalina Barnes.

CHAPTER TEN

I CONTINUE READING, HEARING ALL ABOUT HOW I connected with Isaac, unsure at first, or maybe he was. Either way, I'm at the part where I was debating whether I should have sex with him or wait longer, when my phone buzzes. I glance at it impatiently, not wanting to stop reading, but I see it's Aaron. I look between the phone and the pages, and then set the writing aside and click on the phone.

"Hey," I say. "Deacon said you'd need a few days to find out info on Virginia."

Aaron laughs. "I do. I'm not calling about her. I just needed someone to talk to. Things around here are . . . heavy."

I sit up, concerned by the tone of his voice. "Are you all right?" I ask.

"Yeah," he says. "I'm fine. It's just . . . this case. Dude was messed up."

"How so?"

"I was going through his profiles and everything was peachy, you know? Unrealistically happy. But then I found these notebooks in his closet. Three of them with words scribbled across the pages, and then a bunch of large black spirals. I felt like I was in a horror movie or something."

My heart stops. "I know exactly you're talking about," I say. "I . . . I found something similar in Catalina's things."

"You've seen them?" he says. "That's strange. And they're unsettling, right?" he asks, as if needing affirmation for being creeped out.

"Very," I agree. "What . . . what do you think they mean?"

"I have no idea," Aaron says. "But to be honest, those spirals tripped me out. For a minute it was like I was slipping away. Don't worry," he says firmly. "I'm fine now. I just needed to hear a familiar voice, but Deacon was bringing me down."

"Yeah," I say. "He's not too happy with me."

"He'll get over it," Aaron says. "But dang, girl. He was all torn up this morning, telling me how you left with your boyfriend—"

"First of all," I say, "it's an assignment—not my actual boyfriend. Second of all, if I *did* have a boyfriend, he still wouldn't have a right to complain."

"But he—"

"You know Deacon dates other girls, right?" I ask, maybe sounding a little jealous myself.

"I know Deacon *pretends* to date other girls," he corrects. "He hasn't hooked up with any of them. And believe me, he'd tell me."

I scoff. "What, then?" I ask. "Are they off playing Scrabble all night?"

"Doubtful," he says with a laugh. "But he likes their attention; he likes your attention to their attention. Then he drives them away, long before his tongue ever touches theirs."

"Gross."

"But accurate," he says. "So rationalize all you want, little closer, but your not-so-ex-boyfriend is saving himself for you, even if he doesn't tell you. But I think you already know. *And* I think that's why you feel so guilty for playing house with Isaac Perez."

"Oh, shut up," I say. "What is that supposed to mean?"

"I saw you with him. We've been at this a long time. I'm just worried what you'll take away from this assignment, life klepto. I hope it's not his virginity."

"I doubt that's still intact, but I assure you I won't find out." We get quiet for a moment, the reality of our situations sinking in. "I do think about it sometimes, though," I say quietly. "What it would be like to live like this—to have a family. Regular life."

"Isn't that the biggest danger?" Aaron asks. "The fact that we get to see what normal is like. Only to realize it's not normal at all.

These people hired us to fill in their grief. Never forget the truth, Quinn. They don't love you. They love who you used to be."

"I remember," I say, glancing down at the pages lying on the bed. From beyond the door I hear my mother say my name. "I should go," I tell Aaron, sitting up. "Call me when you find out more about Virginia."

"I will," he says. "And, Quinn . . . stay safe."

I thank him just as my mother opens the door. I quickly pull the phone from my ear, and covertly slide the pages under my pillow. I smile politely and see my mother's eyes flash with curiosity.

"Isaac," I lie, motioning to the phone. "How's Angie?" I attempt to distract her, relieved when I see that it works.

"She's good." My mother smiles. "In fact, I was coming to see if you wanted a sandwich. Maybe help me cut some vegetables for dinner? Your sister's going to join us."

My stomach turns abruptly. "Oh . . . that's great." Although I'm not sure if I'm ready for the emotional abuse Angie will want to hurl in my direction. "Yes," I continue with fake enthusiasm. "I'd love to help."

I climb up from the bed, checking back once to make sure the pages are safely hidden, and follow my mother from the room to assist with dinner. I've already lost my appetite.

My sister sits across from me at the table, her thin arms crossed over her chest. She glares at me, disturbed by my presence. No one has said a word since we sat down. My mother sets a plate of pork chops in the center of the table, the sweet scent of apples wafting up from the glaze that I helped her make. My father tells her it looks great, and stabs one with his fork to plop it onto his plate. Angie doesn't make a move for the food. Neither do I.

Finally my sister groans and looks at my father. "You're seriously going to let her stay?" she demands. My composure cracks, but I see my mother's face twist with agony and pull it back. The last thing my mother wants is a reminder of how not happy our family really is.

My father doesn't react so abruptly, though. He folds his hand in front of him, looking kindly at my sister. "Angie," he starts, but she's already scoffing.

"You always liked her better," she says bitterly, tossing her napkin onto the table. "You even like her impostor better."

"Angela!" he snaps, his booming voice sucking the air of the room. My sister wilts under his authority, and even my pulse has skyrocketed. A moment passes, and my father unfolds his hands, seeming to know the effect of his tone. "This is part of the process," he says in a quieter voice. "You haven't been here." He meets her eyes, and I observe their interaction, tense but ultimately concerned for each other. "We're suffering," he says, cracking over the words. "And having . . . your sister here is helping."

Angie flinches as if he's slapped her. She leans in to the table, her eyes wild. "That is not my sister," she says. "She's a counselor, or an actor, or God knows what. You *bought* her," she says, shooting me a hateful glare. "And if you and Mom don't realize how twisted that is, then you really do need to be in therapy."

"Angela," my mother scolds. "How dare . . ." But she can't finish her sentence. She dissolves into tears and covers her face with her hands. I immediately reach for her and my sister jumps up so quickly, I think she might attack me.

"Stay away from her!" she shouts, rounding the table to stand next to my mother. She puts her arm around her and my mother turns her face in to Angie's side, sobbing. My father is quiet, staring down at his food.

But I'm hurting too. I feel my own body weaken with the rejection and hatred. There's a flicker of recognition in Angie's eyes when she looks over at me, like maybe she's almost sorry. I'm numb as I stand from my spot at the table.

"Excuse me," I murmur, and leave the family to their misery. They've filled me up with it, and I need a minute to process. I walk straight out of the room and through the kitchen and out the patio doors.

Michelle Blake was fourteen years old when she fell down an old well shaft. Her family's property was a sprawling acreage just outside of Salem, and they ended up suing the former owners for not disclosing the hazard when they purchased the home. The girl's body had gotten lodged only two feet below the opening, just close enough that her parents could reach and stroke her hair while they waited for the fire department and ambulance. Michelle had died instantly, though, so she didn't suffer. That was all saved for her parents. Normally those sorts of grizzly details would have been left out, but Michelle's older sister felt it was her duty to inform me of everything. She was the one who had convinced her parents to contact the department in the first place, concerned for their well-being.

She was right to be worried. Her dad attempted suicide the night before I got there. Marie almost called off the entire assignment, but my father assured us that we would be saving the family. Andrew Blake was still in the hospital when I arrived, so I spent the first day with my mother and sister. They were both very helpful and kind, and I quickly diagnosed that my father was the one with symptoms of complicated grief. I gave the family instructions on what to look out for, how to redirect. Technically, it wasn't my job to advise them, but it helped pass the time.

When Andrew returned, everyone in the house was working toward his well-being. His recovery was swift, and even his wife said she found peace when I was around. In the end I redirected them to their daughter Hailey, helped them rebuild their family structure around her while still honoring Michelle.

I liked Hailey. She was a sister to me. Somewhere in my room at home in Corvallis, there's a picture of Michelle and Hailey, sitting together on a porch swing. I took it from one of the photo albums stacked under the entertainment center of the Blake house. I haven't looked at it in a while, but I used to when I first came back. It reminded me of the time I spent with my sister and mother, and how we worked together. There was a camaraderie there built on love and trust. I needed a little bit of that in my life.

And so my thoughts turn to Hailey now as I sit on the porch steps, hugging my knees to my chest. I've never had a real sibling. Not sure it would have worked anyway. Would my father have turned us both into closers? Would it have been cruel to only have one, while the other lived a full life? I feel a wave of homesickness, but not for my actual home. That place is so familiar it feels manufactured. Unlived—especially in comparison to this one.

This is a home . . . and I already miss it. I think back to gardening with my mother and practicing batting with my father. I'm just starting to feel better when the sliding glass doors open.

I turn and see my father, his large mass blocking out the light of the kitchen. His face is a silhouette, and I have a sudden fear that he's here to ask me to leave. *Please, no.*

"Hey, kid," he says. I sway, relieved by his approach, the warmth in his voice. As he sits down, I consider my reaction when he first came out. How much I really didn't want to leave. It's disconcerting to say the least—my attachment. "You okay?" he asks.

He sits on the porch step next to me, and I turn to him, suddenly feeling like a child. I nod. "Yeah. Just . . ." I'm not sure how honest I should be. I've never had this much negative interaction while on assignment—maybe it's that the scale of this one is bigger, but the constant barrage of insults is weighing on me. "It just hurts my feelings," I say, wincing once I do. "Sorry."

"Don't be sorry," he says, turning to face the woods beyond the house. "You're a human being. I can't imagine the pressure you live with." He looks sideways at me. "Can't imagine a parent who would let you take that much on your shoulders, but I'm not here to judge you or them." He nods, lowering his head. I'm no longer in character, but I think I'm the one he wants to talk to.

"I know why you're here," he continues. "And to be frank, I'm grateful. I like having you around. I think the toughest part of losing my little girl was the silence left behind in the house, the damned quiet." His voice tightens, and he struggles with the start of tears. "You've made noise, taken up the empty space. You've breathed life in the empty hole that was left behind, and for that, I thank you."

My own tears match his, and I put my hand on his shoulder to comfort him. "You have a beautiful family," I say. My father bites down on his lip, his bushy mustache overtaking his mouth. He then smiles painfully at me.

"Thank you." He's still for a minute, and then he sniffles. "Look, I know this is probably irregular, but I want to you know . . . we care about you. I care about you. It's becoming this dreaded countdown for us until the time you'll leave. You've become part of us."

My body weakens, overcome by the sentiment. *I'm part of them,* I think. *I'm part of a family.*

"Eva and I talked about this earlier," he says, "and we'd like you to stay longer. We'll pay whatever you want, make any arrangements you need. We just . . ." His light eyes are heavy with grief. "We don't want you to leave us."

I stare at him, shutting off all of the training that wants to redirect. Truth is, Marie never prepared me for this. There is no answer here, only love. These people will love me, protect me. They could give me a normal life, and even the grief department should understand that—even my father and Arthur Pritchard.

I leap forward and wrap my arms around the man next to me, his body too bulky to reach around. He chuckles at my response, and pats my back gently.

"Thank you," I say. "Thank you."

I pull away, and he presses his lips together. I haven't said yes, but he can tell by the smile on my face that his and his wife's offer means the world to me.

"Think about it," he says. My father motions to the patio doors. "Now, we should head back in. I've told Angela to behave herself, but you shouldn't let her get to you. She'll come to accept you in time. I promise. She's been through a lot."

I nod, agreeing that she's endured too much. I let myself feel compassion for her, let it wash away my anger and hurt. She's had a chance to vent, so maybe we can finish the meal in peace. At least I hope so. My appetite has finally returned.

Angie doesn't speak to me at dinner, but she stays throughout the meal, and even talks to her parents about school. She's been running on the track in the evenings and told them it helps her clear her head. She glances at me once when she says it, probably thinking about my death. But at least she doesn't tell me to drop dead or call me a monster. That's progress.

"Banana cream pie," my mother says, bringing it in to set in the center of the table. I notice the dusting of almonds on the top, and my anxiety starts to build. I'm allergic to nuts and I don't eat them. Marie should have advised them about this before I arrived.

My mother dishes out the dessert to each of us. My sister takes a bite immediately and tells my mother it's awesome. For a brief moment, everyone is happy—and I fit with them. I don't want to ruin that.

I pick at the pie, not wanting to eat any of it and risk having a bad reaction when I'm supposed to go out with Isaac tonight. They're all taking a painfully long time, though, and my avoidance becomes obvious.

"Catalina," my mother says. "You haven't had any pie." My father looks over, mildly curious, and this time Angie doesn't flinch at the use of my name.

"Sorry," I say, smiling politely. "I'm . . . really full."

"Nonsense." She waves her fork. "It's your favorite. Eat up." She laughs and takes another large bite. I stare down at the pie, debating letting my face swell just to keep up the illusion. But ultimately, I can't do it.

"I'm allergic," I murmur, not looking at her.

"What's that?" my mother asks, leaning in to hear me better.

I lift my head. "I'm allergic to the almonds."

She stares at me for a long moment, and a passing flash of recognition immediately followed by grief plays across her expression. "Yes," she says, and sets down her fork. "I forgot. I'm sorry."

Everyone's quiet after that, and my mother doesn't finish her pie. My sister only nibbles on hers. At one point I look at my father and he nods encouragingly, letting me know that it's okay. That I didn't do anything wrong. I appreciate his support, his clearheaded resolve in the face of so much tragedy.

So later, after Angela's gone and my parents watch a bit of television with me, I take special care to say good night to my father, giving him a kiss on the cheek before going to my room.

CHAPTER ELEVEN

ISAAC SENDS ME AN INSTANT MESSAGE ON THE computer around eleven thirty, telling me he'll be by in fifteen minutes. Nervousness creeps over me, and I go to the mirror to check my appearance. I brush my fingers through my hair, telling myself once again how much I love the cut. My freckles are hidden, makeup flawless to capture my features just right. Winged eyeliner and soft pink gloss on my lips. I press them together and have a wild thought that maybe they'll be kissed tonight. I quickly spin away from the mirror, ashamed of where my mind went, and walk to the bed to pull out the plastic aerobic step from underneath.

I open my window and see exactly where I would have hidden it in the bushes. I drop the step into place, glad my return won't be as difficult as it was last night. One more check of my clothes: a sleeveless turquoise shirt, not entirely weather appropriate but insanely flattering against my skin. I smile, thinking that Isaac will like this. It's different from what I would have normally worn with him, but in a good way. An idealized way.

I see the shine of headlights quickly flick off, and I know that Isaac is here. Anticipation builds inside of me, and I'm at the window before I realize I left my phone on the side table. I glance back, knowing I should take it in case there's an emergency, either with me or with Aaron. But then, with a careless turn, I leave it behind. I leave it all behind.

The grass is damp, and as I jog across, my shoes slip, almost sending me headlong into the mud. I steady myself, and when I get to Isaac's truck, he's trying to hide his smile.

"That would *not* have been funny," I say, although I'm nearly cracking up myself. He turns, and under the interior lights he gets his first glimpse of me. His smile fades; his eyes widen as they take me in. We sit idling at the curb in front of my house, and I briefly wonder what would happen if my parents looked out the window. Would they be mad that I snuck out? Would it be okay because it was with Isaac?

Isaac licks his lips in that slow way he does before he talks. "You're beautiful," he says, sounding a bit lost. I smile at the compliment, but he lowers his eyes like he's ashamed. "I'm sorry," he says. "I'm afraid I'm being selfish."

"What?" I ask. "Why?"

"Because I want this so badly." He looks up at me again,

his expression clouded by his confusion. "And I don't care if it's real. I . . . I want to believe. Does that make me awful?"

I shake my head. "No," I say, hiding my disappointment. "You're wonderful."

This time, I'm the person who didn't want the reminder of our situation. I wanted to be the one to make him forget, to take away his loneliness. To make him happy. But maybe this wasn't the way. "Isaac," I say, drawing his attention again, "I'm here for your recovery. Just tell me what you need. If this is too much, then we can—"

"I need *you*," he says immediately. "I need her. I don't want to think or talk about it. I just want it to be true." His words are desperate, and I wonder if he's been beating himself up since he saw me this afternoon. Feeling guilty. I press my lips into a smile.

"Then tonight I'm her," I say, my voice thick with compassion but not pity. Earnest resolve to help him through this. Isaac exhales, putting aside the pain and rational thoughts. We sit in the cab of the truck a little longer, and I gaze out the window at the stars.

"It didn't rain," I say, feeling him turn to me. "It hasn't rained all day, just like they promised."

I look at him, and he nods, shifting the truck into gear. He leans forward to check the sky through the windshield, and when he turns to me, I think he's more handsome than I've ever seen him. "Looks like it's going to be a perfect day after all," he says in that quiet, raspy voice.

By the time we're down the road, headlights on, we're both smiling, putting aside the truth in favor of now.

Cars line the street in front of the house, but there are no people gathered outside or spilling onto the lawn. Instead a blue glow emits from the blinds, silhouettes of people behind it. I tug self-consciously at the wisps of my hair as if I could wrap them around me like a security blanket. I like parties just fine—I've never gone to one as someone else, though.

"It's okay," Isaac says, looking sideways at me as we get out of the truck. "They don't know you here. And we won't stay long. I . . ." He pauses, smiling in that shy way that is all flirtation, even if he doesn't realize it. "I'm glad you said yes."

I'm so charmed. "Me too," I say, falling into step next to him. We cut across the soft lawn and climb the front steps. Isaac rings the doorbell before burying his hands nervously in his pockets.

I look from him to the door, my heart beating quickly. Although he assured me that no one at this party would know that I'm a closer, I worry that they'll figure it out. My death wasn't on the news—the story was buried because the family was seeking closure. But there's still a chance they heard. I don't want to be verbally attacked.

The door swings open, and I gasp, having been lost in my thoughts. The guy at the door is slightly older, with a thick beard and a checkered sweater. He smiles at me but then reaches out to do a hand slap/side hug with Isaac.

"Glad you made it, man," he tells him. "Few more months and you'll be out of here for good. One last hurrah, right?"

Isaac grins, proud that he got into UCLA, even if it hasn't been his top priority since my death. The guy in the door turns to me, and leans in to kiss my cheek. "You must be Catalina," he says warmly. I notice Isaac flinch next to me. "Jason," the guy says, poking himself in the chest. "Your boyfriend and I go way back to summer camp and shit. But I've been in Alaska the last few years on a fishing boat." He looks at Isaac. "But he e-mailed me about you. Total fucking sap."

He and Isaac laugh, and I smile along, both saddened and heartened that Isaac took the time to e-mail his old friend about our relationship. I've seen Isaac with other people, and although they like him, he doesn't let them this close. I'm honored that he brought me here. When Isaac looks sideways at me, I smile. It makes him pause—I think the similarity overwhelms him—and he reaches to take my hand. I let him, but my stomach tightens; I wasn't expecting the physical contact. I don't let it show.

"All right, let's get inside," Jason says. "People are starting to dance, but Romy brought over his videos from Belize. Me and the guys are watching him save the world and shit." He turns and walks through the door, leaving Isaac and me on the porch. His hand is warm in mine, and he slowly pulls away, his finger gliding against mine, causing a flutter in my chest.

"After you," he says quietly, motioning me forward. I nod, my hand still tingling, and walk inside the house.

The entryway is dark, but there are more people than I could read from outside. There's wood paneling on the living room wall, lit up by neon signs of various beer brands, and a large-screen TV with a blue ocean scene and a guy narrating, even though you can barely make out what he's saying above the music. A girl walking by accidentally bumps my shoulder, and I stumble sideways into Isaac. He catches my elbow, and we pause, wrapped up in each other. I lift my eyes slowly to his, and I think both of us blush, slowly untangling ourselves.

"Come on," he says, turning to start toward the kitchen, unhooking his arm from mine. "Let's get a drink."

There's a keg in the middle of the kitchen floor, sitting on the tile without any ice around it. I imagine the beer is probably warm and flat, and Isaac and I both scrunch up our noses to say that we'll pass. We laugh, each glad the other isn't about to lower their standards for alcohol. We move to the counter, where there are a few cans of unopened Coke, slightly cooler than room temperature. Isaac starts talking to a friend, and I take a moment to look around the room. I'm examining the others before I realize what I'm doing. Studying their gestures, expressions. It's a terrible habit, and I force my eyes away and take a sip of my Coke.

"So where's your girl?" I hear Romy announce. Instinctively, I look over and meet Isaac's eyes. He hesitates, and it stings—even though it shouldn't.

"Uh . . . ," he says; his brow furrows, and I realize he doesn't want to say. I smile politely, as if telling him not to worry about it. *Pretend I'm not here.* He doesn't want to introduce me to people if he doesn't have to. Jason's one thing, but an entire party? Eventually Isaac will have to tell them I died. They'll know he brought a closer here after the fact. Would they forgive him for bringing something like me around? Some*one*, I correct. There's a sharp pain behind my eyes, and I touch my forehead and wince.

I set down my cup and slip out of the kitchen, zigzagging my way through the people in search of refuge. I find a spot on the stairs where I can sit down. The wood is hard and uncomfortable, and I lean forward, my hands hanging between my knees. After a minute, the ache fades and I'm left instead with loneliness.

Get a grip, I tell myself. *This isn't personal. Isaac's a client.* It doesn't really matter what I think, though, when I feel so slighted. I try not to, but I can't stop psychoanalyzing myself. Could I have done something differently to make him want to introduce me, to jump at the chance? I sigh, turning the situation over in my head. I've never taken this type of rejection so personally before—why? What's different?

You like him, I think, and then quickly shake the thought away. I close my eyes, resettling myself in my role. I'm on assignment. I'm Catalina Barnes, and I'm here with Isaac to help him say good-bye to me. Nothing more. It's okay that he's hurt; it's part of the process. I just have to get him to the other side of his grief.

A shadow rounds the bannister of the staircase, and Isaac pauses in front of me. He's holding two cans and reaches one in my direction. I look at it doubtfully, and the first hint of a smile crosses his lips. "Apology soda," he says. His dark eyes sparkle again, and I'm helpless to resist the charm in his look. I take one of the cans and thank him. Isaac sips from his drink and motions to the stair I'm sitting on.

"Mind?"

I shake my head that I don't and move over so he can join me. His shoulder brushes against mine, and I'm reminded of how we touched at lunch, carelessly. Freely. I look at him as he stares out at the party with an unreadable expression.

"We don't have to stay," I tell him.

"It's a lot like pretending, yeah?" he asks, not turning to me. "Both of us. You pretend to be her. I pretend you're her."

I want to be me, I think. "Yeah," I say instead. "That's exactly how it goes."

He turns, looking me over like he did when he first saw me tonight, as if struck by my beauty. "And what would she say right now?" he asks. "How well did you study her? How much are you like her?"

"I'd say you're bumming me out," I tell him, knowing exactly how I would say it. Cute and gentle, something to bring him out of his bad mood, like I'd do after he lost a game. Of course, I know this is so much worse, but that's the closest experience I have to compare it to.

Isaac smiles, his expression a little faraway, thinking back on something. Around us, the music changes, and the next song comes on, more bass, more swerve. It seeps into our bones, and

I realize how entirely close Isaac and I are sitting now. He licks his bottom lip. "Do you know what I'd say?" he asks.

I'm caught up in his dark eyes. "What?" I ask.

"Let's dance." He holds out his hand, and I'm frozen, wanting desperately to take it, but doubting that I should. Do we really want more attention on us?

Isaac tilts his head, smiling softly. "Come on," he says in that raspy voice.

Dreamlike, I reach and slide my fingers against his, energized by his touch. He pulls me to my feet and then leads us into the crowd. The smell of sweat and perfume is around us, sickly sweet and savage at the same time. Isaac finds us an empty spot near the window.

It's the perfect location, partly hidden in the shadows. The house is old and the windows don't offer the sort of protection from the wind that they should. The pane lets in a cool, gentle breeze. It prickles up my arm and tickles the back of my neck. The song on the stereo is slow and sexy, the rhythm little more than a sway.

I look around at the others, mostly couples. They're not slow dancing; they're each in their own orbit, girls holding their hair off their shoulders, eyes closed. Guys whispering, touching the girls' exposed waists just above their jeans. The bass is heavy; the voice is scratchy. The rhythm is intoxicating, and I move in time with the music. I close my eyes, letting the sound deepen and take me over. It's been a long time since I've given in like this, danced in any fashion.

Despite the cool breeze, sweat trickles down my back, but it feels good. The dampness on my skin is purifying. There's a touch at my hip, and my eyes flutter open. Isaac is closer now, moving with the music, but looking down at my body, his fingers digging into my skin as he pulls me closer to match up our movements.

The song is echoing in my ears, and then Isaac's other hand is at the hem of my shirt, his fingers occasionally making contact with my skin beneath, setting me on fire. My eyes close again, drawn in by the heat, the touch, the sounds. I reach to rest my arms over his shoulders, and he lowers his head so that his mouth is near my ear. I feel his breath, and an ache starts in my stomach. I'm absolutely seduced by the moment, lost in a haze of desire and want. I thread my fingers through Isaac's short hair, and he makes a soft sound of approval, his body pressing into mine.

But then the song ends. The next one has a faster tempo, and the people around us call out for Jason to turn it up. Isaac and I take a step back from each other, his hands falling away from me. I lift my eyes to his, feeling breathless. His skin is flushed, his eyes slightly narrowed as he licks his lips and glances over my entire person. I want to kiss him.

The front door opens, and a cold breeze blows into the room. Isaac looks toward the doorway and his expression tightens. He turns quickly and takes my hand. "We should go," he says.

Confused, I glance at the doorway and find a girl standing

there. I'm immediately hit with a streak of jealousy—but then I recognize her. My heart just about stops. Isaac leans in to whisper.

"That's Kyle," he says. "Believe me when I say that you don't want to run into her. Especially not with me." I look up at him and he presses his lips together as if to remind me that I'm not really Catalina. To remind me that others hate me for just that reason. Instead of appreciating his warning, I'm saddened. My mood takes a dark turn, and I pull my hand from his. *That thing.*

"Yeah, let's go," I say, unable to control my behavior. I'm the opposite of professional right now, but I'm annoyed. Upset that I had to break the illusion—I liked it. I was completely lost in it, and it felt *good*. And I haven't had good in a long time.

Isaac is wounded by my sudden change, and I see him actually consider telling me to stay. But he's right—the last thing I need right now is an altercation in front of all of his friends. That's not beneficial to his recovery, and certainly not to my self-esteem. I step forward, put my hand on his arm, and try to smile an apology. He exhales, relieved, and then tosses one more cautious glance toward the door.

At that moment Kyle catches sight of him and her face lights up. She lifts her arm in the start of a wave, but Isaac quickly turns and grabs me to pull me through the crowd in the opposite direction. I'm surprised, but I move with him. At the entrance to the kitchen, I turn back and find Kyle staring dead at me, her mouth open in stunned horror.

I swing back around, and Isaac and I rush out the back door without a word to anybody, fleeing in our desire to be together.

We sit in his parked truck, a block down from the party. The heat from the vent is blowing over me, but the chill of the night air clings to my skin. I want to regret what just happened inside, regret dancing so closely. Instead I regret that it had to end. Tonight I don't want to be a closer anymore. I want to be real.

I look at Isaac and find him staring out the window, his arms hanging at his sides listlessly. Seeing Kyle affected him, made reality crash back down. He remembers that I'm supposed to be dead, that he's supposed to be missing me. But how can he miss me when I'm still right here?

"You okay?" I ask, my head clearing slightly from concern. My training tries to flood back, but it's still foggy and hard to grasp in this moment.

Isaac swallows hard. "I didn't know Kyle would be there tonight," he says. "She hasn't been around much since you . . ." He doesn't finish the sentence. "She introduced us," he continues, sounding a bit nostalgic. "I've known her since I was a kid; our parents are friends. After you guys started hanging out, she'd drop subtle hints. And the minute I was single, she did everything she could to pair us up."

I twist my leg underneath me and turn to him completely, wanting to hear more of his story. Hear more about us. He looks at me, his eyes weakening as he studies me.

"You're so perfect tonight," he says, his voice low and sad. "I didn't want it to end."

There's a flutter in my chest, and the moment deepens—the energy between us pulling us closer. "Neither did I," I murmur.

He shifts his body, leaning his shoulder into his seat like I'm taking up all of his attention. "Do you remember," he starts hesitantly, "the first time I kissed you?" My stomach flips, and I can actually feel my hands start to shake. Isaac's words are filled with pain, though, pain and resolve. Like he knows he shouldn't bring it up but can't help himself.

"Yes," I answer. It's not a lie, really. It was in the journal. It was detailed; I know every thought that went through my mind, every smile, every butterfly. "You were supposed to be at practice," I tell him, recalling the entry word for word. "But you showed up at Off Campus, right when I was fighting with Kyle. You sat across the room."

Isaac's forehead creases as he tries to hold back the emotions. The memory is coated in pain, but he wants it. He wants to feel it.

"You and I had gone to the movies the night before," I say. "Kyle's idea. But I hate the movies. To make matters worse, you hardly spoke a word to me. I was convinced you didn't like me, and I told Kyle she was a jerk for embarrassing me like that."

I smile softly, feeling the memory as if it's my own. "Turns out you're just shy," I say. "Shy and sweet. You told me later that you couldn't get me out of your head, but you didn't call because you can't stand talking on the phone. You decided to find me instead."

"And what did you think about that?" he asks, able to ask the questions he thought he'd never get the answers to. "What did you think about me?"

"That I would never let you get away," I tell him. "In that moment, seeing you sitting awkwardly as you waited for Kyle to leave, smiling madly at me, I knew that I would fall hopelessly in love with you, Isaac. I'm not sure what it was about you, but I wanted you from that moment on."

Isaac stares at me, tears brimming in his eyes. "But you did let me go," he says in barely a whisper. I've never seen anything lonelier than how Isaac looks in this moment. I can't stand it.

"I'll never do it again," I say without thinking. Say to make his hurt go away. Say because I almost mean it.

So when Isaac reaches for me, clumsy and desperate as he leans over the center console, puts his hand on my cheek, and pulls me into a kiss, I don't stop him. His mouth presses against mine, pausing for a long moment before his lips part and he kisses me again. Again. Warmth flows over my skin, and my fingers clasp the edge of his jacket. My body is electric. My lips move with his, my eyes fluttering shut.

I kiss him passionately, recklessly. And I let Isaac Perez fall in love with me all over again.

PART III
THE REMEDY

CHAPTER ONE

IT WAS ONLY A KISS, **I TELL MYSELF, TRYING NOT TO** let the guilt eat me alive. Isaac and I stopped almost immediately after we'd started, preventing ourselves from making a huge mistake. But I let him hold my hand on the drive home. We kissed once more before I snuck back into my house.

I did all of that. I knew exactly what I was doing.

Staring up at the ceiling from my bed, I can still taste Isaac on my lips. I let myself fall into the illusion, imagine a world where Isaac still loves me. Imagine this is my real life.

I'm curious then about who I used to be, this girl who seemed to have everything. I slide my hand under the pillow and find the diary pages. I click on the light and bend my legs to rest the papers against my thighs, tracing the handwriting with my index finger. I have a great family, perfect boyfriend. But yesterday my mother said I'd been withdrawn before my death, and that even Isaac had noticed. Something had changed.

I sift through the pages to where I left off in the journal. Earlier I was eager to find out about my love life, reading it like a torrid romance novel. But now, as I skim the words, a different emotion takes over.

We were at the lake house, in one of the loft bedrooms because we thought it was tacky to use the large bed in his parents' room. Losing it on a bunk bed—there's some comedy in that that I think we both enjoyed. Despite the cramped space on the mattress, it was exactly what I thought. We laughed and then we didn't. Then we got really serious. It didn't feel good—not like everyone always says it will. But that was the thing . . . it kind of hurt, but Isaac was there, in tune to every movement, watching and careful. Just like always. I think that's what everyone likes about it—the closeness. It's the only time you can ever share yourself so completely, be so completely vulnerable. In that moment, Isaac was mine. And there

I crumple the pages in my hand, my heart racing and sickness in my stomach. My face is hot and I want to cry. I tighten my fist into a ball, crushing the words. I shouldn't have read that. I didn't want to know, not really. The girl I've been playing loved Isaac Perez, and she's right—he is hers. He still is.

I throw the pages across the room, abandoning the words forever. I squeeze my eyes shut, hating how I feel. I have no right, no right to feel this way. Betrayed. Heartsick. I roll over, facing the ceiling again, my mind starting to spin. *This isn't me,* I think. *I can't be jealous of a dead girl.*

But pain continues to gather in my chest, and I reach over to grab my phone—desperate. I stare at the blank screen and finally break down. Who can I call? Not Isaac, not on this phone. A name comes to mind, the person who's always there for me. But thinking about Deacon leads me to a different memory. The one I try not to think about.

Deacon is the only guy I've been with, the only guy I've ever kissed until tonight. We always say that closers don't love, that we can't. But I thought I loved Deacon. We held each other's identities in our hands. I gave him everything of myself, and for a while I thought he did the same. We were a tangle of passion and intensity; we were a blazing fire. But he ended it. With no explanation, he shredded my heart.

"I don't understand," I'd said, standing at the door of the apartment Marie had been renting for him. I'd asked if I could come in and Deacon told me it wasn't a good idea. He'd been avoiding my calls for three days. "Deacon," I pleaded, my skin raw from the cold, wet weather outside. "What's going on?"

I'd always considered Deacon to be the perfect assembly of parts, his every feature my favorite thing. But he was flawed; he seemed different. He wouldn't look at me, and finally I pushed open the door and put my hands on his cheeks, forcing him to meet my eyes.

He closed them, not letting me see. Hiding. But I knew him too well, could feel his pain. And his pain was my pain.

I got on my tiptoes and pressed my lips to his, my fingers sliding into his hair, my body against his. Deacon went completely still, letting me move my mouth over his without any response. There was a flutter of a touch at my hip, but just as my heart began to beat again, he turned his face away, breaking our kiss. He put his fingers over his lips like they hurt.

I fell back a step, wholly rejected. When Deacon finally looked at me again, the mischief was gone from his eyes. Instead his expression was deadened. Cold and uncaring. I'd never, ever seen him look at anything the way he stared back at me. Like I was a stranger, invisible. Like I meant absolutely nothing to him. "Quinlan," he said, "I've moved on. I want you to do the same."

A sharp pain broke across my chest, and my lips started to quiver. I sniffled hard, but the tears brimmed over and streaked down my cheeks anyway. I took another step back, putting my hand over my heart. Feeling it break into a million pieces.

"You should go," Deacon said simply. "This isn't good for you. It's over. It never should have started."

I tried to read the lie in his expression, I *begged* for it, but it wasn't there. No hints of hidden truths—blotchy skin, shifty eyes—nothing. He looked straight at me, reducing me to ash. Not even a week ago we'd been in his bed and he'd been drawing a tattoo in black pen across my bare back, kissing my neck at every pause. If I looked in the mirror, the faded design would still be there. And I didn't mean to ask; I don't even know why it came out.

"Don't you love me?" I murmured, warm tears rushing over my lips. Deacon didn't flinch or show any emotion at all. He held my gaze.

"No."

I stilled, my face and extremities going numb. My broken and betrayed heart stopped beating. We had never said those words before, but I did love him—thought I did, at least. But you can't be in love with someone who doesn't feel the same way. That's not real love.

The world went fuzzy around me, and before I could break completely, I turned and started down the hall, my boots echoing loudly on the floor. I heard Deacon's door shut, and my legs weakened. He didn't try to come after me. I flattened my palm against the cracked plaster wall, steadying myself. Trying to hold back the sobs that would wreck me. Somehow I made it down the stairs and out the front door.

There was no way I could drive my car in that state. I took out my phone, my arm wrapped around my stomach, holding myself up as I hunched over. I dialed, and when my father answered, I cracked at the sound of his voice.

"Dad," I said in a choking voice, "can you come get me?"

He did. Seeing me that broken down is why my father doesn't want me around Deacon anymore. He's afraid he'll keep hurting me. He's right. That's why Deacon and I can't be together. Because even if he wanted to, Deacon would never let himself love me. And I deserve better than that.

I set my phone on the side table, Deacon's betrayal sticking to my skin. At this point, my jealousy over the journal entry has faded to a dull irritation. But I don't want these feelings anymore. I get out of bed and grab the pages from the floor on my way to the closet. I stash them up on a high shelf so I won't be tempted to read them again. *Your life is over, Catalina,* I think, turning away. *It's my turn now.*

My backpack is on the floor, and I kneel next to it and rummage through until I find the picture of me that Deacon drew. I don't unfold it. I crumple the paper into a tight ball. I stand, walk over, and drop it into the wastebasket under my desk. There is an instant of regret, but I block it out. I go to the side table and grab my phone. I click my settings and delete all of my apps, not knowing which is used to track me. I just get rid of all of them.

No one will follow me anymore. I drop the phone onto the table and climb back into bed and under the sheets. I shut off the light and close my eyes, waiting a minute for my old emotions to fade, and then let the night settle over me. I touch my lips, imagining Isaac's on mine. Imagining him at my ear, telling me he loves me. I beg him to say it again. And again. He whispers it against my skin until I fall asleep.

I sleep in, missing breakfast entirely. I wake up feeling refreshed, though, excited for the day. My skin is alive, and I note the glow it seems to have when I look in the mirror. I cover my freckles and put on a new outfit that my mother picked out and head to the kitchen to find my parents.

Both of them are there, content in my presence, and they ask if I'd like to do anything fun today—as if I'm on an extended vacation while everyone else is at school. My father even took time off. I walk over to the patio doors and glance at the sky—not a cloud in sight. I smile and tell them it's going to be a perfect day.

We decide to pack up some hot dogs and burgers and head to the river to cook out for lunch. My father asks if he should hitch up the boat, but I tell him he doesn't have to. We'll just hang out by the water and soak up the rays of the sun.

I pack a bag with my swimsuit and a change of clothes. I

grab sunscreen and a book I've never seen before off the shelf. I take a quick moment to open my computer and send Isaac a message of where I'll be. I tell him I got a new phone, and I give him the old number. Now that it's not traceable, I can take it with me. I walk over to grab it and immediately a message pops up. I smile.

HELLO, BEAUTIFUL, it says.

I drop down on the edge of my bed, my cheeks burning from the flattery. DO YOU WANT TO SEE A MOVIE TONIGHT? I ask. In reality, *I* don't hate movies. I kind of love them.

DEFINITELY, he writes. I HAVE PRACTICE UNTIL SEVEN. I'LL PICK YOU UP AFTER.

I tell him to have a great day, and then slip the phone into my backpack and go outside to meet my parents at the car. None of us mentions anything to break the illusion. Not one word.

"You love the river," my mother tells me from the front seat, beaming as we drive toward the park.

"I can't wait," I say, watching the trees pass outside the window. The sky is a gorgeous blue. It's a new day. A new life. I smile and settle back against my seat.

The afternoon glides by, easy and calm. My father grills wearing a button-down shirt with bold patterns, and a wide-brimmed hat. He looks like he's on vacation in Florida. My mother sits at a picnic table, reading a book and drinking soda out of a can with a straw. I'm lying on a towel in the grass with my chin on my folded hands, watching the water rush by. It's still a little too cold to swim, but in this spot the wind doesn't touch us.

Isaac texts me throughout the day, telling me how he wishes I could be his lab partner in physics class instead of Byron, who's "dumb as shit." He says he's been dodging Kyle most of the day, and that he thinks he's going to fake sick one day this week so he can hang out with me instead. I tell him I like this plan.

"Who've you been talking to?" my mother asks curiously as we sit at the picnic table, eating burgers. I feel myself blush, and wipe off a bit of ketchup that's smeared on the corner of my mouth.

"Isaac," I say, and take another bite. I have a quick worry about their reaction.

"He's better with you," she says, but not dreamily. I look up and find her staring at me, her expression clear. "We thought we'd lost him; no one could get through to him," she continues. "But your sister told me he's improving. That he's been better since you arrived. If you stay . . ." She tilts her head. "I think he'd be really happy."

My mother is saying what I already feel. There's a place for me here, with Isaac and with them. Maybe after Isaac graduates, I can go to California too. Take classes. I can fill in all of their empty spaces and make something of this life that was cut too short.

I set down my food and grab a new napkin to wipe my hands. "I think I'd be happy too," I tell my parents. My heart swells at the idea of being part of their family. I don't let myself think about how impossible it would be—how the department would never let me. In my head, it could be real.

My father reaches to put his large hand over mine. "Then stay," he says.

Isaac and I don't watch much of the movie. The theater was almost completely empty, and we sat in the shadows of the very back row. Now his mouth is on my neck, his tongue occasionally touching my skin and driving me wild. I don't think about anything. My mind is blank and I just feel, blanketed by heat and emotion.

We kiss again, his mouth sweetened by candy. By the time we stop, still breathing each other in, the movie is almost over. We pull apart and look around, glad no one has noticed us, or at least they've pretended not to. I'm embarrassed by our complete lack of control. My lips are raw and swollen, and Isaac is watching me, wild with passion. But then suddenly . . . it worries me. Like this is too much too fast.

"We should go," I say abruptly. Isaac's face twists in confusion, and I lean in and peck his lips. "Sorry," I tell him. "But you're too tempting."

He laughs. "Me?" He looks me over and then moves in to kiss me again. I hold out my hand to stop him. Despite the fact that I'm insanely attracted to him, I'm too aware of us now.

"Come on," I say, taking his hand to pull him up. We skip out before the final scene of the movie, but neither of us cares. Isaac's arm is thrown over my shoulders as we walk through the outdoor mall, and he talks about practice and school—regular things that I don't know much about. But I listen, nod when I should. When a cool breeze blows by, I snuggle up a little closer and he holds me tight, kissing the top of my head.

This is what it's like to be normal, I tell myself. I watch the people who pass us on our way to his truck, watch their expressions and try to mimic them. Try to take their normal.

When I get home, I see I've missed three calls from Aaron and two from Deacon. They've sent text messages too, but I don't read them. I'm tired. I climb into bed and close my eyes. But I don't retreat into any memories tonight. Or the next night. This time, my world is enough to comfort me.

And so I let the week stretch on like a beautiful dream that I never want to wake up from.

CHAPTER TWO

THERE IS AN INSISTENT BUZZING. MY EYELIDS ARE heavy, as if I could sleep for a few more hours. I finally sit up, pushing my hair away from my face, and turn to see my phone lit up on the side table. It's Aaron. I click ignore again and turn my clock so I can read the numbers. It's nearly ten a.m.

I get dressed and find my mother cleaning up the living room. My father has already left for work, and my mother is really focused on getting the details right for my party next week.

We spent Wednesday afternoon going over invites, and I listened to her stories about my parties past. Yesterday we went back to the mall to pick out the perfect dress, one that needed to be let out just a little. Today she wants to run some errands to get the decorations, but I'm worn out from all the planning. She asks if I want to go with her, but when I scrunch my nose, she laughs. She tells me to take the day off.

She leaves soon after, and I make myself scrambled eggs and clean the pan. I shower and get dressed, and by the time I check my phone again, Isaac has messaged to say he left school early and wants to hang out. I smile, and think about my empty house. I haven't seen him since the movies, although our texts have taken a turn for the affectionate. He tells me how he thinks about me all the time. How much he wants to kiss me again. I get butterflies just thinking about it.

In a streak of rebellion, I ask him to come over to my parentless household. When he agrees, I'm a mess of nerves. I've never done anything like this in my real life, had a boyfriend skip school and come over when my parents weren't home. I never had to. Deacon didn't have any parents, so we always had a place to go. I clench my jaw, annoyed with my thoughts. I don't want to think about Deacon right now.

I grab the house phone and call my mother, settled on the idea of sneaking around with my boyfriend. I smile slightly; Isaac *is* my boyfriend. My mother answers the phone, and I straighten up as if she can see me.

"Hey," I say casually.

"Hi, honey," she responds, sounding a bit frazzled. I have a small twinge of guilt, but I quickly suppress it. I need to know how long she'll be out.

"Are you going by the grocery store later?" I ask. "I was thinking of baking some cupcakes together after dinner tonight."

"Oh," she says, like it's a fun idea. "I'd love that. I'll be tied up at the dress shop for a while. I might not be back before your father gets home at three. That okay?"

I grin. "No rush, Mom. See you then."

I set down the phone and spin around to look over my room. My body is tingling with nerves and possibilities. I smooth out my blankets, but my fingernail catches on a loose thread, and the tip snaps off.

"Ow," I say, checking my finger. It broke short, leaving a sting on the skin. I look down at the sheet, and the sight of my bed sends me in a different direction of realization.

Maybe this is a bad idea, I think, nervously biting the edge of my nail to smooth it out. *What if I . . . if we . . .*

The doorbell rings. I furrow my brow, looking at my bedroom door. Isaac must have texted when he was already on his way. I try to squash down the nervousness building up, the out-and-out giddiness I feel about seeing him. Jason called Isaac a total sap, but that's how I feel. Completely and stupidly into him.

I leave my room, brushing back my hair and rubbing my lips together, wishing I'd had time to put on gloss. Excitement flutters through my stomach as I walk into the living room. When I get to the front door, I swing it open, smiling broadly.

My world shatters, falling around me in sharp, jagged pieces that reflect back different images. Different lives.

"Quinlan," Marie says, pronouncing my name carefully as her dark eyes take in my appearance. "I'd like to come in and speak with you."

My mouth opens, but no words come out. I'm shocked, fearful. I glance behind me into the house, and when I turn to Marie again, she presses her lips into a polite smile.

"I know your parents aren't home," she says. "So may I please come in?"

I swallow hard, looking over her shoulder toward the street, worried that Isaac's truck will pull up at any moment. But without another choice, I nod and open the door wider, motioning for Marie to come inside.

Marie's wearing a deep purple pantsuit; her braids are undone at the bottom to leave the ends curly. She's a vision, professional and yet approachable, a complete package designed for the manipulation of trust. I remember her telling me once that every detail is used to bring about an intended feeling in others, planned down to the shade of lipstick she wears. Despite her attempt, her appearance offers me little comfort right now. I'm scared as hell.

Marie takes a seat on the couch and motions for me to sit across from her. When I do, she rests back and crosses her legs. "Would you like to explain to me why I'm getting a panicked phone call from Aaron, claiming you're losing touch?" she asks.

My stomach twists anxiously. "He called you?"

"That's not an explanation," she says.

I have to regroup quickly, portray confidence. "Look," I say, opening up my expression to show honesty. "I'm avoiding him, but it has nothing to do with this assignment," I explain. "He's harassing me about Deacon, total everyday stuff. I'm sorry he dragged you into this." I feel bad for stretching the truth, making Aaron look unprofessional. But he had no right to contact our advisor.

"Say I believe that," Marie says, eyeing me carefully. "Now I'm asking you personally: Do you need an extraction?"

"No."

"Quinlan," she persists. "Are you compromised?"

"No, Marie," I say. "In fact, things are going very well. Exactly as planned. This case will be closed by next Friday."

That may be true, but it doesn't guarantee that I'll leave. And if the department tries to force me to, I'll come back when I'm eighteen. There's nothing that says I can't. No matter what, my career as a closer is over. I don't care about the money, about any of it. I have everything I need right here.

"And to be honest," I add, "Isaac is on his way over right now. He's made huge strides in his recovery. Ask my parents."

"That's reassuring," Marie says. Although I note the slight relief in her voice, the concern doesn't leave her eyes. She leans toward me. "I trust you," she says. "I always have. And whatever's happening, Quinn, you need to clear this up. I can see you're a little confused. The question is, is this enough of an issue to pull you out?"

"No," I say emphatically. "Marie, I agree this is a hard assignment, but the family has finally let me in. Isaac trusts me too. I've even made headway with the sister. Let me finish this. Please."

Marie looks me up and down, weighing my words. She stands, brushing at the thighs of her suit to smooth the fabric. "Fine," she agrees. "But you need to end it with the boyfriend. Give him closure early and exit him from this process. Understand?"

It's a punch to my chest, and it takes everything I have to keep my expression steady. "That's not an option," I tell her, standing up. "His wellness is tied into the family's. They like having him around; they like seeing him get better. It would devastate them if he was cut off."

Marie narrows her dark-lined eyes, and smiles. "Bullshit," she says. My mouth opens in surprise. "Do you think I don't know you?" she asks. "Haven't known you since you were a child?" She steps closer to me, taller than I am in her high-heeled boots. "You've gotten attached, Quinlan," she says. "And for that I should pull you immediately. But the thing is, this case, it's bigger than you. Has bigger implications. And I honestly and truly believe that you're a good enough closer to finish this assignment. Finish it with *you* intact. Assure me that I'm right."

My face burns with shame, but I appreciate what Marie has said. Of course, she's not wrong about me getting attached. I hope she's not wrong about me being strong enough to overcome it.

"I can finish this," I tell her, tightening my expression to show her my resolve. "Just give me until next Friday."

Marie nods slowly and then comes close and pulls me into

a hug. She smells of vanilla, and the scent is familiar, comforting me immediately. I close my eyes for a moment, breathing her in.

We separate, and Marie holds my arm as I walk her to the door. She is the closest thing I've had to a mother in my real life. I've lied to her, and yet we still trust each other.

I open the door, and she steps outside and turns to look back at me. "No more running around with Isaac," she says, pointing her finger at me. "One call, Quinn, one call from a pissed-off friend of his and your father will send you straight into therapy. He has no idea what's happening here, and I have no inclination to tell him about it."

"Thank you, Marie."

She nods, and there is a hint of hesitation in her movement. But after she turns and leaves, a new feeling starts to bubble up inside me. Anger.

I slam the door closed and march into my room, grabbing my phone and dialing Aaron. I'm furious. This is the second time he's betrayed me, and I'm not going to give him another shot at it.

"Quinlan, thank God," he says immediately on answering. I scoff, even more annoyed that he's trying to sound concerned.

"You reported me, asshole?"

"Calm down," Aaron says. "You wouldn't take my calls. Not even Deacon's. I was worried, and I was afraid to come near the house. Not to mention the tracking app has been disconnected on your phone. Coincidence?"

"No," I say. "I didn't want you spying on me."

"It's not spying. It's looking out for you. What is going on over there?"

"I'm doing my job," I tell him, my mouth tight with bitterness. "And if you interfere again, I'll report *you* for trying to derail my assignment. My father will send you to therapy."

Aaron is quiet for a long moment, and even through my anger I realize my threat was too severe. Too cruel. I almost apologize, but Aaron talks before I can.

"Fine," he says. "Do what you want. And when they're scraping your brains off the floor of the hospital, remember that I was trying to help you."

He hangs up, and I toss my phone on the bed. Sickness tears at my stomach—I'm hurt that he told Marie that I was losing myself. Embarrassed that he was kind of right. And I'm ashamed of how I just talked to him. Aaron's my friend, I know that. What I don't know is why I want this thing with Isaac to continue, this risk I'm taking. It's like . . . I can't stop myself. I want it too much.

But Marie's warning stays with me. I put on some lip gloss and a little more makeup, trying to disguise the paleness, my glow snuffed out. When Isaac arrives fifteen minutes later, I meet him on the porch and close the door behind me. I can't have him over now, interact the way I planned. He still smiles brightly when he sees me, and I ask him if we can go to lunch instead because I'm hungry. There's a small hint of disappointment in his expression, but he tries to hide it. Of course, he's not a closer, so I can read him easily. I give him a quick kiss, making it better. Reassuring him on some level. He takes my hand and we walk to his truck, but before I get in, I scan the streets quickly, looking for a car—one that's out of place. One that's watching me. But if there are any, they're well-hidden, because there's nothing out of the ordinary on this street. Nothing but me.

CHAPTER THREE

JASON INVITED ISAAC AND ME TO THE BATTING cages at the park on Sunday morning, and although I'm not supposed to be "running around with Isaac," I thought it sounded fun. And I'm entitled to a bit of fun once in a while.

Isaac and I arrive at the cages and find Jason waiting for us near the little shop that houses concessions, a big wad of gum stuck in the side of his mouth like chew. He's wearing a jersey that's tight over his rounded stomach in an endearing sort of way. I like Jason. I can totally understand why Isaac is friends with him.

"There's my favorite couple," he calls out when he sees us approach. He twirls his bat around a gloved hand in pretend showing off, then drops it with a loud clank and we all start laughing. He nods at me. "Your boyfriend is going to show us all up, just a bit of warning."

"I figured," I say, looking over at Isaac.

"No, you don't understand," Jason says, smirking. "Most nice guys would downplay a little so that their friends don't look stupid. Not this asshole. He'll totally flaunt it."

"Shut up, man," Isaac says, laughing. "You're just extraordinarily bad."

"This is true," Jason says, grabbing a cup of tokens he'd left on the ledge near the door. "So should we let the humiliation games begin?"

I can't stop smiling, immersed in their constant fake bickering. I take a seat on the top of a picnic table, and Jason is first into the cages. He puts in a token and exaggerates his stance. I giggle, and he looks back at me and winks. The pitch comes out, fast enough to make me jump, and Jason smacks it, sending it to the netting on top of the cages.

Isaac lets out a low whistle and sits next to me to watch. "Whaaaat?" he calls to Jason. "Someone's been practicing."

"You think I would've met you here if I hadn't?" Jason asks with a shit-eating grin. The next pitch comes before he's ready, and Isaac lowers his head and laughs. Jason readjusts and takes the next eight pitches to the sky.

I'm surprised how fast the balls are shooting out of the machine, and also a little nervous. The extent of my batting training happened in my backyard the other night with my father, so I'm not feeling super confident. I watch Jason finish his pitches, and then he turns on his heels and points his bat in my direction.

"You're up, Catawampus," he announces. Isaac and I burst out laughing, but there's a soft touch on my heart that he used a nickname in the first place. A sense that I belong. I hop down, turn back to Isaac, and bite my nail like I'm nervous.

"You've got it, babe," he says, clapping his hands loudly to pump me up. I'm all smiles when I get into the cage and pick up the metal bat from the ground. I weigh it in my hands, and then scrunch my nose and look at Isaac. "I have to warn you," I tell him. "I suck and I'm going to embarrass both of us."

He gives me an encouraging thumbs-up. I grab a token from the cup and slip it into the slot. The sound of the motor starts, and I swallow hard, edging up to the batting square. The first pitch shoots out, and I yelp and jump back from the plate. Holy shit that was fast.

I toss a panicked look at Isaac, but he and Jason tell me to be brave—patronizing me, I suppose. Either way, I get back in my stance and the heavy bat bobs unsteadily in my grip. The pitch comes and I close my eyes and swing, spinning myself around. I got a piece of it, though. They clap wildly, again patronizing me, but at least I know I can hit it. By the fifteenth pitch I'm able to hit the ball toward the back of the cage, and the muscle in my shoulder is on fire. I finish, exhaling dramatically and letting my arms fall to my sides.

Isaac jumps up from the table and comes into the cage, putting his hands on my waist, telling me what a great job I did. He leans in to kiss my lips, and then takes his hat and puts it on my head backward.

"He's right," Isaac tells me, motioning to Jason. "I'm going to show up both of you."

I push him, laughing, and then go to join Jason on the picnic table. Jason looks sideways at me. "That kid's a superstar," he says admiringly. "Charmed life, that one." I turn back to Isaac, sadness creeping in to remind me that Isaac's life isn't as great as Jason thinks. But I quickly bury that thought, not wanting to ruin the day.

"Come on, Isaac," I yell to drown out my guilt. "Impress me."

He looks over his shoulder at me, licks his bottom lip, and says, "I will."

I lean forward, my elbows on my knees, and put my folded hand to my mouth because my cheeks are starting to hurt from smiling so much. Isaac turns back to wait for his pitch and all I can think about is how incredibly sexy he is.

He smacks the hell out of the ball. Next pitch, same thing. I straighten, watching with a bit of awe as he handles every pitch as if it's the easiest thing in the world. Next to me, Jason knocks his knee into mine.

"Haven't you seen him play before?" he asks, noticing my reaction.

I probably should have known how great he is, so I smile and say, "Yeah, but he still amazes me every time."

Jason tilts his head, studying my face for a moment. He looks thoughtful, and turns back to Isaac. "I'm glad he loves you," he says quietly. "You're good for him."

My breath is tight in my chest, and I'm so grateful for this day. I'm so glad I ignored Marie's advice, because now this is mine. This memory. Maybe even this life. *He loves you.* I turn to watch Isaac once again, trying to memorize his every movement.

"Not to mention," Jason continues, "that I'm way better than you at baseball. So you're good for me, too." We both snort a laugh.

Isaac finishes, clearly proud of his ass-kickery, and comes back over to the table. He reaches out to take the hat from my head and puts it back on his. "Well, I'm starving," he says, looking between me and Jason.

"I'll get us some hot dogs," Jason says, climbing down from the table.

"I'll come with," Isaac adds. He puts his hand on the table and leans in to kiss my cheek. "You want one?" he asks. I nod, enjoying the closeness. He puts his other hand on the other side of me, boxing me in. He leans in and kisses my lips. And then again. "Be right back," he whispers, and then jogs to catch up with Jason, who is already on his way to a little store on the other side of the cages.

I watch them, feeling content in a way I haven't in a while. I lean back on my arms, my legs stretched in front of me. My phone buzzes in my pocket and my posture stiffens. *I don't want to talk to you, Aaron,* I think, ignoring the call. *Just leave us alone.*

"Quinn?" There's a sharp pain in my heart, and I spin around and find Deacon just inside the fence, not far from where we've been sitting. He lowers the phone from his ear, devastation painting his features. He looks toward Isaac and Jason, who are thankfully out of earshot, and then back at me. I know he's seen everything.

"Deacon," I say, climbing down from the picnic table. He can't be here; he can't let Isaac see him. How would I explain? I'd have to break character in front of Jason. That would ruin everything. "I can't talk right now," I say, shooting a look over in time to see Isaac and Jason disappear inside the store.

I cross the pavement to where Deacon stands and put my hands on his chest, walking him back a few steps and out of direct view. He doesn't fight me; he only stares in disbelief. His fingers close around my wrists, holding me to him.

"What are you doing?" he asks pleadingly. "What have you done?"

His pain rolls over me, and I want to apologize—but doing that would be admitting I did something wrong. And frankly, this isn't any of his business.

"I'm on assignment," I say, pulling my arms from his grip. "I'm working, Deacon. You can't be here."

"You're living. You're not working."

"I'm helping him," I say.

"You're helping yourself."

My soft spot hardens and I cross my arms over my chest. "Don't be a dick."

"Me?" he says. "You've dodged Aaron for three days. Marie's grown concerned. Hell, we're all concerned, Quinn. She sent me to check on you so it'd be off the books—that should tell you something."

The mention of Marie irks me, and I sneer. "What should it tell me?" I ask him. "That they want more control over how I provide closure? That they think you can manipulate me better than Aaron? I'm doing my job, Deacon. Tell them that."

Deacon's face contorts, tightens as if he's in pain. "I saw you," he says miserably. "I saw you kiss him."

Heat rushes to my cheeks, but I do my best to keep up my facade. "I've already told you that I'm helping him," I whisper harshly. "There are only a few days left. I think the department can live without me until then." I take a breath, trying to calm my appearance, and start back toward the table.

"And what about me?" Deacon calls. "What if I can't live without you?"

It's a punch to my gut. I turn back fiercely. "Don't," I say, pointing at him. "Don't you dare." Deacon is not allowed to use this against me, to manipulate me with his feelings of hurt and jealousy. He's already broken my heart twice. I won't give him the chance to do it again.

Deacon stares, surprised by the ferocity of my response but also devastated by my rejection. He glances at the store and then takes a step toward me. "You're killing me," he murmurs.

"Go home, Deacon," I say, and turn my back on him. I feel sick, but I keep my posture strong as I stride away and return to the table. My hands are shaking, but my face is emotionless. I force myself numb. I won't let him in. I can't.

It's quiet behind me, and when the screen door of the concessions shop opens and Isaac and Jason walk out with trays of food, laughing about something, I finally glance over my shoulder. Deacon is gone.

There's a quiet loss, and I turn away. I wonder briefly if he'll report what he saw—me kissing the boyfriend of an assignment. A client, even. But I know he won't. Deacon would never betray me to the department, even if it's for my own good.

CHAPTER FOUR

ISAAC HAS A GAME ON TUESDAY NIGHT, AND ALTHOUGH I've never been to a high school baseball game, I decide to attend. I'm nervous that someone will call me out for being there, but I've been living so effortlessly the past few days that the threat seems far away now. I'll be careful. I'll wear my hood up, keep my eyes downcast. I'll sit in the back.

Those people can't stop me from living. Isaac wants me there, and I want to be with him. It's simple now—easier than any assignment I've ever had. Even at dinner tonight, my parents were all smiles. There was no pain. I've taken it all away.

My hood is up as I sit in the top row of the bleachers. Even so, a few people turn occasionally to stare at me, and I shift uncomfortably under their gazes. I pay rapt attention to the score, clapping when Isaac comes up to bat but not whistling or calling out like I want to. I can't draw that sort of attention to myself. I don't want to embarrass Isaac.

"It's pretty weird," a voice says. I turn to my left as a guy slides onto the empty bleacher to sit next to me. "What you do," he clarifies. "It's weird, if you ask me."

I tighten my jaw and turn to face the field. This is exactly the sort of confrontation I was hoping to avoid. "I didn't ask you," I say calmly. I unfold my palms over my knees, wishing the guy would leave.

There's a cheer from the crowd to my right as the catcher tags someone out at home plate. I've lost interest in the game, though, and glance up at the scoreboard to check the inning. Top of the seventh; it's almost over.

"Name's Nando," the guy says when the noise dies down. "Fernando, but everyone calls me Nando." He pauses. "You used to know that."

I still don't turn, afraid I'll find hatred in his expression. I read about Nando in the diary pages. He was good friends with Isaac and with Kyle. And with me, I guess.

"Anyway," he continues, sounding self-conscious. "I just . . . I wanted to get a closer look, you know? See if you could actually pass for her."

I debate for a moment and then turn to him, wondering if his interest comes from curiosity or bitterness. But his expression is open and kind. The tension in my shoulders releases slightly as I examine his dark brown eyes, his round cheeks. From what I can tell, he's not a threat.

I flip back my hood, and the cool airs rustles my hair. I tame down the wild strands, tucking them behind my ear, and smile—the perfect practiced smile that I know almost as well as my own. Nando takes in a sharp breath; his eyes widen. I watch as he studies my flawless makeup—meant to accentuate my features in the right ways. He looks over my short hair, my clothes. I am Catalina Barnes.

Nando scrunches up his face. My appearance is unsettling if you know who I'm supposed to be, and I regret showing him. I quickly flip up my hood, embarrassed that I thought I could be so casual with a stranger.

"Wow," Nando says, swallowing hard. "You look just fucking like her." It's not a compliment, but it's not a slam, either.

There's another loud cheer, and this time when I look up, the dugout players are flooding the field. Isaac's team lost. Around me the bleachers are starting to empty, and I turn back to find Nando watching me. He smiles sadly.

"What's he going to do when you leave?" he asks. He doesn't have to mention him by name, and the thought of leaving Isaac tugs on my heart. I look at the field and find him talking with some of the other players, laughing despite the team's loss.

"I don't know," I say quietly. "But the hope is he'll be able to move on. That he'll eventually be happy."

"He's happy now," Nando says. "I wasn't sure he'd make it through this. So thank you." I turn to him, but he's staring straight ahead. The bleachers all belong to us now. "But after you're gone . . ." Nando looks at me. "Isn't he going to mourn *you*?"

"No," I say automatically. But I doubt my own words. In regular role play, families get to say good-bye to their loved ones. They move on without ever seeing me as a person. This assignment has been different. I'm a part of this life now. I can't even begin to think about saying good-bye to Isaac. Or to my family. I just want to stop thinking.

"His therapy's going well," I tell Nando, standing up and slipping my hands into the pockets of my hoodie. Nando rises to his feet next to me.

"I'm glad," he says, seeming relieved. "And no offense"—he smiles apologetically—"but I can't wait until you're gone. You've kind of been making everyone around here a little crazy. I just want things to go back to normal."

I nod like I understand, but his words pierce my armor. *Normal.* That's not how they see me—I'm distinctly abnormal to most of them. But not to Isaac. Not anymore. I look at the field just as Isaac disappears into the dugout toward the locker room.

"I have to go," I tell Nando, moving past him toward the bleacher stairs. I take the steps two at a time, trying to disappear from sight as quickly as possible. When I reach the bottom, Nando calls to me from the top step.

"Catalina," he says. It startles me, and I turn to look at him. He holds up his hand in a wave. "It was nice meeting you," he says. His eyes glisten with the start of tears, and I can see his grief. He lost a friend; I'm a reminder of that loss. I'm salt in his wound.

"You too," I tell him. I turn away and walk swiftly toward the parking lot.

Isaac has his duffel bag over his shoulder as he approaches his truck. I'm leaning against the passenger door, and he smiles, looking me up and down. "I gave you that shirt," he says, nodding to it.

"You did?" I ask, glancing down at it. Isaac drops his bag at his feet and scans my face.

"Yeah," he says with a slight edge. "Don't you remember?"

"Uh . . ." I can't recall reading or seeing anything about this shirt. Truth is, I picked it because it was the most comfortable one I could find in the drawer. "Nope. I forgot," I say sweetly, stepping in to him and draping my arms over his shoulders. His hair is still wet from the showers, and the smell of soap is thick around him. Isaac doesn't smile, though. Confusion clouds his face.

"We went to that show," he explains, talking faster. "You wanted that T-shirt, Catalina. That exact one. You pointed it out on another girl and I bought the fucking shirt straight off her body so that you could have it. I can't believe you could forget about that."

I lower my arms and take a step back; dread coils in my stomach. I don't know how I got this shirt because it didn't happen to me. He knows this. "Isaac," I say, keeping my tone steady, "I don't remember."

"Yes, you do!" he shouts, making me jump. A couple of people leaving the game look over at the sound of his raised voice.

"Hey!" I snap at Isaac, startled by his frustration. Heat rushes to my face and tears sting my eyes. I understand the unusual circumstances of our relationship, I really do. But I'm not going to stand here in the school parking lot while he yells at me in front of strangers. I won't let him shatter this illusion.

"I'm going home," I say, and round the hood of the truck. My mom dropped me off earlier and now I'll have to call her back for a ride. I need to get out of here. My mind is racing, flipping between my training and the life I've been living. The lines have blurred. I need a moment to think, but my heart aches with jealousy and clouds my judgment. I'm sick of competing with a dead girl.

Isaac runs up, stopping a few steps ahead of me and holding out his hands to slow me down. When I pause, he studies my face for a long moment before reaching out to touch my cheek. The touch, the affection, eases the pain in my chest.

"I'm sorry," he says desperately. His eyes have softened, painting his features in misery at the thought of me leaving him. "I'm just a little off today," he says, his fingers sliding to the back of my neck as he stares down at me adoringly. I exhale as his thumb strokes over my skin. "I'm so sorry," he whispers, stepping closer.

"You can't talk to me like that," I tell him. "You can't just hurt my feelings whenever you want."

“I don’t want to,” he says immediately. He wraps his arms around me, and I listen to the fast beating of his heart. “I don’t ever want to hurt you,” Isaac murmurs close to my ear. “You’re the love of my life.”

A shiver runs down my body, and I smile. The idea of him loving me, saying that he loves me, is enough to keep me here—in this present—with him. The rest of me falls away—all of my sense, all of my worry—leaving me completely vulnerable.

We stay wrapped up in each other, and Isaac tells me again how much he loves me. I don’t say it back, content enough with hearing it. And after a while Isaac and I go to his truck to continue our night, gluing the pieces of us back together, ignoring the hairline fractures we can’t quite cover.

CHAPTER FIVE

ISAAC SUGGESTS WE GO TO OFF CAMPUS TO GRAB a bite to eat. It's a small café where students go to order fries or smoke cigarettes on the front patio. I spend the drive listening to him recount the game, pitch by pitch, all the way to the final out that snapped their three-game winning streak. When he's done talking, he intertwines his fingers with mine and pulls my hand to his mouth, where he kisses it sweetly—our earlier fight far from his mind. But not entirely from mine.

A headache has started behind my eyes, a dull thud that keeps me from being completely engaged in our conversation. During dinner, I nod and smile in just the right places, but Isaac's frustration resonates with me, making the night a bit surreal. I shake it off before we leave, and press my lips into a smile as he puts his arm around me in the parking lot and kisses the top of my head.

On the way home, Isaac gets a call from Jason. I can hear Jason's booming voice, boisterous and loud, as he asks Isaac to come over for a card game. Isaac hesitates, glancing over at me like he'd rather spend the night just the two of us. I, however, nod emphatically. Hanging out with Jason has been a blast—times that have made me feel completely normal. And I'm craving a moment of that normalcy right now.

Isaac smiles at my excitement and agrees, telling Jason he's on his way. When he hangs up the phone, I lean in and give Isaac a kiss on the lips, distracting him while he drives. He laughs, trying to keep his eyes on the road as I kiss him again, my hand on his thigh. I've missed him, even though he's been right here.

There are a few cars in front of Jason's house, and Isaac parks halfway down the street at the curb. The remainder of the light has faded beneath a gray cloud-scattered night sky. We're reminiscing about the batting cages when Isaac and I climb the porch steps.

Isaac knocks on the front door before opening it partly and calling in our arrival. He pokes his head in and says hey, pushing open the door the rest of the way for me. I'm smiling, comforted by a less crowded version of Jason's house. There is a round table set up in the living room, three guys sitting around. I recognize at least two of them from the party last week.

"Hey," I call to Jason, holding up my hand in a wave. There's only one empty chair at the table, and I glance around at the faces of the other guys. It only takes a second for me to register that something's wrong. Isaac's already on his way over to them to slap hands, completely oblivious.

My smile fades quickly. A toilet flushes in another room; my heartbeat booms in my ears. Adrenaline begins to rush through my veins.

Jason hasn't answered my greeting. His lower jaw is jutted out, his eyes narrowed with disgust. The good-natured teddy bear I spent time with is gone. I glance at the others, finding the same reaction to me.

Isaac's expression falters when no one immediately acknowledges him. And in that moment, I think we both realize the truth. *They know.* Panic flashes in Isaac's eyes, and he turns to me just as footsteps echo in the hallway, quickly approaching.

Kyle enters the room and stammers to a stop, stunned that I'm standing in front of her. At first her face flashes an instant of joy at seeing her best friend again. But it twists into grief, and then anger. Hatred.

I turn to Isaac, and he looks up and sees Kyle. He blinks quickly and steps back from the table of guys, shoving his hands nervously in his pockets. "Hey, Kyle," he says in a quiet, raspy voice.

Kyle stomps past me, banging her shoulder into mine. The force of it knocks me sideways. "Jesus, Isaac," she says in a worried tone. She goes to pause in front of him, looking him over like she's trying to determine if he's been injured. "Are you okay?"

He swallows hard. "Yeah, of course."

Kyle casts a hateful glare in my direction and then puts her hand on Isaac's arm. "I'm sorry we had to do it this way," she says. "But you're ignoring my calls. Look, I know you're grieving, believe me I know." Isaac pulls away from her touch, annoyed at her tone. She reasserts herself, gripping his hands. "That's not her," Kyle says, her voice cracking. "You know that's not Catalina."

She doesn't say it like she's angry. She says it like she misses her best friend. Like she's worried for Isaac. Behind them, Jason rubs his face as if overcome. Then he bangs his fist on the table, making the glasses rattle.

"I can't believe you, man," he says to Isaac. "Why didn't you tell me? She died! How could you not tell me that your girlfriend died?" He looks over at me, bitterly. "How could you bring one of those things into my house?"

A sickened sound escapes from my throat, a swift pain stealing my breath. I press my lips hard together to keep from crying, but my eyes well up nonetheless. *One of those things.* Jason was my friend. I thought he was my friend.

Isaac moves back from the table, glaring at all of them. But nothing can distract me from the way they hate me. This can't be happening.

"You're disgusting," Jason says to me, tears dripping down his cheeks. "What you've done . . ." He holds up his hands like he can't bear the enormity of my deceit. "He was grieving and you took advantage of that. What are you? What the fuck are you that you could do this to another human being?"

What am I? What am I? the voice repeats in my head. The headache that started earlier begins to throb, the pressure building behind my eyes.

"Just get out!" Kyle snaps at me, pointing to the door.

I don't move; I'm not leaving without Isaac. I dart a look at him, but before our eyes can lock, there's a flurry of movement. Kyle's across the room and inches from my face.

"Get out of our lives!" she shouts, bits of spit hitting my cheeks. Her expression is wild, angry. All of her grief tightened into a ball of hatred, directed at me. It's easier if she can blame someone for the loss of her friend. It takes the sharp edges off her ache. She wants me annihilated because maybe if I'm gone, she will stop being reminded of her best friend's death.

In the moment that I'm lost in my head, I don't notice her cock back her arm. I register Kyle's movement at the same time her fist connects with my jaw, sending a vibration through my face and into my head, cracking my carefully constructed reality.

I fall back, off balance, ears ringing. I drop hard onto the wood floor, catching myself to take much of the force with my shoulder. My wrist aches, and I clutch it to my chest with my other hand as I lift my eyes to Kyle's. She covers her mouth, her knuckles still white from her clenched fist. She looks horrified by her actions.

She hit me, I think, stunned. *She hates me so much that she hit me.*

I'm a pile of rubble on the floor, and when I look at Isaac, the sight of me, pathetic and torn down, makes his face go red with anger. He tries to rush toward me, but Jason jumps up from the table and wraps his large arms around Isaac's upper body, holding him back.

"Just let her go," Jason growls into his ear. "You have to let her go, man."

The room erupts in chaos. I watch, devastated by the scene. Isaac yelling, saying that he needs me. Jason pleading with him to calm down. Kyle's guilty looks in my direction before she returns to Isaac, begging him to end this. Tonight was an intervention. Isaac's friends had an intervention to cut the poison out of his life. To cut me out.

Jason lowers his voice, his tight grip turning into a hug. Isaac closes his eyes, listening to whatever Jason is saying. His body starts to shake, going limp. "Stop," Isaac says, breaking down. "Stop." Jason turns him around and holds him up. Isaac cries against his shoulder. "Make it stop," he murmurs.

My tears are warm as they rush down my face, over my aching jaw. Kyle drops into a seat at the table, burying her face in her hands. Isaac's sobs get louder, racked with pain.

I am no longer his girlfriend. I am a pariah.

I'm shaking, cold from the inside out. My soul has finally worn too thin. I climb up from the floor, moaning softly at the pain in my shoulder and wrist. At the blistering headache that's left me slightly disoriented. I walk soundlessly to the door and slip outside. I close it behind me, looking at the road, the sky, the grassy lawns.

Numbly, I move down the steps and turn in what I think is

probably the direction of my house. I'll have to call for a ride, I guess. I wince, the pressure in my head almost too much to take. I can't remember who to call, so I keep walking.

"What do you want to be when you grow up?" a mother asked me once. I can't remember which one.

It was a terrible question to ask a ten-year-old. I wasn't sure if she wanted the actual answer or the answer her daughter would have given. I sat there thinking for so long that my head began to hurt.

What did I want to be? A closer—no, never. I only did that because my father asked me to, told me how good I was at helping people. I didn't want to be a doctor like him and Marie. I wasn't sure what else there was.

I looked up at the mother, studying her pretty features, her soft cheeks and pink lips. "I want to be you," I said. I meant her job, even though I didn't know what it was. But something about my words made her face cloud over. She straightened, backing away from me. She tried to force a smile, but I saw fear instead. I didn't understand at the time what I'd done wrong. Eventually I finished that assignment and moved on.

Now I know what she was afraid of. People don't want to be replaced. They don't want a stranger to come in and seamlessly take over their lives. Because that would mean they didn't really matter. What was the point of them ever existing if I could come in and wrap it all up in a few days? I'm a walking nightmare.

The lights of a car behind me illuminate the street, and I hug my arms around myself. I try to fade away so I won't be noticed. Rain has started to fall, and as the vehicle slows next to me, I realize it's a truck. I turn quickly just as Isaac pulls to the curb.

I'm frozen with fear, with misery. I don't want to hurt him, but more than anything, I don't want him to tell me this meant nothing.

Isaac gets out of the truck and rounds the hood, his face lit up by the headlights. Even from here I can see that his eyes are red and swollen. His face is drawn. My guilt overwhelms me.

"I'm sorry," I call to him, fresh tears springing to my eyes. Isaac continues toward me, and I flinch back just as he reaches out and wraps his arms around me. I take in a breath, waiting, but he's holding me. His fingers slide into my wet hair, cradling my head; his lips brush my ear.

My fear starts to dissipate, and I close my eyes. Close out the pounding that's still behind them. Isaac sways me, rocking me gently, and neither of us says a word as the rain soaks us through. After a few moments he pulls back, wipes the mascara from under my eyes with his thumbs. Checks over where my jaw still hurts. He leans in and kisses my lips.

I see in his eyes that his friends' words haven't changed the way he feels. Although that should comfort me, it doesn't. It only leaves me more confused. Isaac cradles my face in his hands, staring down at me as rain runs over us.

"They can't see you," he says. "But I do. You're right here, Catalina. You never left."

I open my mouth to talk, but no words come out. My thoughts flash back to Jason's expression tonight—the disgust. I think about my sister, my parents. I think back to the first day I met Isaac, wearing a prom dress. "This isn't my life," I mumble, the cold making my voice shake.

Isaac tightens his jaw and gathers me into a hug. "Yes it is," he whispers. "Things just got screwed up tonight, but we'll fix it. Everything will be fine tomorrow. I promise. Now let's go home, okay?" He pulls back to look down at me, checking me over as if daring me to tell him again this isn't real.

But I don't know what's right anymore. I'm weak and cold, beaten down. I nod and let Isaac help me into his truck, the world hazy around me. When Isaac gets in the driver's seat, he gives me a worried glance. I must look terrible. I almost flip down the mirror, but I can't stand the idea of seeing my face.

My body continues to shake, and Isaac blasts the heat. It warms my skin, but I can't get rid of the cold. I lean my head against the passenger window, my thoughts jumbled. My identity is slipping away—but rather than pull it back, I close my eyes and let it go. It hurts too much to pretend anymore. My head just hurts.

"You're almost home," Isaac says, sounding concerned.

"Which home?" I murmur. I don't think he hears me over the sound of the blowing heater, but soon he's pulling up to a familiar grand house on a tree-lined street. I stare at it a minute, confused, and feel Isaac's hand touch mine.

I turn to him, study his features. I feel lost. Isaac takes a deep breath, staring down at the center console, deeply troubled.

"I don't care what they think, you know?" he says, his voice taking on a tremor. "They want to take you away, but they don't understand. You won't leave me again, Catalina. You love me."

Tears wash down Isaac's face and I watch him, unable to do anything to make this better. His grief settles over me instead, too much to absorb any longer. I place my palm on his tear-soaked cheek. Isaac lifts his eyes to mine, his emotions stripped down and bare. "Don't cry," I whisper.

He stares at me for a long moment, and then leans in to kiss me. I put my hand on his chest, holding him back just enough to break contact. There's a flicker of images through my head—different places, people. Real memories and manufactured ones. I don't know which belong to me anymore.

"I love you," Isaac whispers, his breath warm on my lips. But the words are slightly off. Wrong in a way I can't identify. I push him back and press myself against the passenger door, staring at him with an increasing anxiety. Forgetting and remembering his face. Forgetting my own.

"I'm not Catalina," I say in a different voice, a familiar one. Isaac takes in a sharp breath as if I've slapped him. "You're not in love with me," I continue, starting to cry. "And I'm not in love with you. I'm not real, Isaac."

He stares at me, fresh tears gathering in his eyes. "Shut up," he murmurs. "You're Catalina Barnes. You're just confused."

I shake my head, horrified that I don't know if he's telling the truth or not. I just know that I don't *feel* like Catalina.

Isaac rubs roughly at his face, and when he looks at me again, he's not angry. He's desperate. "Why are you doing this?" he asks, his teeth bared like he's in pain. "Why are you *lying*?"

"I'm not her."

"Yes you are!" he shouts, making me flinch back. "You're the . . . the love of my . . ." His eyes weaken and the rest of the words get lost in his sobs. Isaac falls apart completely, his body slumped forward as he begs for me to come back, even though I'm sitting next to him. I realize then that he's no longer talking to me. He's talking to Catalina.

And I no longer exist.

CHAPTER SIX

IT WAS ALMOST TWO YEARS AGO, AND I HAD JUST turned sixteen. There was only a day left on my current assignment, and the father was with me in the kitchen, frying up bacon. Now and again he'd turn away to run his finger down a list of printed items, reciting them to me.

He'd told me and Marie when we got there that, in preparation for our arrival, he'd made a list of pieces of advice he never told his daughter before she died. I didn't know the details of her death—I think her name was Miranda—but I do know she was murdered. The killer had been caught, but her father had been unable to move on due to the circumstances. Marie stayed with me for this case, which was an unusual arrangement, but I welcomed her help with this one.

She was still asleep in the guest room as my father read

items fifteen through twenty-five. But it was at the last one that he paused, choking up. I stared across the room at the back of his flannel shirt, curious about what he was going to say.

He steadied himself, and moved the bacon off the burner, the acrid smell of charred pig starting to fill the room. "Make sure the boy you marry wants you for you," he said, his voice cracking. "Because you deserve the best kind of love."

I'd felt those words then, felt them for a grieving father who would never attend his daughter's wedding. Never meet her husband or her kids. Never see her love anybody.

But now I feel them in a different way. What do I deserve?

Isaac continues to mourn in the driver's seat, and my sympathy grows. I reach over to touch his shoulder, but he moves back against the door and doesn't look at me. "Get out," he says in a thick voice. It's a dagger to my heart. "Get out of my truck."

I stare at him for a moment, rejected. Ashamed. I nod even though he can't see, and numbly reach for the door handle. I climb out and Isaac doesn't stop me.

My body flinches against the cold air, and I stagger, another sharp pain behind my eyes. I wince and put my palm over my forehead. It's like there's a vise squeezing my temples to crush my skull. I blink my eyes open and closed several times. The world tilts slightly, disorienting me even more.

I glance at the house, desperate to be inside and out of sight. Away from this world. I jog for the front door, hoping to acclimate myself. I just need to think so the confusion will clear up.

The front door of the house is unlocked, and I bust in like I'm running from someone. I trip over my feet and have to quickly steady myself against the wall.

"Catalina?" my mother calls, jumping up from the couch. She's wearing a pink set of flowered pajamas, and I gaze at her. "Honey, what's wrong?"

This is wrong, I think with a streak of fear. *That's not my mother.* I spin around the entryway, not recognizing some of the pieces. "Where are the mirrors?" I ask. "The flannel coat? I don't . . ."

The woman comes over and puts her hands on my forearms. I jump, banging into the wall. A picture falls and smashes on the floor near my feet. I yelp, backing away from the shattered glass. On the floor is a picture of my family. *Not my family,* I correct, darting my gaze around the room, looking for something, anything, familiar.

The edges of my world start going fuzzy, and I run my palm over my face. *What is this house?* I think. I stop, and stare at the lady in front of me. "Where are my things?" I ask her. "There should be things to remind me; without them . . . I float away."

Fear tears through my chest, and I push past her and run into the kitchen. There are memories of frying bacon and talk of boys and marriage. I turn back to the woman in pink pajamas as she enters the room; her face has gone stark white. She's staring at me, wide-eyed.

"This isn't me," I tell her, dropping into a chair at the table.

"This isn't my house. Isn't my life. I let mine go and now I can't find it. There's nothing familiar to pull me back. I don't know who I am."

The woman rushes past me and grabs her black purse off the counter. I watch her, my breathing labored as I try to get a grip on my mind. "Do you know me?" I ask her helplessly. When she turns, she's holding a pill bottle. She moves quickly to grab a glass and fills it at the sink. I ask her again, but she refuses to answer. She's scared, but I don't understand why she can't just tell me my name.

"Emily?" I ask hopefully. The woman shakes out two pills into her palm and thrusts them in my direction. I pinch them in my fingers, staring down at them. "Susan?" The woman gives me the glass of water and brushes back my hair.

"Shh . . . ," she says kindly. "Take these. You'll feel better."

I want to feel better. But I want to remember first. *Think, damn it. Who are you?* Different faces flash though my head. I'm everyone.

I set my water on the table and then lay the pills out in my open palm, examining them. "What are these?" I ask her. The house is too cold and I'm shivering.

The woman picks up the glass and tries to put it in my hand again. "Just something to help you relax," she says. "Dr. McKee prescribed them for you. Do you want me to call him?"

McKee? My eyes snap to hers, and I jump up from the chair, nearly making her drop the glass. Startled, she backs up until she's against the counter. I'm struck with a weird sense of déjà vu. "Quinlan McKee," I say out loud to the room, as if arguing with myself. The name is a shock to my system, a cold slap in the face. I'm a closer, but I've been away for too long. Something has gone wrong.

Tears sting my eyes, and my headache won't dissipate. My jaw hurts. My head starts to go fuzzy again, and I look down at the pills in my hand. "No," I say. I turn over my palm, dropping the pills onto the tile floor. "I don't want any pills," I tell her. "I have to get out of here."

My limbs are heavy, but I rush from the room and into the hallway. At the other end a door opens, and a large man with a big mustache pokes his head out, looking sleepy. He holds up his hand as if say hello to me, but I immediately try the first door on my right, finding only a bathroom. The woman appears at the other end of the hall and I'm trapped.

"Honey," she says. "Please calm down. I'm going to call somebody to help you."

I try the next door, and when I open it, it's a bedroom. I rush inside and then slam and lock the door, resting my forehead against it until there's a soft knock on the other side. I step back, my teeth beginning to shatter. "I need to think," I tell the people on the other side. I try to call up my memories, but none of them will stick. It's almost impossible to tell which ones are real, which are part of the assignment.

I run my hands through my wet hair, looking around. *I am Quinlan,* I think, but then the idea gets further away. Other faces pop into my mind, smiling girls. Online journals and video. This isn't right; there should be something—a tether.

There was a picture, I remember desperately. I run to the trash, falling to my knees next to the desk. But when I tip it over, the bin is empty.

"No," I say. "Where is it? There was a picture!"

I pull my knees up to my chest, hugging them to me. I lower my pounding head, trying to piece together my identity. I try to call up the picture, but the image is fuzzy. But where did I get it in the first place? Where is my home?

"Deacon," I murmur, lifting my head. I have to find Deacon.

I use the desk to pull myself up. I'm unsteady, but gaining purpose. I spy a set of keys on the top of the dresser, and I snatch them up and race for the closet. There's a backpack on the floor and I grab a couple of items of clothing and shove them inside. I pull the straps over my shoulders and listen for a moment. The hallway has gone quiet, and I imagine the woman is on the phone, calling for help. I don't want to be here when that help arrives.

I slide open the window and slip outside, dropping onto the ground. Splatters of rain hit my face, and I look up. It's raining again. Or is it always raining?

The key to the Jetta is marked, and I quickly get inside, tossing my backpack onto the passenger seat. I have the vague idea that Deacon lives in Corvallis, but I don't have a way to get ahold of him. I don't remember his number, and I don't know where a phone is anyway. I step on the gas, back out of the driveway, and race toward the freeway, hoping muscle memory will take me where I need to go. The pain in my head is nearly unbearable—it's probably dangerous for me to drive. But I need help. I need something familiar.

The drive is torturous, and no matter what I do, I can't warm up. I've avoided my reflection in the mirror, terrified of what I'll see. Who I'll see. My senses tell me I'm Quinlan McKee, but then there's also Catalina Barnes. *No,* I think. *She was the assignment.* At least I think she was the assignment.

Even though an image of Deacon comes to mind, I can't place him, can't figure out how I know him. My body is on autopilot and I find the exit for Corvallis. The landmarks start to look vaguely familiar, but I can't hold on to any specific memory. I think I'm broken.

My panic continues to grow as random images flash through my mind, splitting open my head with too much information. Too many people. I find the street near the college, sure I'm going in the right direction. I see the small house with a big porch, and now the pain starts in my chest. It starts in my heart.

I shut off the car, shaking uncontrollably as I wait in the driveway. I've lost my identity and I'm not sure how to get it back. What if I'm stuck like this—a collage of other people's lives? Who am I with other people's memories?

I open the door, and the sound of rain hitting the car drowns out my staggered breaths. The rain has soaked through my shirt, and I wrap my arms around myself. It doesn't help.

What if I really am Catalina Barnes and I just ran out of

my house? What if Quinlan is the assignment and I'm confused? Or I could be someone else entirely. I look at Deacon's darkened porch and debate driving back to Lake Oswego, demanding that the woman in the pink pajamas explain everything to me.

I'm so alone. I'm so alone it's like there's a hole in my chest and my life is bleeding out. I don't want to be empty anymore.

I start toward the house, my feet sloshing in my shoes. The soles squeak as I climb the steps, and once under the cover of the porch roof, I ring the doorbell, holding myself up with my palm against the door frame.

The light clicks on above me, and I wipe absently at the rain that's running off my hair onto my forehead. When the door opens, Deacon is first silhouetted against the light in his hallway. I can't see his face. What if I don't know him? What if I'm completely crazy? I cover my mouth, starting to cry because I'm so damn scared.

Deacon springs forward and grabs me, pulling me to him. He's wearing a thin white cotton T-shirt, and his skin is hot in comparison to mine. I can't talk because my teeth are chattering so hard. I close my eyes, pressing my sore cheek into his chest, flattening my hand over his heart.

"What happened?" he asks. He runs his palms over my arms to warm me up. "Jesus, Quinn. Are you okay?"

Quinn. Slowly, I pull back and look up at him. He doesn't hesitate in touching me, brushing away the water running over my forehead, holding my face as his gaze travels over me.

"What is this?" he asks, running his finger delicately over my jaw. His posture hardens and he darts an enraged look into the darkness beyond the porch. "Who did this to you?" he demands.

"I don't remember," I say. I stare at him, recognizing his eyes, his mouth. I like all of his pieces, like how they're put together. "I'm cold," I say in a small voice. The sound of it seems to weaken him, and he wraps his arm around my shoulders and walks me inside the house.

"I've got you," he says gently. "I'm here." He turns and scans the porch, and after seeing nothing in the rain, he closes the door and bolts it.

CHAPTER SEVEN

I'M SHAKING—MY WET CLOTHES CLINGING TO MY body, my lips quivering.

"You're freezing," Deacon murmurs, and brings me into the living room. He sets me down on the couch and grabs the blanket from the cushion behind me, wraps it over my shoulders.

"How long have you been in the rain?" he asks, kneeling in front of me to unlace my shoes. When he removes my sneaker, water pours from the heel. He groans, annoyed that I'd be so careless, and peels off my socks. The minute my skin touches air, my toes feel a little nicer.

"I don't remember," I tell him for the second time. "Maybe a while. I was walking in it, I think."

"God, Quinn," he snaps, clearly pissed off. "Who's watching out for you? They can't just—" He stops and glances up, apologetic for his tone. He motions to my face. "We should put some ice on that before it bruises," he says more gently.

I reach to touch my jaw, but the pain has started to fade. "Doesn't matter if it does," I tell him. "I can't stand to look at myself. Deacon . . . I don't know who I am."

His expression falls, his eyes widening at my statement. "What do you mean?" he asks, sounding terrified.

"I can't remember who I am," I say. "I'm not sure what's real anymore."

Deacon curses, shaking his head. "I told them it was too soon." He reaches to take my hands, leveling our gazes. "You're real," he says sternly. My mind is swirling, unsure, and I squeeze my fingers between his, testing the feeling. It's foreign, as if this is the fake life.

I stare down at our hands, unclear of our relationship. Our past. "He loves me, you know," I say quietly. Deacon flinches. "Isaac told me he loves me."

Deacon is quiet for a long moment, and I look over to find his face haunted. "And do you love him?" he asks.

"I thought maybe I did."

Deacon pulls away and drops back into a sitting position on the floor. He bends his knees, rests his elbows on them, and puts his hand over his forehead to block his eyes. "Well, fuck," he murmurs.

I feel his reaction in my chest, a bright pain that spreads outward from my heart. He's devastated at the thought of me loving someone else. "He thinks I'm Catalina," I say. I'm scared of the next question. "Am I?"

Deacon's throat clicks as he swallows, and when he drops his arm, I see the skin around his eyes has reddened, his emotions bleeding through. "No," he says. He crawls back over to pause in front of me, but he doesn't touch me again. "You are not Catalina."

I don't know what to think. I run my fingers through my wet hair, noticing the short length. My mind flips back and forth between my memories, a picture of me and Isaac, him staring adoringly at the side of my face. "No," I say uncertainly. "I am Catalina Barnes." My voice cracks, and I'm overcome with the heaviest sense of loss. Too heavy to carry. Too dark. Too painful.

"You're not her," Deacon says, moving closer. I'm still shivering, but the heat from his body is fire next to me, radiating warmth.

My memories continue to swirl, but then I remember thinking that Deacon is always here for me. But not anymore. Now it's Isaac. But Isaac can't help me. I can't tell him how I feel because I don't want to make him sad.

"Quinn," Deacon says in a voice that's utterly heartbroken. "Come back. Be here with me." He takes my hand again and brings it against his mouth like he's pleading with me. "Please," he murmurs into my skin.

I blink slowly, watching him as he starts to unravel, worried sick that I'll never come back to reality. Worried that he's lost me for good. The pain in my head flashes bright white, and I squeeze my eyes shut. In that moment I think of Deacon—a memory that I lost somewhere along the way.

* * *

"I have the perfect place," Deacon said, propped up on his elbows while we lay in the overgrown grass in my backyard. He had a red pen, and he was drawing a tattoo on my ribs, tickling me with each stroke.

"Don't say your bedroom," I said, and laughed.

He flashed me a smile, but then leaned in closer to see his art. "No," he said. "That's your perfect place. No, I'm thinking we'll go to Europe. New identities, espionage, all that shit."

I smiled, turning my head to watch him as I lay on my back. "That's the stupidest idea I've ever heard. Besides," I said, "we both have a while on our contracts, so maybe we can pick a place closer to town."

He stopped drawing, glancing up at me. His eyes holding mine, he leaned in and kissed my skin, right where he was drawing. My eyes fluttered closed and I ran my fingers through his hair. He kissed me again.

"Your dad is never going to let you out of your contract," he said, slowly kissing his way up my body. "So Europe, fake mustaches, all of that is in our future." When his mouth got to my neck and he slid his body over mine, I decided I'd go wherever he wanted. He stilled, just short of kissing my lips.

I gazed up at him, completely and totally in love. "Let's run away together," I whispered. To that he smiled—broad and handsome. And then he leaned down and kissed me.

* * *

I take in a sharp breath, the world around me slowly coming back into focus, coming alive as the pieces fill in around me. Deacon is still watching me, lost in his concern, murmuring that I'll be all right, he's sure of it.

"I'm Quinlan McKee," I say weakly. Deacon chokes out a relieved cry. "I drive a beat-up old Honda," I continue, "with the check-engine light on."

Deacon laughs, wiping away the tears that have streamed down his cheeks. "Yeah," he says. "Yeah, your car's a piece of shit."

"And I'm here with you," I tell him, the numbness fading from my skin, my blood circulating again as if I've been holding it frozen in my veins. I look around, taking in Deacon's living room. There are papers and magazines strewn about, like he was in the middle of research. There are embers in the fire although it's nearly summer. Drawings doodled on the backs of pages, some that look like me. Everything's different but still the same. But I'm alive. I'm home.

When I turn back to Deacon, he smiles. "Hey," he says quietly, as if I've only just shown up and didn't come into his house like an emotional tornado.

"Hey." I take a breath and exhale, deep and cleansing. This was what I needed, who I needed to see to remember. I gave him all of my trust once, and because of that, he holds my identity. He can always remind me of who I am.

"Tell me what you need," Deacon says. "Do you want another blanket? Are you hungry? Because I can make you something to eat."

He's good to me. Despite the hurt in our past, I know he cares deeply. And I loved him madly—I think I still do. Those beautiful brown eyes, his serious expression. The freckles across the bridge of his nose. His is the face I see when I think of home.

I reach to comb my fingers through his hair, brushing it aside and off his forehead, gazing at him. Letting my hand run over his cheek, onto his shoulder, down his arm.

This touch is different and he senses it; his chest rises and falls a little faster. He gets up on his knees to come closer, wanting this as much as I do. Everything about him warms to me, calls to me. I lean in and kiss him.

My lips brush over his, softly at first. He tastes like cinnamon and my heart beats recklessly. I kiss him harder. There's a light touch as he licks my lower lip, and I moan, aching for him. He deepens our kiss, sending sparks all over my body. I'm wild and careless; I clutch at his shirt to drag him closer. Deacon pauses, breathing fast against me like he's afraid he's losing control.

"Don't stop," I murmur, wanting to be lost with him. Lost and free.

Without hesitation our mouths crash together again. Deacon yanks off my wet T-shirt, growling his approval when I tug at his. He pushes me back on the couch and pulls at the rest of my clothes, kissing his way down my body. His touch burns my skin and I love it. I love him.

I close my eyes, reminded of our every moment, our every feeling. And it isn't until later, when we're pressed together on this small, cushioned space, that he holds himself above me, breathless and shaky.

"What are we doing, Quinn?" he asks.

"Being more than friends," I tell him.

He doesn't laugh, doesn't say anything else. Instead he looks down at me, completely and utterly defenseless. *He's mine,* I think.

I reach for him, let him consume me. We block out the entire world, and we're left with just us. There's no more pretending or protecting—I give in. We both do. And this time we try to give each other what we've both always wanted most: love, the kind we don't have to say.

I slept in Deacon's bed last night, not in Catalina's, where her parents have probably been up waiting. Maybe they've called Marie, called my father. Instead of worrying about it, I snuggle against Deacon, my thigh over his while he plays with my hair. He was here when I woke up late this morning, long past my internal alarm. He was with me all night. He's different now—I can feel it. He's no longer scared of getting too close to me.

With my fingernail, I trace a heart shape into his skin just above where his heart would be. I draw a little arrow stabbing through it, and hear him laugh.

"That's you," he says. "The arrow in my heart."

"So I'm a wound?"

"Definitely. Deep one too. Lots of scar tissue."

I slap his chest, and he rolls me over, pinning me beneath him. He kisses me on the nose, and then stares down at me.

He looks thoughtful for a moment, and then uses his thumb to scrub my cheek, like he's rubbing off makeup. He smiles, does it again to the other side. "There you are," he whispers. He leans down to kiss my lips and then smiles at me again. "Missed this face," he says. "Missed kissing it."

I laugh and push him off, but like magnets we're snuggling close again. The room is warm, and outside, a bit of light filters in through the gauzy curtains. Shining right on us. My headache is gone; my heart is contented. I told Deacon everything about my time as Catalina Barnes, even the parts where I totally screwed up.

"Still can't believe that girl sucker punched you," Deacon says, not even the slightest bit amused. "What a bitch."

I exhale, relieved it didn't bruise beyond a slight red mark. "She was grieving," I say, although I shouldn't make an excuse for her violence. But in truth, I understand it. Isaac and I were living in a fantasy world—we needed to be stopped.

"I think I've made things worse for that entire family," I tell Deacon. He shifts beneath me, and I know he doesn't really want to talk about it. Mentioning that I thought I might love Isaac was a bit of a dagger, I'm sure, especially after how hurt Deacon had looked at the batting cages. Of course, I understand now that I really didn't love Isaac. I mean, yes, I was attracted to him, but more than anything, I liked the way he felt about Catalina. I liked having a normal life where we could be together and do normal couple things. I liked how easy it was with him. At least for a while.

"What should I do?" I ask Deacon.

He's quiet, thinking it over. "We leave," he says. "I'll get us tickets to wherever you want to go. We don't tell Marie or Aaron. We definitely don't tell your dad." He tightens his arms around me. "We just go."

I sit up and look at him, my eyebrows pulled together. "And leave that family to suffer?" I ask, incredulous. "I made them worse, Deacon. How can I live with that?"

"It's not your fault," he says, adjusting the blanket as he moves to rest against the headboard. "This is all on your father."

"Stop," I say, exhausted with him always heaping the blame on my dad. Yes, my father shouldn't have sent me, but I'm the one who failed.

Deacon sighs and stares up at the ceiling, trying to compose himself. "Fine," he concedes. "Do you want help finding another closer to go in and finish it?"

I lower my eyes, a small twinge of jealousy hitting me at the idea of another person taking my place, even if it's my place as a replacement. I begin to chew on my thumbnail, trying to imagine how I could adjust the family's therapy, redirect them in time for the party on Friday. I shake my head, looking at Deacon and knowing he's not going to like my answer. "It has to be me," I tell him.

He tightens his jaw. "You almost lost yourself," he says in a controlled voice. "You can't go back there. No."

"I have to," I say. "I owe it to her parents. And to Isaac."

"You don't," he disagrees. "You really don't owe anyone

anything, Quinn. You can walk away. We can walk away."

"I have to put this right. After that, I'll talk to my dad. See what can be done about the contract. But I won't turn my back on the Barnes family. It's not right."

Deacon stares at me like he can't believe what I'm saying. "What else do I need to do?" he asks. "I'll give you anything, Quinn. But what else can I possibly do to make you stay?"

"This isn't about us."

"It is to me!" he says, raising his voice. "I made a mistake eight months ago, I know that. It killed me to see what I'd done to you, how I'd hurt you. I promised myself I wouldn't do it again. I promise it every time. And then you came here last night. I was defenseless. I was completely open to you. So what, Quinn? You let me back in so that you could leave me? Tear out my heart and punish me?"

"I'm not punishing you, Deacon!"

"That's what it feels like! If you care about me at all, you'll quit your contract. Right now."

"You can't ask that!"

His mouth tightens as he fights back his tears, his face raw with emotion. He takes my arms and pulls me to my knees in front of him. We stare at each other, and I watch him try not to fall apart. His breaths are quick and shallow as he leans to rest his forehead against mine. He closes his eyes. "Please," he whispers. "Please, Quinlan."

And it breaks my heart when I murmur back, "I'm sorry."

* * *

After a shower and a change of clothes, I'm downstairs in the front entryway, my backpack straps over my shoulders. Deacon is sitting on the wooden staircase, staring at his feet. I wait a beat and then call his name. His face is miserable when he looks at me between the slats of the railing.

"You saved me last night," I tell him. "Thank you." My heart is begging me to stay with him, but I won't be that selfish. I couldn't live with myself if I left that family to suffer. The fact that Deacon could makes me question if we belong together at all. Maybe closers aren't meant to love each other. How can we when the world thinks we're heartless? They could be right.

Deacon holds my eyes for only a second, and then looks away. "Take care of yourself, Quinlan," he says coldly, as if I'm a total stranger. The sound is a slap in the face, so reminiscent of the day he broke up with me that it sends a chill down my spine.

I press my lips together, holding back the tirade of broken-hearted words I want to yell at him. He knows how he affects me, how he hurts me. I wait for him to look over and apologize, but he doesn't. Last night, I thought we'd changed. But it's clear we haven't.

I close my eyes and turn my back on Deacon. I swipe under my eyes before any tears can fall, harden myself against the outside world, and open the door. I'll leave this baggage here, stow it while I finish my job.

Without another word I walk out Deacon's front door and slam it shut behind me.

CHAPTER EIGHT

I HALF EXPECT THERE TO BE A ROADBLOCK WHEN I return to Lake Oswego, but the town is as picturesque as it was that first day. I've called Isaac's phone several times, but he hasn't answered. Once I smooth things over with my parents, I'll find him. I'll make sure he's okay.

My heart has begun beating faster as I worry about Mr. and Mrs. Barnes' reaction to my outburst last night, my disappearance. They might not even let me back into their house. I have to be prepared for that.

I pull up in the driveway, worried when I see both of their cars parked out front, along with a white Lexus I don't recognize. It's not Marie's or my father's, but who knows who could have been sent in their place. I park and then take a minute to gather my courage.

I walk up to the house, debating whether I should knock or just enter. My face is makeup free, but ultimately, I'm going to try to act like Catalina. I take on her persona and facial expressions the minute I walk in the door.

"Ah," a man in a gray suit says without missing a beat. "And there she is." He smiles warmly from the couch; my parents are seated in chairs across from him. I look between him and my family, trying not to let my confusion show. The man turns back to them. "Told you she'd be along shortly."

He stands, brushing his hands over his slacks to smooth them out. He has salt-and-pepper hair and a neatly trimmed beard. From my experience I see that he carries himself like a doctor, and I wonder if he's been sent by my father.

"Catalina," he says, nodding to me, "I told your family that you needed a short break, and that we had failed by not providing you one. I take it you've been able to sort things out and have returned to prepare for your party?"

"Yes," I say carefully, and then look behind him to my parents. "Sorry if I scared you," I say. "I had . . . I had a tough night and I should have handled it better. Or at least asked for help." I'm uncomfortable with my lie in this man's presence. I can't read him, not like I can read most people. I have no idea what he's thinking beneath this polished exterior.

My mother grabs on to her husband's arm, swaying with relief. "We're just glad you're okay," she says. "I was so worried."

I press my lips into an apology, scared when I look at my father that he'll be angry. But instead he's just happy that I'm back. The transition is easier than I imagined it would be, and I wonder if this man prepared them for it. I take my backpack off my shoulders, about to go to my room to fix my makeup, when the older man reaches out his arm to me, like he wants me to take it.

"Would you walk me out, Catalina?" he asks kindly. I look between him and my parents, waiting for them to call him out for being creepy. My mother takes a step toward him.

"Thank you, Dr. Pritchard," she says. My stomach sinks, and I flash a look at the man. He turns away to tell my mother it was no trouble at all, but my heart is racing. He's Arthur Pritchard. He's the one who created the remedy, and this assignment was at his request. *Shit.* He must know how badly I screwed it up.

Although I don't want to, I drop my bag and take Arthur Pritchard's arm, smiling politely at him. I tell my parents I'll be right back, wishing they would stop me. I'm afraid the doctor is going to chew me out, or worse, throw me in the back of his car and drive me straight to therapy.

I don't let any of my fear show as we walk onto the front porch, and I shut the door behind us. Arthur pauses at the top at the stairs, looking around like he's taking in the scenery. He slides his cool hand over mine, holding me in place. I consider asking him about his daughter—what role Virginia Pritchard has played in all of this. But something in his demeanor tells me it would be dangerous to do so. That this entire conversation would become more dangerous. I swallow hard and look sideways at him.

"So what happens now?" I ask, waiting for the inevitable.

"Well," he reasons, "it depends. Are you competent enough to finish this assignment?"

There's a sting at his words. "I am," I say, wishing his cold hand wasn't over mine so I could move away from him. We'd seem like old friends if my parents were to look out the window, but there's a tension between us that's palpable.

"May I ask where you've been for the last fifteen hours, Miss McKee?" He stares at the flower bed in the yard, admiring it.

"No offense," I say, turning to him, "but it's none of your business."

He chuckles as if I've just made a highbrow joke. His grip on my hand tightens. "Yes, I suppose it isn't. I just don't like when my closers lose contact." He turns to me, his lips pursed. "I worry about them."

I narrow my eyes. "I'm not *your* closer."

"All of you are mine." He pats my hand and then lets go, starts down the stairs without me. He slips his hands into the pockets of his coat and turns to look over his shoulder. "By the way," he asks. "Have you spoken to Deacon Hatcher lately?"

"No," I say, like I'm surprised he asked. He studies me for a moment, and then nods thoughtfully. Inside, my stomach is in knots, and I wonder if he can read my lie. "Well, then," Arthur says pleasantly, "good luck on your assignment, Qu—" He stops and snaps his fingers. "Catalina," he finishes. And then he turns on his loafers and walks to the white Lexus parked in the driveway.

I stand there, stunned, as I watch him drive off. First of all, Arthur Pritchard just came out to my assignment and basically told me to pull my shit together. But more alarming, why did he mention Deacon? How did he even remember his name? They only met once for an evaluation, and Deacon told me he was a stuffy old dude. He left out the part where the good doctor is intimating and creepy. Thanks, Deacon.

Does Arthur Pritchard know where I was? Has he been watching me? Paranoia chills my skin, and I wrap my arms around myself and look at the street. The idea of being spied on is suffocating, and I have to try hard to shake it off. I'm on an assignment. I have to keep my head.

I won't think about Deacon, or even Arthur Prichard. I came back to Lake Oswego for a reason. I need to set this right. I turn toward the house, gathering up my courage, and then I go back inside and find my parents waiting for me on the couch.

I'm a nervous wreck as I go to sit across from them in the seat Arthur Pritchard just vacated. I feel like I'm on a job interview, a really screwed-up one, and I fold my hands neatly in my lap. I'm still wearing my contacts from yesterday, and my eyes are itchy. My freckles are visible, but at this point I'm not sure that matters. I look at my mother, guilt gnawing at my insides. The normally neat house has items out of place, the normal routine of chores ignored.

"I really am sorry for what happened last night," I say, sounding like her daughter. "I've never . . . I didn't mean to freak out. I sincerely apologize."

"No need," she says kindly, waving away my sentiment. She turns to her husband, and he nods as if he knows what she's about to say. My mother looks at me again. "You don't have to pretend anymore," she tells me. "It's okay. *We're* okay."

I don't respond at first, mostly to make sure I understand. Part of my job is to let patients lead their own recovery. Now I need to ascertain if she's saying what I think she is. If this assignment has just ended.

"I'm the one who should apologize. Dr. Pritchard asked us not to talk about it"—she lowers her voice as if he's still listening—"but I feel terrible for not warning you. You should have been prepared."

I narrow my eyes as I concentrate on her words. She's referring to me as a closer, not as her daughter. I've never had a client end the assignment first. It's not against the rules . . . it's just unexpected. It also hurts a little in an entirely selfish way. "What do you mean?" I ask her, Catalina's voice falling away. "Prepared for what?"

She folds her hands in front of her lips, gathering her composure. "Catalina was sick . . . before she died," she says. "The counselors don't want us to dwell on it—they even had us sign a confidentiality agreement to not discuss it—but they should have told you. Last night, you reminded me so much of her. It was terrifying, and I didn't know what to do. I called everyone at the department. This morning, Dr. Pritchard showed up and said it had nothing to do with this case—that breakdowns were a common occurrence for . . . people like you."

On the inside, I bristle at the words "people like you," but I don't let it show. Just yesterday I thought I could have a life with this family, be a part of it. I see now that it could have never worked—no matter how much I wanted it to. With a bit of sadness, I let go of the illusion completely. These are no longer my parents. This is no longer my life. These people want to talk to *me*. Marie can't fault me for that.

"What do you mean when you say Catalina was sick?" I ask carefully, at first uncomfortable being out of character in front of them. But what disturbs me more is Arthur Pritchard's lie. This is *not* a common occurrence. Especially not for me.

Mrs. Barnes winces, and I can see that this is difficult for her. Her husband doesn't step in or cut her off. He lets her talk, and I admire him. The respect he gives her feelings. I have a moment of longing for him to be my real dad, but then Mrs. Barnes starts talking again, and I look away.

"About three months ago," she says quietly, "Catalina and Isaac had an argument. Nothing earth-shattering, but when she came home she sat at the kitchen table and just . . . cried. It was totally unlike her. My Catalina was always joking, happy. This was right around the time she met that Virginia girl, and I guess Isaac didn't really like her. He told me later that he'd only seen her once, but that he thought Virginia was a bad influence on Catalina. Said she was morbid."

"Have you ever met Virginia?" I ask.

"No," Mrs. Barnes says, shaking her head. "And Catalina only mentioned her twice, three times, maybe. Why?"

"Just curious," I say. "I never did find her name in any of Catalina's things."

"I'm not surprised," Mrs. Barnes says. "Catalina had stopped hanging out with her usual friends. And from what the doctors told me, her journal and pictures had been *tampered* with." She laughs sadly. "Catalina did that herself, but they called it tampering, like it was evidence. Tell me, how can you tamper with your own life? Isn't it up to us what we show others?" She purses her lips. "That statement has always bothered me."

I knew that the images on Catalina's profile seemed too perfect. Maybe she knew this would happen somehow. Maybe she was preparing for it.

"Anyway," Mrs. Barnes continues, "I think Virginia was just someone to talk to. Isaac said he never brought her up again after the day they fought. Catalina's reaction scared him. But no matter what we did, Catalina continued to spiral." She stops her story. "You know," she says. "I asked the therapists about Virginia, and Dr. Pritchard contacted me personally to say he'd already spoken to her and that she had lost contact with Catalina weeks before she died. Truth is"—she sighs out a shaky breath—"we don't know what happened to Catalina."

Arthur Pritchard didn't tell them Virginia is his daughter. What did he find out? What else is he withholding?

"I'm sorry to ask this," I say carefully. "But . . . how did Catalina die?"

Mr. Barnes gets up from the chair, and I nervously glance over to him. He doesn't say anything, just walks out of the room and into the kitchen. I look back at his wife. "I'm sorry," I say, feeling horrible for upsetting him.

"It's fine," she says quietly. "He doesn't want to hear the details."

I'm about to tell her to forget it, hating that I'm making them dredge up painful memories, but she looks over at me, her face so terribly sad it breaks my heart.

"They were my pills," she says. "I'd been taking them for anxiety. She . . ." Mrs. Barnes wipes away the tears that fall onto her cheeks. "She swallowed a ninety-day supply. Her dad and I were out to dinner. We got a call from Angie about eight, just before dessert. She said Catalina was locked in the bathroom and wasn't answering. We told her to call 911. Angela . . . Angela used a baseball bat to break off the door handle and get inside. And, um . . ." She sniffles hard. "She found Catalina on the floor, covered in vomit. Uh . . . there was some blood. Angie tried to resuscitate her, but she said her sister wouldn't wake up. The paramedics got there before we did, and they had to sedate Angie because she was hysterical."

The air in the room is so heavy I can barely breathe. The story is awful, so much worse than I imagined. I wish she didn't have to relive it just now. Or ever. Mrs. Barnes looks down at her pants, wiping at the tearstains. I watch her, and go numb from her grief.

I get Mrs. Barnes a glass of water from the kitchen, my hand shaking as I fill the glass. Catalina Barnes killed herself and no one told me. The grief department must have known, and that terrifies me. Because if that's true, that meant my father let me take on this girl's life, subjecting myself—in an already precarious emotional state—to whatever it was that triggered Catalina's behavior. He could have killed me. He must have known he could have killed me.

I bring the glass back to Mrs. Barnes, and she takes it and thanks me. I can see she wants to be alone, and I decide I won't press her any more about Catalina's life. I'm not supposed to focus the therapy around these memories, around death. They won't help her heal. I give her a minute to mourn now that her denial has been swept away.

Wandering back into the kitchen, I notice the light is on in the backyard. Mr. Barnes is probably out there, hitting baseballs into the woods. I think back to that first day he let me into his life, how nice that moment was. How much I wished it could have been real.

I open the patio doors and walk outside, finding him sitting at the table. He glances up when he sees me, and I stop as if asking him if it's all right if I join him. He waves me forward, watching me approach with a thoughtful expression. The wind blows through my hair, and I tuck the strands behind my ears.

"I apologize for leaving so abruptly," he says when I sit across from him. "I'd rather not think of her like that."

"You don't have to apologize," I tell him. "It's completely understandable. I just wanted to say . . ." I trail off, not sure if it's selfish for me to continue. But ultimately, I hope my words can set at least one part of him at ease. "You were a great father," I blurt out quickly. "The best I've ever had." I look at him, smiling sadly. "Catalina was lucky to have you. I just . . . I wanted you to know that."

His expression weakens for a moment, and he stretches his neck from side to side as if his grief is a pulled muscle. He looks at me again, his face cleared. "I know this situation is unorthodox," he starts. "But I'm glad you came to us. *You.* I'm not sure how you separate yourself from what you do, but I wanted you to know that you matter. Even if you're not my real daughter, you matter to us because we care for you. We want good things for you."

My breath catches, and I have to put my hand on my chest to subdue the ache that's started there. I'm speechless.

"Maybe you thought you were playing my daughter flawlessly," he says, smiling softly. "But the real you was always there. I could always see the difference."

I have a quick flash of embarrassment because I *did* think I was portraying her perfectly. But I guess it really doesn't matter anymore.

"When you came out that one night," he says, glancing toward the trees, "I was still angry. But when I saw you, really looked at you, I realized you were just a kid. And I couldn't figure out for the life of me why your parents would let you do this job. If you were mine, I never would have. After that, I wanted to protect you. I wanted to be your father."

"I liked being your daughter," I say, tears flooding my eyes. "I really did."

Mr. Barnes sniffles, and lowers his head. He brings his fist to his lips, holding back his cry. "Yeah," he says in a choked voice. "I really liked it too."

We both sit and cry for a bit, a sad little moment that is just as much a good-bye for me as it is for him. I don't want to leave, I realize. I wanted this so much. I think it might be all I've ever wanted. Someone to love me. Someone to look out for me. And this time, I found it. And it was almost real.

CHAPTER NINE

THE PATIO DOORS OPEN, AND I QUICKLY WIPE MY face and turn, finding Mrs. Barnes looking out at us. She walks over, her face tearstained. She sits on the arm of her husband's chair, putting her hand supportively on his shoulder.

They're a picture, sitting like that—holding each other up. I realize then that they'll be okay. Neither one will let the other fall. "You have a wonderful family," I tell them sincerely. "I wish I could change things for you, take away what happened. I really do."

"I know you do, honey," Mrs. Barnes says. "And maybe you needed someone too. I hope . . . we hope"—she smiles at her husband—"when this is all over, you'll still come see us once in a while. Would you consider that?"

I nod. "Yeah," I say. "I'd really like that."

"Good," she says, clearing the emotion from her voice as if it's settled. "Now, I was thinking you should go see Isaac today. His mother called me last night, very worried. His friends contacted her, expressing worry about your . . . relationship. I was hoping you could . . ." She shrugs slowly, waiting for me to supply the answer.

"I planned to talk to him," I assure her. "Things got out of hand, but I'm going to set things right."

"I'm glad," she says. "He's a good boy, but he has a lot of guilt. What happened to Catalina, it wasn't his fault. He needs to know that."

"It wasn't your fault either," I say quickly. Catalina's decision to end her life had nothing to do with them. They're not to blame. Mrs. Barnes nods silently, and I see a small bit of acceptance, just enough to break the spell of complicated grief. That guilt of not having stopped Catalina's death will never go away, but we all have guilt. It just can't be all that we have.

I stand up, glancing around the yard once more, knowing that my time in this house is almost over. In fact, I could probably leave now if they wanted me to. I turn to Mrs. Barnes. "About the party . . . ," I start, but she holds up her hand.

"It's a celebration," she interrupts. "A celebration of Catalina's life. We've invited her friends and extended family. It was time."

There's a moment of sadness when I realize I won't be part of the celebration, but ultimately I know that my attendance would make people uncomfortable. I'm a closer, after all. I nod, and start toward the house, unsure of what that means for this assignment. Is it officially over?

"Hey," Mr. Barnes calls. I turn to look back at him. "You really can stay as long as you want," he says. I thank him, considering at least spending one more night here.

"Oh," his wife adds, holding up her finger. "Can we . . . Can you not mention this to your supervisors?" she asks, looking slightly worried. "We signed that agreement, and—"

"My lips are sealed." I pretend to lock my lips, and she laughs. My gaze flows over to Mr. Barnes. He stands, and I wait as he makes his way toward me. I'm already crying when he gathers me into a big bear hug.

"Just in case we don't see you again," he murmurs, "you take care of yourself. We'll be here if you need anything. Understand?" I nod against his big shoulder, clutching on to his shirt. "You're not alone."

I pull back with an embarrassed laugh, sort of humiliated that these people seem to be more helpful than me. His eyes are sympathetic as he looks down at me.

"What's your name?" he asks, as if he's been wondering for a while.

For a moment, I'm speechless. I've never been asked by an assignment before. They never wanted to know who I really was. "Quinlan," I say, breaking another of Marie's rules. It feels good being able to speak it out loud to him. He smiles.

"That's a pretty name," he says.

I can tell by the fading sun that it's starting to get late in the afternoon, and I need to find Isaac and talk to him. I tell the Barnes family good-bye again, tell them I might see them later tonight. They say they hope so.

I grab my backpack on the way out and borrow the Jetta for another trip. I have to talk to Isaac.

When I get outside, I pull a hoodie from my backpack and slip my arms in, knowing the day will only get colder as the sun goes down. I'm in the middle of zipping it up as I round my car near a large set of overgrown bushes.

There's a flurry of movement and someone grabs me from behind, one hand over my mouth, the other around my waist. I'm struck down with fear, and I try to shout for help. I kick back my foot as hard as I can, connecting with a leg and sending my attacker to the ground. I spin, chest heaving, stomach churning.

"Aaron?" I say, incredulous. I shoot a look at the Barneses' house before kneeling down next to him to check his ankle. My sneaker scuffed off a good chunk of skin, and a thick line of red blood runs down his leg. His eyes are pained, but before he can lecture me, I stand, putting my hand on my hip. "Are you nuts?" I whisper forcefully. "Didn't you think I'd fight back?"

"I was trying to keep you quiet so we could talk in private."

"Uh, how about you call my name?"

"I was afraid you would run."

"What?" I ask confused. "Aaron—I wasn't thinking straight

the other day, but I'm better now. I should have called you. I'm sorry."

He nods as if he understands, rubbing at the skin just above the cut on his leg. "I was looking out for you," he says, but not bitterly. "You should have known better."

I smile, lowering myself to the ground next to him. "So you're here to say I told you so?"

"Not hardly. I had to talk to you," he says. "The guy—my assignment, Mitchel? He knew Catalina. They were friends."

I furrow my brow. "Are you sure? I haven't seen anything about him." Although now it's obvious that there was a lot about Catalina I didn't know.

"Yeah," Aaron says. "After Catalina died, Mitchel, he . . . he killed himself. Took something he called QuikDeath—a poison cocktail, I guess."

I fold my legs underneath me, this revelation a punch in the gut. Two suicides so close together—this town must be reeling. And yet no one has mentioned it. The fact that Mitchel and Catalina were friends is especially troubling.

"Catalina committed suicide too," I tell Aaron quietly, feeling like I'm betraying her by revealing this secret. "Coincidence?"

"Well, if it is," Aaron says, "it doesn't end there. Guess who Mitchel's girlfriend was."

I'm stumped at first, but then my breath catches. "Virginia Pritchard?" I ask in disbelief. Aaron nods, and I turn back to the house, wondering if I should go inside, ask for their help.

But I can't tell them about Arthur Pritchard's connection to their daughter's death. They're just getting well, and this could compromise their entire recovery.

"We have to call Marie," I say. She's the only person I can think of who might know how to help.

"And what would we tell her?" Aaron asks. "Marie *knows* everything. Do you really think she didn't know about this before sending us in? She practically runs the department."

There's a pit in my stomach, a hint of betrayal at the thought of Marie purposely putting us in harm's way. I'm not sure I'm ready to believe that yet.

"Then what do you want me to do?" I ask him, unsure of a next step. "I'm almost done with my assignment. I'm ready to go home."

"You have to find Virginia," Aaron says. "My contract is almost up, Quinn. Sooner than you think. There is something big happening here."

The words are ominous, and they crawl over my skin. "Meaning?"

"Mitchel left all sort of pages, scribbled notes, creepy shit. He even started drawing spirals, just carving them into his bed frame. It was . . . psychosis or something. I don't know. Anyway, he would write about dying. About him and Catalina and Virginia, all of them dying."

"So you think this was a suicide pact?" I ask.

"All I know," Aaron says, his face clouding over, "is that everything got real dark, real fast." He puts his hand on the ground and gets to his feet, hobbling slightly because of his injury. "Look," he adds. "Marie's already contacted me for extraction. She's going to pick me up in a few hours. I'm not going to tell her about Virginia or the suicides; it shouldn't be part of the debriefing. But the other stuff . . . this is on us."

"What do you need me to find out?" I ask.

"I think there are others," he says. "Suicides listed as 'undetermined.' Deacon's been researching for me, but we think the grief department has been covering them up. They've been using us and other closers to do it. But more than anything, you have to find Virginia Pritchard. Last I checked she was in Roseburg. Quinn, you have to find her before she kills herself. Find out what she knows about all of this."

"And if I don't?" I ask, having no idea if I want to chase down Arthur Pritchard's daughter.

Aaron shrugs. "Then I guess we'll see if this is bigger than a suicide pact."

I tighten my jaw, more worried than I want to admit to him. I understand why Aaron needs me to find Virginia. She'll know what happened to Catalina and Mitchel; she'll provide some background. Catalina's life has been scrubbed clean of her intentions. I have to believe part of that is coming from Arthur Pritchard's daughter. Who else would have known what the department would be looking for when duplicating someone's life?

Aaron takes out his phone and looks at the time. "We'll talk more about it after your debriefing," he says, and steadies himself on his bad leg. I'm glad the bleeding has stopped, the gash clotting dark red. Aaron slides his phone into his pocket and pulls me into a hug. "You be careful," he says near my ear. "I'll be back to extract you. Okay?"

He looks at me, and although he doesn't say it, there's a hint of worry there. Worry that he won't come back at all. That he'll be sent to therapy, and then who knows when I'll see him again.

"Yeah," I tell him, forcing a smile. "You'd better." A streak of paranoia runs its course, and I look around the street, checking to see if we're being watched. There isn't a white Lexus in sight, but the feeling doesn't entirely abate.

Aaron says good-bye, bumping my fist, and then he limps down the driveway and disappears around the corner.

I'm unsettled, turning over all the information in my head. Putting it together with what I learned today. I get in the Jetta and take out my phone. Deacon hasn't contacted me since I left him this morning, but I try not to let that in. *This isn't about us,* I told him. That's especially true now.

I text Marie to let her know there's been a change in scheduling and I'm close to finishing my assignment and will be done before Friday. I don't tell her about seeing Aaron or even Arthur Pritchard. I don't mention suicide at all. There's a possibility she already knows what's going on here, and that she and the entire grief department have played us for fools. But part of me wants to believe she's still on my side. No matter what.

Marie texts back that she'll notify Aaron of my pending extraction—not mentioning that he's leaving his own assignment. She doesn't break procedure. She also doesn't ask how I am, and that is an immediate red flag. She would have known about my meltdown yesterday, been made aware especially if Arthur Pritchard got involved. And yet she didn't warn me he'd be here. Didn't track me down at Deacon's.

My advisor is hiding something. Seems we all are.

CHAPTER TEN

I WONDER HOW MANY "UNDETERMINED" DEATHS there have been over the past fifteen years. How deep the cover-up goes. How much my father is involved. Catalina Barnes committed suicide. She was lost in a way that was just her own, isolated and apart from everything and everybody. She didn't reach out for help—she didn't want it.

Catalina Barnes killed herself and no one was able to predict it. Her family wasn't able to stop her. Suicide clusters have existed for years, one death influencing others with no other known stimulus. A ripple effect. It's why they don't detail suicides on the news, afraid of the public reaction. But now is that what the grief department is using closers for? To control the perception of death?

Undetermined. What a bunch of bullshit. They knew how

Catalina Barnes died and they didn't tell me. Instead they used me to help cover it up. I have to find Virginia Pritchard and find out what she knows about the suicides. *If* Virginia Pritchard is even still alive. A chill runs down my back at the morbid thought, and I quickly refocus on my current situation.

Before I can go to Isaac and finish this assignment, I need to talk to Angie. She was there the night Catalina died. Maybe her sister said something to her. Or maybe Angie knows more about Virginia—maybe she can tell me about the connection.

I drive toward the school. I know Angie sometimes hangs out at Off Campus after classes. I head that way, hoping I'll see her car and know she's there. Getting her to actually speak to me might be a different issue altogether.

I slow as I pass the lot, relieved when I find the red SUV I recognize from her sixteenth birthday pictures parked there. Angie's inside. I pull up next to her ride and shut off my engine. I watch the café through my window, waiting for her to leave. I catch my reflection in the rearview mirror, and I'm startled by my eyes. They're brown—but they're not supposed to be.

I hold up my index finger until I feel the contact cling to it, and I take it out and drop it into the cup holder, and blink rapidly to help the stinging. I do the same with the other eye and then check my reflection again. Blue eyes. I feel like it's been forever since I've seen them.

I'm comforted a bit by my own face. I think of Deacon, how much he would have liked to see me now. How I occasionally catch him gazing at me like I'm his favorite thing in the world. Last night he admitted that he's been keeping his distance, said it was because he was afraid he'd hurt me again. But then he let me close; he was open to loving me. I felt it. This time I walked away. Maybe one of us always will.

A rush of sadness rolls over me. I miss him, and I wish things were different. Wish *we* were different. But I don't think either of us can change.

Out of the corner of my vision I see movement, and when I look up, I notice Angie, her long hair blowing across her face so that she has to pick it out of her lip gloss. She's walking with a friend, one I recognize from that first day at the bleachers. My heart starts to race, and I consider leaving without ever uttering a word. She sees me and it's too late.

Angie's posture stiffens, and she turns to say something quiet to her friend. The other girl turns to me quickly, horror on her face. She says good-bye to Angie and heads in the other direction. I get out of the car and move around to the front, slipping my hands into my pockets to look casual. Less combative.

Angela walks past, aggressively ignoring me, but then stops and turns. She jabs her finger in my direction. "What?" she asks, her face screwed up in disgust. "Are you here to tell me again what a terrible daughter I am? Because I don't really want to hear it."

"Angie," I say in my own voice. She starts, surprised that I don't sound like her sister. She stares at my eyes, noticing the color. But it only succeeds in making her more afraid. After all, I am a closer. "I'm leaving today," I tell her. "But I wanted to talk to you before I did."

A flash of grief crosses her face, but she forces herself to be angry again. "You've been running around with my sister's boyfriend," she says bitterly. "Stealing her identity. And you think that I'd want to talk you? You're delusional."

"Angie," I say, moving toward her. She throws up her hands, falling back a step like she's repulsed by my existence. She turns to stalk away, but I can't let her leave without knowing the truth about Catalina. "Angela," I call, sounding exactly like her sister. Angie stops, frozen. Slowly she turns back to look at me, hurt registering in her expression.

"Don't do that," she says, her voice weak. "Don't . . ." But instead of chewing me out again, Angie dissolves into tears, covering her face.

I hurry around the car to where she stands and awkwardly pat her back, telling her it will be okay. Her reaction isn't entirely unusual. I've seen it before. Even though Angie didn't want me here in the beginning, I did represent her sister. Once I'm gone, Catalina's gone for good.

To my surprise, Angie turns around and hugs me, clinging to me as she cries against my shirt. I brush my hand over her hair, my heart aching at her loss. I've never had a brother or sister, at least not one of my own. I can't imagine what it would be like to lose them. How much it would hurt to have your blood, your friend, taken away. I close my eyes and hold her close, trying to absorb her pain.

"I miss her," Angie mumbles. "I don't know how we'll be okay without her."

"You will," I say. I take her by the shoulders to straighten her up, and she wipes her face, fighting back her flood of emotions. She's failing at it, though. "Your mom and dad," I continue, "they're some of the best people I've ever met." She squeezes her eyes shut, choking on another cry, only this time it's because she knows how lucky she is. "To be honest," I tell her, "they're the best parents I've ever had."

She looks at me, confused at first, but then she sees that I'm trying to lighten the moment, even if my comment is entirely true. She laughs self-consciously and takes a step back, trying to regain her composure. She smooths down her hair and clears her throat.

"I like you better like this," she says. "It was too hard to talk to you as Catalina; it . . ." She shakes her head and decides not to finish the thought. There's a boom of thunder, and we both look up at the ominous gray clouds. Angie motions to her car. "Want to talk in there?" she asks tentatively. "It looks like it's going to pour."

I smile, grateful that she's letting me talk to her at all. In a way, I think she wanted to connect before, but was scared. Now that I'm leaving, it's her last chance. We climb into her SUV, and she turns on the engine to get the heat running. For a moment we both stare out the windshield at the road, watching cars drive by.

"I heard about the intervention last night," she says quietly, looking over at me. "Kyle told me she hit you. She felt terrible about it."

There's a sharp stab of humiliation and hurt, but I shrug like it didn't matter—even if the cruelty of it all still stings. "They were worried about Isaac," I say. "I understand."

"You're worried about him too," she says, like she's figuring me out. "Is that why you're leaving early?"

"No," I tell her. "I'm leaving because your parents don't need me anymore. They've accepted that Catalina's gone. They need you. They need to get their lives back on track."

Angie lowers her head, thinking that over. After a second she turns to me, her eyes slightly narrowed. "But you liked him, didn't you?" she asks, turning the subject back to Isaac.

"I liked the way he loved your sister."

She closes her eyes, overcome by the statement, but when she opens them again, she flashes me a watery smile. "They were sickening together," she says. "So gross."

We both laugh, and I can only imagine how happy Isaac and Catalina had been once. Before Virginia came into Catalina's life. "What happened?" I ask. "What changed?"

Angie rests her arms over the steering wheel and leans forward, staring outside once again. "I don't really know," she says. "They were inseparable, but then Catalina wanted to be around him less and less. One time Isaac came to me for advice, and when I told Catalina, she got pissed. Called me a traitor. Said she couldn't trust anyone."

"Do you think she stopped loving him?" I ask, unable to figure out why she was trying to cut Isaac out of her life.

"No," Angie says easily. "In fact"—her expression clouds over—"the day she died, she came to my room and gave me a set of pages. Asked me to hide them for her. When I asked her why, she said she couldn't bear to destroy them. She didn't want to lose the memories. I ended up stuffing them into her mattress. Stupid place, I know, but what else was I going to do with them. I read the entries and they were basically about how much she loved Isaac." Angie pauses. "And then . . . those damn spirals. She'd draw them everywhere those last few weeks. Just absently draw them. I asked her once what they meant, and she told me they represented her soul lost in a deep, dark nothing."

"Did you know that she was going to kill herself?" I ask gently. Angie scrunches up her face like she's about to cry, but she fights and keeps her composure.

"No," she says, her voice thick. "But I should have. She was my sister. And I should have."

She lowers her head, and I reach to put my hand on her arm. I tell her it wasn't her fault, tell her all the things she needs to hear. I give her closure, even though I wasn't hired to do so. When we finish talking, Angie wipes the sleeve of her jacket over her lips to wipe away the tears that have settled there. She sniffles hard, and looks over at me.

"You're not horrible, you know," she says, her pretty brown eyes rimmed in purplish red skin, raw from crying.

"Thanks."

"I'm sorry for being a total bitch to you," she adds. "It's just that what you do is sort of . . ."

"Creepy?" I suggest.

"Yeah. But you're a counselor, too, right?" she asks.

I tip my hand from side to side. "Kind of. I mean, I've been trained, but mostly I'm a mimic, a representation of loss. Think of me as an empty vessel for your emotions."

Angie widens her eyes. "Sounds like the worst job ever."

"It is sometimes." I pause. "But it's not all bad. Like now, here with you. Meeting your family and Isaac." Now my own emotions threaten to boil over. "It was the best assignment I ever had," I say, trying to oversimplify it. Before I can embarrass myself, I pat her leg and tell her I have to go. She looks stricken for a moment, but then she nods. Again she surprises me by reaching over to give me a hug.

"Thank you," she says. "Thank you for helping my parents."

"It was my pleasure," I say, staring out the window over her shoulder. Wishing I could have stayed a little longer. I move to get out of the car, but then pause and look back at her.

"Angie, have you ever met your sister's friend Virginia?" I ask.

"No," she says with the shake of her head. "Catalina mentioned her a few times, but she never came over or anything. Why?"

"Just tying up all the loose ends," I say. The truth about Virginia is still a mystery—one Angie doesn't need to be involved in. She has a chance to rebuild with her family now. I won't leave her with any lingering doubts.

My resolve to find Virginia is strengthened by my want to set things right. Learn her part. I tell Angie good-bye, holding up my hand in a wave, and then I close the door just as the first drops of rain start to fall.

CHAPTER ELEVEN

ISAAC MUST HAVE KNOWN SOMETHING WAS WRONG, I think as I drive toward his house, the windshield wipers on my car streaking against the glass. He must have been worried if he went to Angie, upsetting Catalina even more. During this assignment I thought I was learning about Isaac and Catalina's relationship, but really, I was seeing his idealized version of it. Maybe even my idealized version of it.

Isaac's house is on the other side of town. I've never been inside, but we've stopped there a few times so he could grab his baseball gear. When I pull up, his truck is the only vehicle in the driveway. I'm glad his mother isn't here, because even though I've successfully avoided her during my time, the woman terrifies me. I flip up my hood and jog to the door. I freeze there, afraid to knock.

How do I tell him good-bye? How can I give him closure when I'm not even sure he'll talk to me again? I close my eyes, trying to imagine a way to set him at peace, but all I can see is the way he'd smile when we were together. How happy it made him. How heavy his grief was last night when he told me to get out of his truck.

This is it, I tell myself. *The true test of your abilities.* I look at the doorbell, fear making my hands shake, and then I press the button. I curse immediately and spin around, watch the street. The wind is cold, but it's nothing compared to the cold reality of this situation.

The door opens, and I straighten my expression before I turn around. Isaac's lips part when he sees me, surprised. He's a mess, though. Pale and drawn. I wonder what he's been doing since I left him last night.

"Can I come in?" I ask. The sound of my voice, my regular voice, makes his eyes widen with a flash of confusion. But then he nods and steps aside so I can walk past him. I glance up when I do, and find him watching me intently. Trying to figure me out.

He closes the door, and stands awkwardly like he doesn't know how to greet me. Everything must look new to him, the way I stand and my expressions, the blue of my eyes and my freckles. I'm not trying to be Catalina anymore.

"I . . . um . . ." I look around the house, nervousness growing in my gut. "I wanted to talk to you. About Catalina."

He sways slightly and then motions to the couch. "Okay,"

he says, sounding distant. He walks ahead of me and takes a seat, blinking quickly as if his eyes are already starting to sting with tears. I sit next to him, wondering if he'll open up at all while I'm Quinn.

"I'm sorry," I say, guilt gnawing away any clinical thoughts that try to rise up. "I fucked up." Isaac watches me, and he's an open book. I can read all of the emotions as they play across his face. It's always been so easy with him. "I got attached, Isaac," I explain. "I let it go too far, and then last night . . . it was my fault. I'm sorry your friends had to step in. I'm sorry I didn't—"

"Stop," he says, shaking his head. "Stop apologizing." I wait a beat to see where this conversation is heading. I wipe under my eyes, feeling tears about to brim over. "I was there too," Isaac says. He lowers his head to stare into his lap. "And I'm not sorry."

My heart skips, and there's a small sense of validation. My default is to take the blame because I should have known better. I'm the professional. But part of me wants to believe the relationship was mutual, at least partly.

"Being with you," Isaac says quietly, "it took away the pain. I wasn't ready to be reminded of it—not like that. And now it's back." He looks up at me with the saddest eyes I've ever seen. "But you're not going to fix it this time, are you?" he asks.

I press my lips together to keep from crying, and slowly shake my head no.

"The counselor called and told me you were leaving," he

continues. "But what if I'm not ready for you to go? Would you stay?"

His emotions bleed over to mine, and everything I felt for him over the last week floods in. Without thinking, I reach to take his hand, needing to comfort him. Needing to stop his pain. He closes his eyes when I do, maybe hurting more because of my touch.

"You deserve better than this," I tell him. "You deserve something real."

"Maybe," he says, meeting my eyes. "But it was a lot easier to pretend. Especially with you." There's a flutter of attraction still there, but now that I'm thinking clearly, I know it's just that—attraction. Isaac doesn't even know me.

I take my hand from his, fold my fingers together in my lap. My training tells me that Isaac's avoiding Catalina's memory, filling up her space with anything he can. He's afraid. But if he wants true closure, he has to be honest. And he has to let her go.

"You need to talk about her, Isaac," I say. "The real her. No one's going to replace her—no one can. But I know something went wrong with your relationship. What secrets are you keeping for her? What happened to Catalina?"

He winces like he's going to refuse to answer. But then, slowly, I watch him turn it over in his head. Work through the things he wants to share, but doesn't because it feels like betrayal.

"You can tell me," I assure him. "I'm here so that you can tell me. I'm here for you." My words seem to comfort him slightly, and he sits back, staring straight ahead as if looking into his memories.

"Catalina and I were in love," he says, as if I'd argue. "Madly in love. We wanted to go to college, get a place. Shit. We even talked about our kids' names. I wanted that, even if other people thought it was stupid. Said I had too much to experience. But why? If I loved her, why should I end it to screw around with people I didn't care about? I . . . never understood it.

"Then one day," he says, "Catalina told me about a couple she met, found them on some forum. They wrote dark shit, poems about death and stuff, and she would tell me to read it. See how good it was. I'm a not a big reader," he explains. "Things started to change. After a few weeks, I asked Angie if she'd noticed Catalina's mood shifts at home. When Catalina found out, she accused me of spying on her. Said I'd been watching her, and what was I, some kind of handler? I didn't know what the hell she was talking about. I told her that she needed to drop those new friends. That they were messing with her head," he says, sounding defiant.

"We didn't break up, but she'd stare at me sometimes, like she stopped trusting me." Isaac squeezes his eyes tightly shut. He's quiet for a moment before continuing. "I'd find these pages," he says. "Lying around her room and in my car. Black spirals. I hid them." He looks at me. "That's the thing—I didn't mention her darkening mood to anybody, even though she was getting worse. But I didn't want her to be upset with me." His voice cracks, and he cries the last few words. "I knew she was suffering; I saw it. I thought I could make it better, so I didn't tell anybody. I kept her secret. I kept her fucking secret and then she killed herself. It's my fault, my fault for not getting help. Tell me," he begs, staring at me with tears dripping from his eyes, "tell me how she could ever forgive me for that."

I cover my mouth, absolutely overcome by his guilt. I jump forward and wrap my arms around him, holding him so tight I don't know how he can breathe. Isaac doesn't pull away, and I hold on to him, especially when I feel him shudder. Hear the first hitch of a cry.

"It's okay . . . ," I whisper close to his ear, running my fingers gently over the back of his neck to comfort him. "It's not your fault," I say. "It's not your fault." He whimpers into my shoulder, broken and lost. I absorb his guilt, telling him that he didn't know what she was going to do. And that she would never, ever saddle him with this misery.

"I miss her," he says miserably. "I don't think it'll ever be okay again."

"It will," I promise him. "So many people love you. And they need you, Isaac. They need you. Please trust that Catalina loved you, but something happened to her. She got sick and she didn't tell anybody. Nobody knew, Isaac."

"I did."

"Not the extent of it," I tell him, pressing my cheek to his. "You didn't know how bad it really was. You're not to blame. You have to let that guilt go. It's not yours."

"She's the only one," he says, sniffling back his tears, his body starting to calm. "The only one I'll ever love. Did she know that?"

I want to tell him that she did, tell him anything he wants to hear just so he'll smile again. Isaac Perez is one of the sweetest people I've ever met, and he loved his girlfriend. He truly did. But I can't lie to him. I won't lie to him anymore.

"No matter how much you told her," I say, "I don't know if she believed it. I don't know if she could at the end. But you're still here, and I have to trust that if she could see you, if she was no longer in pain and could see you, she would only want good things. She loved you too, Isaac." I pull back to look at him, running my hand over his cheeks to clear his tears. "I know that for a fact."

He catches my hand, holds it on his face. For a minute I worry that he'll kiss me, that he hasn't been listening. But then in his eyes I see that he has. I see that he's ready to let go of Catalina Barnes. It hurts a little. Because I know it also means he's saying good-bye to me.

"It's time to say good-bye," I say, standing in the middle of the room. Isaac asked me to go through the motions in the typical way, said he was curious about how it worked. A weight seems to have lifted from his shoulders, and I see a hint of the guy I met those times when we were with Jason.

Isaac stands in front of me, and it's all very formal. Very awkward. He nods, and for a minute it's almost like we're about to say our wedding vows. He smiles. "Would it help if we sat down?" he asks.

I exhale. "Yes, please." I walk back over to the couch, relieved to not have to stand in front of him. Isaac sits, fascinated by me, the closer, now that the brunt of his guilt has left him.

"This is where you say all the things you wanted her to know," I tell him. Isaac looks down sadly, but in his face I see a bit of nostalgia, and I imagine he's thinking about the good times they had together. Thinking more about the love they had, and less about the pain he felt after her death.

"It's weird," he starts, "because I still love her so much. What can I do with that kind of feeling—where can it go?"

"To yourself," I say. He presses his lips together, and turns to me. "Love yourself and your memories. It doesn't have to *go* anywhere."

"I'll always love her," he says simply. "I'll love her my whole life."

In that instant, I wish she could be here to see him. To see how much he loves her, would have done anything she asked. I think about what she would tell him. I close my eyes, and when I look at him again, my expression has changed. My voice is different. "I wrote about you in my diary," I say. Isaac's breath catches, and he watches me. "How much I loved you. All of our private moments. They're in the closet in my room. Up high. You should have them. I . . . I think I left them for you."

"Catalina, I'm sorry," Isaac starts. "I just need you to know how goddamn sorry I am."

"I forgive you," I whisper. "I forgive you for loving me too much." He sways, and tears race down his cheeks. My heart breaks, feeling the loss of Catalina and Isaac, their story cut short in the wake of a tragedy. I lean in and kiss softly at his lips, just once, and then wrap my arms around his neck to hug him. I close my eyes. "Good-bye, Isaac."

His voice is barely a breath. "Good-bye, Catalina."

We stay locked together for a while longer, not speaking because we know that this assignment is done, and that when I pull away, Catalina will be gone too. Isaac holds me, and then finally he lets out a long breath, and he moves back.

His eyes are swollen, but there's a sparkle behind them. I wait for him to tell me he's going to be all right. He swallows, and looks toward the hallway.

"I . . ." He stops to clear his throat. "I got you something for the party, but since you won't be there, I wondered if I could give it to you now."

My stomach sinks, and I worry that he's still confused. "I'm sorry," I say in my own voice. "I'm . . . I'm not Catalina . . . anymore."

He smiles. "I know," he says. "But I got it for you."

Butterflies tickle my stomach, and I feel a blush rise to my cheeks. "Me?" I ask.

"I bought it a few days ago," he says. "It made me think of you." When he sees how flattered I am, he grins and jumps up. "Wait right here," he says. I watch as he darts down the hall and disappears.

I put my hand over my heart, thinking that maybe this assignment was the best thing that's ever happened to me. That it's shown me love and compassion. This is what I should strive for. This level of normalcy.

When Isaac returns, he's carrying a rectangular jewelry box. He sits on the coffee table, facing me, and holds it out. He seems nervous as he waits for my reaction.

"You shouldn't have," I say, but he motions for me to open it. I click open the box and find a thin silver bracelet—delicate and beautiful. Modest and romantic. "It's lovely," I say, running my finger over it. I've never been given jewelry before, I realize. Closers don't typically own any of their own.

"Do you like it?" he asks impatiently. I lift my eyes to his and smile.

"I love it," I tell him. "I really love it." My voice is threatening tears, and I quickly have to look away. I miss him. I miss Isaac already. "Will you help me put it on?" I ask in a choked voice.

He takes the box from my hand and unhooks the bracelet before laying it over my wrist. His fingers are gentle on my skin, maybe lingering a little longer than necessary, but I don't mind. I don't mind at all.

When it's clasped, I hold out my arm to admire the bracelet. I bite down on my lip, making eye contact with Isaac. And I can see that he's going to be okay. No, he'll never really get over Catalina. But he was carrying the guilt of her suicide with him. It wasn't his to bear.

A few minutes later, Isaac walks me to the door. We pause for a long moment, and I think we both consider leaning in for one last kiss. But that would be unethical. And I won't lead him on again. So I smile, and tell him good-bye, and wish him the best life possible.

I park the Jetta at the Barnes residence twenty minutes later. Sitting in the front seat, I grab an old receipt and a pen from the console and tearfully scribble out a good-bye note. When I'm done, I climb out of the car. The rain has stopped completely, and I slip the key into the mail slot, along with the note. Angie will be home soon, and together the family can continue to heal. A family I wanted to be a part of. I pause, looking over the house. Maybe I did—for a little while, maybe I did belong to them. The idea of it is agony and comfort at the same time, and I hold it to my heart and walk away.

CHAPTER TWELVE

I SIT ON THE OUTSIDE PATIO OF THE COFFEE SHOP, my hood popped up so people in town don't immediately recognize me. I used my own money last night to crash at a motel, unwilling to intrude on the Barnes family anymore, but not ready to return home, either. When I called Aaron for extraction, he sounded better than he has in a while. I guess it really was the assignment that was bringing him down.

There's still ten minutes before Aaron is supposed to arrive, so I take the time to observe. A mother sits with a little girl in a stroller next to her. The mom is talking on her phone, while the toddler stares up at her, waiting for any sign that she's paying attention. My eyes shift to an older couple, the man in a wheelchair, and a server stops to take their order, impatient as they ask questions. Toward the outer edge, near the railing, is a young guy, his laptop open, his expression faraway while he stares out at the street, his fingers poised on the keys. Daydreamer.

A girl around my age walks in, takes stock of the place, and then goes to sit in the corner. She's impatient, glancing around for the server. Her eyes fall on me and I quickly look away. When I notice the server leave the old couple and head in her direction, I glance up again. The girl has long brown hair and deep-set dark eyes. She points her finger at the menu, asking a question. Without thinking, I mimic the movement, tilting my head and tightening my jaw. The server nods after taking her order and quickly closes the menu, fanning the girl's hair.

"Casing someone?"

I jump, and turn to find Aaron standing at my table. I quickly get up and hug him, smiling ear to ear. He's wearing too much cologne, but I don't care. He holds me tight as if saying that we've been through some shit here in Lake Oswego. Before I can start tearing up with relief at seeing him, I pull back. Hide those emotions because I'm a closer and I shouldn't be so easy to read.

We sit down at the table, and Aaron reaches for my water, drinks it until he drains the glass empty. I laugh, missing his selfish charms. Still, I notice that he's different, even though I can't quite place what's changed about him.

Aaron sets down the glass with a clink and wipes his mouth with the back of his hand. He leans toward me, his elbows on the table. "So what's with that girl?" he asks, nodding his head at the other table.

"Nothing," I say. "Just killing time."

"You were mimicking her," he says, clicking his tongue. "That's weird."

I press my lips into a smile. "Yeah," I say. "I know."

"So long as you know," he sings out. He studies me, taking inventory of my mental state, and when he's sure I'm me again, he flashes me that all-knowing smile and whistles low under his breath. "That poor bastard," he says.

I roll my eyes and sit back in the seat, folding my arms over my chest. Of course our conversation would turn immediately to Deacon. "He told you?" I ask.

Aaron raises his hands in a *What did you expect?* motion. "Deacon's my boy. And damn, girl. You blew his mind."

"Don't be gross."

"I'm not. It's about time. I thought the sexual tension would last forever."

"Shut up." But I laugh again and take back my glass as punishment, even though it's empty. Aaron looks elated, like he has something to do with my and Deacon's rekindling relationship. Obviously, Deacon didn't tell him the entire story, though. I didn't go to him blinded by passion and lust. I'd lost my mind, myself. He brought me back. And then I left him sitting on his staircase.

"How is he?" I ask, lowering my eyes to the table. "I . . . haven't talked to him since yesterday morning."

"You mean before you went back to your fake boyfriend?" he says conversationally. I shoot him a dirty look, but he continues. "Uh . . . I wouldn't say he took that well," Aaron adds. "But you know Deacon. He hates the system, but he'll eventually understand. You had to finish the job."

I pull my hands into my lap, picking at my fingers in order to look casual. "Have you seen him?"

"Yeah. He came over this morning, asking about you. Myra called him out immediately, and Deacon broke down and told us about your night together. I mean, he was vague on the details, but knowing the two of you it was pretty obvious what happened. Myra wasn't pleased, mostly because Deacon looked miserable. But after talking for a bit we realized he was probably just worried." He smiles at me thoughtfully. "He didn't want you to leave."

"Yeah," I say with a touch of regret. "He made that part clear."

"You should give him another chance."

"How many?" I ask. "He's already broken my heart twice. How many tries does he get?"

"You're the one who left this time," he points out. "And I understand. I do. But Deacon's changed, Quinn. He's always loved you—everyone could see that. I think this assignment made him realize it too."

I don't answer, turning over the words in my head. My heart. "It's almost funny," I say after a moment. "I make a living sorting out other people's lives when I have no handle on my own."

Aaron smiles. "That's why you're such a good-ass closer," he says. "You're too kindhearted. You give your clients everything." Only this time he says it as a compliment and not as a criticism he'd point out to Marie.

"I am pretty awesome, huh?" I say, grinning. "Like, the best . . . ever?"

"Relax over there, egomaniac." He laughs, and then pushes back his chair to get up from the table. "It's late," he says. "We should head home. You ready?"

I take a moment, looking around the restaurant patio, around at the trees. The air is crisp but comfortable. Wind is blowing and swaying the trees. I'll miss Lake Oswego. I'll miss a lot of things. I say my final good-bye before nodding to Aaron, and follow him to the Cadillac.

In the quiet of the car, my thoughts turn back to my assignment. I check my phone and see there are no messages or missed calls. Nothing from Isaac or the Barnes family. For a moment nostalgia takes over, and I wonder if I really could have stepped into Catalina's shoes and lived her life forever. Run off to college with Isaac.

Tears sting my eyes, and one drips onto my cheek. I'm jolted back into reality and quickly turn toward the window to discreetly wipe it away before Aaron notices.

I know better, of course. It wouldn't have worked. But the buildup of grief can be overwhelming this soon after an assignment. That's what Marie's going to help alleviate.

Aaron checks his phone, and his posture stiffens. He clicks

off the screen and stares at the road, seeming troubled. "Can we take a detour?" he suggests, his voice deepened.

"Now?" I ask.

"Marie hasn't returned my calls," he says, tossing his phone into the center console. "I'll keep trying her, but I don't know where she's at. She set up the extraction, so she knows we're on the way." His expression clouds over, and then he looks at me, realizing how much of himself he's revealing. "It's nothing," he says with a quick smile. "Let's stop off at Deacon's until I get ahold of her."

"Aaron," I say, shaking my head. "Is that was this is about? Getting me back with Deacon? Because—"

"No," he says so seriously that I know he's telling the truth. "But it's a safe place," he adds, turning away from me to face the road. The words hang in the air between us, cold and haunting. The assertion being that the other places we'd go, like home . . . may not be safe anymore.

We pull into Deacon's driveway a half hour later, and Aaron cuts the engine. He picks up his phone, checking it again, and nods toward the house. "You go ahead," he says. "I want to call Myra and let her know we'll be back soon."

I curl my lip, letting him know that he's acting crazy. "Seriously?" I ask.

He exhales impatiently, pursing his lips as if I'm the one being difficult. "I'm pretty sure you and Deacon have drama to sort out," he says. "All I want is a few minutes to let my girlfriend know that we're running late and that I'm okay." He pauses, maybe realizing his rude tone. "Go kiss and make up with him," he says with the hint of a smile.

Although I love the optimism, I don't share it. Instead there's a wave of sickness, regret, and I get out of the car and start toward Deacon's front porch. We haven't spoken; he hasn't tried to call. I'm suddenly devastated at the thought. Maybe he thinks he made a mistake. That *I'm* his biggest mistake.

My heart thumps against my ribs, and I pause at the steps, unable to move forward, until I notice the shadow move in the window and I know Deacon has seen me. I can't stand in front of his house like a stalker. I have to talk to him.

I climb the stairs with a mix of dread and longing. I shoot a panicked look back at Aaron, but he has the phone to his ear, talking. He doesn't notice me. By the time I get to the top step, the front door opens and Deacon's there, waiting.

Although I'm not sure Deacon can ever look bad, this is easily the most disheveled I've ever seen him. He's wearing shorts and a faded T-shirt that he won at the Oregon State Fair two years ago. His expression is completely unreadable as he watches me approach, his eyes studying me in that careful way.

I pause at the door, staring back at him, and when I can think of nothing to say, I lift one shoulder in a shrug. Deacon rolls his gaze to the sky like it's painful to see me; his jaw tightens as he tries to keep control of his appearance. A downfall of being around closers so much, I guess. We're always conscious of being read.

"I saw how happy you were there," he says, "that day at the batting cages. So when you walked out my door, I didn't think you'd ever come back." This time when he looks at me, it's an arrow through both of our hearts. A sharp, piercing pain, a fatal wound. I screwed it up—even if it was morally right, I screwed *us* up. "I asked you not to leave," he says. "I fucking begged."

"It's not just about us, though," I tell him, even though I'm not sure he can understand. "I couldn't abandon them, Deacon. Not even for you."

"Him," he corrects. "You couldn't abandon him."

"No." I shake my head and take a step closer. *"Them."* Deacon's posture weakens, his resolve to be angry with me already fading. I'm his only insecurity, the only person who could ever hurt him. Maybe that's the real reason he's kept his distance.

Deacon stills, vulnerability painting his features. "And is it over?" he asks.

I nod. But I hate the thought of Catalina's life being over. I hate how it ended, who she left behind. There's so much that still hurts, and I don't know where I fit into the world. But I look around, and I'm sure it's not here. Not anymore.

Deacon lowers his eyes, unable to hold my gaze any longer. He pinches his lower lip with his fingers, like he's thinking. "And if I . . . if I told you I was sorry?" he asks, darting a look up at me. "If I say that I'm a total shithead for not believing you earlier, would that matter?"

I know he's sorry. He's always sorry when he shuts me out. But deep down I know he'll do it again. He'll break my heart every time.

My body is worn down from the past few weeks, and my feelings are too jumbled to sort out right now. There's a wave of exhaustion, the start of another headache, and I close my eyes and rub my temples. For the first time in probably forever, I'm looking forward to a debriefing.

Deacon asks if I'm okay, and there's a light touch on my arm as he reaches for me. Just as everything comes back into focus, Aaron calls my name from the car. "Quinn, we gotta go," he yells, holding up his phone to signal he's talked to Marie. He shifts his glance to Deacon. "Sorry, man." Obviously, he can tell from our stances that this reunion isn't what he'd hoped it would be.

When I turn back, Deacon's watching me with a solemn expression, and I wonder if he's come to the same sad conclusion that I have. That this is terrible—the thought of not being together feels . . . terrible. But it's right.

Deacon lifts his chin; the light reflects the film of tears in his eyes. "I'll see you around," he says quietly. He doesn't move, as if he's waiting for me to stop him from going back inside. I could. I see that Aaron is right—Deacon's changed. With a word I could have him. Even if he's bad for me. But mostly because I'm bad for him.

"Yeah," I say, instead of the million other thoughts racing through my head. I turn and walk numbly down the stairs back toward the car; Aaron's staring at me with his mouth open. His disbelief doesn't fade when I get in, but he doesn't press me for details. He doesn't ask *why*.

Instead he backs out into the road and drives us toward Marie's apartment.

CHAPTER THIRTEEN

AARON PARKS MY FATHER'S CADILLAC AT THE CURB in front of Marie's building instead of using the lot. He doesn't turn off the engine. When I look at him, his fingers are tightly wrapped around the steering wheel, knuckles white. My heartbeat kicks up, and Aaron blows out an unsteady breath before he turns to me.

"What's going on?" I ask him. His expression devastates me, fills me with abandonment even before he says it.

"It's time to say good-bye," he says, smiling at the irony. "I have to leave, Quinn. You won't see me again."

My heart constricts, and I breathe out, "No."

"Your car's in the back, keys in the visor like always," he continues calmly, like I'm just an assignment. "Marie had it brought here for you earlier. I'm going to drop off your dad's car and then Myra and I are leaving town."

"But your contract—"

"Canceled. My contract's been canceled and I've been paid for my services. I leave today or I get nothing, do you understand? I've signed a confidentiality agreement and I can't say any more."

"From who? Aaron, you can't just not tell me what's happening. We're partners."

"Not anymore. And let's be honest," he says with a sad smile, "you never needed a partner."

I reach out to grab the sleeve of his jacket, determined to hold him until he explains what's going on. "Did my father do this?" I ask, incredulous. "Marie?"

Aaron gently unclasps my fingers from his sleeve, and then squeezes my hand with his. "It doesn't matter," he says. "My last assignment was to drop you off here. I wasn't even supposed to say good-bye." He tilts his head, looking me over with the admiration of a friend. Of my best friend. "But I wasn't going to leave you without giving you closure. Hell, I didn't want to leave you at all. But the grief department has ended my employment. My severance package is dependent on me skipping town within twenty-four hours."

I plan to find out what role my father played in this, but I won't let those thoughts steal away my last moments with Aaron. I lean in and hug him, my head resting on his shoulder.

His familiar cologne filling my nostrils. "Does Deacon know?" I ask.

"Naw," Aaron says, resting his chin on the top of my head. "That boy is going through something, and I don't mean you. I didn't want to add to his stress. Not to mention he'd be pretty pissed."

"He's going to kill you," I agree, sniffling as I pull back to face Aaron for the last time. "And when he asks me about you?"

Aaron brushes a tear off my cheek. "Tell him the truth. I ran away without saying good-bye to him because it hurt too much to do it any other way. He'll understand."

"He's going to be heartbroken."

Aaron nods. "I know. Which is why you can't leave him. He needs you. And whether you like it or not, Miss Badass, you kind of need him too."

"He's badass; I'm hard-core, remember?"

Aaron laughs and then closes his eyes, smiling and shaking his head like he can't believe this is happening. When he looks at me again, he's crying, but the tears aren't just sad. I know the truth, and once I get over how much it hurts, I'll be happy for him.

"I can't believe it," I whisper. "You're actually free of the system."

Our gazes linger for another moment, and then Aaron casts a look at the apartments outside my window. "You'd better go," he says. "Marie said she'd be waiting. And you know how much she hates waiting." Determined to not let this moment last forever, I reach behind the passenger seat and grab my backpack.

"Quinlan," Aaron says hesitantly. "If you go after Virginia Pritchard, promise me you'll be careful."

I pause, tilting my head as I try to determine if there's more to his warning, but he doesn't go on. "I always am," I tell him. Aaron smiles to himself and then nods his good-bye.

I climb out of the car and start toward the oversize apartment doors, stopping to look back. Aaron doesn't lower the window, but he lifts his hand in a wave. I stand there and watch him shift gears, turn away, and drive off.

I gasp in a breath and put my hand over my heart. In the past two days I've lost so much that I'm starting to wonder what's left. What's really left of me.

I'm sluggish as I walk up the stairs, drained of emotion. I'm building myself up to throw my shoulder against Marie's hard-to-open door when I stumble to a stop on the fifth-floor landing. Marie door is ajar, the room dim inside. I swallow hard and take a tentative step forward, looking around at the other apartments. All of the other doors are closed; the only sound is a low murmur from a television behind one of them. Silence radiates from Marie's apartment.

Aaron said she was waiting for me. My heartbeat pounds in my ears. "Marie?" I call softly, moving closer to the door. I wish Aaron had come upstairs with me.

I call my advisor's name again, but the room beyond the door stays silent. Well, I'm not about to get murdered here. I take out my phone, but the minute it's out . . . I realize that

Aaron is the person I'd call for this. A wave of sadness rushes over me. I consider calling Deacon or my father, making them stay on the line while I poke my head in and check on things. I don't think I need to call the police or anything—it's just an open door of the apartment of a person who's expecting me.

I debate what to do, but ultimately, I send out a quick text to Deacon, just in case I disappear: AT MARIE'S. I slip the phone back into my pocket and approach the door. I push the heavy door open a little farther, peering in. The overhead light near the sink is on, casting the room in a soft glow. I take a step inside the room and slide my hand along the wall until I touch the switch and flip it on.

The apartment has changed. The furniture has been pared down; her most treasured knickknacks are gone. The bigger pieces—sofa, coffee and kitchen tables—still remain, but the room is no longer eclectic and alive. It's been stripped of all personality. Marie is gone—I know it immediately. It's not a complete surprise. She and my dad have been at odds for a while, so I knew that one day she would leave. This was just a really shitty way to do it.

Numbly, I walk over to the couch and sit facing the door. I let the knowledge sweep over me. The loneliness. I take out my phone and skip the return text from Deacon to dial my father's number. Part of me worries that he's gone too. That I've been completely abandoned by everyone I love. The line rings, and as it does, I glance around the now-plain room—missing

Marie. Waiting to hear the jangle of her bracelets. My eyes fall on the kitchen table, and I jump to my feet. There's a file.

I hang up the phone and move quickly toward the kitchen. If Marie took off, she wouldn't have left this behind. She has to be coming back. Wild hope seizes me, and I sit at the table—maybe she's on a different assignment. I turn the folder around to the look at the name on the tab.

The world stops and the hairs on my arms stand up.

QUINLAN MCKEE

This is my file. Why do I have a file? My hands are already shaking as I open the manila folder, pick up my birth certificate, and check the name to make sure it matches. Yeah, it's mine. Has Marie been keeping notes on me? I mean, closers are careful not to give away too much because we fear being copied, but that's never actually been done. The fear . . . I thought it was almost irrational. But my advisor has an assignment folder with my name on it.

On the inside cover someone has printed CASE 20859. I shift through the papers, surprised that much of the information is severely outdated. There's my mother and father, smiling in a copy of the same picture that hangs in the entryway of my house. I find a photo of me, blond-haired and pigtailed. There are drawings from when I was in kindergarten, SUPERSTAR sticker from the teacher and all. I don't understand—why have a file on me and not update it?

I find more candid photos with my parents, although I'm not sure I've seen these ones before. My stomach knots as I sense that something is off. Why wouldn't I have seen these pictures before?

There's a photo of me next to a trampoline. My father's lips are pulled into an exaggerated frown, and I'm next to him with a cast on my arm. A cast . . . on my arm. I look down at my left wrist, forearm, elbow. Not only do I not remember breaking anything, but there's no sign of trauma. When was this taken?

I whip my hand through my hair, pushing it back and out of my face. I sift through the pages more quickly, hungry for information. There are no journal entries, even though I've been required to write them before. Why aren't they in here? My fingers are trembling so badly, I can't even read the pieces of paper I hold. I smooth them down on the table, my body in complete panic mode.

When I see the page, I begin to hyperventilate. The room tips from side to side, my eyes blur with tears, and I brush my palm roughly over my face to clear them. I start to whimper, scared because I don't understand what this means. I don't know what's happening.

I'm holding my death certificate.

CHAPTER FOURTEEN

I DROP THE DEATH CERTIFICATE BACK INTO MY FILE, my entire body shaking. I can't comprehend what this means, the idea so awful my mind won't latch on to it. Taped in the back of the file is a DVD with my name printed across the middle with Sharpie. I wonder what other terrible secrets Marie has left for me. How could she do this? She sent Aaron away. *She left.* She left me with this. I need my father now. I need my dad. I call his phone, alternating between crying and failing at not crying as I wait for him to answer. I hang up when I get his voice mail. I just need to hear his voice. Hear that I'm okay.

After trying a second time, I put my phone away. I take my death certificate and fold it up before stuffing it in my pocket. I grab the DVD and start toward Marie's office, hoping her computer is still here. I step inside the small room and find the file cabinet still hanging open. I wonder for a moment if Marie left in a hurry because she had been in danger—if *I'm* in danger. But my advisor wouldn't have let me come here if that were true. Wouldn't have left me a file. She gave me her secret—I just don't understand. I'm sick over it, yet I won't accept what it means.

In the cabinet, I see multiple folders, a different name on each tab. I close the drawer and make my way to the desk, and pull the computer keyboard toward me. I shake the mouse and the monitor comes to life. I stare a moment at the password entry, and then click a few buttons to see if it'll clear. It doesn't.

I need to know what's on this DVD. I pause, thinking about the file that was left on the table. I type in 20859 and hit enter. The screen clears, displaying a bright white background. My heart beats wildly, and I lean down to put the DVD into the drive. I click it open. I'm terrified.

A video pops up—the freeze screen set on a stark room, not unlike the early case rooms I've seen in old photos. In the beginning, advisors used to introduce the closer to their clients at the facility and document the meeting. Based on the interaction, they'd decide if the case would go forward. Nowadays counselors just send us to the family and collect their money—not that it's just about money. It helps, though.

I click the play button, leaning in to watch as the video begins. The client is out of the frame, only a pair of men's shoes visible in the shot. The metal door opens, and I recognize Marie immediately, although she's younger. She has a small child with her. The camera zooms in on her face, and I take in a sharp breath when I realize it's me. I'm the little girl with Marie.

"Come on, honey," Marie says kindly, leading the girl to the chair. The child sits down, feet swinging because she's too small to reach the floor. She looks around curiously, not scared or anxious, and Marie smiles to the client, whose shoes shift as he leans closer.

"This is our next candidate," Marie says, taking a seat next to the girl. She puts her arm around the back of the chair to offer the child the feeling of comfort and safety. The girl rests against her, eyes wide.

"It's uncanny," the man says, his voice thick with grief. "She looks just like her."

I cover my mouth, stunned. That's my father's voice. What's happening? I don't remember any of this.

"She's very sweet," Marie says, brushing at the girl's hair lovingly. "I think she's just perfect, Tom. She'll make the perfect daughter. We've already filled her in on the assignment."

My father is quiet for a long moment, and I imagine from the way the little girl is watching him that's he's studying her, too, looking for differences. Then there's a sniffle, and the soft sound of my father crying.

Marie's face registers his pain. "Tom," she says sympathetically, rising to her feet. But then the little girl who used to be me climbs down from the chair and crosses to him, my father's face still off camera. "Don't cry," she tells him in a closer's voice. "Don't cry, Daddy."

I turn away from the laptop and get sick all over Marie's wood floor.

I ejected the DVD and put in my backpack, careful to wrap it in my old Rolling Stones T-shirt so it wouldn't break. I cleaned up my mess, intermediately stopping so I could sob. I'm a closer. I'm a closer for my own life. I hiccup in another cry, standing in the middle of Marie's apartment, unable to move. My phone buzzes in my pocket, and I fight to pull myself together, my mind racing with possibilities.

"Hello?" I mumble without checking the caller ID.

"Quinn?" Deacon breathes out. I cradle the phone to my ear, wishing Deacon was with me now. Saw what I just saw. "Are you okay?" he asks. "I've called you like five times."

"No," I tell him, my voice scratchy from crying. "Something's happened. Something awful."

I squat down, using one hand to cover my face as I start to cry again. I can't imagine how this must all sound to Deacon, but I manage to get a few words out. "I'm a closer," I tell him. "I'm a fucking closer."

"I know you are," he says soothingly, not understanding the true meaning of my words. "And I'm sorry I asked you to quit. I'll support you in whatever you want. But right now I'm worried. Are you still at Marie's? Let me talk to her for a minute."

"Aaron and Marie are gone," I say, sucking in my cries.

"They're gone, Deacon. It's all been a lie. Every damn thing."

"What do you mean they're gone?" he demands. I hear him moving, his voice taking on a frantic edge. "Okay, Quinn, listen," he says. "I'm coming to get you. Don't move."

"No," I tell him, shaking my head and getting to my feet. "You can't save me from this." I take the phone away from my face and try to regain my composure. The grief and shock begin to wear off, but now I'm flooded with thoughts. With anger. I have to find my father.

When I bring the phone back to my ear, Deacon is talking quickly and I hear a door closing, the sound of wind as he gets outside. "Don't come here," I say, my voice calmed. "I have to take care of something first."

I have to go home. *Home.* I can never go back. I'm not even Quinlan McKee. My entire life is a lie, and I would be irresponsible to drag Deacon into that. "I love you, Deacon," I murmur into the phone. "I've always loved you." I hang up. I let the phone fall from my hand to smash on the floor, not wanting to be tracked. Even if I have removed the app, I can't trust anything. The two people who loved me most in the world have lied to me. I start toward the door, fighting back the emotions, forcing myself clear. I need to deal with my father and figure out what happened to me. How I got here. I need to find out the truth.

The tires on my car squeal as I take a sharp turn into my driveway. My adrenaline is pumping and my mood is frantic. I'm slightly more rational, needing an explanation more than a cry at this point.

I slam my car into park, jutting forward in the seat. I jump out and rush up the front porch, trying the door but finding it locked. My hands shake as I try to use my key, the metal skipping along the hole. It takes a few minutes, but I finally get the door open, pushing it hard enough that it hits the wall, sending several frames crashing to the floor, smashing the glass panes.

"Dad!" I scream, looking wildly around the entryway. I start walking through the hallway of lies that are meant to remind me of who I'm not. "Dad!" I scream again, and even saying that word makes my throat burn. I curse, and toss the keys on the kitchen table and trample up the stairs.

I head directly for his room and flip on the light. He's not here. The bed is neatly made as always, all of his items arranged on his dresser and desk. I'm so upset, I can barely think. I immediately pull the drawers out of his dresser, letting them fall to the floor with a clatter. I bend down and sort through his things, throwing his clothing aside, and I look for anything he might have hidden. I check underneath the drawers, in his closet and his desk. I look everywhere, but I find nothing.

Nothing. No papers at all. I still, thinking about that. My father's entire life revolves around keeping files. And yet there isn't one paper out of place here. Not one piece of information that he's left unchecked.

"He's too careful," I murmur to myself, spinning to exit the room. He'd never leave evidence, not something I could find. There's nothing here.

I stand there for a moment, my resolve slipping. I step toward his bed and run my hand over his pillow, my eyes filling with tears. It smells like home in here. Like love and safety. He's my dad.

I sniffle and snatch back my hand as if I've been burned. He's a liar. He's a stranger who kept me.

"No," I say out loud, shaking my head. "No, I don't belong here anymore." Without a backward glance, I walk out.

I get downstairs and start to pace, knowing I'll have to confront him. There's no other option. I grab a kitchen chair and drag it into the living room, letting it scrape the gloss-finished wood floor. I set it in front of the couch, not wanting the comfort of a sofa—*false comfort,* I remind myself.

I'm sure Deacon has contacted my father, so my dad has probably left work and is on his way now. I'll go upstairs to pack my bag—one that will have to carry everything I need. Because once this is over, I'm never coming back.

I was eleven years old when my father told me I'd have to sign another contract. I'd completed my first three years, and more than anything I wanted to be a regular kid. Sixth grade was supposed to be my time to do that. He'd promised me that every time I begged to quit.

"The McKees are not quitters, Quinlan," he said sternly.

"We've taken an oath to help these people, given them our word. Would you really want them to suffer for your selfishness? I can't believe I raised you this way."

I was ashamed, lowering my eyes to my now-cold dinner. *He's right,* I thought. *I am selfish.*

"If your mother was here," he said, taking a sip of his iced tea, "she'd be very disappointed in you."

My heart broke, and I covered my face and started to cry. I missed my mother, even though I couldn't remember her. My father told me that was normal, that I'd been a little girl when she died. But all the other kids, they had a mom to braid their hair and make them lunch. I wanted a mom too, and I promised that if I ever got one, I'd be so good to her. I'd never cause her trouble. So the idea that I had disappointed my mother absolutely broke me down.

"It's okay," my father murmured, coming to kneel next to my chair. He pulled my hands away from my face, and his eyes were so sad. I sniffled, and he reached to touch lovingly at my cheek. "You look just like her sometimes," he said dreamily. "It's like she never left at all."

In that moment I hugged him, telling him how sorry I was. That I would sign the contract if he thought I should. That I wouldn't disappoint anyone again.

I swipe my finger under my eyes now, sitting in my living room. It's dark outside, but I don't turn on the light. My anger has bubbled over, and this memory only helps cement the fact that my life is a lie. I realize now, especially after all the time I've spent with grieving parents: He wasn't saying I looked just like my mother that Saturday night. He was saying I looked just like Quinlan McKee. His daughter.

My back aches, and to distract myself I twist my torso a few times to loosen it up. I sit back in the chair and prop my black boots up on the coffee table. It's been over a half hour since I left Marie's. I know my father will be here any second.

After packing, I took the time to strip my emotions—to try to lose myself so I could become numb enough to handle this. Brave enough. Strong enough so that he won't be able to manipulate me. That's the thing that Deacon doesn't realize. Looking back now, my father has always been able to bend me to his will. Make me believe that I want to be a closer, that I want to help these people. But really, he studied me. Knew me well enough to push the right buttons to get the reaction he wanted.

It's probably why he hated Deacon so much when we broke up. He saw that Deacon had the power to affect me too. My father had lost a bit of his hold on me. Could have been why he let Deacon out of his contract early, in the hopes of keeping us apart.

My father didn't count on the fact that I have power over myself. I've been doing this long enough to understand my emotions now, to be fully self-aware. He won't get inside my head again. I won't let him.

Headlights illuminate the windows, and I sit up with a start as a car pulls into my driveway. My heart beats frantically, but I take a breath, reminding myself that I have to keep cool. I can't show him any weakness.

The front door opens, and my father rushes in, stopping when his shoes crunch on shards of broken glass. "Quinlan!" he yells, stricken with worry.

I don't move. I sit half in the dark, staring straight at him. He sets his briefcase near the door and shrugs out of his coat, examining the mess of frames on the floor. He glances toward the staircase.

"Quinn?" he shouts.

"I'm here, Dad," I say calmly.

He spins, startled, and clutches his chest. "My God," he says. "You scared me." He comes into the room, squinting his eyes in the low light. He stops at the lamp and clicks it on. "Deacon called me and said—" He abruptly stops when he sees me in the light.

I study every tic of his facial expressions. Flashes of worry, fear, realization. He tries to quickly cover it with parental concern, but I've already seen behind the curtain. I tilt my head to let him know I'm not here for his bullshit. When he still doesn't budge, I reach into my pocket and pull out a folded copy of my death certificate. I toss it onto the coffee table between us, and my dad picks it up and opens it.

His throat clicks as he swallows, and then he drops onto the couch, devastated as he stares at the paper in his hands.

"Who am I?" I ask him. "Because obviously that's not me."

"You're Quinlan McKee," he says, but there's no force

behind the words. He lowers the paper onto his lap and takes off his glasses, rubs his eyes with the heel of his palm. He slips the spectacles back on and looks at me. "You're my daughter—"

"Don't you dare!" I shout, kicking the table and startling him. "I read the file. Saw the video. I remember bits and pieces." I grit my teeth, anger and hurt bubbling up. "You're not my father, are you?"

He holds my eyes, refusing to answer. In his stubbornness I see a bit of myself. My personality that I've adapted because he's been my father for the past eleven years. I wilt slightly, the enormity of his lie breaking my will to find out the truth. I still love him.

"Please," I say, my voice a little weaker. "Please tell me."

My dad looks down at the paper and clears the emotion from his throat. For the first time, I see how tortured he truly is. I don't know how I haven't seen it before, or maybe he's brilliant at hiding it. But that death certificate is his truth tea.

"No," he says quietly. "No, I'm not your father."

I begin to shake, not my hands or feet. My insides tremble, my heart broken into a million pieces. There's a quick flash of our lives, the times we've sat together laughing, moments when he held me while I cried. I don't know when I lost the truth—how I *became* my assignment. But his love is all I've ever known. And it's all been a lie. My whole life is a damn lie.

I feel I might throw up again, but I fight the sickness. I can't walk away now and give him a chance to regroup. He's too good. He'll find a way to cover, make me believe his false truths.

"What happened to your real daughter?" I ask, the words painful to say. "The certificate only lists the cause of death as an accident."

My father sits quietly for a long moment, and then he leans his head back against the cushion, staring up at the ceiling. "Quinlan died when she was six years old," he says.

I flinch at the name not being attached to me. I'm betrayed by the sound of it. But I don't interrupt. I need to know what happened. How I got here. And what this all means.

"Quinn and her mother were on their way to school," he continues, "when a tractor trailer that had been clearing snowbanks swung out a little too far. My wife died on impact, but Quinn held on. She survived long enough to give me hope that she'd recover. Long enough for me to accept my wife's death and pin all of my dreams on her broken little body.

"A month," he says. "My little girl fought for a whole month. She never woke up, but I was there for every minute. I would sing to her and brush her hair and cut her nails. I would bend her legs so they didn't grow too weak. I wanted her to be able to play again when she woke up. It didn't matter that the doctors told me her spinal cord had been severed. I didn't believe them. They also told me she wouldn't survive the night, and there she was, four weeks later."

My father looks at me, and I'm completely heartsick.

"I loved her more than I loved anything else in this world," he says, "including myself. I would have given anything, anything possible, to keep her with me. She was my baby. She was my everything.

"It was late on a Sunday night when she died. Soundlessly, like she just drifted away on the wind. I heard the monitor, and I grabbed her and begged her to stay. I yelled and screamed and told her not to leave her daddy. But she couldn't stop it. I couldn't stop it.

"When I finally left the room, Marie was sitting in the hallway in a chair they'd brought for her. She'd been my closest friend for years, longer than I even knew my wife. I told her Quinn was gone, and rather than crying like I knew she wanted to, she jumped up and grabbed me by the shoulders, looking me dead in the eyes.

"'You'll get through this, Tom,' she said sternly. 'This will not break you.' But her fierce expression couldn't last. Her lips began to quiver, and then we were a huddle of grief in the children's hospital wing."

I'm only human. Even through my anger, his grief is palpable. I have to fight back my sympathy, refusing to be weak in front him. "Where do I come into this story?" I ask.

"Marie," he says. "She went to Arthur Pritchard and asked what could be done. I don't know the details," he tells me. "I didn't want to know, didn't want to be pulled from the illusion. Marie showed up with you seventy-two hours later, the third girl she tried. She never told me your real name."

"She stole me from my family?"

He shrugs. "I don't know," he says. "I don't know where she

found you. And I don't know what Arthur Pritchard had to do with it—why you fit so well." He presses his lips into a watery smile. "Although you won't believe this," he says, "I do love you, Quinn. I raised you. You're my daughter."

"Don't call me that," I say, fiercely. "My name's not Quinn."

"You can't see this now, but there are bigger things happening, things I've tried to protect you from. Same with Marie." He hesitates, but continues. "I've signed a confidentiality agreement—a pretty severe one—so I can't give you more information. But I need you to know that the department doesn't plan to let you walk away. They never did. They have custody of you until you're eighteen, but even after that, they plan to transition you."

"What?" I ask. "How is that—"

"You're a ward of the state," he says. "You all are."

I don't have a family, I think. *I don't belong to anybody.* Maybe in some way I knew this. It could be why I've felt so lost, so alone. "And what the hell does the department plan to 'transition' me into?" I demand.

My father shakes his head. "That I don't know. But I've tried to protect you, institute rules when I thought they would keep you safe. The department will keep pushing you as a closer. Find ways to make you agree. Marie was angry with me for letting you sign the latest contract, and when she found that you're expected to sign the next one, she begged me to stop them. But I don't have that power."

"Who does?"

"Arthur Pritchard, maybe. But he's just one man. In the end, we're at the mercy of a board of directors. A corporation."

"Then what do you suggest?" I ask, even though he's the last person I should be taking advice from. Guess it's old habit.

"You should run," he says. "Take whatever I have. It's not much, but I can't get your contract money, not without setting off red flags. I'm sorry I failed you."

I can leave it all behind, leave the department, my father . . . if I can still call him that. I'm a danger to everyone around me—a bargaining chip the department could use against them. I'll have to leave everything behind. Even Deacon. Especially Deacon.

Scared, paranoid, I stand, grabbing my bag and pulling it over my shoulder. My father quickly takes out his wallet and hands it to me. "There's isn't much," he says. "The credit cards will give you a head start, though. Take out a cash advance, the pin number is our address. I won't report them stolen, but when you don't show up at Marie's for debriefing, then—"

"Marie's gone," I tell him. "Aaron, too."

He rocks back, absorbing this information. "Oh. That's good, I suppose."

His most trusted confidant left him without a word. If there's anyone who knows what it feels like to be alone, he's sitting right in front of me. I take his wallet and stuff it into my bag. Before he got here, I dreamed of telling him to rot in hell. Telling him I don't need anything from him—he's done enough. But I can't erase the time I've spent here, the love I have for him. Even if I hate him right now.

And the truth is I'm terrified of being on my own. I know how to assimilate, how to blend in. But I'm not going to live some quiet life in the country. I'm going to find Virginia Pritchard. And after I talk to her, *if* I can talk to her, I'm going straight to her father for answers. But I can't do any of that without money.

I readjust my bag and glance around the living room, the one that's looked exactly the same my entire life, to always remind me. Remind me that I'm real. But even that was a forgery. It's the most devastating feeling in the world. Knowing that I don't exist. I died when I was six years old.

My heart is heavy as I walk to the front door, my boots cracking the glass on the floor. Just as I reach out for the door handle, I hear my father's voice.

"You were always my daughter," he says. "I know you're hurt right now; you have every right to be. But I do love you. I swear to you I do."

I flinch with grief, but force my face straight and turn to look back at him, watch as he bites hard on his lip to hold in his cry. The man I've known only as my father. How many times has he wanted to tell me the truth? To tell me about his real daughter?

And I realize that if I wanted to, I could give my father closure. He's never had to accept the loss of Quinlan McKee until right now. I can make it easier, tell him it'll be okay. Tell him I forgive him. A good person would forgive him.

I'm not that good.

"You're not my father," I say instead, bitter. Hurt. He dissolves, but before I have to listen to his cries, I walk out the front door into the cool night. I pull out the keys to my car, knowing I'll leave it at the bus station. I don't want to be tracked. I'll find Virginia. Last Aaron heard, she was in Roseburg. So I guess that's where I'll start.

I shiver once in the cold and then tighten my coat around me. I look back at my house and worry briefly how my father will get along without me. But then I remind myself about what he's done and harden my heart against him. Promising to never let him in again. Refuse to give him any more power over me.

I head toward my car, my expression stoic. I know now why I always felt so alone. It's because I always was.

CHAPTER FIFTEEN

I'VE TAKEN FIVE HUNDRED OFF EACH OF MY FATHER'S credit cards. I bought a bus ticket to Roseburg, and at a pay phone I called Deacon—leaving him a message when he didn't answer. I didn't tell him where I was, but I did tell him the truth. I'm not Quinlan McKee; I'm her closer.

It hurt to recite it, even in a condensed version. But in a way, I'm glad Deacon didn't answer. I might not have told him if he did. Unable to speak the horrible words. Unable to say good-bye to him.

The bus rolls up—a picture of the Oregon Zoo painted on its side—and I wince as the brakes squeal and hiss in front of the station. People around me on the benches get up and clamor for a spot in line, but I hang back, afraid of the next step.

"So you're going to leave it all behind?" a voice asks. I smile, turning slowly. Deacon stands away from the crowd, his face blotchy red like his emotions have gotten the best of him. My stomach does a little somersault, and I try to hide just how thrilled I am to see him. I try—but I've never been able to keep secrets from him.

"That was the plan," I say. He hikes his duffel bag onto his shoulder, and I glance at it before looking at him questioningly. He shrugs.

"I figured," he says. "The bus station was a lucky guess."

"And what does that mean for you? What's your plan, Deacon?" I ask, moving over on the bench so he can sit next to me. At first he studies me with his careful gaze—assessing me like an advisor. He darts a look at the bracelet Isaac gave me, the delicate silver snug against my skin, and then Deacon meets my eyes with an expression that's completely open.

"To be with you," he says in a low voice.

No matter what Deacon and I have been through, it always seems to come back to this. The fact that we just can't stay away from each other. I consider all of the baggage Deacon will have to deal with. How the department will come after him now. Use him as leverage against me.

"I'm not good for you," I tell him.

Deacon doesn't hesitate. "I don't care."

"You're not good for me," I say instead.

"I know," he responds. "But I could be."

I close my eyes, the words hurting me with their possibilities. But I don't think he truly understands my situation. "We don't make sense anymore, Deacon," I say, looking up at him again. "I'm not who I thought I was. I'm not even Quinlan McKee."

"I heard your message," he says. "But that doesn't matter to me. Because wherever we are, whoever we are—we always make sense. I think we're the only things that make total fucking sense. We belong together." He says it like it's a fact, an unchangeable part of this world. And even if I didn't agree, it wouldn't change how he felt.

What Deacon doesn't realize, or maybe he does, is that those words are the ones I've wanted to hear. Ever since I was a child, I've wanted to belong to somebody. I could always take care of myself; that wasn't the problem. But to have a real family, people invested in your outcome, well, that's something completely different. I wanted to be loved. I accepted my father's lies because I wanted it so much. I don't know what happened to me before I was left at the McKee house. But I'll find out. I have to.

"I don't even really exist," I murmur, the familiar hurt crawling up my throat. I look at Deacon. "I don't even know my real name."

Deacon lowers his bag and sits on the bench, his shoulder against mine as he stares toward the bus. "You exist," he says in a low voice. "Quinlan, you take up my whole world. I assure you, you exist."

My heart hurts, a deep ache that's been caused by loss and lies. And although I'm brave, I'm not sure I'm brave enough to walk away from this. I love Deacon too much. "We're both coldhearted closers," I whisper. "How do we keep from hurting each other again?"

"We try really hard."

He turns to me, all of his beautiful parts combining in my favorite way. He's both friend and more. I think there's no way I can lose myself again so long as Deacon's with me. He's my touchstone. My tether.

"I love you," I say, not caring if he ever says it back.

Deacon lips pull into a slow smile. "Can I kiss your face now?" he asks.

I laugh, and my heart is full, my loneliness abating. "Yeah," I say. "You definitely should." He sighs, relieved, and leans in to press his mouth to mine. Kisses me sweetly. Lovingly.

The driver steps off the bus and makes the last call for passengers. Deacon and I pull apart slightly, but my fingers clutch his shirt to keep him close. "You sure you want to come with me?" I ask Deacon, motioning to the bus. I'm scared of his answer. I'm asking him to leave it all behind too—his entire life. His future. But without a moment of thought, Deacon kisses me again, this time more fiercely, passionately.

When we stand up a moment later, he takes my hand as we walk to board the bus. He gives me a look that says, *This is not friend hand-holding,* and I laugh. We make our way down the aisle, and the air is stuffy and tinged with the smell of sweat, but we find two seats together in the middle of the bus. I push in toward the window and drop my bag on the floor. Deacon does the same and then unzips his bag to pull out a package of Twizzlers (for me) and earbuds (for him). The windows rattle as the bus pulls away from the station.

We'll have to find a new home, but I don't even know what that means anymore. For the past eleven years I've been an experiment, a homegrown remedy created by my father and Arthur Pritchard. I want to know who I was, where he found me. But first I'll have to find Virginia Pritchard and discover her role in all of this. And then I'm going after her father.

As if sensing my swirling thoughts, Deacon takes my hand, his fingers intertwining with mine again. Warmth floods me, and I give his hand a reassuring squeeze. Then I open the package of Twizzlers and pass him one.

He takes it, smiling softly. He rests back in the seat and slips the earbuds into his ears, turns up the music. Roseburg is about two hours away, and Deacon and I settle into a comfortable silence, tired and hazy—worn down by our emotions.

I can hear the hum of Deacon's music while he stares out the windows across the aisle. There is a quiet buzz, and I glance down to his open bag at our feet. His phone, casually tossed on top of his clothes, is lit up with a message. I'm about to tell him, but I catch the words on his screen. Words that prickle their way over my skin until they stop my heart dead in my chest.

I shift my eyes to Deacon, but he hasn't noticed. He's as serene and beautiful as ever. He's perfect—like always.

By the time I glance back at the phone, the message has faded to a black screen. But I know what I read. A question from a number I don't recognize. A thought that will haunt me because now I really don't know who to trust.

HAVE YOU FOUND HER YET?

I swallow hard and turn to face the smudged bus window at my side. My heart kicks alive again, pounding against my ribs as the enormity of my situation closes in. I haven't escaped the grief department, escaped my life as the remedy for a sick world. I'm here with Deacon, but now I have to wonder:

Who else is looking for me?

EPILOGUE—EIGHT MONTHS EARLIER

ARTHUR PRITCHARD PAUSES AT THE END OF THE table, undoing his jacket button before sitting in the hard metal chair across from Deacon. "Mr. Hatcher," he says in greeting. Deacon stares blankly at him, unimpressed with his appearance. "I'm here to talk to you about Quinlan McKee," Arthur continues smoothly. His tone unnerves Deacon, and the closer shrugs like he has no idea who the doctor is referring to.

"I understand you're close," Arthur says.

"Depends. What do you want?"

The doctor leans his elbows on the table, a movement meant to signify a bond forming between the two men. "I'll take that as a yes," Arthur says good-naturedly. "I'll get to the point," he says. "There's something special about her."

"Yeah, I noticed," Deacon says.

Arthur Pritchard laughs softly. "Beyond the obvious, Mr. Hatcher. You see, Quinlan is a special case for us. We've taken extra care with her, trained her differently. I need eyes on her to make sure she's progressing. To find out if there have been any . . . setbacks in her behavior."

Deacon's purposefully empty expression starts to falter, patches of red brightening on his cheeks. "What are you talking about?" he asks. "Trained differently? How?"

Arthur holds up his hand as if urging patience. "It's very complicated."

"Well, I'm very smart."

Arthur nods. "Yes, you are. You've tested through the roof in intelligence. Shame you dropped out of high school."

"Not really," Deacon says. "After I'm done with this contract I'll be set. At least for a while."

"Would you like to be set for life?"

Deacon's expression darkens. "Why am I here, Pritchard? What do you want from me, and what does it have to do with Quinn?"

"I want you to monitor her, note her behavior, and report back to me. Quinlan McKee has undergone an untested behavior modification: memory manipulation."

Deacon jumps up so fast, his chair clatters to the floor behind him. Arthur rises slowly, his eyes carefully trained on Deacon in case he decides to attack him.

"What have you done?" Deacon demands.

"We've fixed her," Arthur says. "I've fixed her. All I need

now is for someone to keep tabs on her. I'm sure you've noticed that her attachments are growing, both to you and to her assignments. But her condition is precarious, and overstimulation or a traumatic event could cause a break with reality. A meltdown, if you will. You would see to it that this doesn't happen. I have no time to test another subject. Quinlan *is* my case study. I need to know everything about her."

"Case study for what?"

Arthur straightens his back and adjusts the buttons on his jacket. "Things are changing, Mr. Hatcher," he says, sounding suddenly clinical. "There is a shift going on in our society, one with momentum. An epidemic. I can't control it. I can't stop it. At least not yet. I need to know if this is a viable course of treatment."

Deacon scoffs, incredulous that this man came to him in the first place. Arthur closes his eyes, sighing heavily before steadying his gaze on Deacon once again.

"I want what's best for her," Arthur says. "And I know you do too. All I'm asking is for you to watch her and let me know if there are any changes. This is privileged information, so I would need you to sign a confidentiality agreement. In return, I will pay you the full amount of your closer contract along with a lump-sum payment." Arthur takes out a small notepad from his jacket, a pen from his front pocket. He writes a number on the paper and rips it off. He outstretches his hand to Deacon.

At first Deacon doesn't acknowledge the motion, but then, mostly out of curiosity, he takes the paper. The dollar amount makes his breath catch, twists his stomach in anxious knots, like he's already guilty of something.

"This . . . ," Deacon starts, not finding the words to attach to his feelings.

Arthur nods. "Understand, if there was another way to get the truth, I would take it. But as it stands, Quinlan is not being honest with her advisor; her advisor is not being honest with us. You're the only person who can do this job."

Deacon's eyes well up. The money is more than he could have imagined—he'd never have to work as a closer again. He could buy a house, go back to school, maybe even college. He could have a future—something he never really dreamed was possible. But at what cost?

"No," he whispers. Deacon crumples the piece of paper in his hand and tosses it violently aside. Tosses his dreams aside—for her. Always for her. "I can't do it," Deacon says as tears spill onto his cheeks. He shakes his head, helpless. "I love her," he breathes out.

Arthur is quiet for a long moment, his brow pulled together in sympathy. But then his expression brightens, and he steps forward to put his hands on Deacon's shoulders, leveling their gaze. Arthur Pritchard smiles sadly.

"I know you do, son," he tells him. "And that's exactly why you're the perfect person to be her handler."